THE
EMPEROR'S
ASSASSIN

AUTUMN BARDOT

FLORES PUBLISHING

THE EMPEROR'S ASSASSIN

AUTUMN BARDOT

Enjoy the adventure!
Autumn Bardot

FLORES PUBLISHING

Cover design by Sweet 'N Spicy Designs

Interior Designs by Sweet 'N Spicy Designs

Photos © Deposit Photos

Photos © istockphoto

ISBN: 987-0-9882092-9-9

WEEDS
&
WEDLOCK

ONE

Northern Province of Roman Empire
48 AD

A month was a long time to wait. It felt like a lifetime. But now it was done. Negotiations were complete and my future decided. There remained only one more formality.

I skipped down the hall, stopping only to pet the guard dog sprawled in the atrium near the rectangular rainwater pool. Shining through the roof's opening, the sun's rays danced upon the water and shimmered with a thousand sparkles. I felt the same, effervescent with excitement and luminous with expectation. Today I would find out when I meet my betrothed.

At the entrance to Father's study, I peeked around the thick drapery that cordoned off the doorway.

Seated at his writing table, its marble top aglow in the morning sun, Father hunched over a parchment.

We greeted each other, and I noted his cleared-eyed gaze with relief. Father was alert and lucid today.

"Faustinus agreed to join us for dinner tonight." Father frowned, his eyes dropping to the documents.

"You look unhappy." I fussed with the gold bracelets at my wrist. "Is something wrong?"

"This!" Father swept a few scrolls to the floor. "Taxes! Rome bleeds us dry. Emperor Claudius may add to Roman coffers with new conquests, but he sucks profits from hard-working citizens like me to finance his projects."

"What sort of projects?" I picked up the scrolls and set them back on the table, my attention fixed on the list of taxable items—land, dwellings, workers, livestock, income, furnishings—and not Father's loud litany of Roman schemes.

Father's fist struck the table. "Aqueducts. A new port. A lake-draining tunnel. Ridiculous! And we pay for it. Bah! Claudius is a drooling, limping fool who imagines himself a great builder. He's as bad as Caligula!"

I set down the scroll I was reading and rolled my eyes.

"Come, daughter." Father beckoned me forward. "Do not let my ravings mar this delightful day."

I rounded the desk and kissed the top of his smooth head. "And you should not let a Roman fool ruin yours."

"An excellent idea." Father pushed aside the offending documents. "However, there's one thing we *will* enjoy like Claudius and that Roman rabble."

"What's that?"

"Why celebrating Rome's eight hundredth anniversary of course. There's no better time for you to meet your future husband than while we drink wine from our vineyard and feast on fatted capon." He lifted my chin and smiled. "Faustinus will wed the most beautiful woman in Gaul. With a beauty that rivals the goddess Venus and a fair knowledge of healing plants, you'll make a commendable wife. Expect a

2

large gift tonight. Jewelry worthy of your new status, perhaps?"

I clapped my hands, then remembering more adult behavior was required, dropped them to my side.

"Now, away young bride, your father has unpleasant business to finish." Father waved his hand and returned to his documents.

I hugged him, hurried from the office, and almost collided with a houseboy as I raced past the sunlit atrium.

"Pricilla!" I pushed away the heavy linen drape that partitioned off my bedroom and bounded inside.

My favorite servant sat by the narrow window, her head bent over a stola draped across her lap. She glanced up, full lips and amber eyes smiling with expectancy. "When do you meet him?"

"Tonight." I plopped down on the bed and touched my bare neck. "He might even give me jewels."

"He'll want to give you more than that after the wedding." Pricilla glanced at my belly.

"Babies." I looked down, imagined my stomach rounded like an inflated pila that the boys kicked about in the fields. "Will I be a good mother and wife?"

Pricilla shook her head. "You will not be good at all."

My eyes widened. "Why?"

Pricilla twisted her mouth, a mischievous gleam in her eye. "You'll be nothing less than excellent."

I sighed. "Am I ready for such responsibilities?" I wanted to make my husband happy and Father proud.

"No woman is ever *really* ready. You worry too much." Pricilla folded the stola, set it aside. Has dominus told you anything about this man?"

"Only that his first two wives died." I recalled the first time Father mentioned negotiations with Faustinus.

"He's old."

I grimaced. "Don't say that. He might be young." But Pricilla had never been wrong before. About anything.

Ten years ago, Father purchased the fourteen-year-old Pricilla to take care of me after Mother's death. As the years passed, Pricilla's duties changed, from nursemaid to tutor to handmaid to confidante. Although a servant, Pricilla's position in the household was less burdensome than those with lesser skills.

Pricilla was educated. She taught me to read, write, and calculate sums despite Father's belief that women had little use for such learning. I disagreed with him. I loved reading Plato and Socrates. Found delight in answering questions correctly. Found even more delight in solving riddles or equations. My studies were useful! It gave me satisfaction.

"As long as he's not *very* old," I said.

Pricilla narrowed her eyes. "How old is very old?"

"Wrinkled and gray."

"Family Parisii is too wealthy to permit anything less than an advantageous financial match." Pricilla squeezed my fingers. "Prepare yourself. Faustinus will be old and wrinkled and you will lay with him and bear his children."

I chewed on my lip. "Did you ever lay with an old man?"

Although it was not men Pricilla favored.

Pricilla was beautiful, with amber eyes and ivory skin taut over athletic limbs. More than once she hinted at the other servants' jealousy over our friendship. I thought it more likely they were envious that Pricilla was permitted to leave the estate, earned a few coins from her herbal remedies, and engaged in indiscriminate behavior with like-minded women. I adored Pricilla and her affairs did not prevent me from loving her as much as my own family. In truth, her boldness made her more endearing.

"I did. Long ago. I was forced to be with several displeasing men. More than several. I dare say I had my fill of men." Pricilla's eyes hardened with memory.

"I'm sorry." I pressed my lips together. Pricilla did not like being reminded of her former master, a man with a vile temper who treated his servants with contempt.

"It's the past." Pricilla shrugged. "Will you take me to your new home?"

"Of course. We will both need you."

"We?"

"Yes, because if Faustinus is as old as you suspect, you'll have to give him a tonic to increase his virility, and I'll need one to make me a willing wife." I hid my worry with a giggle.

Pricilla saw through my fears and set a soft hand on my shoulder. "Those tonics are easily made."

"Will you teach me how to make them." I only knew how to make a few herbal potions. Drinks to soothe a sore throat, ease monthly cramps, and calm worries. I wouldn't mind one now. A calming draught ought to ease the knot in my stomach. "Tell me about the wedding night."

"What do you want to know?"

"Everything. How can I be a good wife if I know nothing about the art of love?"

"You confuse love with lust. Love is a feeling of the heart. Lust an action of the body."

I crossed my arms and tried to scowl but blushed instead. "Tell me! I want to do it …right."

"Marital relations between a man and woman can be wonderful." Pricilla offered an indulgent smile. "You'll be Faustinus's third wife, I'm certain he'll be a skilled lover."

"What does it feel like? What must I do?"

"It's not something you can study. Anyway, I dare not tell you erotic secrets. Faustinus will question your virginity. Do you want him to send you back to your father in shame because you know things you should not?"

"I would never disappoint Father like that."

"Don't look so distressed. I'll tell you what to expect a few days before the wedding."

I stood, paced the room, fiddled with my bracelets, spun them around my wrist. "A year is a long time to wonder about sexual intercourse."

"You can watch your uncle's horses mate." Pricilla's eyes glinted with mischief.

"That's not the same." I flipped my hair. "Well, if I'm to be the mare, then I suppose it's time my groom style this into the mane of a goddess."

I tugged on her hand, pulled her down the hallway towards the baths and didn't let go until I ducked under the drapery.

Enfolded in the steamy cocoon, I took a deep breath and inhaled the sweet musky scent of the linden tree just outside the window.

Father had built the baths several years ago. Insisted cleanliness was a necessity not a luxury. Proud of his marble testament to hygiene, he made the baths available to our friends and family.

I stood in the circle of sunshine that poured through the skylight and pulled off my tunic.

Pricilla untied the soft leather strap around my breasts. "Don't wear this tonight." She held the restrictive binding between two fingers.

"Why not?"

Pricilla gave me a pointed look, wiggled her own unbound bosom.

"Oh." I snatched the binding, threw it over her head, and

looked down at my nakedness. These blossoming curves did not feel like they belonged to me.

Pricilla lifted each breast, cupped them in her hands. "Always use these weighty assets to your advantage."

The thought of Faustinus touching my breasts made my cheeks blaze with embarrassment. I descended the steps into the bath where my breasts floated weightless in the cool water. "An advantage like getting my own way?"

"Sex is a great persuader. Intelligence and beauty too." Pricilla kneeled down and placed a folded towel at the edge. "You have all three, so I'm certain Faustinus will be clay in your hands."

"But I'm the one who needs to be molded into a worthy wife and mother." I rested my head against the towel, looked up at the circle of blue, and imagined married life.

I was young when Mother died, too young to recall anything about their marriage. For as long as I could remember it had always just been Father, Camilla, Varinius, and me.

"Who will help Father when I leave?" I asked. "His muddled moments are becoming more frequent. What will happen when he's no longer able to manage the estate? Varinius isn't capable."

My brother, the eldest, avoided social events, rarely made eye contact, became agitated by loud noises, and laughed indiscriminately. We often found him lying in the vineyard, daydreaming the afternoon away.

Pricilla told me she had met his kind once before. Varinius, she had explained, possessed select talents that surpassed those of other men. Father had since given up finding Varinius a wife, but since my brother never noticed women, I doubted this troubled him in the least.

"Calm yourself." Pricilla stroked my forehead. "Varinius

7

is not simple-minded. Far from it. He's good with numbers and counts grape yields with more speed and accuracy than anyone we know."

"It takes more than calculations to manage the vineyards. Perhaps Uncle Amando can find a trustworthy overseer."

"Locusta, if you want to look like a serene goddess tonight, you must stop worrying about your father and the vineyards."

I closed my eyes. "Then distract me."

She did. With village gossip about cuckolded husbands, thieving servants, and merchants with rigged scales.

Cooled and refreshed, I emerged from the bath, and left a trail of wet footprints behind as I went to the next one. My favorite.

"I had no idea there were so many dishonest merchants and cheating wives." I stepped down into the warm bath.

"No one is amused by stories about good folk," said Pricilla, "at least not for long."

My head on a pillow, my body floating in peaceful suspension, I daydreamed about my nuptials. I envisioned myself in the traditional orange veil and saffron-colored wrap. Saw my hand sign the marriage contract. Watched the goat sacrifice. Imagined the grand party and delicious food. My mind painted a beautiful picture. A perfect picture. Despite my not knowing *all* of the women's rituals.

I knew a few. Married women relatives would stand by my side and demonstrate the proper method to smear the doorpost with oil and confirm the number of times I touched the hearth. The other rituals would be revealed before the nuptials. At least, that's what Aunt Diana promised.

My eyes snapped open. "I must make a gift to the gods today. I'll ask for a marriage like Aunt Diana's." Though it had not begun as a love match it had become one. Uncle

Amando, ten years older, doted upon my aunt. He lavished her with jewels, costly trinkets, and exotic perfumes. How Aunt Diana expressed her gratitude I had no idea, although I began to suspect it was in womanly ways yet unknown to me. I never once heard them utter a cross word or saw a disparaging look between them. They seemed like the best of friends.

Aunt Diana treated me like her own daughter after Mother died. She made sure my sister, brother, and I performed all the rites of passage, observed religious holidays, attended festivals, and hosted parties. She planned the banquet that marked Varinius's entry as a full Roman citizen and accompanied him to the Hall of Records for the official enrollment. Only one task was beyond her abilities: Finding a wife for Varinius. Word of his odd personality made securing a woman with equestrian status a challenge for even someone with my aunt's abundant associations.

Warm and rosy from the second long soak, I emerged ready for the female masseuse to oil, massage, and scrape my skin. With a third immersion in the hot pool, my ablutions were complete.

Back in my room, Pricilla dried my waist-length hair with a thick towel and unsnarled my dark curls with an ivory comb.

"I hope Faustinus is good-hearted," I said.

Pricilla sprinkled a few drops of lavender oil onto her palms and smoothed my hair. "You deserve nothing less."

I pressed my hand to my fluttering stomach while Pricilla plaited my hair and coiled the braids around my head.

"Calm yourself." Pricilla slid a pearl-tipped pin into the braids.

I couldn't, instead I shifted from foot to foot, wiggled as Pricilla draped a sea blue tunic over my shoulders and squirmed even more when she attached three jeweled broaches.

I pinched the shimming sash around my waist. "I don't think it's tight enough."

Pricilla tugged on the fabric, pulled until it no longer swept the floor. "I thought you might want to breathe."

I laughed. She always knew the right thing to say.

Pricilla dabbed ochre-colored balm on my lips and cheeks. "Be still." She drew the thinnest black line around my eyes. "Perfection." She stepped back to admire her handiwork.

"Not quite." I lifted Mother's pearls from the lion-footed chest and passed several lengthy strands to Pricilla.

Pricilla put them on me and then held up a polished metal plate. "No goddess is your equal tonight, Locusta."

I looked at my reflection. It was a distortion. My innocence was eclipsed by kohl and ochre. It gave my face a depth and luster of one far more worldly.

I turned away from the mirror. "Would Mother approve?" Perhaps it was silly to worry what my long-dead Mother might think. I thought about her often. Wondered what herbal remedies might have prevented my sister's blood-soaked entrance into the world from costing Mother her life.

Pricilla smoothed my stola. "She would be proud of you."

"What advice do you think she would give me?"

"Mmm...I don't know, but if I were a mother, I would tell my daughter to be herself. It's dishonest to pretend to be anything less or more. Falseness hurts both the deceiver and the deceived. At least in this case."

"Be myself." I squeezed Pricilla's hand. "I can do that."

Pricilla draped a sea-green mantle across my left shoulder, wrapped it around my back, and adjusted it over my right arm. "Faustinus will be besotted."

"I hope so." I crossed the room and looked out the window.

A sinking orange sun bathed the courtyard in golden light. In the center, a marble Bacchus cast a long shadow over the fountain, his chiseled arm stretched forth holding a grape cluster. It was usually a comforting view but not tonight. A thousand thoughts swirled about. I rubbed my hands together with anticipation. A hundred emotions churned in my belly, reason and logic mixing with excitement and nervousness.

It was time.

TWO

I turned around, found Camilla behind me. We did not look like sisters. Camilla had fair hair, a round face, and ivory skin like Mother, while I had Father's dark hair, high cheekbones, and olive skin.

"Father said a timely arrival is long overdue. Everyone is present. Everyone!" said Camilla. "What are you waiting for?"

I chucked her gently on the chin. "Pricilla said I must make a grand entrance."

"I don't recall saying that." Pricilla tucked a disobedient lock into my coiffure.

"Are you dining with us?" I asked Camilla.

"Pffft! Father says I am allowed to dine with the adults but only if I *sit* in a chair! I'm *almost* a woman! Any day now, I know it! I refuse to eat on a chair like a child or servant! I told Father I *must* recline on the couch with the other guests or I will not attend!" She thrust out her bottom lip.

Despite her insistence, Camilla still looked like a child,

her hair tousled from running, her hem speckled with vine-yard mud.

"Maybe if you bathed and Pricilla adorned your hair…"

A quiet cough alerted me to another presence.

A female servant hovered nearby. "Dominus summons you."

I hugged Camilla but looked at Pricilla. Her eyes shone with love and pride. For a fleeting moment I imagined they reflected the spirit of Mother's approval.

The waning light cast long shadows across the marble floor as I walked through the hall toward my future. This encroaching darkness was chased away by servants who lit the tall bronze lamps that stood like so many centurions in the corridor, each new-lit lamp fading my fears.

I passed the atrium where marble-headed ancestors whispered glad tidings of health and fertility from atop stone pedestals. Hips swaying, breasts pushed forth, each step forward I shed the vestiges of youth so I might cloak myself with a woman's demeanor.

I heard the guests first. Merry sounds of laughter floated into the hall. Which voice belonged to my future husband?

With feet heavy as granite, I hid near the entrance and toyed with my bracelets. A new life awaited. A woman's life. I did not know if I was afraid or excited. Probably both.

I looked over my shoulder, and saw Camilla standing in the doorway of my room. For I moment I envied her. Wanted to be a child again. Then I recalled a bit of wisdom by Heraclitus. *There is nothing permanent except change.* With a courageous breath I squared my shoulders and entered the dining room prepared to face my destiny.

THREE

T he cyzicene hall was Father's favorite place to dine, its décor a reflection of his two favorite interests: the gods and wine. In each corner, finely wrought lamps shaped like bronze branches mimicked the grape boughs of our vineyard. Supported by claw-footed pedestals, they flickered with flame, dancing light upon the fanciful murals. On the south wall a muscular Jupiter threw thunderbolts at the trident-bearing Neptune who emerged from a foamy sea on the east. Above, grape-heavy arbors covered the ceiling in soft washes of color.

Beyond the open doors, the vineyards in the distance stretched like rows of verdant Doric columns over low hills. It was a sublime sight, one I never tired of. But tonight, my attention was on the guests. One in particular.

I looked past the servant who held a plate of olives and cold-pickled fish and counted six people lounging on the sofas. Father, Aunt Diana, Uncle Amando, and three gray-haired strangers.

Old men.

A heaviness fell, a weight that squeezed all my hopes out

through every inch of my skin. I sucked in a ragged breath and affected a cheerful demeanor.

Father had abdicated his spot—the head seat—to a stern-faced gentleman, which meant he had high status. Surely this wrinkled stranger could not be my future husband. He was far too old, perhaps as old as Father.

"Ah, the late arrival of Fair Youth. My daughter Locusta makes a grand entrance." Father plucked an olive from the plate and plopped it in his mouth.

"Greetings." I removed my sandals with trembling hands and took a place beside Aunt Diana, whose mouth curved into a knowing smile.

Father introduced two men without ceremony. With a sweeping gesture, he indicated the third. "Faustinus, this is the most beautiful maiden in all of Gaul, my daughter, Locusta."

My heart heaved and constricted. My stomach clenched. All appetite vanished. "Greetings." I widened my polite smile.

An old man! Father and Aunt Diana arranged a marriage to an old man!

Father beamed with happiness and rubbed his hands together. "I hope everyone is hungry."

I stole a glance at Faustinus as the servant poured wine into my goblet and diluted the vintage with water.

Old. So old.

He looked stern too with his hooded eyes, hair that curled from the nostrils of a large hooked nose, and his hard-set mouth.

I looked at Aunt Diana and tried to convey my disappointment with a pained smile. She pretended not to understand and looked away.

I regretted appearing as a marriage-ready prospect. I

wanted to wipe off the ochre from my lips and cheeks. Pull the pearls from my ears. Shake the pins from my hair. Revert to the girl-woman I was an hour ago. I wanted Faustinus to see I was far too young so that he would tell Father there had been a mistake.

But it was too late for that. Father and Aunt Diana must have reasons for choosing Faustinus. A prudent intention beyond his wealth and status.

I glanced at Faustinus again. Perhaps a kind heart laid behind his grim looks. I must not judge him too quickly. Yet, it did not matter. My life was dictated by others. I swallowed the lump of disappointment and pretended good cheer. Aristotle said happiness depends upon ourselves. I would make the best of it and hope Faustinus was a good man.

While servants set meat-laden platters on the table, the conversation shifted from weather to politics to the latest gossip about Rome and Emperor Claudius. They discussed senatorial conspiracies, criticized double-dealing petitions, and debated the merits of foreign wars. I nodded, smiled, and said "how interesting" at the appropriate times and covered the occasional yawn with a small linen mappa.

"Emperor Claudius is so afraid of being assassinated he only sups with an armed guard present and after his food has been tested for poison." The man with a ruby ring pointed at his plate.

"Claudius imagines he sees conspiracy in every senator," added the bearded noble.

"I hear his idea of entertainment is watching wild beasts devour men in the arena—that he cheers as loudly as the uneducated rabble." Ruby Ring leaned forward. "A friend, known for his candor, confessed that he saw Claudius drool while watching a lion maul a thief. He swore the emperor leapt from his seat in a frenzy and danced about as the animal tore open the thief's stomach."

"Emperor Claudius is no less merciful to his political enemies." Bearded Man paused to belch. "It's common knowledge that Claudius will kill anyone if his advisor so much as whispers of treachery, false or not."

"Have you heard the recent rumors concerning the emperor's marital escapades?" Faustinus aimed a crooked grin at Aunt Diana.

"I heard whispers," Aunt Diana replied. "They seem preposterous."

Faustinus licked his lips and flicked his eyes my way. "The truth is always more sordid than any lie a Roman citizen might fabricate." His voice was grating, like hundreds of rocks shifting about in his throat. "The truth is Emperor Claudius is a hapless fool when it comes to women. His first wife did not fare well. The second died on their nuptial day. The third, Urgulanilla, had two children during their marriage. The first lived only a few days."

"What about the second?" I attempted to participate in the conversation.

His dark eyes slithered toward me, his top lip twisting into a smirk. "Urgulanilla's second child was not the emperor's."

"Not his?" The question slipped unbidden from my tongue, my naïveté exposed.

"Not. His." Faustinus repeated, a mocking edge to his gravel-filled voice. "He divorced the treasonous Urgulanilla to wed Paetina, only to divorce her after her brother's disgrace. Messalina was the emperor's next ill-advised choice. She is a renowned beauty with high status, although of all Claudius's wives she's the worst."

"Why is that?" I pretended not to notice his disdainful manner of speaking

Faustinus smiled, but not kindly. His was a sneer of superiority. "Her unquenchable lust for other men." Cold eyes bore into mine.

My smile quivered. Was this a warning? Did Faustinus see something in my manner or appearance that made him think I would be a faithless wife? Was it the ochre on my lips and coal-rimmed eyes?

"Oh Faustinus, you taunt us with this gossip. Tell us more." Aunt Diana clapped her hands in delight and leaned close to whisper in my ear. "He teases you."

"What sort of guest would I be if I did not indulge the hostess?" Faustinus's thin lips spread into a sinister snigger. "Messalina was only eighteen years when she married the fifty-year-old Claudius. Her beauty is as renowned as her appetite for men. You see, it is no secret that she leaves her palace bed in the middle of the night to visit local brothels where she lies on stained coaches and plays the prostitute."

"She beds men like a common whore?" asked Father.

"Indeed, and yet the brothels do not slake her unbridled lust."

"You jest." Aunt Diana flapped her hand.

"I would never stoop so low as to mock the emperor's wife. I'm no weaver of tales and speak the truth," said Faustinus. "Commoners, nobles, senators—Messalina spreads her legs for all of them. A trustworthy source claims he was present on the very night she held a competition with a well-connected prostitute." He paused to sip wine.

Roman women, I decided, were as wicked as their patrician husbands.

"You're a clever guest to keep us in such suspense,

Faustinus." Aunt Diana wagged her finger at him. "What were the particulars of the contest?"

"To discover who could fornicate with the most men in one night."

"No. Faustinus, you tell stories." Aunt Diana's ringlets shook with laughter.

"I do not engage in storytelling."

"Who won the competition?" asked Uncle Amando.

"Messalina, of course. Her victory over the prostitute came after fornicating for the twenty-fifth time that day."

"Twenty-five times?!" My hand flew to my breast.

Everyone looked at me and laughed.

"Outrageous." Aunt Diana cocked an eyebrow at her chuckling husband. "Such scandalous behavior from our empress."

"I've heard this before," said Father. "Gossip about Messalina reached even our small town, but no one dared believe such tales. Is it true Messalina fancies herself a nymph of Bacchus?"

"She does indeed," said Faustinus.

As winemakers, our family paid homage to the god of the grape, and yet we also recognized the darker side of this most immoral of gods.

Faustinus plucked a piece of pork from a plate. "Messalina's prior escapades were trifling compared to her latest. This one may even destroy the emperor."

"Don't torment us any longer, Faustinus," urged Aunt Diana.

"Yes, tell us," I said. "This gossip is more interesting than anything that happens in our village." Patrician women crossed decency's lines and engaged in unthinkable acts. Their behavior was as enthralling as it was horrifying.

Faustinus gave me an odd look, dabbed his mouth with

his mappa. "Messalina's current sexual conquest is Senator Silius. He's become so besotted he banished his wife from their villa and let Messalina move in. Messalina even had the audacity to bring her servants and furniture from the emperor's palace. She uses every opportunity to flaunt her adultery to the Roman elite."

"Noble wives are a curious breed." Uncle Amando chuckled.

Faustinus was not amused. "Empress Messalina is a debased and shameless woman. Claudius should have her killed."

"Why doesn't he?" I hoped my question was not too politically ignorant.

"Claudius is a coward."

"Oh."

Faustinus's answer was a disappointment. Was Claudius afraid of his wife? Afraid of what the Roman senators might do if he murdered her? Was Claudius *really* a coward or just overly cautious? I opened my mouth to ask but felt Aunt Diana's hand on my arm, staying my questions. She shook her head quickly, mouthed 'no.'

I suppose she knew Faustinus did not like explaining the finer points of politics to an innocent.

For the remainder of the meal, the men discussed government policies. Rome sounded like a terrible city. The men spoke as though it was a hub of decadence fraught with intrigue and harboring a nest of political vipers. Nothing could compel me to visit such a debauched city.

I was relieved when Father finally poured the last of the wine on the floor as a bacchanal offering.

"Good evening." I rose from the sofa. Decorum required an early leave taking.

I plodded down the hall but stopped before a marble

ancestor in the atrium. "My betrothed is old," I whispered into his stone ear. "And stern." I looked toward my room. Pricilla waited for me and would be eager to hear all about Faustinus.

I patted the ancestor's head and went to the kitchen instead. I passed three kitchen workers washing dishes, walked out the back door, and headed for the vineyards. Although it was night, the moon was large and bright, its light guiding me into the indigo rows that stretched over the hillside.

I grazed my fingertips across the silken leaves and inhaled the comforting scents. A brisk walk always helped me think, the exercise and grape-heavy air a balm to my spirit, the soft soil beneath my sandals cushioning my heavy heart. And Mother was here.

I liked to believe Mother's spirit lived among the curled tendrils and cordons of purple clusters. She must! Because I could not bear to think she was imprisoned in Hades' depths or submerged in the River Styx. I refused to consider the tormented hell described by Virgil in *The Aeneid.* Mother did not deserve such suffering. I also rejected the belief that she was carried off by genii into caves under the earth or that she drifted in a godless limbo after judgment by Minos. I preferred to believe Mother cavorted in the Elysian Fields, and by some mystical means, those fields joined with our earthly ones. Father scoffed at my notions of afterlife. Asked why I wanted her to wander in dark places like a lemure. He did not understand that it was not Mother's ghost but her spirit who spoke to me.

"Mother," I whispered into the vines.

Mother answered with a bird's screech. Its piercing cry commiserated with me, matched the tightness in my chest. A childhood severed by a betrothal to a stern old man. A wrinkled, saggy-jowled, hairy-eared, arrogant man.

Mother spoke again. This time through a nightingale's song. *Find the good and honorable in the man, find a melody in his somber personality.*

I snapped off a leaf, recalled Faustinus's gossip about Messalina and how her wanton behavior was an insult to Emperor Claudius and Roman decorum. Her desire for adventure and romance neither controlled nor quenched.

Had Faustinus sent a veiled warning to me? I kicked at a pebble. I was no Messalina. I had no desire for drama and intrigue. The promiscuous behavior of Rome's elite was far removed from these vineyards and herbs and sunshine. A kind husband, children, a good book, and a fertile garden were my only ambitions.

I shivered in the cool air and rubbed my bare arms. Thick clouds crossed the moon, the darkness transforming familiar boughs into sinister apparitions. Mother was gone, her spirit fled with Luna's light.

I walked swiftly down the path, back toward the villa and Pricilla's comforting arms. I was ready to tell her about Faustinus.

As I approached the collecting station with its grape-sweet tang thick in the air, a figure slunk out from the darkness.

FOUR

Faustinus crossed his arms and blocked my way. "My bride enjoys midnight strolls?"

My chest tightened, fear crushed against me like a taut leather binding. "Good evening."

"Do you often wander the vineyards at night?" Although his face was shadowed, the contempt in his voice was obvious.

"The scents and sounds help me collect my thoughts." I forced a smile. "Like those about our upcoming marriage."

"Is that so?" Faustinus rubbed his chin. "You must know these paths well. They're difficult to see without moonlight."

"I walk these vineyards so often my heart sees the paths with more clarity than my eyes."

Faustinus stepped forward, his face emerging from out of the shadows. "I find your behavior odd." He scowled. "Where are your servants to light the path?"

"I'm quite capable of walking alone." Every muscle in my body tensed. I wanted to run yet did not. How disrespectful and foolish that would be. Faustinus would think me daft.

"Did you meet your lover?"

I laughed, but the taste of his accusation was sour. "You'll be my only lover." I recalled Pricilla's advice to disarm suspicion with kindness.

Faustinus stretched his arm towards me. I took his hand and he yanked me forward. Too hard. Too close.

"We haven't been acquainted long enough for me to measure the truth of your words." His gaze dropped to my breasts. "Your father neglected to tell me how beautiful you were."

"Father finds virtue the worthier quality." My false smile quivered. Did he see my fear?

Faustinus's arm tightened around my waist. "I doubt your virtue is unsullied."

His breath was heavy, and anger clung to him like a dank mist.

"I *am* a virgin." Panic choked my voice, made it sound like a lie.

"I intend to discover the truth for myself." Faustinus spun me about. Crushed my body against the wood frame of the collecting vat.

My cheek pressed against the surface, the smell of resin mixing with the taste of terror in my throat.

"I'm not waiting for the wedding night." Faustinus wrapped one hand around my neck. With the other he yanked up my stola. His mouth clamped over mine and his tongue pushed in. It was my first kiss. It was violent and demanding and not at all how I imagined. I started to gag.

I tried to push away. He held tighter and forced my legs apart with his knee.

"Please, not this way." I stopped struggling. "I beg of you to wait for—" I yelped.

The pain surprised me. The violent end of my virginity

choked all rationale. I felt only the burning sting of my surrender below.

He heaved against me. His nails dug into my arm. Each new stab was a vicious initiation into womanhood.

So this was sex... it was humiliating. And it hurt. Fighting back was futile. Faustinus was merely taking advantage of an ancient Roman display of dominance, one that began long ago when Romulus urged his men to kill the Sabine men and rape the Sabine virgins. Thus despoiled, the women were forced to accept the Roman abductors as husbands.

I whimpered, but this only enflamed his lust. So I clenched my teeth and discovered the meaning of hate. The kind that leaves you as cold and hard as marble.

Faustinus groaned. His body collapsed against mine. His teeth sunk into my earlobe. I felt the stain of his domination. My blood, his seed—the residue of his violence stuck to my skin.

The gods had cursed me. Cursed this marriage. Dreams of a tender wedding night melted into tears that ran down my cheeks. I stared into his cold eyes and saw my destiny. A life of humiliation and pain.

His three fingers dug into my chin and turned my head. "Now that we've dispensed with that unpleasant formality, I feel compelled to tell you that I prefer other methods."

"What—"

Faustinus struck my face. "Silence." His mouth covered mine again.

I turned my head and shoved him away. "You're hurting m—"

Faustinus pinched my nose closed. I sucked air through his mouth. Twisted and kicked. He tightened his grip. A creeping blackness narrowed my vision, my head spun...

Faustinus released me and laughed as I gulped the air. Then he wrenched my knee forward with his leg and sent me sprawling into the dirt face down.

"Shhh." He pinned me to the ground.

He straddled me, his mouth on my ear and his hand tight over my mouth. "I don't want any more children. Do you understand?"

I did.

Pricilla had once told me about this method of fornication. It was common, she said. Sometimes it was an expression of the loving friendship between two men. Other times it was the dominant asserting power over the weaker. Often, it was the master over the servant.

The next violation came without warning. The pain lanced my body. I cried out but his hand clamped over my mouth.

"There will come a time you will beg for this," he grunted.

Tears flowed down my cheeks, silent sobs that choked my breath.

"Good." Faustinus removed his hand. "You're a docile and obedient girl, however, I prefer women who cry and struggle. You'll learn soon enough the best ways to pleasure me. I'll tell your father to move up the date of our nuptials. Would you like that?"

Words stuck in my throat, fear of inciting either his lust or wrath.

Faustinus pulled my hair. "Answer me."

I swallowed, found my courage. "Your will is mine."

He squeezed my breast. "I'm glad we reached an understanding. Your father taught you well."

Except Father had spent little time preparing his children for the harsh realities of life. Pricilla was my teacher. She taught skills to be a successful equestrian—cunning flattery, clever repartee, obedience when necessary, and defiance with charm. Skills I would need to survive this marriage.

"On your knees." Faustinus pointed to the ground.

"My handmaid will be worried," I rolled over, kneeled before him. "I'm gone longer than usual." I kissed his hand and looked up into his cruel face. "She'll send servants to find me."

"You're safe with me." Faustinus yanked me to my feet.

My jaw dropped. Safe?! Did he mock me? Did he honestly believe I was safe in his presence?

"Was it painful?" His disdainful gaze roamed my body.

Yes? No? What was the right answer? And then I remembered his desire for a woman who cried and struggled.

I burst into tears.

"Good, that pleases me." Faustinus tilted his head, satisfied and smug. My misery was his delight.

I staggered away on shaking blood-streaked legs, hate propelling me forward.

"I have ten children from my first two wives," Faustinus called out. "I have no need of more."

I knew then what my fate would be.

FIVE

I stumbled into the bedroom and found Pricilla asleep on the sofa, one arm flung across the cushion.

"Pricilla!" I threw myself on her, burrowed my face in her neck, and soaked her skin with my tears.

"He can't be that bad." Pricilla stroked my back.

"He…he…" I sobbed and gasped for air, my voice lost to pain and humiliation.

Pricilla tugged on my soiled clothes and pulled a leaf from my messed hair. "Did he rape you?"

Rape. That single word loosened my voice. Justified my hate and shame. I told Pricilla everything. Each repugnant detail.

"My life is over. No kindness. No children. No love." My dreams for the future scattered like dry leaves in the wind. I pulled Mother's pearls over my head and threw them on the bed. "I should have bit off his earlobe! Scratched out his eyes. Ran away. I didn't. I couldn't. I had no choice." I tore off my bracelets and hurled them across the room.

"We all have choices, Locusta." Pricilla ran her fingers through my hair. "You chose to submit to your future husband. You did what you thought was right, but I'll make certain he never treats you that way again."

"How? Are there plants for suppressing male urges? What if he suspects? Or his impotence makes him more violent? No." I shook my head. "I must learn to endure."

"You want a life of pain, humiliation, and subservience? You resign yourself to this unhappy destiny? Don't you remember my stories of ill-fated women? Not only will you never experience the wonders of a loving intimacy, you'll be denied children. This is acceptable? Locusta, this is only the beginning! His actions tonight are merely a small taste of the marital suffering and degradation to come. He may be old, but it seems he's still vigorous in his sexual demands."

I burst into hot tears. "What recourse do I have? I can't slip your herbal potions into his drinks every day for the rest of his life."

"You're right. He'll suspect something." Pricilla's finger tapped her lips, her gaze faraway. Until one corner of her mouth curved upwards. "Take off these clothes. Wash his cruelty and filth from your body. After that, purify your spirit with offerings to the gods and goddesses." She touched my cheek. "Faustinus stole your virginity and fouled your idea of passionate love. Don't let him take your strength here." She tapped my head. "And here." Curling my hand in hers, she set both over my heart. "Don't let him destroy your capacity for love and truth. Never give anyone that power over you."

I wiped the tears from my eyes and on trembling legs let Pricilla lead me down the dark hall that hours ago echoed my joy.

"You're wrong, Pricilla. A man like that will be determined to break me. Mind, body, and soul. He could forbid me from reading, from gardening…from you."

"Most certainly." Pricilla pushed aside the drapery to the baths.

"How am I supposed to remain strong?" I tore off my stola.

"You will and you must." Pricilla lit the smallest lamp.

"How? I have only one option. I must learn to appease him." I sank into the hottest pool. Its heat soothed my skin but not my spirit.

"I'll be back." Pricilla adjusted the palla over her shoulders.

"Now? Don't leave me. What if he comes in here?"

Pricilla crouched at the pool's edge. "I need to gather a certain plant."

"Why?"

"To make a tonic that will vomit a man's seed from a woman's womb."

I clutched my belly. "You've made it before?"

"The village women ask for it often." Pricilla stood and poked her head around the drapes. "Do you want a servant to guard the entrance?"

"Get two." I looked toward the linden tree. I could always climb out the window to escape. This time I *would* run.

"I'll be back soon," said Pricilla.

I moved to the far side of the pool, my eyes trained on the entrance, and waited. Moments later I heard two servants murmur behind the drapery. I sighed with relief. Now I just needed a plan to postpone the marriage ceremony.

I could pretend to be sick, become hysterical, or run away. But to fake a sickness for months was not believable. Neither was hysterics. And there was nowhere to run.

Would Father and Aunt Diana believe me if I told them the truth? They ought to. I never lied to them.

I glanced at the entrance. What was taking Pricilla so

long? Locusta's Oasis, the small plot of land where we grew herbs and flowers was not far from the villa. I should have gone with her. Helped pinch off buds or dig up roots. Waiting made me anxious. Besides, the garden, with its straight rows, verdant hues, and savory scents always made me happy.

SIX

Locusta's Oasis. Each year Pricilla and I added different plants. A few came from distant lands, clippings and seeds carried across great distances by Pricilla's friends. I never learned the names of these furtive astrologers and augurs, only benefited from the gifts of nature they left behind. Not all the seeds sprouted. A few withered away in spite of Pricilla's deft coaxing. As a vintner's daughter who understood the effects of climate, weather, soil, and cultivation, I found great delight when a new plant took root and flourished.

Many of the plants were harmless herbs and flowers. Except for those in the southwest corner. That was the location of the plants whose beauty belied their toxic secrets. Most of those were gifts from one particular visitor. Pricilla said the woman was her great aunt, a prophetess and sorceress. I had scoffed at this. How could a woman with ebony skin be related to the fair-skinned Pricilla? Unlike the others, who with furtive hands slipped seeds from one basket into another, this woman walked like an empress. Despite her faded clothes and worn sandals.

Each time she visited she spoke to Pricilla in a strange lyrical language, handed her a satchel of seeds, and gave her a long hug. For me, she had only sharp words and dark looks. I had asked Pricilla what portents the prophetess saw in my face that she looked at me with such contempt. Pay no heed to her dour looks, Pricilla had said, she's old, her mind addled with age.

"Where did you go?" I said when Pricilla walked in with a steaming bowl.

"To the far meadow." Pricilla knelt at the edge. "Drink."

I pointed to the bright green leaves and pale lavender buds that floated on the surface. "These looks familiar."

"They should. Do you recall the tall plant that stretches into the air with blooms stacked high like pale purple dandelions?"

I nodded. They were delicate small-orbed blooms, beautiful and wild.

"It's pennyroyal, very common and found far and wide. Steeped in boiling water, it will encourage your womb to bleed and expel his seed."

"But what if this is my only chance to have a child?" I inhaled the minty steam.

"Do you think he'll believe it's his? Or let you keep it? Especially after he told you he wanted no more children. I know his kind. He'll kick you in the stomach until either you or the baby dies." Pricilla's eyes clouded.

I glanced at her stomach.

"Not me. A friend who died long ago with my first master." She sighed and gestured to the bowl. "Drink."

I wiped my tears away and lifted the bowl. Although the scalding brew burned the memory of his brutal kiss, I shivered in the warm bath.

Water rinsed the dirt from my skin and hair. Pennyroyal

would purge his seed. But nothing would heal my broken spirit.

"Release your pain tonight," said Pricilla. "Cry like Neptune himself loosens the rage of seawaters from your eyes. Flush out your sorrow. When the tears stop—and they will—when you're exhausted with spent emotion, make me a promise."

My brows furrowed. "A promise?"

"Vow you will never again shed tears over this misfortune."

I gulped down the contents of the bowl. "That's ridiculous."

Pricilla folded her arms. "Then you give him great power. Is this what you want? To be haunted by his deeds? The possibility of a happy future destroyed because you wallow in misery?"

I clamped both hands over my ears and submerged under the water. Pricilla asked too much. Never cry over this again? Impossible! I never wanted to forget. How could I? A joyful marriage would never be mine. A lifetime of anguish and degradation was an unjust substitute.

Then I saw it. The wisdom in her advice. Strength of mind was one thing Faustinus could not take from me. He might refuse me children, love, and happiness, but he did not have to ravage my soul. That was mine. To destroy. Or nurture.

With my lungs demanding breath, I emerged to find Pricilla waiting patiently.

"I will not allow one man to destroy my life," I said. "He may use my body, but he will not conquer my spirit. This I vow to you."

"And to yourself." Pricilla wrapped a towel around me as

I stepped from the bath. "This morning you were a pampered maiden. Tonight, you became a woman who shares in the sorrows of our sex."

Back in my room, I did as Pricilla suggested. I wept one last time. I sobbed so hard my chest hurt. Pricilla stroked my hair and wrapped me in her arms until I fell asleep.

Sometime during the night Pricilla brought another cup of the pennyroyal brew.

"Tell me what herbs will make Faustinus unable to… to… hurt me," I said.

"I will, but I think it best if you never speak his name again."

"How can I wed him and never say his name?"

"I'll make it possible." Pricilla's breath came soft in my ear. "This is my pledge to you. Now go back to sleep."

I gazed at Pricilla with wonder. Though her amber eyes were soft and her brow smooth, her voice was thick with grim foreboding. My stomach tightened and I slunk beneath the covers.

That night I dreamed thousands of multi-colored leaves swirled about me so thick and fast that Fau—That Man— could not penetrate. A cocoon of leaves twirled, spun, and whirled around my body. I felt powerful and afraid at the same time.

A single shaft of bright sun in my face woke me the next morning.

Pricilla stood at the foot of my bed, another bowl of the brew in her hand. "I overheard that vile man."

I rubbed my eyes, puffy from last night's weeping. "How?"

"He stood outside the kitchen while I made this." She lifted the bowl. "It's worse than we thought."

"Why?"

Pricilla gave me the brew. "His wickedness extends beyond rape."

"What did he say?" My heart beating double time, I put my lips to the bowl.

"He beat his servant because his porridge was not to his liking."

"Only a fool treats a servant like that." Everyone knew a bondsman did tasks best when treated with kindness and tolerance.

"Then the world is full of fools." Pricilla waited while I drank, her usually serene face now furrowed with dismay.

"You heard something else, didn't you?"

"He told another servant to saddle his horse so he could—and I repeat his exact words—assess the worth of the vineyards before the stupid old fool wakes up."

How dare he! Father was not a stupid old fool!

I threw off the covers, crossed the room, and looked out the window to the green rows beyond. "Surely Father did not include the vineyards as part of the marriage contract." I turned around. "Unless F—That Man knows about Father's ailment and schemes to defraud him after we wed."

"He's wicked. I put nothing past him." Pricilla drew back the bedding.

There was a bright smear of blood on the linen.

"There should be more." Pricilla frowned. "I'll apply a plant oil to encourage your womb to contract." She crouched in front of the large coffer and lifted the lid.

Inside were perfect rows of clay pots filled with essential oils, extracts, roots, seeds, and dried leaves. Pricilla withdrew a tapered vessel, lifted the stopper, and sniffed. She shook several drops of oil into a small bowl, added a splash of olive oil, then applied the mixture to her palms.

"Your feet." Pricilla pointed to the chair.

I sat, lifted my feet. "Can I stop him?"

"He wants your father's vineyards, and he knows your brother is easily manipulated."

Pricilla's strong hands massaged my feet and heels. She poured more oil on her hands and rubbed my shins and calves. Next, she lifted my tunic and massaged my stomach.

"There must be something I can do."

"Talk to your Aunt Diana. Tell her she must find a wife for Varinius, preferably one with a shrewd father."

"Varinius is not interested in women."

Pricilla snorted with laughter. "I saw him with Dora."

"Dora?" She was the new sweet-faced kitchen worker.

"Yes, and his interest was on prominent display." Pricilla giggled and made a thrusting motion.

"Varinius and Dora?"

"Why is that difficult to believe? His peculiarities do not include celibacy."

"He's awkward with people. I never thought…" I rubbed my forehead. "I'll tell Aunt Diana when I see her again."

"We should visit this afternoon."

"No." I drew my knees to my chest. "I'm not ready to leave my room and see people."

Pricilla returned the vessel of oil to the coffer. "Didn't you tell me That Man planned on seeing you again today?"

I buried my head in my arms and groaned. "We'll go to Aunt Diana's as soon as possible."

Pricilla stroked my head. "Camilla's handmaid will tend to you."

I looked up. "You're leaving me again? Why?"

"You know the reason."

"More pennyroyal?"

"No, a different plant." Pricilla selected another small clay vessel from the coffer and left the room.

I stayed in this curled position until Camilla's handmaid brought my porridge. I devoured it, even though she had not added enough sweet berries. After she dressed me and braided my air, I peeked out into the hallway.

"Where is Father's guest?" I asked a servant who scrubbed the floor.

"He's with dominus in the vineyards."

With a sigh of relief, I walked towards the front entrance, pausing to greet two of Father's clientalia in the atrium. These men, like the others, waited by the rainwater cistern each morning to solicit favors, borrow money, or ask for legal advice.

Camilla stood in the vestibulum with her hands on her hips and tapped her foot. "Pricilla is out front. She says you're visiting Aunt Diana. Can I come?"

"Not today." I swayed, the tile mosaics of fish and fowl blurring beneath me.

"Why not?"

"It's not a social call. It's business," I stepped outside onto the portico after the servant boy opened the wide front door.

"Fine! I don't want to go anyway!"

I sank down on the marble bench, put my hand over my gurgling stomach, and flexed my right foot, which began to tingle.

Pricilla, basket in hand, appeared from the west terrace.

"I'm sweating, my foot is numb, and I have cramps," I whispered when she was near.

"Side effects of the tonic," said Pricilla as metallic squeaks and clopping hooves announced the carpentum's arrival.

I climbed inside. "Pull back the shades. The stuffy air makes me nauseous." I lifted my shaking hands. "Is this another side effect?"

"It is." Pricilla withdrew a clay cup from her basket. "Time for another dose."

"How much more do I need?"

Pricilla dabbed at my damp brow with the edge of her mantle. "Your monthly blood must flow like a stream after a heavy rain."

"Fine." I gagged it down.

The carpentum crested the first hill and I ordered the driver to stop. I heaved myself out the door and vomited over the grass.

"I'm ill, Pricilla." I threw up again. "I want to go home."

Pricilla rubbed my back as more of my morning meal splattered the weeds. "Do I need to remind you that he's there? Waiting for you."

I spit bile on the road. "I'll post guards in my room. He wouldn't dare violate me knowing the whole villa will hear my screams."

"Home is not the place for us now."

"For *us*?"

"For you."

I returned to the carpentum and rapped on the roof to signal the driver we were ready to continue on.

"You'll feel better soon." Pricilla laid a soft hand on my shoulder. "It's important you tell your aunt about your brother's romantic adventures."

I rubbed my belly. "Can you make a soothing drink the moment we arrive?"

"Of course." Pricilla patted her basket. "The ingredients are all in here. I even brought more indigestion tonic for your uncle."

Twice more we stopped so I could purge. By the time we passed through the Doric-columned entrance to Aunt Diana's villa, I was weak and thirsty.

Noting my pale face and sluggish step, Aunt Diana scolded Pricilla for not insisting I return home.

"Locusta was insistent, domina. She has important news concerning Varinius."

Aunt Diana slipped her arm about my waist. "Such a good sister you are, Locusta. Come, rest on the veranda. A cool breeze and refreshing drink will do wonders."

It did. As did the soft pillows and fruited wine. But nothing took away the humiliation and hopelessness lodged deep in my gut.

Aunt Diana's eyebrows rose in surprise when I told her about Varinius and Dora.

"I'll begin looking for a wife immediately," said Aunt Diana. "A simple-minded young girl would be perfect."

How unfair, I thought, that girls must resign themselves to wedding older men with property while young men reaped the benefits of youth and beauty.

"I disagree with you, Aunt Diana. A girl with a quick mind will serve Varinius better." I plucked a wine-soaked berry from the goblet. "A recent widow with intelligence complementing Varinius's limitations would make the best match."

"A young widow. Mmm…I'll make inquiries."

Aunt Diana's friends and associates stretched across the land. Uncle Amando traveled frequently to Rome and Athens. Aunt Diana often went with him on these business trips but that was before managing three children and a large household kept her home.

Aunt Diana nibbled on a spiced asparagus spear. "Do you like Faustinus?"

I should have expected her question and prepared an answer, but the pennyroyal's effects left me slow-minded and pre-occupied.

At least my initial anger at Father and Aunt Diana had faded since last night. The morning had brought a new understanding. How could I blame them when That Man appeared likable enough at social gatherings? Aunt Diana was forthright, her intent only to wed me to a man of wealth and status. Still, I wondered… had she heard gossip about his hostile nature? Or had she disregarded the rumors as jealous prattle by snubbed maidens? One thing was certain. He must have been the best prospect. Maybe the only one. Families of equestrian rank were few in this region according to my aunt.

I loved and trusted Aunt Diana. I would not lie to her. Nor would I tell her the truth.

"He has cruel eyes." I dabbed at the sweat on my brow.

"Oh, Locusta. He's a good man. Perhaps you mistake his stern looks for sorrow. His previous wife committed suicide —ran Faustinus's own blade through her breast in front of him."

"How awful!" The woman must have been desperate after so much abuse.

"He told me she was prone to hysterics, and after the birth of her fourth child went mad. Did nothing but weep and rant against the gods. Perhaps, Faustinus's stern looks stem from this."

My stomach lurched and contracted. The horror of my future turned my insides liquid. "How did his first wife die?"

"In childbirth. I don't know the particulars."

"His wives met unfortunate ends."

Aunt Diana touched my forehead with a cool hand. "You're not yourself today. Illness and anxiety over your upcoming nuptials burden your heart. I insist you remain here until you feel better."

But that did not happen. Father arrived shortly before dinner to deliver the news in person.

Faustinus was dead.

SEVEN

We departed with haste. Father, Pricilla, and I were silent most of the ride home.

I did not dare look at Pricilla. Did not want to see the truth in her eyes. She murdered Faustinus. I was horrified. It was immoral and vicious. Her audacity astonished me. My dearest friend, my loving handmaid, my skilled teacher of herbs, murdered my betrothed! For me. To save me from a life of misery. To stop That Man from seizing the family estate through unscrupulous means.

My insides twisted with spasms of confusion, relief and horror and guilt writhing like three snakes in my belly. I took deep ragged breaths and looked down at my trembling hands. Pricilla claimed dark-skinned Babylonians foresaw a person's life from the web of creases crisscrossing one's palms. What future did mine reveal now that Pricilla changed my destiny?

I slid my gaze to Pricilla. Her hands were steady, clasped, fingers laced together. Her demeanor poised and calm. Innocent.

"This is a terrible tragedy." Father broke the silence. "I'm glad you were not there when he died."

I lifted my head. "What happened?"

"Faustinus appeared fit and strong all morning." Father looked out the window, his gaze resting on some distant hill. "I was talking to the overseer about purchasing more dolia—some of the older earthenware jars were cracking—when I ran into Faustinus returning from the vineyards. He asked questions about crop yields and told me he might want to buy a vineyard since grapes yielded more profit than vegetables."

So that was his ruse, pretending to expand his livelihood. If Father only knew!

"We continued our conversation in the baths and that's when… " Father turned to me. "Are you certain you want to hear this?"

I wanted to know every detail, wanted to ask a hundred questions. Instead I only nodded.

"Faustinus cried out and pawed at his throat. He tried to speak but his words were nonsensical, and then…"

"Go on."

"Foam bubbled from his mouth." Father grimaced and shuddered.

"Do you think he has the falling sickness like Julius Caesar?" I had to know if Father suspected murder.

Father rubbed his chin. "Possibly. An astute observation, Locusta. But those with the falling sickness don't usually die from an attack. Julius Caesar hid his condition for many years, and it didn't prevent him from becoming a great conqueror and driving the warring Celts from our land. In fact—"

"Father." I rested my hand on his arm. "I must know how my betrothed died."

Father patted my knee. "Faustinus began to vomit. His arms flailed about like a goose taking flight. I grabbed him before he sank under the water, but his body was already limp."

I finally managed to look at Pricilla. She looked back, blinked, all blameless pity.

"Such a tragedy," Father continued, "and it was such a good match. Faustinus was so charmed by you."

The sour taste of guilt rose in my throat despite my innocence. Or was I to blame? Were my tears and despair the reason for Pricilla's murderous deed? I chewed on my lip and stared into the distance, willed the green hills to tell me just how responsible I really was for his murder. Was all this my fault? Was I—

"When I was a boy I ran through these fields for miles and miles." Father stuck his arm through the window. "I told my tutor I was going to run all the way to Rome. You can't catch me! I missed many lessons and my tutor got angry. He punished me and made me speak nothing but Greek for a week—when the rabbits died."

"Rabbits?"

Father grinned, his gaze far away, his mind in another time.

I patted his arm. "Tell me about the rabbits."

Father was no longer in the present and had returned to the past. During these episodes I learned to play along. Previous attempts to roust him only made him irritable.

"Father killed them with rocks and clubs. Too many. *Whack*! Mother said it wasn't her fault. Trap them. Eat them. Bunnies falling from the sky. I had to find them all."

As Father rambled, the orange sun sank into the horizon and the sky turned the color of blood.

I did not make eye contact with Pricilla again until the carpentum stopped in front of our villa.

The servant opened the door, but it felt like another door opened for me as well. I stepped from the carpentum freed from an abusive husband. A new future awaited.

"Take Father to his room," I told a servant. "Today's misfortunes have tired him. His mind is fixed on looking for dead rabbits. If he leaves, follow him wherever he goes."

The servant bowed his head. He was familiar with Father's failing mental health. "Would you like some wine, dominus? I'll bring some to your room." He led Father inside the house.

"Show me the plant," I said to Pricilla once we were alone in the courtyard.

"Why?"

"I'm curious." But it was more than that. Knowing about curatives was not enough anymore. Not when I saw what real knowledge could do. It made one powerful. In charge of one's life. I wanted that kind of power. Not that I would use it —I could never kill someone. But knowing I *could* might bring peace of mind.

"It'll be dark soon."

"There's time." I put my hands on my hips. "And the moon is full."

"Once you go down this path there's no turning back." Pricilla gave me a hard look, her eyes sharp with warning.

"Knowledge is not dangerous," I said.

"Don't be naïve." Her voice was low. "Knowledge of deadly plants is the worst kind, both to you and the people who know you have this knowledge. It will end all innocence —shine a light on your soul—make you see the dark workings of your mind and heart—make you question the truths you cling to."

Her grim tone did not discourage me. "Socrates said an unexamined life is not worth living."

Pricilla arched her eyebrow. "Then prepare to examine the murky depths of your beliefs." She turned about and headed for the west terrace.

EIGHT

I followed Pricilla.

We passed Locusta's Oasis and took a meandering trail away from the villa, away from the vineyards, and toward a hill bordering the estate. We plodded up to the summit.

"There." Pricilla pointed in the distance.

Beyond was a wild meadow where nettles, alfalfa, and scraggly weeds I did not know the names of grew in abundance. We traipsed back down and walked through tall grass until Pricilla stopped at a plant that looked like a wild carrot. Purple spots dotted its thick knee-high stalks, and its tiny-clustered white blooms and lacy leaves fluttered in the evening breeze.

Pricilla crouched down, hands dangling over her bent knees. "This plant killed Socrates."

I crouched next to her. "Hemlock."

Everyone knew the story of the philosopher's death. He was forced to drink an infusion of hemlock as punishment for his irreverent attitude about the Greek gods. Crito, his faithful student, had marked his final words and symptoms as the poison took hold.

"It's quick-acting." Pricilla ripped off a leaf from the plant, crushed it in her hand, and brought it to my face.

I wrinkled my nose. It smelled like rotten vegetables.

"All parts are poisonous. Roots. Leaves. Seeds. It's easy to disguise in food or wine, and usually fatal."

"Usually?"

"Given in small doses, hemlock calms muscle spasms, quiets a person's mind, and suppresses sexual urges."

"It was an accident, right? You gave him too much? You only wanted to keep him from…from hurting me again."

Pricilla lifted her chin, regarded me with bright golden eyes, and said nothing.

"Did you or did you not mistake the dose?" I had to know. Too much hemlock meant Pricilla had not willfully murdered That Man. It made his death a lucky accident. One I would not agonize over. Not feel responsible for.

Pricilla released the crushed leaf. It fluttered to the ground where it lay among bits of weeds, stones, and dirt. "It's getting dark and you look as pale as the moon."

I rubbed a hemlock leaf between my fingers. "Was it an accident?"

Pricilla turned and walked away.

"Pricilla?"

She said nothing.

Was her silence meant to keep from incriminating herself? To protect me?

"Pricilla, tell me."

She hummed a tune and kept walking. Never looked back. Never answered.

It was the first time she had ever refused to answer a

question. It was my first ethics lesson in poisoning. Confess to no one.

I COLLAPSED ON THE BED. My head, heart, and body were exhausted, and yet I tossed and turned all night. The day's events—blood and murder and hemlock—circled like a chariot race in my mind.

Sometime during the night Pricilla brought me a hot draught that encouraged sleep. I drank, hopeful that with the morning's light my womb would be healed and my conscious eased.

It did not. Instead, it brought more blood. I bled for more than a week. Pricilla assured me it was normal.

Nine days of blood. Nine days I did not leave my room. Nine days I stared out the window. Nine days I replayed every scenario and conversation in my head from that fateful night. Socrates said that wisdom began in wonder. I did not feel wise. Quite the opposite.

"Get my sandals, I want to walk the vineyards and work in my garden." It was my tenth day of self-imposed confinement.

Pricilla did something I never saw her do before — she wrung her hands. "Too much exertion might reopen your womb."

I set my hand on my belly. "I feel fine."

"You might feel well enough; nonetheless, the body takes a month or more to heal properly." Pricilla interlaced her fingers. "The muscles must weave together to be strong."

I paced the room. "I need to do *something* to keep my mind busy."

"I have an idea." Pricilla ran from the room and returned with a green sprig.

I sniffed. "Elderberry?"

"You want to know more about plants. I'll tell you."

My lessons began in earnest that afternoon. And my love of plants blossomed.

I studied minute differences in the same plants. Listened while Pricilla explained how variations provided different degrees of medicinal essence. Some days I identified plants from a tiny clipping, a crushed leaf, or a dirty root. Other days, Pricilla told me to close my eyes and identify plants by smell alone. An herbalist, she claimed, needed to enlist every sense.

When I recovered enough to venture outside, my herbal instruction bloomed like a hawthorn tree. No longer a girl's idle diversion, Locusta's Oasis became a woman's diligent pursuit. And as was often the case when seeking knowledge, I asked questions Pricilla could not always answer.

"Does a plant's attributes—like its poison or curative—transfer to the insect or animal that eats it?" I asked.

"Nobody knows," said Pricilla.

"A Greek botanist might." I nudged her with my elbow.

"Of course, they do," she laughed. "Greeks think they know everything."

Plants fascinated me. Each flower, shrub, tree, and weed held a secret. I was determined to learn every one.

I was a diligent, eager student and examined every plant with meticulous care. The silky powder on a plum. The pointed edge of a thorn. The serrated edge of a leaf. The velvety hair on a stalk. The sticky ball of sap.

Pricilla was an equally thorough and enthusiastic teacher. Flowers, she claimed, were like people, female and male, or sometimes both. Male parts were pollen-filled, whereas female parts contained seeds within its swollen base. She described the toxic inconsistencies between a young and mature leaf. Pointed out those plants reaching full potency after maturity and those whose effects peaked while in bud.

I learned which had lethal seeds, and which deadly blooms. I learned about the plants with shallow roots and those that sent out long tentacles, their shoots emerging far from the parent plant.

Each day my knowledge about plants increased, until one afternoon when I learned another deadly secret.

"Where are we going?" I asked Pricilla as we hiked through the field where the hemlock grew.

Pricilla veered from the trial, wended her way through a meadow of wild flowers and scrubby weeds. "Patience."

"Oh dear, that's not my best quality." I pulled out a thin reed clinging between the fibers of my thick sock.

"There." Pricilla pointed to a few straggly trees huddled together in the distance.

We waded through a sea of tall grass, the ground soggier with each step, the bog thick with weedy stalks that obscured the pond's edge. Startled, two long-legged birds flew from the grass, wide wings flapping. The surface-skimming dragon-flies and low hovering wasps, however, were not bothered by our arrival.

"What plant are we looking for?" I pulled my mud-soaked foot from the muck.

"I'm not looking for a plant." Pricilla pointed to a patch of green-gray weeds growing in the water. "Do you see it?"

I frowned, stared at the weeds, and saw only the ugliest of creatures. "A toad?"

Pricilla crept toward it. "A toad's skin is extremely poisonous."

"Varinius catches toads all the time."

"Touching one is harmless. Eating its skin is fatal." Pricilla's voice was a whisper, her body motionless and poised for jumping. "First, the eyes, nose, and throat start to hurt. Vomiting follows. By the time the victim begins to hallucinate, death is imminent."

As if sensing its own imminent death, the toad stood tall, four legs braced in a defiant stance.

I shifted my foot, snapped a twig, and the toad leapt into the safety of the tall rushes.

"Hop away, warty toad. I'll find one of your relatives." Pricilla pointed to the water. "Do you see the mucus strings with black flecks? Those are eggs. All the female toads come to this pond to find a mate."

Oddly enough, this reminded me of my last discussion with Aunt Diana. She had said Gaul was a pond with few fish, whereas Rome had a sea of suitable men. I pushed back the thought of another betrothal. "Is there a remedy to counteract the effects of the toad's skin?"

"None I know of."

Our countryside was rife with toads. Who might have thought such a peaceful pond harbored so many deadly creatures?

We lived in a poison-filled world.

NINE

I spent the winter sketching. Stem, leaves, flowers, seeds. All the plant life I could find. And as I pressed the stylus into the wax surface of my three-page tablet, I recited their attributes and growth patterns. I wish I could have kept my sketches, but Father refused to provide more pages. He said a maiden was not a scholar. Only boys could aspire to such lofty ambitions. Unable to persuade him, I had no choice but to commit each illustration to memory.

Nature's flora fascinated me, and by the following spring I knew the medicinal properties of every local herb, tree, mushroom, weed, and shrub in Gaul. Pricilla claimed my obsession for plants was a substitute for what I really wanted. A husband and children. Maybe she was right.

I often accompanied Pricilla to a sick villager's home. Pricilla thought it improper, but I saw no difference between Father's duty to help his clientalia's financial problems and my treating their physical ailments. Besides, I loved doing it. My mind hummed with excitement and I felt giddy with pride when a remedy worked. The afternoons passed swiftly during those visits.

A few of those house calls dredged up memories I thought I had gotten over. Like when I prepared valerian roots for a nervous young bride. But most visits were ordinary. Dried leaves and flowers in hawthorn-infused wine for an old woman claiming that the goddess, Vesta, squeezed her heart. Bright yellow petals of goat-weed for a mother whose despair over her husband's death caused her to neglect her children. Serrated leaves from a chestnut tree for an overseer troubled by such frequent bowel movements it impaired his work.

Although months slipped by as I happily etched plants on wax tablets, made cuttings, mixed infusions, dried leaves, and memorized remedies, I noticed a change in my body. I no longer bled with regularity. Pricilla tried various potions and tinctures, but all proved ineffective.

"Is this all?" Pricilla pulled the blanket back and pointed to a small red stain. "Two months—Maius, Iunius—and only a smear of blood?"

At least it was red. Sometimes the stain was the color of a dried autumn leaf.

"Perhaps my humors are not in balance." I shrugged as though it was not important. But in my heart, I suspected Pricilla had given me too much pennyroyal after the incident with That Man. I did not tell her this. Did not blame her. Never asked if I was barren. I considered it the cost of being saved from a horrific marriage. "I'll make more offerings to Fecunditas."

The year was uneventful, and yet that was the year my life changed. Aunt Diana's efforts to find a wife for Varinius and a husband for me were unsuccessful. Father stopped entertaining friends and no longer accepted invitations. And because dinner parties provided opportunities to make new acquaintances there was little chance of meeting eligible marriage prospects.

Each month Father's condition declined, his mind increasing fixed on the distant past of his childhood. He often wandered about the estate until I sent servants to find him and bring him back. Twice they found Father naked and speaking Greek to the vines. Another time, and to the overseer's dismay, Father climbed into the trough to stomp on the grapes.

When Uncle Amando was not in Rome on business, the daily administrative tasks of Parisii Vineyards fell to me. My days were consumed with crop yields, debts, payments, and household management. Any free time I had was spent learning about plants. Varinius was busy as well. That summer, Dora, the kitchen worker, gave birth to his child. A son.

Pricilla and I had been summoned when Dora's womb poured blood moments after the babe entered the world. While the midwife dabbed at the sweat on Dora's forehead, I held my brother's child and soothed his lusty cries. I stroked his downy hair, inhaled the scent of his skin, damp from the lilac-infused bath, and yearned for a child of my own.

"Locusta," said Pricilla.

"What?" I looked up, the infant's tiny, balled fists and miniature toes stole my attention.

Pricilla tugged at my sleeve, a lank weed clutched in her hand. "There will be time for doting later."

"Look how beautiful and perfect he is. Hungry, too. See how he turns his head and seeks my breast?"

Pricilla leaned close. "I see that you're not paying attention to what I'm doing."

I moved closer to Pricilla, watched her crush the stem, small white buds, and root with mortar and pestle. After a thorough mashing, she scooped a dollop on her finger and returned to Dora's bedside. "Put this under your tongue." She smoothed back Dora's sweat-soaked hair, then looked over her shoulder at me. "Locusta, the second tincture must be prepared."

I reluctantly surrendered the infant to the midwife because Dora was too weak to hold him.

First, I transferred the pulverized weed into a cup, then added hot water and a dollop of honey. While the ingredients steeped, I hovered near the babe, admired his blue eyes, Varinius's eyes, and wondered if the boy inherited his father's curious mannerisms and temperament.

I glanced at the tonic. The water had changed hue and it smelled slightly bitter.

"It's ready," I said.

The tonic's main ingredient was shepherd's purse. The unassuming weed grew everywhere. It was so prevalent workers cleared it weekly from grazing areas because it tainted the goats milk. Pricilla claimed the plant was a gift from the gods who, foreseeing the complications of child-birth, generously sowed the weed over the earth.

"I'll make offerings of gratitude to Vesta, Minerva, and Jupiter for a healthy child." I offered the cup to Dora.

"You're very kind." She sipped and grimaced at the taste.

Pricilla and I waited. Left nothing to chance. We would not leave until the tonic stemmed the flow of blood to a trickle.

But waiting was difficult and demanded duplicity. Outwardly, I must appear confident, because it inspired confidence in the patient, which aided in their healing.

Inwardly, I must watch for signs of adverse reactions. Inwardly, I must think of alternative remedies in case the current one failed.

The appearance of confidence, I learned, was an art. One I was determined to master.

"How can I be certain Dora's child is Varinius's and not another's?" I asked Pricilla as we headed home.

"You cannot. Only the gods know the truth, but I'm certain the babe is his. She loves him."

"Loves him or his wealth?"

Pricilla frowned. "Someday you must learn to trust again."

"This isn't about me. It's about Varinius not being taken advantage of."

Pricilla, however, knew otherwise. "Do you remember your promise to me?"

"Of course, I do." Never would I allow That Man to destroy my ability to love. "My heart is a bird in flight," I said, "the air beneath its wings, my hope."

Pricilla paused to pluck a purple bloom from a vine. "You're young and beautiful. Your aunt will find another man for you."

"Aunt Diana has little time these days, she's with child again."

"Be patient awhile." Pricilla tucked the flower into my hair. "Little good comes from worrying about things you can't control. Perhaps the gods wish you to remain with your father for now."

But the gods are an inscrutable crowd, and that spring they played a vile trick.

TEN

"Locusta! Locusta!" Camilla burst into my room. "The Roman army is at our door!"

I looked up from the ledger and blinked. Camilla's outbursts tended toward exaggeration.

"The entire Roman army?" My voice dripped disbelief. "Thousands and thousands of soldiers? They must be very quiet because I hear nothing but the twittering of birds outside the window." I cupped my hand to my ear.

"I didn't count them, Locusta! But a centuria, at least!"

"They're *all* in our courtyard?" I set down the stylus.

"No, but a centurion *is* in our atrium. A centurion! A giant centurion! And he asked for *you*. By name." Camilla grabbed my hand and pulled.

"Me? Are you certain?" My heart dropped into my stomach. Had I forgotten to pay taxes? Did the emperor send the Roman army to collect them? Was Father in trouble? Or Varinius? Or Uncle Amando? Why would a centurion ask for me?

"Hurry. He looks dreadfully fierce and most impatient.

Father is with him now—and in one of his moods. Last time we had a visitor, Father ranted about dead rabbits."

With trembling hands, I covered my head as decorum required, and walked slowly with Camilla towards the atrium.

"There he is." She hid behind a marble column.

The centurion's back was to me as he talked to Father, who appeared quite composed as he reclined on the couch.

Head held high, I entered the atrium. As though sensing my arrival, the centurion turned around. He was exceptionally tall and broad of shoulder, the transverse-crested helmet of plumes adding extra unciae to his already magnificent stature.

I had never seen a centurion up close before and studied him like I would a new species of plant.

Chain mail hung over his waist, and a leather chest piece revealed his Herculean musculature. His front breastplate bore many medallions of valor and rank. A fine-woven cloak draped from his left shoulder. I recognized the emblematic eagle on the hilt of his sword. From his embellished belt, straps of metal-tipped leather fell over his kilt. My gaze traveled downward to the silver armor greaves protecting his shins. He was intimidating from head to toe.

Though the helmet obscured his face, I felt his eyes upon me.

I stiffened my shoulders and looked up. "Salve. To what pleasure do we owe a visit from the Roman army?"

"Salve, domina. I must speak to Locusta. The villagers told me she resides in this villa." His deep voice matched his physique, yet its smooth timbre was at odds with his aggressive posture.

"I'm Locusta."

He stepped forward. "You're the daughter of Quintus Metallus Parisii?"

"Yes, as I said." I looked past him at Father, whose eyes

were fixed on some faraway vision as he mumbled incoherently.

"Greetings." The centurion bowed his head and removed his helmet. A blonde-haired, blue-eyed Hercules regarded me with surprise. "Forgive me. I thought you would be an old woman."

Faced with such a handsome man, my cheeks grew hot. "The villagers said I was old?"

"No. They said a wealthy woman with knowledge of the healing arts resided at the Parisii estate. It appears my assumption was incorrect." His eyes narrowed. "Is there another by that name?"

"No." I swallowed, and my stomach fluttered.

"You're a healer?"

"I possess some knowledge, but I think it's my handmaid Pricilla you want. She has more skill than I."

The centurion moved closer. "The villagers told me to find Locusta. No other name was uttered."

With each step, my heart thumped louder. His nearness both unnerved and thrilled me. I let my eyes linger too long on the flaxen stubble which emphasized the cleft in his chin.

"I'm at a disadvantage," I said. "You know my name, but I don't know yours."

"Forgive my poor manners. I'm Marcus and," he gestured to the helmet in his hand, "as you see from the plumage, a princeps posterior in the army."

With no knowledge of army ranks, I did not know the level of respect or awe he expected me to show. "How may I help you?"

"For many months my manservant has been grumbling about pain in his toe. He's a proud, uncomplaining man so his pain must be great."

"The largest toe?"

"Yes." Marcus frowned, rubbed his chin.

"Is the skin inflamed?"

"Yes. You're familiar with his illness?"

It was a common complaint. Treatable but not curable. I had helped an old noble with the same problem. Unfortunately, he refused to limit his excessive eating and drinking. And none of my warnings convinced him.

"He has gout. I can help him," I said, "but unless his eating habits change the attacks will continue."

Marcus winced. "That's not likely to happen, he's obstinate." He tapped his chin. "But perhaps a beautiful woman will change his mind."

My heart skipped at his flattery. "You're a kind master to see to his pains."

"There's no one who polishes my armor better."

"I only meant…" My cheeks flamed with embarrassment. Centurions were not kind. They were the fiercest of officers, chosen for valor and leadership.

"Can you keep a secret?" One eye narrowed.

"Yes." I spoke the word slowly, unsure of what he might reveal.

"I plan on releasing Sol from his servitude when we return to Rome. That way I can buy a healthier manservant." His eyebrow quirked and he folded his arms. His mouth twitched, then broke into a wide grin. "It's a surprise. After this mission, I'll be able to grant him manumission and give him a large sum."

"Your secret is safe with me." I could not stop smiling.

Our eyes met for too long. I looked away, and Marcus cleared his throat.

"I'll return with the preparation shortly," I said, my heart galloping like a horse.

"May I accompany you? Many seasons have passed since

I've had the pleasure of such attractive company. I'll gather and carry the plants for you."

"Yes. No." It was difficult to think when all I could focus on was his sparkling eyes.

Marcus cocked his head.

I tugged on my scarf, pulled it over my brows to hide the blush spreading across my cheeks. "I already have the ingredients. I only need to prepare the mixture."

"Ah, I see." Marcus sounded disappointed. "Well, if you'll excuse me, I'll tell Sol a beautiful herbalist will soon attend to his pain." His full lips curved into a smile. "I'll be here when you return." Helmet swaying from his hand, he walked from the atrium.

I exhaled, set my hand over my hammering heart, and looked about. Father was gone. I never noticed he left!

"Your face is red." Camilla came out from behind the column.

"It's hot today."

"Not *that* hot."

My cheeks grew warmer. "Hot enough."

"The centurion didn't seem so fierce after removing his helmet," said Camilla. "He was rather handsome. In a rough sort of way. His jaw is a bit too brutish for my taste."

Brutish? It was chiseled to perfection. "I didn't notice."

"Did you notice the size of his arms?"

"I didn't pay attention to that either." I scowled at her and walked past. But my excitement could not be contained. I broke out into a wide grin thinking about Marcus's strong, muscled limbs.

"Either you're lying or you're becoming as daft as Father," said Camilla.

I spoke over my shoulder. "Send a servant after Father, he wandered off."

I was halfway to my room when Camilla's taunt resounded down the hallway.

"I know you paid attention when he said you were beautiful. Don't pretend you didn't!"

I lifted my stola's hem and dashed around the corner, Camilla's laughter mocking my every footfall.

Gout was a frequent complaint of old men, so Pricilla and I always harvested enough of the meadow saffron in the fall when its purple blooms were at their peak. With unsteady hands, I lifted the coffer of dried herbs and grabbed the clay pot. It slipped from my fingers.

This was silly. I had talked to handsome men before. Anyway, Marcus was a centurion, a soldier who had none of the refinement of a patrician or equestrian. He was well beneath my own equestrian status.

My heart did not seem to care. Neither did my trembling hands. I set a dried tuber in a bowl and picked up the pestle. And dropped it. I took several deep breaths and began again, mashing the tuber into a pulp while Marcus and his smiling eyes and wheat-colored hair consumed my thoughts.

I looked down, surprised to find the meadow saffron pulverized to the perfect consistency.

And panicked.

I snatched the reflecting plate and held it to my face. Marcus said I was beautiful. It was not the first time someone had told me that. Family, servants, and old men had told me the same, but I had paid no attention. Relatives were bias, servants mere flatterers, and old men entranced by youth. Marcus was none of these. He was young and handsome and made me think about things an unmarried maiden should not.

The bowl clutched in both hands, I returned to the atrium.

"This is a grand villa." Marcus spread his arms wide. "Are you mistress of this estate?"

He thought I was a married woman!

"No, although I do what I can to help Father."

Marcus smiled with compassion, his eyes softening. "He was very concerned about dead rabbits."

"Those rabbits are frequent subjects of conversation." I held out the bowl. "Where's the patient?"

"Sol is outside." On long athletic legs, Marcus strode through the marble-tiled ostium, pausing to pat our dog's head.

I giggled, even the huge guard dog, his tail a-wagging, was under Marcus's spell.

"Did you know all the patrician's homes in Rome keep a guard dog like this? Sometimes two," said Marcus.

"That's why Father insisted we have one. I don't think we need protection in the country. We know everyone."

Marcus chuckled. "That's precisely who patricians fear. Everyone they know."

We found Sol sitting against an outside wall, one foot without a sandal. Nearby, two legionnaires held the reins of four horses under the linden tree.

I looked down the long drive of our villa. "Is the Roman army nearby?"

"Only a centuria, eighty men camped near town."

"Are you on your way to battle?"

"We're on a diplomatic mission." Marcus crossed his arm and stared down at Sol. "This is the domina of Parisii Vineyards."

I hunched down beside Sol. "Hello, my name is Locusta."

"You have my gratitude, domina." Sol shifted his foot, which was bright red and swollen.

"What land do you call home, Sol?" I learned from Pricilla to ask questions while examining a patient. Small courtesies put people at ease and distracted them.

"My home is by my master's side."

"Marcus is a giant to be sure, but he's not so massive as to be considered an empire."

Marcus rumbled with amusement.

"He's both a giant and a great master," said Sol. "As for my home, these old eyes haven't seen its beauty for many years. It's far east of here. A land of milk and honey. Of sweet dates and farting camels."

"What's a camel?" I set the bowl on the ground beside him.

"A large beast bigger than a horse. They have a fair temperament and a foul odor."

"Beasts of burden?"

"Indeed, they carry men and their loads across deserts as vast as a sea."

"I hope one day you'll see your home and these smelly camels again." I pointed to the bowl. "You must eat a small portion of this mash."

Sol pinched a lump between his thumb and forefinger.

"Not that much."

Sol shook off a globule. "Is this enough?"

"Perfect." I gestured at the sundial in the yard. "After an hour passes, take another bite. One small bite every hour."

"And when night falls?"

I pointed to the sky. "Any good soldier follows time by the moon's path across the sky."

"What if the clouds cover the moon?"

"Make an offering to your gods for a cloudless night." I could not help but smile at his questions.

"I pray to only one god."

"Well, I hope he's powerful then," I said.

"The most powerful of all." Sol wiggled his foot. "When will the pain ease?"

"You should feel relief in a few hours. I can prepare a hot dandelion brew to speed healing if you like. There's a side effect." I lowered my voice. "You'll need to eliminate more frequently."

"Eliminate?" Sol guffawed. "Who cares if I piss like a war horse if the pain is gone."

"You compare yourself to a war horse?" Marcus pulled a long stick from his belt and tapped Sol's thigh. "Only if it's one that's been put out to pasture."

Marcus and Sol shared a laugh. Their closeness reminded me of my relationship with Pricilla.

I looked up at Marcus. "I'll need to examine Sol's toe during the night."

"Is there someone else who can examine him? A servant whose reputation will not be sullied by a nocturnal visit?"

"My handmaid Pricilla can, but for her sake I insist Sol stay in the servants' quarters tonight. I don't want her walking through a centurion camp."

"Yes, of course. Sol will remain here." Marcus tapped Sol's side again. "Heal fast, old man. We will not impose on this gracious woman's hospitality a second night."

I stood, looked at the two legionnaires waiting in the shade. "Well…" There was nothing else to say, nothing else to keep this handsome centurion from his men.

"Well…" Marcus shifted on his feet, tucked the long stick back into his belt. "I'll be back tomorrow morning to see if Sol survived the night without me."

"Will you join us for dinner?" The words tumbled from my mouth.

I did not want Marcus to leave. A wonderful warm excitement coursed through me. Was this love? Did Varinius feel this with Dora? Was this why Pricilla snuck away at night to caress the dark-eyed servant girl?

I had followed her a month ago. Watched from a dark alcove as the servant spread her tunic on the cold tile floor and opened her arms to receive Pricilla's embraces. They kissed, suckled, fondled, and moaned until their bodies writhed. I did not turn away, even when Pricilla lowered her lips between the servant's legs. I was transfixed. Listened. Barely breathed. Afterwards, I had climbed between the blankets and wondered about love. And lust. And if it would ever happen to me.

Marcus frowned. "It's a tempting invitation, except I must decline. My centuria have traveled for many days and haven't had an opportunity to bathe."

"We have the finest baths around." I sounded too eager, too bold.

Marcus's smile lit up his face. "How can I refuse? I'm honored and humbly accept."

His eyes met mine and my body warmed under his smile.

Sol's exaggerated coughing startled us. I blushed. Marcus issued a terse command in Greek, which caused Sol to scramble to his feet and hobble away.

Marcus knew Greek? It was the language of the educated elite.

"You speak Greek to your servants?" I asked.

"To those who want to learn."

"Why?"

"When they earn their freedom, they'll be able to speak to anyone worth speaking to."

"You're a good master." I picked up the bowl Sol left behind and held it out to him.

"Shhh, my reputation will be ruined if my men hear you make such a preposterous claim." He took the bowl from me.

Our fingertips brushed against one another. Something

passed between us. Something warm and wonderful and exciting. His touch traveled up my arm and into my heart.

I mumbled directions to the baths then, as skittish as a young colt, hurried inside to tell the kitchen workers we had a dinner guest.

ELEVEN

L aughter echoed down the hallway. When had Father laughed so heartily? I could not remember.

I peeked between the drapes but saw nothing. Marcus and Father must be in the cold bath, out of my line of sight.

"Spying?" asked Pricilla.

I startled, let the drapes fall closed. "Back so soon?"

"The girl wasn't sick, just pretending. It's good you stayed here. Her father was as angry as Mars when I told him she was faking her illness to avoid getting married."

"Can you blame her? Had it not been for you..." My meaning swirled with the escaping steam, thick and heavy with the anguish of my own fateful betrothal.

"I heard a rather robust centurion paid a visit this morning." Pricilla's brows lifted, her eyes bright with curiosity.

I pointed to the drapes. "He's in there with Father. Oh, Pricilla, he's the most handsome man I ever saw. He is Hercules in centurion armor."

"Is he now? I must see this fine specimen for myself." Pricilla pushed aside the drapery and strode inside.

As a house servant, Pricilla was able to venture where I

could not. Whereas it would be improper for me to enter while men bathed, she was not bound by rules protecting her virtue. Sadly, although Pricilla was a bondswoman and I was free, neither of us had the same freedoms as equestrian and patrician men. Women were not permitted to hold public office and children belonged to the husband. Our statuses were very different and yet we shared a common master. Men.

"Did you see him?" I asked when she returned.

"Every luscious inch. He's quite well-endowed."

My cheeks exploded with heat.

Pricilla sidled close. "Do you want him?"

I did. I think. But That Night with That Man had made me distrustful and afraid. "Is there an elixir to encourage love?"

"I know a plant that heats the loins but not one that mimics love."

I frowned and started back to my room.

Pricilla walked beside me. "I see the lust in your eyes and the bloom on your cheeks. If you desire this centurion, lie with him. Nothing stops you from experiencing the greatest of pleasures."

"I want to but…" Pleasure? I recalled only pain and humiliation.

"I see how you gaze at young men, your eyes fixed too long on a muscled calf or a broad shoulder," said Pricilla. "I understand your desire for fleshly pleasures. Better a handsome centurion than a poor village boy."

I walked into my room, dropped into the chair, and put my head in my hands. "I don't want to talk about it."

"You must. Your feelings are normal, natural. If you were married your yearnings would be fulfilled. Do you plan to wait for a husband until you know this delight?"

I looked up. "What if I get with child?" Although I

believed my womb was damaged, I needed to give Pricilla an excuse other than that I was afraid.

Pricilla grinned. "Don't worry about that."

"I don't understand."

"Do you recall the woman who almost bled to death after her fifth child?"

"Of course. She asked for something to prevent her from conceiving anymore children."

"I'm giving you the same herb."

I leapt from the chair. "Without my knowledge?! Without my consent?!"

Pricilla set her basket of herbs on the table and put her hand to her heart. "I'm protecting you."

"How dare you!"

Unaffected by my outburst, she lifted the lid and returned the clay vessels to the herbal coffer. "You no longer have a virginity to protect. You should be happy. Now you can frolic with the centurion."

"I still have a reputation."

"Then I suggest you be discrete."

I slammed down the lid of the coffer. "Send a servant to tell me when the men leave the baths. And tell Camilla's handmaid to attend to my hair and dress. Leave me be."

"I—"

"Go." I turned away and folded my arms.

Pricilla departed the room and I slumped back into the chair. Pricilla loved me, had only the best intentions. I knew that, but this was an odd way to show it. This wasn't Rome. I could not be promiscuous! I had to wait for a husband.

But what if Aunt Diana never found one? What if I had to live here an unmarried woman all my life? I would never know what a real kiss was. I would never experience the pleasures of sex.

Did I *really* want Marcus? Or was it just sexual curiosity? I stood and looked out the window. What *did* I want? Neither the vineyards nor the statue of Bacchus gave me an answer.

Before dinner, Pricilla crept into my room with a small bouquet clutched in her hand. "Am I forgiven?"

I slid a bracelet over my wrist. "No."

"I brought these for your hair." Pricilla held out the pink flowers.

"Fine, but I'm still angry with you." I sat down.

"I'm sorry. I should have told you. I did it for you. So you could have some happiness if the situation presented itself." Pricilla's head tilted sideways, her eyes regarding me from behind the tendrils that escaped her braids. "And it did. Marcus is a present of luscious manliness."

"He is, isn't he?" I giggled. "I'm torn, Pricilla. What if sex with Marcus is awful? I'll blame you for encouraging me to do something I'm not ready for."

"What if it's good?" She wove the blossoms into a flowery crown.

"I suppose I'll have to forgive you then." I managed a weak smile. "And slip a few coins into your hand to express my gratitude… even though you overstepped your position."

Pricilla adjusted the palla over my left shoulder. "You're a daughter, sister, and friend to me. I did it out of love."

"Love or not, you should have told me. I have the right to make my own decisions. I'm not a child." I held the polished plate to my face. "Should I or shouldn't I?"

"You need to decide soon. Your handsome centurion will leave any day. Will you savor a night of passion or lament a missed opportunity for a lifetime?"

TWELVE

"Father is lost," said Camilla while we waited in the cyzicene for Marcus.

A maiden of marriageable age now, Camilla put effort into her appearance and showed interest in the world beyond our villa. Especially eligible marriage prospects.

"Not again." I turned to two attendants. "Find Father."

Each day he became more disoriented, more prone to wander farther from the villa. I stared into the distant vineyards and prayed they found him before dark.

"Who are we waiting for?" Varinius bounced his foot against the sofa.

Before I could answer, Marcus strode into the room.

Camilla gasped. The intimidating centurion was gone. In his place was a sophisticated man in a finely woven tunic and toga. Attired in this formal manner, Marcus's muscled limbs all but disappeared under the fabric. Only his right arm, tan and brawny, suggested the mighty physique beneath.

"Welcome." I introduced Camilla and Varinius. "Father will join us shortly."

"Thank you again for your hospitality." Marcus reclined

on the sofa near Varinius. "I can't remember the last time I dined surrounded by such beauty—a grand villa, fine artwork, and two beautiful women. I'm humbled by your gracious welcome."

The room fell silent and I regretted my invitation. There was nothing an immature maiden, a skittish loner, and a lustful herbalist could say to interest a centurion. At least not for very long.

"It's we who are thankful. We don't get many visitors." I signaled the servants to serve the meal. "Do you have any news of Rome?"

"News is boring," said Camilla. "Do you have any gossip?"

"There's no shortage of that, unfortunately, it's not suitable for young ears," Marcus said.

Camilla waved her hand around. "No one here with that problem."

Marcus looked to me for approval. I nodded my consent, his gesture making me feel wise beyond my years. Delighted by his unspoken compliment, I almost forgot how ignorant I really was. I knew nothing about the world.

"Mmmm," Marcus drummed his fingers on the table. "Did you know Emperor Claudius had his wife Messalina killed after she publicly wed senator Silius?"

"How can she be married to two men at once?" asked Camilla.

Marcus shrugged. "She can't. Not legally."

"She deserved to die," said Camilla.

"Marcus," I said, "our villa is not so remote we haven't heard that bit of information already."

"Nobody told me," Camilla pouted.

Marcus tossed me a knowing smile. My heart warmed to see him indulge Camilla's youthful temperament.

"Ah," said Marcus, "but did you know the lovers plotted to assassinate Emperor Claudius for the purpose of making Silius the new emperor?"

"Silius? Her lover? Why isn't a woman allowed to rule?" asked Camilla. "Cleopatra did. She was the pharaoh of Egypt."

"Only until Augustus raided her lands," I reminded her.

"No Roman army will ever follow a woman," said Marcus.

"Then they're stupid." Camilla plucked a bit of fish from the plate.

"Not stupid." I tried to softened Camilla's rude remark. "The army must obey the tradition of male rule." I turned to Marcus. "Tell us more of the assassination attempt. That sounds interesting."

"Emperor Claudius grew suspicious—"

"I'm confused." Camilla interrupted. "How does Messalina wed another man when she's already married to the emperor? How does Emperor Claudius not know what's going on in his own palace?"

"The emperor's palace is much larger than this villa," said Marcus. "Both Claudius and Messalina have their own suite of rooms. They may go days or weeks without seeing one another. Also, living in Rome is much different from living in Gaul. Here, the women marry men of equal wealth and status. Husband and wife reside in the same villa and work toward common goals like family and business. In Rome, the patricians marry for a different reason. Fathers use their children to forge political alliances, manipulate diplomatic accords, and broker senatorial votes. By cementing a bond with their progeny, the power-hungry senators achieve power, gain new lands and titles, and increase their wealth. Senators don't care about things like love or temperament. The political soil produces little love between the two people matched only for political gain. That's why husbands and wives take lovers, although wives are expected to be discrete."

"Like Emperor Claudius and Messalina." Camilla wrinkled her nose.

"Exactly. I doubt they spent much time in each other's company except to beget an heir."

"How did the emperor know she was married to another man?"

"Roman walls have ears."

"Don't tell Father," I said, "or he'll order our walls be immediately fitted with Roman ears."

Marcus nodded. "I think that's one decoration best left in Rome."

"How did Messalina die? Did Claudius kill her during…" Camilla covered her mouth and giggled.

"Nothing as sordid as that," said Marcus. "Claudius sent his guards to the Gardens of Lucullus where Messalina often engaged in—" Marcus paused and glanced my way, "carnal activities." He cleared his throat. "They found her in a private grotto, and—in deference to her nobility—presented her with a sword to commit suicide. Messalina held the blade to her neck just so." Marcus lifted the table knife to his throat. "And like this." He shifted the point to his chest. "And here." He tapped the blade over his heart. "But she didn't have the courage to kill herself."

"What happened?" If Camilla leaned any closer, she would topple from the couch.

"The senior guard, disgusted by her cowardice, snatched the blade and plunged it into her stomach." Marcus pantomimed the gesture, complete with a theatrical groan of death.

"Oh!" Camilla's hand flew to her mouth.

"Unfortunately, Claudius has learned nothing about how to choose a worthy woman. His current wife, Agrippina, is far worse and even more devious than Messalina."

Agrippina. The name meant wild horse.

"Another adulteress?" I asked.

"She's the sister lover of Caligula." Marcus plopped a fig in his mouth.

"The gossip is true?" I shook my head. Were all Roman patrician women without morals? Or was their outrageous behavior born out of necessity and the will to survive? What about Rome made the elite so outrageous and immoral?

"Many swear they witnessed it with their own eyes."

"What's a sister lover?" Camilla set down her goblet.

I pursed my lips and my gaze met Marcus's.

"Caligula lay with his sisters—together—all of them together," I said.

"Eww." Camilla grimaced.

I turned to Marcus. "Why would Emperor Claudius wed such a woman?"

"It's whispered that Agrippina has the ear and another persuasive appendage of Emperor Claudius. Also, she's young and beautiful and conniving... and his niece."

Camilla's eyes grew as wide as platters.

"Deplorable." I shuddered.

"Indeed, it stretches even the Roman elite's ideas of propriety," said Marcus. "Even worse, Agrippina's previous husband died under mysterious circumstances."

"Did she poison him?" asked Camilla.

"That's the rumor."

"Poison who?" Father, with mud-splashed ankles and wrinkled tunic, came in from the courtyard.

"Agrippina, the woman betrothed to Emperor Claudius." I

rose from the couch, flicked off a leaf from Father's shoulder and guided him to his place at the table.

Father bid everyone hello, settled himself on the couch, and reached for a plate of bread.

"How did Agrippina poison him?" said Camilla.

"Camilla." My chest tightened and cold sweat beaded on the nape of my neck "That's not suitable discussion for the dinner table."

"Oh, and stabbing and blood and fornicating are?" Camilla plopped an olive in her mouth.

"Talk of poison upsets your sister." Marcus mistook my worried expression for annoyance.

"Not likely." Camilla flapped her hand about, almost toppling her wine goblet. "Locusta can poison someone as easily as heal them. Isn't that right, Locusta?"

The heat of embarrassment flamed my cheeks. "I don't know anything about poisoning." I lied. I had to.

"I doubt that." Camilla picked up a mushroom and turned to Marcus. "Locusta and her handmaid Pricilla go out almost every day to gather leaves and berries and dig in the dirt like common field workers."

"Camilla." Father ripped off the thigh of the capon and wagged it at her. "I suggest finding an interest in something other than watching how Locusta spends her time."

Camilla's lower lip puffed out.

"Locusta's time in the garden is well spent," said Marcus. "The villagers respect her skill and speak about her with affection."

My heart leapt at his words.

Camilla sighed. Much too loudly. "I don't want to hear about Locusta's weeds. Tell me more about Agrippina."

"Agrippina. Mmm..." Marcus swirled his wine glass and stole a glance at me, his eyes bright with unspoken desires.

"There's talk that Agrippina married Emperor Claudius for only one reason."

We all leaned forward.

"To make sure her only child, Lucius, is next to the seat of Roman power."

"She sounds like an ambitious woman." I nibbled on a bit of honey-drizzled cheese.

"Most of Rome will agree. Her first two marriages certainly increased her power and wealth."

"Claudius is her third husband? How old is she?" I asked.

"Thirty-four years."

Camilla spit out an olive pit with more force than necessary. "I'm going to Rome to find a husband. Three husbands?! Three?! When Locusta and I can't find any?!"

Marcus looked surprised. "I find that difficult to believe."

"Aunt Diana says we'll have to go to Rome to find husbands," said Camilla. "Locusta *almost* had a husband a few years ago but he died the day after they met."

"I'm sorry to hear that." Marcus did not look sorry at all.

"He was old." Camilla's face puckered into a grimace.

"Camilla." I looked to Father, hoped he would stop Camilla from further embarrassing herself. And humiliating me. But Father, his mouth full of food, was grinning at Varinius, who swayed to some silent rhythm while counting the floor tiles.

"Did you have feelings for him?" Marcus directed his question at me.

"We met once," I said, "and exchanged only a handful of words."

"Do *you* have a wife?" Camilla asked Marcus.

"No." Marcus's eyes sought mine. "But it was prophesied that I would meet my true love during a military campaign."

The room grew silent, even the servants paused to listen.

Marcus glanced about the room. "I see I have captured everyone's interest in the ramblings of an old soothsayer."

"Oohhhh, a great romance." Camilla clapped her hands. "What else did the soothsayer prophesize?"

"He claimed my true love would be brave, possess skills far surpassing my own, and be feared for her power."

A knot of envy gathered in my gut. What a wonderful prophecy. Like an ancient legend. "A woman warrior?"

"I hear Africus has vicious female warriors," said Marcus, "but I've never encountered any."

"Do you believe the prophecy?" I hoped he didn't. But if he did, it would make him a romantic. And all the more charming.

Marcus shrugged. "Soothsayers' prophecies are ambiguous and puzzling, and always seek to deceive."

Camilla clapped her hands. "A love story like Baucis and Philemon. Poor but happy peasants who die in each other's arms."

"You left out a lot of the story," I said. "And Marcus is not a peasant."

Marcus rubbed his chin. "I might become one if my men find out my so-called true love is a better warrior than me."

We were all laughing when Varinius jumped up from the sofa.

"I take my leave." He rushed from the room.

"Well," said Marcus, paying no attention to my brother's rude behavior, "shall we trade romance for adventure?"

The rest of the evening Marcus regaled Father, Camilla, and I with stories of Roman bravery in the battlefield, of bold deeds and valiant men. He spoke of giving thanks to Mars, the god of war, and also to Mithras, the slayer of the bull of cosmic darkness, the deity who offered redemption to his followers.

Marcus's stories entertained everyone. But while Camilla and Father listened to his words, I was enrapt with my own imaginings. The taste of his lips. The feel of his chiseled chest. Our bodied intertwined.

That evening, I did not taste the food or savor the wine's flavor. I did not see the colors of the sunset or hear the nightingale's trill. I did, however, listen to every word Marcus spoke. Cherished his every smile.

Camilla yawned and I realized the room's burnished glow came from the lamps. I had not noticed the servants lighting them or clearing the table.

Marcus made the world disappear.

As the night cooled and the moon climbed high into the starry sky, our too frequent glances grew more heated.

Did I want a night of passion? Or a lifetime of regret?

THIRTEEN

"Marcus the brave. Marcus the kindhearted, Marcus of the bulging muscles. You're quite smitten." Pricilla teased while helping me undress. "I confess, I've heard enough about Marcus for one day." She pulled off my bracelets and anklets. "Sleep well." She spread a fine-spun linen sheet over me.

"Don't forget Sol," I reminded her although I myself had forgotten about him until this very moment.

"I won't. Dream of Marcus." Pricilla closed the drapery behind her.

Marcus. Marcus…

I stared at the ceiling, dreams of love and intimacy enfolding me like a mist. My body tingled with yearning. My mind relived every shared smile, each stolen glimpse. I lay there forever. Or maybe a minute. Romantic thoughts were like surf against the shore, relentless and without regard for time.

"Locusta." The voice was low, hesitant, a whisper that floated on the breeze.

I sat up. A silhouette loomed in the doorway. There was no mistaking the broad shoulders and height.

The drape swung closed behind him.

I leapt from the bed and crossed the room. Marcus and I met in the middle. We did not touch, stood a hand's breadth apart, the moonlight casting our lust with a golden glow.

"Do you want me to leave?" asked Marcus with a huskiness I had not heard before. "I'll leave if you don't want me."

I reached out, and his warm hand enclosed mine.

"Tell me, Locusta, what do you want?" He leaned forward and his lips brushed against my cheek. Gentle. Warm.

I wanted more.

He lifted my hand to his mouth and kissed my palm. Every hair on my body responded to his touch.

"Marcus." The name was a sigh, a breath. My consent.

With a deliberate slowness that set me aflame, he kissed each finger. Liquid fire coursed up my arm, raced into my belly, and bloomed downwards. The heat nestled between my legs. My knees buckled.

Marcus wrapped his arm around my waist and gathered me in his arms. He kissed me. It was soft. Unhurried. A slow exploration. His tongue flicked across my lips. I parted them, and the kiss deepened. My mouth melted into his. Now I understood. This is what it was supposed to be like.

I grabbed his hair and pulled him towards me, greedy for the taste of him. I pressed my lips against his, met each flick and thrust.

A moan escaped, long and soft. Mine. His. Ours.

Marcus broke the kiss. "Are you a virgin?"

"I…" Did he want a virgin? I looked away.

"It makes no difference." Marcus touched my face, stroked my cheek. "And *all* the difference. Look at me."

I did. "I don't understand."

"Is this your first time?"

"No." I shook my head. "My betrothed... he didn't have my consent and... 123he was cruel."

Marcus winced. "I'll be gentle." He ran his fingers through my hair. "Are you certain you want this?"

"More than anything."

"Then I'm yours to command." Marcus dropped to his knees, rested his stubbled chin against my belly, and gazed up. "I'm a centurion, Locusta. We are forbidden to wed. Our lovers must content themselves with following us from camp to camp. Noble women do not wed centurions."

"You don't need to remind me."

"Oh, but I do. I'm not a suitable bridegroom. We both know this. Yet, I confess, the moment I saw you in the atrium, I knew—felt it deep in my bones—that you were the one. The gods are cruel, though. We can never be man and wife."

His words coiled around my heart like a snake, writhed and squeezed with the truth of our ill-fated love. "There must be another way."

"There isn't. Do you want me to leave? I don't want you to do something you'll regret."

My chest heaved. "Stay."

Marcus smiled, took my hands, and sprinkled them with kisses. "I leave in a few days."

"I know." I did not want to think about that now.

Marcus released my hands and touched the top of my feet. He stroked my ankles, crept up my calves and over my knees. Each time he moved upward, his eyes sought consent. I nodded. I wanted him to go faster. To slow down. To stop time.

His fingertips trailed along my thighs. I gasped. He moved higher, slipped under my thin tunic, and brushed his hand against the thatch of hair. My breath came in quick pants the further he journeyed. He lingered at my hips, then ran his hands over the curves of my buttocks.

I sighed, his caresses turned my body into molten liquid, melted away all my nervousness.

"I envy the man who will wed you," he said.

I drew a ragged breath and dug my fingers into his hair.

His hands grazed over my belly, climbed higher, circled my breasts, skipped across my nipples. I whimpered as he brushed across the rigid buds twice more.

"Do you want me to stop?"

I thrust his face into my bosom where his hot breath filtered through the thin linen like a zephyr. His mouth latched on to the tip, the heated tug a torturous pleasure.

I cast off my tunic, dropped it on the floor, and stood before him naked. My body a fleshly offering.

Marcus did the same, a grinning shameless Dionysus with his toga at his feet.

In a heartbeat our hands were everywhere, ardent and possessive. Our mouths, greedy and insistent. Marcus scooped me up, crossed the room, and set me down on the bed.

He stepped back, his eyes hungry for me. "You're so beautiful. Like a goddess." He squared his shoulders, his desire stretched towards me. "A goddess who must be worshipped."

I took his hand and drew him near. Marcus lowered his body over mine and caressed my inner thighs until they parted.

I waited for Marcus to thrust into me. He did not. Instead, his fingers slid between my folds. He moaned, my wetness his delight, and covered my mouth with his.

I writhed and sighed with his touch. Wiggled and panted

until, like a wave crashing over rocks, my body erupted with waves of release.

Marcus glided into my lust. His length summoned another crashing wave. We moved to a blissful rhythm, my legs tightening around him, our bodies pulsing to a single desire.

Marcus whispered. Endearments. Honeyed sentiments. He likened me to Venus, goddess of love and beauty. He, as Adonis, was smitten by my charms.

In the warmth of his arms, I treasured his words, the musky scent of our union, and the salty taste of his skin.

And then we did it again. And again.

Marcus left before dawn.

FOURTEEN

I awoke, a smile on my face, to find Pricilla setting a bowl of porridge on the table.

"Did you tell Marcus to come to my room?" I sat up.

"After you scolded me for interfering" The glint in her eyes said otherwise.

I touched my inner thighs, sticky with our lust. "I love him."

"Oh, Locusta," Pricilla sat on the bed. "You enjoyed a night of pleasure. Nothing more."

"You make it sound sordid. This is different. He believes I'm his true love, the woman prophesied by a soothsayer."

Pricilla stroked my hair. "The centurion is a skilled lover, no doubt. He knows the art of seduction."

"We love each other!" I kicked off the blanket and marched to the table where steam curled from the herb-laced porridge.

Her brow furrowed. "Don't take the promises of a naked centurion—slippery from your nectar—to heart."

I threw the bowl to the ground. "How insolent you are!"

Pricilla regarded the porridge's splatter with indifference. "Will you run away with this Hercules? Follow him through dangerous lands with heathen hordes not as a wife—because centurions are forbidden to wed—but as a servant to his pleasures? Are you content to make your home in a tent, wash his clothes, and sire his bastard children?"

"Marcus said…he said…" I sank onto the chair, wiped a tear from my cheek. "He reminded *me* that my status makes it impossible for us to wed."

"Then do not talk of love." Pricilla scooped up the spilled porridge with a jagged pottery shard.

Pricilla was wrong. Marcus loved me. I was not a servant to his pleasure. Not an innocent he wooed with words. He had made no promises because there were no promises we could keep. In a few days Marcus would leave. Forever. It had been my choice to make memories to last a lifetime.

That afternoon, under the pretense of retrieving Sol, Marcus paid a visit.

"Thank you for your hospitality. You have my gratitude. And Sol's. He's much improved." Marcus spoke formally in front of the eavesdropping servant.

"You're welcome." My tone matched his own.

The moment the servant left the atrium, I rushed into his arms. His leather and armament prevented a more satisfying embrace, but I didn't care.

We kissed, our tongues entwining, greedy for the taste of each other.

A sound down the hall made me pull back.

I cleared my throat. "May I interest you in a tour of the Parisii family villa and vineyards?"

"I'd like that." His smile as warm and bright as a sunny day.

Pricilla was wrong. Marcus did not seduce me. He cared for me. I saw it in his eyes, in the curve of his smile. Heard it in the warmth of his voice. Felt his sincerity in my heart.

I looped my arm through his. "This way." I led him through the wide marble halls and ordered a servant to bring a light meal to the courtyard. "This is the winter dining room," I pointed into the triclinium. "Last night we supped in the cyzicene."

"The view rivaled any villa in Rome."

"Really? Do you prefer green vineyards to marble temples?"

"Neither, I refer to the raven-haired beauty beside me."

We stole a kiss and continued to the next room where I showed him the small bronze tripod table in the corner of the exedrae. "Father claims Grandfather purchased this in Greece from a man who claimed kinship with Hercules."

"Your father has fine taste. From floor to ceiling. Does he host many parties?"

"Not anymore. He's old and prefers quiet." And living in the past.

Marcus smiled sadly. "It's always difficult to watch a parent's health decline." He squeezed my hand.

"Your father too?"

"He had a different illness. One that left a big strong man barely able to walk." Marcus paused to study the miniature shrine to Lares and Penates, our household spirit-gods. "These carvings are remarkably intricate."

"Father always had an eye for line and form."

"As does every man." Marcus's eyes swept over me from toe to top.

My face flushed with pleasure. "The guest chambers are much less remarkable." I pulled back the drapery.

"Mmm, it seems your father prefers to let the windowless room and old wooden stool speak the words he's too polite to say."

"Father loved parties, but he didn't like guests over-staying their welcome."

We continued to the courtyard where the table was set with honeyed wine and plates of vegetables, bread, salted fish, and cooked eggs.

Marcus made a sweeping gesture at the rows of grape vines that blanketed the hills. "Where is Locusta's Oasis?"

"You remembered." My brows lifted with delighted surprise.

"Of course. Will you take me there?" Marcus set his helmet on the bench.

Had it not been for his centurion uniform and my good manners, I might have tossed aside my clothing to consummate our desires on the table. Instead, we sipped sweet wine and nibbled on savory food—a poor substitute for our true hunger—and talked.

Marcus told me he was the son of a favorite servant, one owned by a distinguished patrician. Marcus became both the personal servant and companion to the patrician's own son. And as such, he benefitted from the same elite education and athletic training.

On Marcus's seventeenth birthday he was permitted to join the Roman legion where he demonstrated exceptional bravery, intelligence, and literacy not found in the common legionnaire. Marcus soon became a favorite of his superior officers. This favor extended to the patrician who, as a reward for his faithful service, wrote Marcus a letter of introduction. This provided Marcus the opportunity for military advancement far beyond his servant status.

"I hope to achieve equestrian status by the end of my twenty-fifth-year of service," said Marcus.

"Uncle Amando says emperors fill important government posts with equestrians." It also meant we could wed, our status the same.

"Yes, but first the gods will have to bless me with invincibility and fortune to outlive my obligations."

Marcus spoke the truth. Centurions were easily identified by their feathered helmets. They led battle charges and stood their ground to the bloody end.

"I'll wait for you." I brushed my fingers across his helmet's plumes. The tall quills acted both as a target for his enemies and as inspiration for his men.

"The choice is not yours to make," he whispered.

He was right. I had no choices. Father and Aunt Diana would make them.

I looked away and swallowed the sour taste of reality. When I composed myself to trust my voice, I met his gaze again. "Would you like to see Locusta's Oasis?"

Marcus put down his goblet and rose from the sofa. "I upset you."

"The gods mock us." I stood and crossed the courtyard to the statue of Minerva holding an owl. "But I'll make offerings for your safety anyway, especially to your god Mithras." I held out my hand, smiled bravely. "Locusta's Oasis awaits."

We descended the wide marble steps and followed the stone pathway.

"I'm impressed," he said as we walked beneath the stone arch and into my well-tended and orderly garden.

"This is meadow saffron." I crouched beside the lilac-colored flowers. "It helps ailments like Sol's."

"Such an unassuming flower." Marcus bent low and traced his finger down the petal's length.

"Sol should learn how to make the mixture himself, but he must be careful, too much results in death."

Marcus shook his head. "Neither of us have your skill or knowledge. To us, one weed looks like another."

"I'll replant one in a pot suitable for travel."

"Soldiers do not carry potted plants, Locusta."

"Then it's a good thing Sol is a servant and not a soldier." I tapped one of his medallions. "Do you want to see another more private oasis?"

Marcus cocked an eyebrow. "Lead the way."

Years before my birth, Father had built a pergola in the midst of a grove. Over time, the bougainvillea wended a pink path through the green tunnel of trees that stretched across the Doric columns to form a shady retreat. Wicker couches, sprinkled pink with petals from the flowery canopy above, made it the perfect place for napping on a hot afternoon.

I led Marcus here, to this hidden place where two tall statues stood like sentinels at the entrance. The first was proud Jupiter, god of thunderbolts and chaser of women. Opposite him was Daphne, the fleet-footed wood nymph who rebuked his advances. The sculptor expressed this metamorphosis from maiden to laurel tree by chiseling her legs into shapely branches that emerged from twig-covered ankles rooted to the pedestal. The nymph's bough-shaped arms reached out in terror, finger-slim leaves of marble clawing the air.

"Beautiful," said Marcus. "But I prefer skin to stone." He clasped my hand, brought it to his lips.

We sat on a sofa that was secluded in our shaded cloister. I wrapped my arms around him, inhaled his scent, and wished we could stay here forever.

"I think I solved the riddle of the soothsayer's prophecy," said Marcus after covering my neck with kisses.

I laughed, pinched his arm. "You unraveled the Delphian knot?"

"More of a tangle than a knot." Marcus twirled a lock of my hair. "The soothsayer's description led me to believe my true love is a soldier. And, in a way, she is."

I thought...I twisted in his arms to escape. I had no desire to hear about his true love.

Marcus tightened his grip. "Locusta, you fight human suffering brought on by illness and infection. You're a warrior for health and vitality. Your weapons are plants. You're the woman the soothsayer foretold of."

I sprinkled kisses on his cheeks, lips, and neck. Warmth suffused my body, and my heart felt light and full at the same time. I had never felt such happiness.

Marcus lifted me onto his lap. I straddled him, and there under a flowery ceiling of pink we rocked until sated.

I invited Marcus to dine with us again. Unlike last night's flirtatious glances, this evening we could not keep our eyes off each other. My shyness from yesterday was gone. In its place was the confidence of a woman who knew what she desired.

Camilla felt the difference. I saw it in her quizzical stare. Was it so obvious? Were our feelings that evident?

Camilla wrinkled her nose. "You two look at each other like you share a secret."

Marcus scratched his cheek. "We do. We both know I'll be having dinner here tomorrow night as well."

"As long as you don't run out of stories," said Camilla.

I had my own secret though. One I could not tell Marcus. One my head had been whispering to me since this afternoon and my heart knew to be true.

My body and heart were traitors. They hungered for an

ill-suited and forbidden man, a warrior who would leave me. I had to end it. Tonight. Before I fell too hard. Or did something foolish. Or was found out. Father would be furious.

I would tell Marcus after the meal. After all, I tasted the pleasure of his love. I did not need to gorge on it.

FIFTEEN

"Meet me in the baths," said Marcus when everyone had left the room.

I shook my head. "I can't. It's best we don't…"

Marcus traced my lips with his finger. "Don't what?"

His touch melted my resolve. "Get caught." I grabbed his finger and sucked hard. Twirled my tongue around it.

Marcus moaned and nuzzled my neck.

That night I discovered the sensuality of warm water and buoyancy. Marcus was my teacher. I, the eager student. I learned his every carnal lesson with immeasurable pleasure.

I no longer disapproved of Varinius and Pricilla for their fleshly weaknesses. The lure of salty flesh and sweet lips overcame all reason.

"When my military service is finished and I've attained equestrian status, I'll look for you," said Marcus the next afternoon as we curled around each other on the meadow grass.

My throat tightened with sorrow, yet I managed a brave smile. "Do more than look. Find me." I tickled his chin with a blade of grass.

By week's end, our lovemaking grew desperate, each coupling more urgent. How was it possible to be happy and miserable at the same time? How did two such opposite emotions claim my heart and mind with such equal intensity?

The centuria broke camp on the sixth day.

Marcus rode to the villa to say goodbye. Dressed in full regalia and atop his war horse, Marcus appeared severe and unapproachable, every inch an indomitable centurion. The man before me was not Marcus, my lover. It was a warrior looking down from his steed, blue eyes shining, not with love but with an eagerness for adventure. For conquest and battle.

I knew the truth. Our paths would never cross again. And so, I drank in his person, seared his image, our kisses, and every fevered embrace into memory, forever branded my heart with our impossible love.

Camilla rushed outside and peered down the lane. "Oh, I thought the entire centuria would be here, but it's just him."

Just him. Only him.

Marcus bowed his head. "Camilla. Locusta. I owe you much gratitude for your hospitality." His eyes bore into mine. "Optimum est pati quod emendare non possis."

It is best to endure what you cannot change.

Camilla scratched her nose. "What's that supposed to mean?"

Our love, for now, was not meant to be.

I did not answer Camilla, instead I took one last long look at the man who showed me how to love and how to be a woman.

"Ave atque vale," Marcus said.

Hail and be well.

With that farewell, he kicked the horse and galloped away.

Marcus did not look back. I wondered if I was already forgot.

SIXTEEN

"Those publicani are ruthless." Uncle Amando shook the scroll in his hand. "They say they'll seize ten percent of the crop yield."

I took the scroll from my uncle, unrolled it, and gave it a cursory look. "Father didn't pay his taxes?"

"He doesn't remember." Uncle Amando threw up his hands. "The thieving publicani took advantage of that." He crossed his arms. "They also know of Varinius's peculiarities."

I gestured to the wall of honeycombed shelves stuffed with parchments and papyrus. "Father must have kept a record."

"If he did, I can't find it." Uncle Amando shook his head and glanced at Aunt Diana. "The taxes must be paid. Aut viam inveniam aut faciam."

I will find a way or make one. The phrase, attributed to General Hannibal, was often quoted by Father.

Aunt Diana clasped her hands together. "Locusta, your family needs you. Parisii vineyards needs you. You must go to Rome and beg for an extension from Emperor Claudius."

"Rome?" The scroll dropped from my hands. "How will I get an audience with the emperor? What would I say?"

Uncle Amando and Aunt Diana exchanged a glance weighty with secret collusion.

"Tell him the truth." Uncle Amando rested his chin atop his fist. "Youth and beauty make even a stubborn man merciful."

"You're an esteemed equestrian," I said. "Roman senators buy your racing horses. Surely your chances of gaining the emperor's ear are better than mine."

"Not likely. We move in different circles. But a beautiful maiden like yourself is her own circle, which compels men to revolve around her. "

"But—"

"I'm certain Emperor Claudius will take pity on you and grant an extension. I've heard he's easily swayed by a pretty face."

"But—"

"You're unmarried. Who knows what may come of the meeting?"

Like marriage to another old man?!

I rounded the desk, kneeled before my uncle, and set pleading lips on his hand. "I beg you, don't send me to Rome." Hot tears welled in my eyes. Rome was far away. Far from my family, my garden, and the vineyards. Far from where Marcus could ever find me. Farther than I had ever traveled before. "Those people are unscrupulous."

"Pfft, it's gossip." Aunt Diana flapped her hand. "Those living in Rome are no more unscrupulous than the potter making urns designed to break. Think of it as a grand adventure, a chance to see the center of the world and all of its majesty." She placed a soft hand on my shoulder. "It's all been arranged. You'll stay with Gaius

Theon. He's a patrician who has purchased many horses from Amando."

"But—"

"You have no choice," said Aunt Diana.

I stood, put my hands on my hips. "Send Camilla."

"Camilla has neither your guile nor beauty," said Uncle Amando.

"You will attend magnificent dinner parties." Aunt Diana's eyes took on a dreamy look. "You will meet patricians and senators. It's a chance of a lifetime."

"You *will* do this, Locusta." Uncle Amando rose from the chair.

He was right, of course. I was the only one capable of appealing to the emperor. Camilla was too silly. And Varinius was...Varinius.

"You will travel under the protection of my most trusted guards and stay with friends along the way."

Will. Will. Will. I had no choice but to obey Uncle Amando's will.

"I must take Pricilla." I could not bear to go so far without her.

"Of course. Do you want to take another servant as well?"

"That's not necessary." I only needed Pricilla.

"It'll be a quick trip." Aunt Diana kissed my cheek. "And then you'll regale us with stories of all the Roman splendors."

"The only Roman splendor I'm interested in is getting a tax extension."

"THERE'LL BE OTHERS." Pricilla folded a pale green stola into the trunk.

"Other what?"

"Men."

I drew my knees to my bosom. "I wasn't thinking of Marcus," I lied.

"You'll have to lie more convincingly in Rome."

I shrugged and rested my cheek on my knee.

"How long do you intend to sulk about him?"

"You don't understand."

"I understand this love between you was untested and professed too quickly. Love like that flares hot and burns out." Pricilla folded another palla into the trunk. "Marcus has no fortune, no property, and no political connections. All he has are swords, muscles, and a big hard stick."

Embarrassed, I clapped my hands over my ears, but Pricilla was still talking when I removed them.

"—tomorrow we leave for Rome. A city of opportunity and parties and power. If you mope around Rome with thoughts of nothing but Marcus Marcus Marcus you'll miss everything. Embrace Rome and all it has to offer."

"You mean embrace the shame of giving obeisance to a crusty old emperor while begging for mercy? Embrace the pretense of flirting with a pack of old men? I'm too young for this responsibility."

"You're the perfect age for intrigue and love and adventure. This is the perfect opportunity to learn from the shrewdest women in the empire." Pricilla tapped her temple. "Intelligence. Prudence. Beauty. You possess all the ingredients necessary for a woman to succeed in a pit of vipers. Listen and learn." Pricilla clasped my hands. "Locusta, don't scorn all the opportunities that will come to you. Don't let your impractical Hercules keep you from finding a suitable husband."

"I'll do as I'm told to save the vineyard. But do not lecture me on the state of my heart."

FAMILY AND SLAVES stood under the front portico to see me off.

"I wish I could go to Rome with you." Camilla pulled me aside and clung to my arm. "Father grows more forgetful every day. I refuse to spend the whole day following him."

"I assigned three servants to look after him. Your only job is to look after them."

"Ugh." Camilla threw back her head.

"Stop that. You're fourteen-years-old. Most girls your age are married and managing a household. Besides, Aunt Diana and Uncle Amando will make all the important decisions." I kissed her forehead and noted the thin line of kohl on her upper lid.

Varinius gave me a quick hug. "Don't worry, Locusta, I'll take care of everything."

"Thank you. No one calculates better and faster than you."

His son's fingers pinched his nose.

I laughed and kissed the toddler. He was a sociable child who had not inherited Varinius's mannerisms.

Varinius's woman, standing by his side, rubbed her swollen belly and smiled shyly.

Father gave me a long hug. "I'll make offerings to the gods for your safe return."

I kissed his cheek, gave him a long hug, and climbed into the carpentum.

"Good bye! Ave atque vale." I waved and shouted as the carpentum rolled away.

The sprawling villa was more than my home, more than a domicile to generations of my family. It was my solace, my

Elysium, my link to Mother's spirit, Father's approval, and my family's love.

Just yesterday Varinius's son had toddled across the peristyle courtyard and Camilla popped out from behind the column to play peek-a-boo. A week earlier I sat under the portico with Father. He insisted the rosemary and lilac vied for dominance at the courtyard's edge, an herbal battle he would soon take an axe to.

Was it only a few years since Varinius, Camilla, and I climbed up the wide boughs of the old ilex trees? It seemed like a lifetime ago.

I inhaled the fragrant breeze. Listened to the birdsongs. Cherished the rolling hills and wild meadows of Parisii estates. I held all these sights, sounds, scents, and echoes of the past in my heart.

SEVENTEEN

The road to Rome was notorious for its thieves. Some were ingenious in their thievery. Others brutal with butchery.

I did not worry. Our caravan consisted of four sword-bearing guards, a surly archer turned driver, an axe-wielding groom, and a javelin-toting horse handler.

This excessive protection wasn't for me. Uncle Amando's prized stallions were worth a lot of money.

The trip was long and tedious. Every day before dark, we stopped to spend the night in the home of one of Uncle Amando's friends.

Each additional halt to our journey—when I told the driver Pricilla and I needed to stretch our legs or relieve ourselves—was met with dour looks and grumbling. The driver was especially impatient whenever a late morning start detained us. Each day his indignation grew, his scowls and sour looks increasing.

Except for today.

"Quid agis mane." The driver smiled when I climbed into the carpentum. "Servus sum."

"I'm doing well this morning, thank you." I turned to Pricilla as the carpentum rolled onto the road. "What happened to him?"

Pricilla buried her face in her hands, her shoulders shaking with glee.

"What's so funny?"

She looked up. "I changed his attitude."

"With an intoxicating potion?"

"Intoxicating yes, but not a potion."

I recognized Pricilla's grin. "I thought you preferred women."

"Usually, but I found him rather appealing."

I wrinkled my nose. "He's rude and thick about the middle."

"That's not the only place." Pricilla snickered. "You know, I quite forgot the pleasure found in a man's rough skin and persistent appendage."

"But he's so grumpy."

"He's a good man with the big responsibility of taking four steeds and one filly to Rome."

"I suppose I'm the filly. Do you think my future husband will check my teeth?" I opened my mouth wide.

"No, but he'll certainly want to feel your flanks before riding you."

We laughed until breath left us and our cheeks were wet with merry tears.

Our glee spent, I pulled bread and salted fish from a satchel. "You make it seem easy." I offered her half. "You see someone you want, man or woman, and take your pleasures."

"Pleasure was not my initial intent. His sour mood was spoiling the journey."

"You manipulated him." I lowered my voice, even though the driver could not hear us.

Pricilla lifted her chin. "Women wield a mighty power."

"You're wrong. We're powerless."

"Not at all. Our power is subtle. Smooth skin, a fair face, a whispered promise of future pleasures—few men are able to resist a woman's charms. Men seek to unite with, to ravage, to sink themselves into the depths of our body. Even Jupiter cannot overcome his lust for women. How many nymphs and women has he lay with? How many demi-gods has his divine organ sired?"

My eyes narrowed. "Are you saying men have no control over their lust?"

"They don't, and a clever woman uses this knowledge and power to advantage."

"Like the emperor's wives, Messalina and Agrippina?" I frowned and shook my head. "Using your body for personal gain is wrong."

"Don't be quick to judge. Oftentimes it's a woman's only weapon."

I shrugged. It was not a weapon I ever wanted to use.

THE TRIP WASN'T ALWAYS BORING. Pricilla and I often put our healing skills to use. Almost every home we visited had a relative or servant plagued by some malady. A grandmother needed our goat weed and lavender remedy for anxiety. A young boy, as youth are wont to do, played with fire and required a mixture of macerated goat weed flowers and olive oil to sooth his burn. A young wife suffered from eczema— her condition bought on after discovering her sister and husband were lovers—and required a topical concoction of oleander.

My knowledge of plants made for lively dinner conversations. The host often summoned a torch-bearing servant to illuminate a field so Pricilla and I could gather the necessary ingredients by moonlight.

On several occasions, a patient's condition required Pricilla to keep vigil through the night. Exhausted, she fell asleep in the carpentum moments after departing. As her weariness grew more frequent, I suspected her passion-filled nights with our yawning yet contented driver was to blame.

"Pricilla?" I nudged her. "Not again. Wake up. I'm bored. Talk to me."

Pricilla mumbled something, shifted position, and went back to sleep.

One warm afternoon we stopped at a stream to water the horses. I climbed out, glad for the exercise, and watched Pricilla disappear into the nearby woods with the driver.

"Lucky man, maybe she'll give me some," said a guard.

"Maybe she'll take us all together," said another.

"I'll shove my cock in her mouth and you stick your—"

I stomped away. I could no longer overlook Pricilla's brazen behavior. She made me look bad. Like an indulgent master. Or worse, like one who could not control her servant.

Hot with indignation, I glowered at the guards, paced back and forth, and kicked at the dirt.

Finally, I returned to the carpentum, my anger festering while I waited. Both she and the driver took advantage of my youth to do as they wished! This was inexcusable! Such disrespect was dangerous. It fostered insolence. What was to keep the guards, groom, and handler from doing whatever they wanted? My hands balled into fists.

Pricilla climbed inside and closed the door.

"The guards mock you," I growled. "Your wantonness embarrasses me."

Pricilla flicked a leaf off her tunic. "Why? You weren't

embarrassed to frolic with your centurion in the baths, the grove, your cham—"

I smacked her across the face.

Pricilla's eyes hardened and she flung open the door.

"Where are you going?"

Pricilla jumped out.

EIGHTEEN

"What are you doing?" I scrambled after her.

Pricilla lowered her head. "You hit me. I thought we were more than servant and master. I thought we were friends." She pushed past the stunned groom.

"Domina," the guard touched the hilt of his sword. "Should I retrieve your handmaid?"

"Not yet." I hurried by him. "Pricilla!"

She kept walking. Fast resolute strides down the road.

"Pricilla." I was afraid to tell her to stop. Knew she would not. Knew the guards watched.

"Don't leave me." I caught up and grabbed her wrist. "I own you."

"Your father owns me," Pricilla said.

"And if he were here, he would accuse me of being a negligent mistress."

Pricilla lowered her gaze. "I beg forgiveness, domina. My remark was disrespectful."

"But truthful." I released her wrist and chewed on my lip. "Marcus and I…" I peeked over my shoulder at the curious guards. "I understand how it is between you two. You will come back." It was more question than command.

"As you wish, domina."

I winced at her subservient tone. "Are we friends again?"

"You misunderstand the nature of friendship." Her lips wilted into a disheartened frown.

"I understand nature—what you've taught me—and I understand *you*. I don't know how or why you came to be an indentured woman, but I know you're both my friend and my servant."

"I doubt the two can share one heart."

"Perhaps," I said, "they can share one truth. And the truth is, I need you. I need your good counsel in Rome. You're far wiser than I in the ways of the world."

"As you say." Pricilla stared at the ground.

The air was heavy, thick with my regret and her misery. I drew a ragged breath and tasted the bitterness of my superiority.

I stepped close. "I'm sorry."

Pricilla rubbed her red cheek and shrugged.

I bobbed my chin toward the guards. "I was angry at you, the driver, and the snickering guards. They made lewd comments about you."

"So you take it out on me?"

I hung my head.

"If you want to be friends, true friends, despite our stations in life, then you must seek not only to understand me but appreciate our differences."

"And you, my point of view." I stepped close. "I can't have the guards think I'm a weak-willed woman they can take advantage of."

Pricilla chewed on her lip. "I hadn't thought of that."

"We're both bound by stupid rules that dictate our behavior." I blinked back a tear.

"I would rather obey a few rules than live like a godless heathen. Anyway, rules are bendable." She gave me an impish grin.

"Not the most important one. Manumission."

Her eyes narrowed. "What do you mean?"

"Only Father can grant it, but I will plead for your freedom the moment we return home."

Pricilla's face brightened. "You would ask him to release me from servitude?"

"Yes. Even if means I never see you again."

Pricilla held my hands. "I'll never leave you, Locusta. Who would I discuss herbal remedies with? Or love like my own sister? Or share secrets and jokes with?"

I glanced over my shoulder. The guards feigned disinterest didn't fool me. They were as still and quiet as statues.

"I promise never to raise a hand to you again." I hugged Pricilla tight despite how improper it appeared to the guards. Our friendship was too important.

Pricilla squeezed back. "And I promise never to taunt you about Marcus. You still pine for him, and why not? He is Hercules made flesh. I, too, would grieve for the loss of such manliness."

"He's a soldier of exceptional masculinity, isn't he? Which makes me curious." I flicked my eyes toward the carpentum. "I saw you slip something into our driver's wine this morning."

"I suppose the time has come to share a few more herbal secrets," Pricilla whispered.

That afternoon, Pricilla revealed the plants of pleasure. Mandrake for lustful euphoria. Nightshade and thorn apple for increased sensuality.

Pricilla had scarcely finished extolling the mind-altering virtues of henbane when the carpentum came to an abrupt stop.

The driver opened the door. "Forgive the intrusion but I thought you might enjoy the view."

"What view is that?"

"Rome."

HERBS
&
HEALTH

NINETEEN

R ome!
I leapt from the carpentum. Far across a vista of blue sky, amid rolling hills of green, laid the city of Rome. Seat of power. Center of the world. Even the Tiber River yielded to its authority and curled around the metropolis like a besotted mistress.

I pulled Pricilla to my side. "It's bigger than I expected."

"And populated with more slaves, freedmen, merchants, and senators than you can imagine," she said.

"The seven hills?" I pointed into the distance.

"Indeed, domina," said the driver. "The hill closest is the Quirinal. That's where the temples of Sancus and Mars are located and…" he stroked his chin in thought, "the gardens of Sallust. I have never been there myself, but I heard it has marble pavilions, flower-filled arbors, and shrubs shaped into all manner of creatures."

"Sounds wonderful," I said. "Tell me the name of the nearby plateau."

"Viminal."

"What temples are on that hill?"

"The shrines of the Argei and an old Serbian fortress." Frowning, the driver glanced at Pricilla. "The valley nearby is the Subura district. Not suitable for good people like yourselves. I heard it's a place full of wickedness and industry."

"Of course," said Pricilla knowingly. "Where you find business, you find wicked people making foul deals."

"Oh, so you've been there?" The driver cocked an eyebrow.

"I've been to Athens. Different city, same people."

My brows lifted. Locusta had never mentioned Athens before.

The driver nodded. "Well, in this part of the city, I hear that the wicked hold hands like old friends. Harlots and hustlers. Cabbage and bread. Cobblers and metalworkers. All eat, love, fight and live together. Most dwell in rat-infested insulae. If you need a rare herb, you'll find it there. But it's no place for a noble woman."

"I'm sure I'll never need to go there." Purchase an herb? The thought never occurred to me.

"Do you see the hill beyond Viminal?" The driver pointed again. "That's Esquiline Hill. Maecenis's Persian gardens are quite close to the Gardens of Lamia."

"And the hill near the Tiber?" I asked. "What's the name of that enormous temple?"

"That's Capitoline Hill. Home to the temple of Jupiter Optimus Maximus Capitolinus."

I tugged on Pricilla's arm. "That's the temple the senators locked themselves inside after murdering Julius Caesar."

"There," the driver hand aimed at some fixed point in the Roman landscape, "are the Imperial and Romanum Forums."

"And beyond?"

"Palatine, the heart of Rome. Home of many patricians and senators."

"Probably even more wicked and foul than the Subura district." Pricilla nudged me.

The driver guffawed. "I wouldn't know. But I can tell you it's the location of Apollo's temple."

"Is it true the temple doors are carved from ivory?" I asked.

"That's what I heard."

Pricilla put her mouth to my ear. "He hasn't seen anything, but he sure hears a lot."

I bit my lip to keep from laughing. "What's the hill farthest from the Tiber?"

"Caelian Hill. Where Rome's wealthiest nobles live. It's our destination."

I squeezed Pricilla's hand. "Our journey has ended."

"No, Locusta." Pricilla squeezed back. "Your journey is just beginning."

I considered her words. How might a young woman like me enter a city of power and splendor and *not* be changed? There were libraries to visit. Gardens to tour. Markets to explore. Temples to admire. People to meet.

"Tell me the name of the hill that's farthest from our vantage point?" I asked.

"Aventine. Hill of legends," said the driver. "Virgil claims Hercules found the fire-breathing Cacus hiding in a cave, concealed among its rocky slopes. It's the same hill where the brothers Romulus and Remus argued over naming the town." He shook his head. "Now, however, Aventine swarms with foreigners hawking exotic and illegal merchandise. It's another dangerous place for a woman of noble birth."

I stood transfixed at the vista before me, fearful and thrilled in equal measure. Rome rose from the countryside like a beacon of opulence. A stronghold of Roman conquest and domination. Surely, no greater city existed in all the world.

"Divine and Base. Beautiful and ugly," said Pricilla, her awed expression matched my own.

"One city. Many worlds." I imagined how Rome might suck a country girl from Gaul into its wanton whirlpool like Charybdis. Or how the six-headed Scylla might pose as gossiping wives and devour my old-fashioned opinions. Rome had the power to swallow me whole. "I've never seen anything so magnificent." I pretended confidence.

"Magnificent and dirty and crowded," said the driver. "Fear not, domina, I'm certain Gaius Theon will take you only to suitable places."

"I want to see everything," Pricilla announced. "The senate house, Circus Maximus, the Temple of Jupiter, the Temple of Vesta, the Theatre of Marcellus, the gardens, the statues—we must see it all."

"Onward," I said, Pricilla's infectious enthusiasm remedied my anxious worries.

Once inside the carpentum, I pushed aside the window coverings. I didn't want to miss a thing.

The nearer we drew, the more crowded the road became. With people, animals, livestock, carts, wagons, horses, and carpentum. Farmers took their flocks to market. Men rode horseback. Others drove wagons heaped with vegetables. In a blink of an eye the once empty road became a bustling thoroughfare. Merchants pushed carts. Women carried bundles on their backs. Families with children scampered about.

We rounded a bend and saw a great wall looming before us. "Look! The Servian Wall. It must be four stories tall." I stuck my head through the window.

Pricilla gave a gentle tug on my arm. "Be careful. This

isn't your village where everyone knows and respects you. Some thief is liable to rip off your gold earring."

I tucked my head back inside, but never took my eyes off our approach. The gate was enormous, wide enough to accommodate several carpenta, and taller than any tree. Its arched entrance hinted at the paradox of Rome. The grand archway was built to encourage trade, yet it also served as an imposing reminder of Roman superiority.

"Is there only one entrance?" I asked the guard riding by the window.

"There are sixteen entrances, domina," he said from astride his horse. "We enter through the most famous north gate of Porta Salara o Collina."

"Why is it famous?"

The guard swept his arm from right to left. "This is the gate the invading Gauls entered before they sacked Rome. The Servian Wall was built soon after and has kept many northern armies at bay."

"It's a tragic gate, then."

"Not at all, for Sulla defeated the Marion forces here. And Hannibal camped outside before he decided the Romans were too great for even such a formidable general as he—elephants and all."

I recalled this bit of history. The fortified gate had stopped Hannibal and his army of men and beasts from entering Rome. They had crossed a vast mountain range to the north, endured hunger and cold, only to be left standing like beggars at the entrance, unable to breach Roman defenses.

The carpentum crept forward through the throng. It rolled past the poor with their arms outstretched, vendors selling food, and street musicians playing lutes and drums for coin.

The driver shouted and waved a stick. No one moved

aside. The guards, annoyed with our slow progress, reared their horses back.

"Make way," they shouted.

The crowd parted. But just barely.

"They have no fear of being crushed under a carpentum," I said to the guard.

"Many a Roman citizen has met an untimely end under the wheels of a carpentum or chariot," he said. "Especially any chariot driven by the emperor or his messengers. Imperial chariots slow down for no one."

"What bird is that?" I asked Pricilla as a bird swooped down over our carpentum, missing it by inches. "Is it a fortunate omen?"

"I'm looking ahead, not above." Pricilla leaned against me as we stared out the window. "Look at all the people and shops. We must go to the markets. Imagine the herbs and plants we'll find."

I wrinkled my nose. "The smell of humanity leaves much to be desired."

Pricilla laughed. "It's the fragrance of Rome. A mixture of sweat, food, and perfume."

"What's the name of this street?" I asked the guard.

"Alta Semita. It runs along the Quirinal to the Vicas Iugarius—one of the main streets to the Forum. That's where you'll find more warehouses, shops, and apartments."

"People *live* in these buildings?"

Although the shops appeared enticing enough, the floors above were crooked, ramshackle, and made of rough-hewn beams.

"Shopkeepers, freedmen, merchants, and the poor must live somewhere," the guard said. "My parents live in a building like this on the other side of Rome."

"Oh, yes, of course." Embarrassed by my gaffe, I moved

away from the window. "The poor in the country have better living quarters than those in Rome," I whispered to Pricilla.

"Sometimes people must trade the countryside for better opportunities."

Rome was a city of opposites. From its multi-storied insulae apartments constructed of mud brick and wood to the wide marble steps that led to towering columns of white edifices.

"My eyes grow weary from looking." I had never seen so many dome-covered shrines, concrete fountains, statues of past emperors, and sculptures of gods and goddesses

"I should hope not." Pricilla patted my arm. "Trees and vines never inspired such awe."

The carpentum turned onto a steep street and slowed down for an ornately carved sella on the way down. Four slaves, poles on their shoulders, walked swiftly past. Its gold-threaded drapes concealed the elite occupant within.

"I would like to travel by sella," I said.

"You'll have to wed a senator." Pricilla adjusted my palla, which had slipped over my shoulder. "We must make sure you exit this carpentum like a goddess. Your hosts must not see you as an unsophisticated country girl but as a genteel goddess from the land of Bacchus." She smoothed my hair into place, adjusted my stola, tugged and arranged the folds.

My stomach fluttering with anticipation, I peered outside to get a good look at the patrician homes. But the grand villas were concealed behind high walls and long curved driveways.

The carpentum stopped at an imposing marble entrance.

"We're here," I whispered.

Our driver passed a scroll to a guard posted at the gate. He read its contents and waved us in.

Gaius Theon's lawn was lush with trees, shrubs, and

flowers. Amid the greenery, stood erotic sculptures of Bacchus, Venus, and the Greek god Priapus.

"It appears Gaius Theon is enamored with wine, love, and fornication," I said.

"And who isn't?" Pricilla pointed to the statue of Priapus. "His phallus is larger than his leg."

"That statue belongs in a brothel," I giggled and closed the curtain when the villa came into view.

The carpentum came to a stop. Our driver and a guard exchanged greetings and instructions.

The driver opened the door. "The servant goes to find his dominus," said the driver. "Domina, you're to wait in the atrium. Pricilla, follow me to the servant's entrance."

I gave Pricilla's hand a quick squeeze. "This is it."

"This is the first of many 'its'." She squeezed back.

With head held high, I stepped from the carpentum, prepared to embrace all that Rome had to offer.

TWENTY

G aius Theon was not in the atrium. His wife, Annona, welcomed me instead.

"Oh, you must be Locusta. Welcome. Your trip was without trouble? Good, thank the gods. My husband is in the stables inspecting his new race horses. Come in, come in, don't be shy. Men and their horses. He thinks and talks of nothing but his Blue racing team." Her thin lips pressed into a thinner smile. "Call me Annona. No sense being formal." Her gray eyes took me in with a feigned politeness. "Well, aren't you lovely? I bet you need to stretch your legs. Let me show you around."

Annona was a tall, plain-looking, bony woman with gray-streaked hair and angular features. Quite the opposite of her elaborate garments and extravagant jewelry. Like her attire, the villa was equally ostentatious with marble statues, jewel-encrusted tables, Egyptian artwork, and bronze couches strewn with embroidered pillows.

"I've never seen a grander home." I paused to admire a relief of the Greek nymph Io's arrival in Egypt.

"Our villa in Rome is one of several residences. All

equally beautiful." She gave me an insipid smile. "Will you join us for wine on the portico? My son, Lucius, is there."

Without waiting for my answer, she strode away, confident I would follow.

The portico, furnished with potted trees, plush sofas, and marble statuary overlooked a garden paradise. In the center of the luxurious space, a young man reclined against a mountain of cushions, a servant fanning him behind a couch made of elephant tusks.

"Lucius, where's your tutor?" Annona ruffled her son's hair.

"I sent him away. I have neither the skill nor interest in studying Julius Caesars's military strategy. I much rather discuss Ovid's Ars Amatoria—the Art of Love. Non omnia possumus omnes."

You can be good at anything you set your mind to.

"Of course, you're the son of a great man." Annona glanced at me. "We have a guest."

Lucius turned his head, his mouth curling into a lewd grin. "What fair nymph do you bring me, venerable Mother?"

"This is Locusta, niece to one of your father's friends. She'll be our guest for a brief time."

Lucius was too young to grow a beard; his body lean with youth. We were about the same age. He looked like his mother, but the angular features suited him far better.

"Where do you call home, Locusta?" Lucius stroked an elephant tusk, his languid caresses meant to fluster me.

"Gaul. My father is a winemaker and my uncle a horse breeder."

"A peach, mother. You bring me a peach." Lucius stopped his lewd pantomiming and sat up. "This ripe fruit needs to see all the sites. I'll take her to chariot races and gladiator games. Would you like that, Locusta?"

"That's very gracious of you, son, however, your attentions lay elsewhere." Annona lifted a wine goblet from a golden tray.

I took the proffered wine, sat in the chair, and avoided Lucius's curious stare. Annona sipped wine and pointed in the distance to temples I could not see and gossiped about people I did not know. When the conversation began to wane, I asked my hostess if she might permit me to make myself presentable for the evening meal.

"Of course." Annona signaled the servant for a refill. "You must be weary from the journey."

With two sets of eyes on me, I walked from the portico with dignified steps, head high, as though at ease in a patrician's home.

"Look how spacious and grand this room is," said Pricilla when I entered my chambers. "Have you ever seen its like?" She draped a blanket over our coffer of herbs.

The room was nothing like Father's meager guest rooms. The bed was huge, the headboard carved like a lion's head, the feet shaped into griffin's claws. It was swathed in silk, even the canopy. A cushioned settee by a wide door offered a fine prospect of the gardens. There were two chests, two tables, and two chairs. All finely crafted. The walls were washed with a pale shade of blue. One depicted a meadow scene. Only the narrow cot meant for Pricilla was less than elegant.

"Why are you hiding the herbs?" I patted the covered coffer.

"I don't want anyone to know."

"Our herbs present no dan—" I covered my mouth. She was right. Maybe we shouldn't have brought them to Rome. But then we wouldn't have been able to help all those people along the way.

In a city where poisoning one's competition was the most expedient way to gain advantage, a guest with a chest of herbs might arouse suspicion.

Pricilla unclasped the broach that secured my stola. "I requested a large bowl of water." She gestured to the great tub in the corner. "Five servants dragged this in."

"They bring the bath to me. How thoughtful."

"I've never seen a household with so many servants. Annona is attended by three." Pricilla untied the breast-binding leather strap.

"Three? I'm not surprised. It must take at least that many to bedeck her with jewels every morning."

"A handmaid told me the evening meal will be served early today because the dominus leaves on urgent business."

I climbed into the basin, which was warm and fragrant with rose petals. "Perfect."

Pricilla picked up my arm, brushed a soft cloth down its length. "You must be careful of every glance and each word."

"Are you trying to frighten me?"

"Not frighten, enlighten." Pricilla glanced over her shoulder. "The servants are hungry for juicy tidbits of gossip. Friendships are precarious. A friend this week may have been a former enemy the month before. Or become a future rival. The Roman elite murder their children, sisters, brothers, wives—anyone standing in their way."

"I know." I cupped my hands, let the rose-scented water run through my fingers,

"Don't put your trust in appearances."

"I know." I lifted my leg from the water, wondered why Pricilla thought a vintner's daughter from Gaul would interest a pack of Roman wolves.

TWENTY-ONE

We dined in the west triclinium.

It was the best place to watch the sunset, Annona explained.

There's a cooler breeze, Lucius whispered as we took our places.

Gaius Theon entered last. He strode across the marbled floor and heaved himself onto the sofa. A plump man with rosy cheeks and red lips, his thick gray beard was a hairy replacement for the few strands left on his head. His ears stuck out and his lobes were fleshy pendulums. He looked jolly and approachable. Nothing like Annona.

"Good evening, Locusta. Welcome to my home." Gaius Theon picked up a golden goblet. "I hope Amando's horses are as swift as he promised." He guzzled the contents of his goblet.

"My uncle's horses have no equal," I said.

Gaius Theon grinned and signaled the servant for a refill. "My wife will take you to the Circus Maximus where you will cheer for the Blue team and see the truth in your boast, eh? There are twenty-four races each day. I insist you watch at least half of them."

"I'm certain our guest will enjoy seeing a real race." Annona turned to me, eyes already glassy from too much wine. "There's nothing like the thrill of watching chariots collide. Last time, a charioteer was thrown off and torn to bits when his body was trapped in the wheels."

"What a sight." I smiled with as much sincerity as I could muster despite my horror.

"The Green team lost four fine horses that day," said Gaius Theon, "and I won enough money to buy my wife new jewels."

Annona touched a thick strand of rubies around her neck.

"Father tells me you hope to petition the emperor," said Lucius. "That's no easy task, even for someone as esteemed as my father. Emperor Claudius has no desire to hear the appeal of a young woman with no political connections, especially one begging postponement for overdue taxes." One side of his mouth slid into a lecherous grin. "Unless your plan includes other skills of the tongue."

"Lucius, how impertinent," Annona scolded.

"But accurate," said Gaius Theon. "Emperor Claudius has no reason to grant audience to a woman without political alliances. Romans breathe politics and devour favors like honeyed dates." He plucked an olive from the platter. "Perhaps I can make an appeal on your behalf to one of the emperor's aides."

"Ah," Annona flapped her hand. "There are other ways to achieve an audience. We'll host a dinner party announcing Locusta's visit. Such a pretty addition to our household will not go unnoticed. Are you betrothed?"

"My fiancé died. My aunt has not found another suitable prospect."

"Excellent." Annona realized too late her insensitive comment. "Well, perhaps your misfortune is now an advantage. There are a number of bachelors to choose from in Rome."

Lucius snorted.

"Not Lucius." Annona wagged her finger. "He's far too young."

And I was far too politically irrelevant.

Annona set down her goblet, only to pick it up again, her finger caressing the stem. "You're a lovely maiden who will soon be surrounded by suitors."

"And infamous flatterers." Lucius lifted his goblet in mock toast.

"I have no intention of imposing on your hospitality for any length of time. Uncle Amando was very specific about the purpose of my trip."

Annona cocked her head. "Surely, you're not so naïve as to believe your aunt and uncle sent you here only to petition the emperor? They obviously felt the prospects were limited in your village. No one, dear girl, does something with only one purpose in mind. Your Uncle Amando did not attain his wealth by being shortsighted."

Lucius dragged his eyes away from the plump buttocks of a pretty servant and burst out laughing. "Mother, we've acquired a newborn chick in the Roman cock house. It's not safe for her to walk the streets alone. She'll fall for every trick and flattery if left unattended." He thumped his chest. "I'll guard her, Mother. Leave her Roman schooling to me."

Annona tossed Lucius a disapproving glance. "You're much too busy with your own schooling."

"Thank you for your gracious offer, Lucius." I smiled sweetly. "I expect Annona has other plans to find me a worthy suitor."

Annona signaled for a refill. "Indeed, I do. Tomorrow we'll go to the baths and hear the latest gossip."

Gossip? Listening to the idle chitchat of matrons? How dull.

"Your hospitality is overwhelming. I can think of nothing more enjoyable than visiting Roman baths and meeting your friends."

Lucius raised an eyebrow at my remark, then shifted his attention to the fat-bottomed serving girl who bent over to pour his mother's wine.

"It's settled." Gaius Theon dug into a platter of roasted pork.

I did not ask exactly what Gaius Theon thought was settled, but his comment left me feeling more unsettled than ever.

I DREW the blanket up to my nose and stared at the mural on the ceiling. Sleep did not come when the mind runs faster than a Roman sprinter. Especially after Pricilla reminded me that a jeweled viper was concealed in every patch of Roman grass. And a toga-wearing lion hid behind every Roman shrub.

But it seemed snakes and beasts conspired in Gaul as well. My hosts had revealed Uncle Amando's and Aunt Diana's true intent. I did not fault them too much. To find eligible prospects for me required them to throw a wide nuptial fishing net. Rome, evidently, qualified as deeper waters.

I turned my head, the steady rise and fall of the blanket a sign Pricilla was fast asleep.

A soft footfall caught my attention and I turned my head

to look. But it was too late. Someone leapt on top of me.

TWENTY-TWO

A hand clamped over my mouth.

"Shhh, Locusta of Gaul. It's me, Lucius." His mouth pressed my ear. "Is it true what they say about all you country girls? I heard they roll in the hay and ride their lovers in the fields."

I remained still, my eyes boring into his.

"I'll remove my hand but if you scream, I'll hurt you. Understand?"

I nodded once.

"Intelligent girl." Lucius lifted his hand. "Your slave sleeps like the dead. No doubt she drank too much wine. If she wakes, I'll enjoy her too. A country bitch and her stupid servant will be my solace this night."

My gaze shifted toward Pricilla. Surely, she knew Lucius was here. Never had I known Pricilla to sleep so soundly. Or had Lucius drugged her?

I opened my mouth to scream. Lucius's hand smashed back down.

"Bad girl. On second thought, shout as loud as you like. Mother is a follower of Bacchus. She drinks wine until she's unconscious and she'll sleep like the damned until early afternoon. Father, as always, is panting atop one of his mistresses. Maybe several at once." Lucius's body pressed against me, his arousal obvious. "We're a wealthy and important family. It would not benefit you to disgrace yourself by telling lies about their honorable and dutiful son."

I swallowed, willed Pricilla to wake up.

"Are you as virginal as you pretend? If you are, I'll enjoy paying tribute to the god Hymen. If not, we can enjoy a blissful night of lust."

I peeled his hand from my mouth. "I'm not the object of your desires."

"Oh, but you are." His arousal pressed into me, he shoved his hips forward a few times. "This is our secret. And if you display any skill at all I'll see to it every worthy suitor makes a beeline for our front door."

I met his wine-glazed eyes with my sober ones. "I'm a poor substitute for the woman you really desire."

He wrapped his finger around a lock of my hair. "Who might that be?"

"The servant girl at dinner," I said. "It's her you desire, not me."

Lucius frowned. "If I wanted her, I'd have her."

It was true. The master of the house could have sex with any servant he desired. But I saw how he had looked at her. And it was more than lust.

"You want something else," I said. "I think you have tender feelings for her."

Lucius's brow creased. "Why do you say that?"

"It was written on your face, your eyes lingered on her during dinner."

He let out a frustrated grunt. "Am I that transparent?"

"Love has no boundaries." I thought of Varinius and his

servant, now mother to his children. "I can help you win her love."

"You?" Lucius laughed. "How?"

"Get off me and I'll tell you."

Lucius smoothed back my hair with an oddly affectionate touch. "Tell me now."

Fear was lodged in my throat, so I spoke slowly. "I can make her desire you."

"You lie," he hissed and squeezed my breast.

"I'm an herbalist. I can make potions to make her lustful."

Lucius tilted his head. "I'm listening."

"I know a tonic that will cause her such desire she'll happily submit to your advances."

"A love potion?"

"Get off me and I'll tell you." I squirmed beneath him.

"You think I'm a fool?"

"No, but I would be if I lie to you. I speak the truth. This potion produces physical desire, nothing more. It's up to you to prove your love with words and actions during the act."

"Mmmm, so this potion makes her vulnerable to my advances?"

"Yes."

"She'll confused lust with love?"

"Hopefully."

"Why haven't I heard about this potion? Why do you know more than the local apothecary?"

"I…I don't know. But I do know the medicinal properties of every plant and creature. How one berry induces vomit and another cures a cough. How a single leaf alleviates a headache but two blur one's vision."

Lucius looked skeptical. "How swiftly does it take effect? How long will it last?"

"It works almost immediately and lasts about a day."

"Tomorrow, then." Lucius tugged on a lock of my hair. "Mother will appreciate knowing our guest is a skilled herbalist."

My breath caught. No one could know.

Pricilla had warned me too often about the Roman's love of conspiracies and sordid murders. I knew what I must do. And it required mixing more than a love potion.

"I have no problem with your mother knowing my skills. Just as I'm certain she will understand your devotion to a servant."

"Nooooo, we can't have that, can we?" He nipped the tip of my nose. "This will be our secret. You and I. Conspirators of love. We'll be great friends—if your potion works." His lips breezed across my cheek. "Know this, my pretty herbalist, if you're lying to me expect another midnight visit. One where my caresses will not be as pleasant." Lucius rolled off and departed the room.

Several moments passed before my pounding heart returned to normal.

"Well played," whispered Pricilla from the corner of the room.

I rolled onto my side. "You heard everything?"

"Every word. You'll do well in Rome. Already you formed an alliance and are involved in an intrigue."

"Why did you pretend to be asleep?"

"You needed the practice. If you can't handle a young man, then Roman society would surely eat you alive."

"What if he raped me?"

Pricilla adjusted the blanket. "You're not the same girl you were then."

She was right. I would have fought back. And, in a way, I had.

Pricilla yawned. "Watching two young plotters was amusing."

"What herbs do I use? There are several to choose from."

"We can decide tomorrow." She closed her eyes.

I rolled on my back and stared at the ceiling. Mandrake. Nightshade. Thorn apple. Henbane. Mushrooms. Poppy. I considered each plant's properties. Which was no lullaby. I pondered all the possible outcomes of Lucius's love potion. I finally fell asleep, but it was fitful. Even my dreams were filled with ingredients.

I woke the next morning with a new idea for a tonic. One I had mixed in my dreams. I bounded from the bed and opened the coffer of herbs.

Pricilla placed a plate of bread and fruit on the table. "You must eat."

"Not yet." Elbows on the table, cheek in my hand, I heaved a sigh.

To the untrained eye, the bits of leaves, seeds, and roots appeared harmless. An herbalist, however, saw the botanical promise.

I chose two more tiny satchels, untied the string, and unrolled the leather. What if I combined these two? One made the skin pleasantly sensitive. I experienced its effects myself. The other increased heart rate and produced feelings of euphoria. Together they would mimic the feelings of lust. And lust was confused with love—or so Pricilla reminded me after Marcus had left.

Marcus. The memory of my centurion never faded. I heard his voice in my thoughts, felt his touch in my dreams.

"Which will you choose? This one will turn even a passionless woman into a willing bedmate." Pricilla poked at the leaf. "What are you using the other for?"

"I'm combining them. A bit of euphoria goes a long way.

I remember the way I felt with…" I pushed Marcus from my mind and focused on the plants. "The proportions must be correct."

"How do you plan on administering this concoction?"

I looked up. "You will."

"Me? How?" Pricilla crossed her arms.

"You'll share wine with the object of Lucius's affections."

"How can you be certain her amorous attentions will be directed toward the young master of the household?"

"Lucius will wait nearby."

Pricilla sucked air through her teeth. "This is risky." She pointed to the leaves. "What if they interact with each other and cause unintended effects?"

"We'll test it on someone."

Pricilla threw up her hands. "Not me."

I looked out the window and into the gardens. "It was easy at home, no one cared if we fed herbs to a goat."

Pricilla sidled next to me. "I have an idea. While you're at the baths with Annona, I'll make friends with a stable hand. Or a cook. A villa this large must keep a few chickens or goats somewhere."

"Do it quickly. Because if I kill the object of Lucius's desire, we'll have to flee Rome."

TWENTY-THREE

Annona's hand fluttered about. "Amazing, isn't it?"

"It's beautiful." I blinked, the white stone edifice almost blindingly brilliant.

"The exterior is a clam shell compared to its pearl-like interior. Come, Locusta, it's time you meet every influential woman in Rome."

"They all bathe here?"

"If they don't, then they're inconsequential nobodies." She mounted the steps, her three handmaids close behind.

"Where are the men?"

"This is the woman's entrance. Don't fret, we'll see them in the baths."

Men and women had separate entrances and yet they shared the same baths. Rome was indeed a city of contradictions.

Somewhere between walking up the steps and reaching the door, Annona's handmaids disappeared.

"Where did they go?"

"You're a fresh-picked peach, aren't you? Servants use a different door."

We went down a short hallway and into a large and crowded outdoor courtyard. Men exercised while young women in sheer tunics sauntered past them. It was a place to flaunt muscles, curves, beauty, and wealth.

"Annona!" Arms wide, a squat stern man in a blue tunic shuffled towards us. "A pleasure to see you. You'll be pleased to know several charioteers and important gamblers took advantage of Gaius Theon's generosity." The balneator's eyes flicked at me, then dismissed me as unimportant in an instant.

"Wonderful. I'm delighted my husband's kindnesses are appreciated." She touched my cheek. "Mark well the face of this young beauty from Gaul. She's our guest."

The balneator inclined his head. "So marked, Annona. Now, forgive me, I must beg your leave. I see several men who haven't the privilege of Gaius Theon's fee waiver and try to bathe without paying." He curved his head in farewell before lumbering toward the group.

Annona drew me near. "The man fancies himself the emperor of the baths. Never get on his bad side."

As I walked with her across the courtyard, I realized my clothing was rather plain.

"Locusta, I must speak truthfully, I'm not pleased that you did not bring your handmaid. You're overly indulgent with her."

"Well, I…" Pricilla was more than my servant. She was my friend, my confidant, my mentor. And today, my co-conspirator. "She felt poorly. I thought it best she stays home. Please forgive the inconvenience. I'll employ one of the bath's workers to attend me."

"Nonsense. I can spare one. But I insist you see to it her health improves. My handmaids are busy enough with their own tasks." Annona pointed to an advertisement. "I adore the wild beast games. They're quite thrilling. The last time I went a rhinoceros tossed a bull into the air before gouging it to death. It was wonderful!" She paused at the door to the women's dressing room. "The capsarii are notorious thieves with large ears."

I giggled. It reminded me of Marcus's comment about Roman walls having ears.

The soft-spoken and deferential capsarii helped me undress and hung my clothes on a peg. I had nothing of value to steal. No valuable gossip to share. On Annona's whispered advice, I left on my gold rings and bracelets.

The baths were an artistic marvel. More beautiful than anything I could have imagined. The dome was a vivid blue and shimmered with stars. I could have gazed at the romantic rendering of the heavens for hours.

"Locusta, come along," Annona urged. "Don't look so…impressed."

How could I not? The bath's grandeur was overwhelming. Every wall was embellished with frescoes and friezes. Peacocks and chimaeras. Gods and nymphs. Gardens and seas. The murals merged together in a circular fantasia.

Annona nudged my arm. "We'll stop by the perfume seller's booth later. They sell the most exotic oils in the world."

"I'd like that." I smiled uneasily. It wasn't the rare perfumes that made me uncomfortable. It was sharing the baths with men.

"My least favorite pool." Annona rolled her shoulders, her robe slipping off with a practiced and seductive move. She stood proud, small breasts thrust out, one hip lifted, and flung out her arm to drop her robe with a dramatic flourish. Her body, as angular as her face, caused several male heads to turn, although none of their gazes lingered. She stepped down slowly. "I assume that in Gaul you still adhere to the old-fashioned formalities of separate bathing?"

"Yes, both in the public and private baths." I averted my eyes when an old man with testicles to his knees walked by.

"In your own home?" Her voice was pierced with disbelief.

"Father's rules." I shrugged. "I don't know what others do."

"Romans are progressive." Annona beckoned me in. "Come, come, Locusta. If you stand there covered any longer, everyone will assume you're a heathen foreigner."

I handed my robe to a slave—without the dramatic flourish—and stepped into the bracing water.

The men stared. I felt their studied gaze. Was this how one found a husband in Rome? By flaunting your nakedness to the elite? It took all my courage to act like I was not out of place. That I was at ease with men's interested glances. I imitated Annona. Tossed jaunty smiles. Pretended interest in the conversations around us.

"Ready for the next bath?" Annona did not wait for my reply.

I followed Annona's example and walked naked to the tepidarium.

Annona's friends were gathered in the warm water. In this room, painted a deep red and furnished with chairs and bronze benches, servants smoothed oil on the patrons.

Annona led me into the viper pit. "Dear friends, permit me to introduce Locusta. She's recently come from Gaul and is a guest in our home. Locusta, these are the most influential women in Rome."

TWENTY-FOUR

That afternoon I met women of wealth, status, and intellect. Daughters of prominent senators destined to wed rulers of exotic lands. Wives of powerful men who dined with the emperor. Mothers of ambitious sons eager for intrigue. And lonely widows who eyed elder patricians.

My equestrian class did not warrant an introduction to the most pot-bellied patricians of rank, nevertheless, Annona assured me they had taken note of my youth and beauty. She claimed a newcomer with an unsullied reputation—one not yet tainted by malicious gossip—gave me advantage over my unmarried competition.

"I heard they want to separate the men and women again," said a silver-haired matron.

You already separate yourselves, I wanted to say but held my tongue. Very rarely did I see the sexes mingle. Even Gaius Theon, engaged in an animate discussion with a man across the heated pool, paid no attention to Annona.

"The men don't want us to see them frolicking with their mistresses." A stout matron with a double chin raised her arm and waved at her husband.

As the women cackled, I looked across the sea of flesh. Only the servants were clothed.

"Locusta, we would be delighted to attend any party Annona has in your honor," said a frizzy-haired friend. "Any woman whose father supplies Rome with wine is a friend to us."

Silver Hair adjusted her braided bun. "Tell us, dear, what misfortune came to pass that a young beauty such as yourself is not yet a wife?"

"My fiancé died before we wed."

Double Chin laid a flabby arm around my shoulders. "Don't you worry. We'll find you a husband." She bobbed her head toward a group of wrinkled old men with sagging bellies and hairy backs. "Take your pick. They're all in need of a wife. Which one do you want?"

I wrinkled my nose and that sent them howling with laughter.

"Wed for luxury and status," said Double Chin. "Pleasure yourself with a younger man. No Roman woman will fault you."

"Especially Empress Agrippina," added Silver Hair.

"I heard a disturbing rumor yesterday." A matron with breasts sagging to her waist glanced around.

The group huddled together. Gossip about Empress Agrippina and her son, it seemed, was their favorite pastime.

"A most reliable source—"

"Slave or friend?" asked Double Chin.

"A trustworthy source—I swore not to reveal—said mother and son exhibit unseemly behavior when together." Saggy Breasts lowered her voice. "They kiss each other on the lips like lovers and were found napping together. My source—an esteemed person I dare not name—confessed to seeing Agrippina and her son emerge from their carpentum looking altogether disheveled and flushed."

"Does your source claim they have an incestuous relationship?" asked Anonna.

"My source only reported what she saw with her own eyes. Draw your own conclusions."

Frizzy Hair scowled. "What other conclusion is there? Agrippina is a dangerous woman. Her thirst for power is unquenchable. Claudius should be careful."

"Claudius is a simpleton," said Saggy Breasts. "Agrippina will stop at nothing to see her son ascend the throne."

"How is that possible, when he's Claudius's adopted child?" I asked.

Four pair of eyes bent toward me and narrowed into disbelief.

"Annona dear, do give your young guest a civics lesson before the dinner party." Double Chin rolled her eyes upward.

"Lucius—"

"Aa-ah." Saggy Breast wagged her finger. "He's calling himself Nero now," said Saggy Breasts.

"Is that so." Annona brows jumped. "Well then, Nero has legal claim to the throne."

"What about Britannicus?" I asked. "Isn't he the rightful heir."

"Not if Agrippina has anything to say about it," said Saggy Breasts.

The women made a few more uncomplimentary comments about Agrippina's ambitions and then the conversation turned to less provocative gossip.

We lounged about the rest of the afternoon, nibbled on fruit, nuts, olives, and fish, sipped spiced wine, and discussed the week's upcoming games.

"THE RABBIT DIDN'T DIE," said Pricilla when I returned from the baths.

I yawned, the baths made me drowsy. "I didn't think it would."

"Ah, but rabbits aren't people." Pricilla settled back in the chair, one leg swinging over the other. "So I had a bit myself."

All sleepiness vanished. "And?"

"Your love elixir was perfect. My skin was pleasantly sensitive to the touch. I felt happy and …eager. Like a horse before a race." She tapped her chin. "Like a dog wanting to be pet."

"Really? Sounds like it brought out the animal in you."

"I'm glad I only had a nip."

I picked up the clay container. "Let's hope the servant girl submits to Lucius's advances." I wasn't fully confident. Sometimes our potions had different effects on different people. One woman's relaxing brew made another agitated. "Lucius told me that after dinner, Annona usually retires to her chamber and Theon visits his mistress."

"And the servant?"

"She washes dishes in the culina."

Pricilla nodded. "I'll give her our special wine then."

"Only if she's alone."

"Where will Lucius be?"

"Waiting nearby. I told him not to declare his intentions until her face is flushed."

"A blissful seduction." Pricilla rubbed her hands together. "Are we watching?"

"Pricilla!"

"Not his seduction. We should watch the love potion's effects before he drags her off to the bedroom."

"I hadn't thought of that. But you're right. And that gives me another idea." I sat at the table, picked up the stylus, and wrote down the quantity of herbs on the wax tablet. "How much did you ingest?"

"This much." She tapped her thumbnail.

I wrote it down. "How soon after ingestion did the tonic take effect?"

"The time it takes to cook an egg."

"Did you feel any ill effects?"

"None," said Pricilla. "Don't look so worried. What harm can come from making a love potion?"

TWENTY-FIVE

D inner passed with tedious slowness.

Gaius Theon discussed the differences between four and eight-horse racing teams.

Annona shared the latest scandals and prattled about upcoming wild beast games.

When Lucius didn't ogle the servant, he fidgeted and sent me impatient glances.

Whether the servant's indifference to Lucius was womanly guile or girlish innocence, it increased her appeal. Maybe she knew that. History was rife with wealthy masters who wed their beautiful servants.

The last course consumed, we rose from the table. Annona snatched a carafe of undiluted wine, feigned exhaustion, and bid us good night. Theon pretended he had urgent business with a horse trainer in the city's Ninth Region.

Lucius sidled next to me in the hall. "If you're lying to me and this is a trick, I'll make good on my promise to ravage you."

I pretended to be disappointed by his lack of faith. "Stay near while she attends her duties. Don't approach until her face is pink and her eyes glisten. Those are the signs that the potion took hold." Despite my heart fluttering like a leaf, I set a light hand on his arm, a gesture that linked us to the deed. "I provide only the seed of desire. You must water her feelings with love."

"Spoken like a girl who digs in the dirt," he smirked.

"Said by the boy in desperate need of her help." I smirked back. "Come." We strolled down the hallway.

Pricilla approached, her hand wrapped around the tainted goblet of wine.

"Domina," she said, her eyes lowered.

Lucius's brows shot up. "You trust your handmaid?" he whispered as we trailed Pricilla to the culina.

"With my life."

His mouth hovered over my ear. "I heard she already made friends with the groundskeeper and his daughter."

"Pricilla makes friends easily."

He stopped walking, drew me close "Friends of the carnal kind."

I traced the carving of Ceres set in the small niche near the culina to mask my surprise. Pricilla had neglected to tell me that. "Pricilla's beliefs don't require sexual restraint."

His eyes lit up. "It's a pity she hasn't swayed you to join her theology." He tugged on a tendril of my hair, then crossed the hall to peek into the kitchen. "Your servant offers mine the wine goblet." He stepped forward.

I flung my arm across his chest. "Not yet. Let her drink it. Be patient."

Lucius folded his arms, his hands tapping his biceps. He stole frequent glances into the culina. He shifted from foot to foot while Locusta and the servant sipped wine and gossiped about the peculiarities of their masters. Finally, Pricilla pretended she had forgotten about an important task and hurried away. She gave me a quick nod as she walked past.

Lucius was ready. He squared his shoulders, then gave me the oddest look. Fear, worry, relief, desperation—a tangle of emotions flashed across his face.

"Go on," I said.

On my nod, he went in.

Pricilla waited for me at the end of the hallway. "She's a sweet girl. I hope Lucius is kind."

"He will be. He's smitten."

"There's a narrow window on the far side of the kitchen," said Pricilla. "We can watch from there."

We hurried outside, turned the corner, and peered through the narrow casement.

The girl stood at the basin washing dishes while Lucius leaned against the wall and talked about Annona's upcoming dinner party. She answered obediently, her eyes rarely lifting from the chore.

"Oh!" She swayed. The wet goblet slipped from her hand and crashed to the floor.

Lucius rushed to her side. "Are you unwell, Abelia?" He set a steadying hand on her shoulder.

Abelia's face flushed pink, her eyes sparkled.

"I feel so…so…" Her knees buckled.

Lucius caught her, helped her to a bench.

"You're ill, Abelia. You must drink something."

"Oh no, dominus. I'm not ill. I just feel strange."

Lucius caressed her cheek. "Perhaps you need water? Your cheeks bloom like roses."

Abelia smiled, covered his hand with her own. "You're very kind."

Lucius set his other hand on her knee. "Your beauty inspires kindness."

The girl sighed. Her eyelashes fluttered.

Lucius traced her lips with his finger.

"My heart races. Can you feel it?" Abelia moved his hand over her breast.

"Mine too." Lucius guided her hand to his own beating heart. "Whenever you're near."

Her eyes widened. "You…you desire me?"

He nodded and pulled her close. Their kiss was long. Very long. And it made me think of Marcus.

Abelia pulled back and licked her lips. "Such a kiss…" she swallowed. "My lips…tingle."

Lucius kissed her again, then whispered in her ear. Abelia wrapped both arms around him. There was nothing tentative about the next kiss.

I turned from the window. "I think this love will be consummated on the culina floor."

"I'm proud of you." Pricilla gave my hand a quick squeeze. "You invented a quick-acting and potent potion."

"I hope so, but…" I started back to the house.

"But what?"

"Let's wait until morning before we decide anything."

I could not sleep. Thoughts swirled like a whirlpool. Too many What If's. What if the sensual high developed into an emotional low? What if she lost consciousness? What if she became sick?

Pricilla, however, slept soundly.

Lucius did not appear at breakfast. It was not until well after the midday meal when he stumbled into my chambers.

He was sleepy-eyed, disheveled, and wearing a simpering grin. "I made love all night and all morning. Locusta, you have my gratitude." His smile widened. "Abelia says she loves me."

"Will you wed her?"

"Are you daft? Father is negotiating terms of betrothal to a girl with important political connections. I already met her." He dropped into the chair and scowled. "She's a hideous waif."

"Does Abelia knows you're promised to another?"

"I don't know how they do things in Gaul but Abelia is a bondswoman. I'm a patrician. I'll do what all patrician men do. She'll buy her a small home and make her my mistress. She'll have a very comfortable life and her own servants."

"Will you grant her freedom?"

Lucius shrugged. "One day, perhaps, if she gives me sons." He looked at me like I was stupid. "She's content with my proposition."

"I thought you loved her."

"I love to love her." Lucius sat up straight and crossed his legs. "You must understand Roman politics, Locusta. Father is a senator. He needs allies to strengthen his political positions. I'm a pawn. A handsome pawn with aspirations to walk in his senatorial footsteps. He forged a union with an associate's daughter. He had to. That's how both he and I advance." He glanced at the uncovered herb coffer in the corner. "Does your knowledge of herbs include concoctions other than love elixirs?"

I dared not boast. But I could downplay it. Cures for travel sickness, constipation, diarrhea, skin rashes, and insect bites were common enough. Something any apothecary could make. I would never tell him that Pricilla and I knew how to make deadly potions.

I flicked my eyes at Pricilla, who pretended to be engrossed in repairing a loose thread on my tunic.

"I know a little," I said.

"You insult my intelligence." Lucius brushed lint from his shoulder.

"How so?"

"The difference between incendiary and soothing words is but the arrangements of the letters. The same is said of knowledge."

"My herbal vocabulary is lacking."

"I doubt that." Lucius stood, extended his hand. "We're friends, yes?"

"Friends."

Pricilla looked up from her task after Lucius departed. "I would not wish Master Lucius as an enemy."

Me either, because behind his smooth facade was a man who would stop at nothing to achieve his desires.

TWENTY-SIX

The days assumed a predictable schedule. In the mornings, Gaius Theon donned his purple-striped toga and met with clientalia and other senators. Even though Lucius could not begin his career until age twenty he often accompanied his father to the Forum.

Annona and I visited the temples and gardens in Rome. During one outing to Villa Borghese gardens, Annona took me to the site of Empress Messalina's execution, the very spot where the bloody savagery of Rome's elite seeped into the ground.

The self–proclaimed Priestess of Passion and mother to Britannicus, Empress Messalina had soiled her reputation with vulgar exploits. And her husband Emperor Claudius had murdered her for it. Even though she had given him a rightful heir.

But did Emperor Claudius learn anything about ambitious women? No. He fell for the devious Agrippina. Married her and adopted her son, which made his own blood progeny second in line to the throne.

How could I possibly plead for a tax extension to an

emperor with no morals or compassion? He was more likely to kill me.

"Locusta." Annona looped her arm through mine. "Why so grim? You look as if you see Messalina's blood on the ground. Come, stroll the gardens. It will distract you from whatever terrible thoughts your mind conjures."

In a small way, it did. The profusion of flowers, topiary, and exotic plants soothed my longing for home. I would have been happy to visit a different garden every day. However, Annona preferred the blood and excitement of wild beast games to greenery and quiet reflection.

Annona took a perverted glee in the beasts' violent deaths. She cheered until she became hoarse when panthers were pitted against tigers. She whooped with joy—she won the bet—when a lion killed a bear.

In one bloody spectacle, four thieves walked into the ring. Annona almost swooned as they hoisted long lances into the air to rally the spectators. The crowd stomped their feet and shouted, their screams reaching to a fever pitch when three lions prowled in.

The lions made swift work of the thieves. One ripped the first thief in half. Dragged his carcass by the leg across the arena. Not content with the carnage, the audience cried for more blood. A lioness pounced on the second thief, her jaws clamping down over his head. The crowd roared as the thief's limbs flailed about and his blood soaked the dirt. The slaughter scarcely satisfied Roman bloodlust. They howled for more more more.

Chariot races were another bloody sport. Of course, we had to cheer for the Blue. The magistrate needed only to drop a white cloth into the arena and the fans screamed so loudly the gods heard it on Mount Olympus. The trumpet's blare signaled the gate's release and the horses were off. Most races were four-horse teams but on occasion two-horse teams competed. Annona squealed with delight whenever a chariot wheel collided with the curb and catapulted it into another in a cloud of dust and blood.

Annona nudged my elbow. "The victor of this race is a rich man. He was once a slave. Now he beds famous courtesans and wealthy widows."

A man could change his fortunes in Rome quicker than a lightning flash. If he had the right opportunity or connections.

We spent afternoons at the baths. Gossip, food, and strolls through art galleries kept us busy. Annona shunned the library. Claimed it was full of old academics who preferred learning to entertainment.

"Mark the senator." Annona pointed toward a tall arched doorway where a saggy-bellied old man lurked. "See where he's going? Behind that door are rooms for wicked purposes."

"Liaisons?"

"Sex and politics. The two go hand in hand in Rome."

More likely their hands went to other body parts.

Not every day was filled with games and long afternoons at the baths. Many times, Annona had to take care of household tasks or visit a friend. I liked these days best because that was when Pricilla and I visited local markets.

At first, the smells and crowds overwhelmed our senses. There were many stalls! Thousands, perhaps. And the merchandise was beyond our imaginings.

Pretty boys stood in front of booths and extolled the quality of their linen and silk. Merchants praised the value of brightly pigmented carpets from the East. Vendors hawked fetishes and carvings of Roman, Greek, and Egyptian gods.

Indian spices permeated a tent where a sharp-eyed old man guarded gaudy bracelets and cheap rings. There were pushcarts piled with African ivory. Peddlers weaved among the crowd and shouted in foreign tongues. Their pleas required no translation. 'Buy my merchandise' sounds the same in every language.

Each time I came upon a figurine of the bull-slaying Mithras, I thought of Marcus. That was his god.

After the third trip to the markets, the jostling crowds stopped overwhelming me. I learned to keep my coin purse under my palla, away from nimble fingers. I did this despite the fierce-looking male servant Annona insisted accompany us. Pricilla believed his task was more about spying on us than protection.

In the evenings, I attended dinner parties with the family. These seven-course revelries lasted late into the night. Lucius always participated in the drinking games after the meal, often imbibing until he passed out.

During one party, I met his betrothed, Sarra. She was a plain girl with a long nose and pursed lips. Her costly stola found no curves to cling to and her stride was without grace or sway. Her legs moved but her body did not. Lucius paid scant attention to her, no matter how often she attempted to engage him in conversation.

"You treat Sarra horribly. You should talk to your future wife," I said one evening.

Lucius belched in my face. "My obligation doesn't require discourse, merely procreation."

I waved away his wine breath. "You need the first to have the second."

"Not in Rome." He snorted with laughter.

Several months passed before Gaius Theon was able to arrange an appointment with Emperor Claudius.

"Emperor Claudius granted you a brief audience tomorrow morning," he said one afternoon.

"You have my eternal gratitude." I clutched the basket filled with exotic herbs and roots—today's cache from the market—and told Pricilla to return to my room.

"This was no small feat," he said. "The emperor avoids executive tasks and prefers to attend games or write historical accounts of Roman conquests."

"Thank you again."

"You must state your petition with truth and speed. Have you crafted an appeal?"

"A formal appeal?"

"Yes, Locusta. Did you travel all the way from Gaul without a formal petition or practiced rhetoric?" He warmed his hands before the brazier.

"Uncle Amando neglected to inform me of this requirement."

Gaius Theon mumbled something unintelligible under his breath. "Limit your petition to two sentences. No more than three."

"I'll do it now." I spoke with more confidence than I felt.

"If you're clever—and the spark of intelligence behind those bright eyes suggests you are—you will craft an appeal that includes a benefit for his granting the request."

"A benefit?" A weight dropped into my belly.

"Yes, of course. You have one, I presume." He rubbed his hands together.

I had nothing. Could not imagine a single possible political, personal, or monetary inducement. "I'll think of something."

"Think of an excellent something." Gaius Theon's gaze traveled the length of my body. "Lucius speaks well of you."

"Your son is a fine young man."

"Mmmm, yes. He's betrothed to a young woman from an exceptional family."

"I had the privilege of meeting Sarra. She—"

"Lucius talks about you with improper fondness." His voice was as cold as a winter rain. "He's betrothed to another. Is my meaning clear?" His normally jovial-looking face hardened into stone.

I was an unmarried woman without social or political associations. Gaius Theon saw me as a tiresome annoyance and a sexual temptation for his son.

"I'm grateful for the hospitality you've shown me," I said. "I cannot thank you enough for your help. Hopefully, it won't be necessary to impose on your welcome much longer."

Gaius Theon's face relaxed, his jolly expression restored. "Amando is a friend, and my home is your home, Locusta. Let's hope your petition is well received."

We parted in the atrium, he to his study and I to my room.

"What did the dominus want?" asked Pricilla.

"He thinks I seduce his son." I pushed the basket into Pricilla's hands. "I haven't met any eligible bachelors, and there's little chance the emperor will grant a tax extension. This trip was pointless."

She set the basket down, her herbal purchases already spread over the table. "Patience. Locusta. These things take time." Pricilla pointed to several mushrooms. "Look at these."

"I have an audience with the emperor tomorrow and you want me to look at mushrooms?"

"Not any mushrooms."

"They look common enough." I poked at a white one. "Oh, this one looks different."

"It's called Destroying Angel. Very toxic. The other is known as Dead Cap."

"Both are deadly? Where did you get these?"

"While you haggled over ginger root, I found these at another stall." Pricilla lifted the lid on the herb coffer. "A toxic addition to our collection."

"You plan to poison someone?"

"Not today," she giggled.

I studied the fatal fungi. "Extraordinary. It looks exactly like the kind we eat."

Pricilla lifted the mushroom by its stem. "Not quite. There are several differences. Notice the green tint." She flipped it over to reveal its underside. "The white ribbons don't extend to the edge."

"Barely discernible. Any other differences?"

"The best way to determine the poisonous from the edible is by drying the mushroom on a bit of parchment. The Death Cap leaves white dust. The edibles, pink-hued." She held it to my nose. "Smell."

"Roses." I shrugged. "It's an interesting purchase but I'm too worried about tomorrow's meeting to think about poisonous mushrooms." I flung open the lid of my clothes trunk. "Which stola will impress an emperor? More importantly, what will I say to him?"

"You worry too much. Simply make a heartfelt appeal. The emperor will certainly grant your request."

Pricilla was as naïve about Roman politics as I.

TWENTY-SEVEN

Roman citizens crowded the reception room. All men. All holding scrolls.

It took only a few foul looks from the petitioners for me to sink into the shadows of my hooded cloak. Like a skiff in a storm of togas, I was jostled about. The men pushed and shoved, their rude maneuvering for one purpose only. To reach the front.

Gaius Theon did not tell me I would be one of many. This was not an audience, it was a mob. I was no match for this masculine horde.

The crush of people surged forward. I was trapped. Powerless to do anything but stay upright. They pushed and shoved and elbowed. Sometimes forward. Sometimes sideways.

I drew closer and closer to the dais where Emperor Claudius sat in his imperial chair. Before I knew it, only one whale of a man blocked my way. The whale lurched sideways, and another brute tried to shove me aside. He thrust me forward instead.

I stumbled, tripped, and fell. My hands and knees slapped the ground before the emperor. It was a posture of obeisance exhibited by no previous petitioner.

Emperor Claudius gestured to the senators at his side. "Ah, proper supplication from a young woman. Make your petition known."

I rose on quaking knees and gawked at the most powerful man in the world.

Tiberius Claudius Caesar was a tall man, his limbs extending past the gilded chair. Despite his sixty-three-years, he was still handsome and had a full head of white hair.

"I-I...b-b-b," I stuttered.

The emperor's smile crumbled.

He thought I mocked his speech impediment.

Emperor Claudius's eyes tapered. "Speak."

"I b-b-beg an extension for the t-t-taxes due on Parisii vineyards."

"An extension? That name...Parisii." Emperor Claudius pointed at me. "Are you from Gaul?"

"I am, your excellency."

He settled back in his throne and looked at me as though I was an insect to be crushed. "You came all this way to beg?" He lifted his chin and spoke loudly. "See this girl begging before the might of Rome. People of Gaul know their place. They are beggars."

My mouth opened, but my tongue was leaden. Rational thought deserted me.

"Tell me, girl from Gaul, what reason prevents you from giving Rome its due?"

"My father is old and—"

Emperor Claudius roared with exaggerated laughter. "If I deferred everyone's taxes because of old age, Rome's coffers would be empty. How do you think the Port of Ostia was built? Or the aqueducts?"

"We can make gifts of wine."

"Wine? I have enough wine." The emperor waved his hand dismissively. "Denied."

A guard grabbed my arm and dragged me back into the crowd.

I slunk away, covered my face with my palla, hid my angry tears. How dare the emperor insult me. Insult Gaul. How dare Uncle Amando not prepare a proper appeal for me. How dare Gaius Theon—with all his political scheming and gloating over his favored position—subject me to such a hostile venue. They must have known there was no chance of success. My blood boiled with indignation.

I pushed my way through the Roman wolf pack. Prodded a few men who refused to let me pass. A few bold shoves later, I tramped into the corridor.

Pricilla leaned against a marble column. "Did the emperor give you an extension?"

"No. He mocked me. Called me a beggar."

"A lion does not concern itself with the problems of sheep."

"Then it seems I'm a lamb in a great flock."

"I may have found another way to pay the taxes." Pricilla's eyes darted from right to left. "There's someone you must meet."

"Who?"

"While you were waiting to speak to the emperor, I explored the Forum and happened to overhear two women while I admired a statue of Diana."

"Overheard? Or spied on?"

"This is Rome. Is there a difference?"

Roman walls have ears. I never imagined they would be Pricilla's.

"How can these two women help me?"

"By helping them."

I was not in the mood for word games. I wanted to go home—my home in Gaul—and lick my wounds. "You speak in riddles."

"Hear their tale of sorrow. Decide if you'll help."

Will help? Or can help? There was a big difference. "Pricilla, you're a fisher of intrigue, and I, the bait."

"Me?" She pressed her heart and pretended surprise. "Indeed not. Locusta is the fisherman; her humble handmaid, the fishing pole." She affected a quick bow.

"Fine." I smiled, Pricilla's wit brightened my dour mood. "Take me to the fish whose scales will tip the balance of taxes owed."

We hastened down a marble corridor of statuary and secrets. Here, men conversed in alcoves, senators whispered in corners, scroll-toting scribes disappeared behind drapes, and servants scurried after their masters. It was a busy political hall where pledges were sworn, and policies decided. A hall with many ears.

Pricilla and I passed under a domed fresco of golden constellations and into a courtyard.

I looked about, the only figure a robust marble Neptune spewing water into the air. "I see a pond but neither fish nor Roman citizen."

"The south gate exits into an alley." Pricilla pointed. "They're waiting in a carpentum."

Two women. How could two women possibly help me? With a loud sigh, I crossed the courtyard and swung open the gate.

A fresh-painted carpentum waited curbside. It was

without markings, insignia, and decoration. Plain and forget-table. Only the two finely-bridled horses tethered to a new breeching strap revealed the occupants' wealth.

I rapped on the carpentum door. "It's Locusta."

A hand pulled back a curtain. "Please sit with us."

I looked across the courtyard to Pricilla. She bobbed her head.

Two women sat side by side. A middle-aged woman, her eyes swollen with tears, draped her arm around another, whose face was lost in the shadows of a hooded cloak.

I clasped my hands together. "Salve."

"Salve, Locusta. I'm Romana." She sniffed, blinked back a tear. "Your handmaid spoke highly of you and said you could help us."

"What kind of help do you need?"

Romana patted the other woman's shoulders. "This is my daughter, Rhea."

Rhea pulled the mantle from her head. She was my age, with tear-filled eyes and trembling lips. She lifted her chin. A wide bandeau and long veil covered most of her hair. But not all. Her long braids peeked out beneath.

I gasped. I had only heard about women like her. Only saw them from afar.

Rhea untied the ribbons on her cloak and pushed away the fabric to show me the distinctive vestments of her sect.

"You're a Vestal Virgin," I whispered.

"I was." Rhea rested her hands on her belly. "Your handmaid boasted of your talent with plants. She claims you harness unknown forces found in all leaves and flowers."

"She overestimates my skill."

Romana reached forward and clasped my hand. "She spoke of your humbleness."

"What troubles you?" I directed my question to the Vestal Virgin.

"I haven't bled for two months," Rhea said.

"Women are often late with their monthly courses."

"My daughter is with child." Romana squeezed my fingers, her voice fractured with desperation. "Should the Pontifex Maximus discover she's no longer a virgin she will be buried alive in the Field of Wickedness."

"He'll cast me in a pit." Fresh tears ran down Rhea's cheek. "And cover me with dirt."

Buried alive. Rome's penalty for breaking a vow of chastity. As the city's guardians, Vestal virgins maintained the sacred flame. Rhea's transgression defiled blessed laws and put Rome at risk.

"I'm sorry but—"

"You don't understand," Romana cried. "I see by the look on your face you make false judgment against my daughter. If she willingly broke her vow, Rhea would accept her fate. But she did not. A man of great power—political power—raped her and—" Romana buried her face in her hands. He shoulders shook with muffled sobs.

"I had no choice." Rhea blew her nose. "He…he…" She shuddered. "He swore to kill me if I exposed him."

"Will he be punished, as well?"

Rhea wiped her eyes and nodded. "They would flog him to death in the Comitium."

"I'll whip him myself." Romana balled her fists. "That vile scum rapes my daughter—desecrates a living testament of our faith with his foul seed and—" Her voice faltered, her breath wracked with strangled whimpers.

Rhea covered Romana's clenched hands with her own. "He raped me, Locusta. Then told me that defiling a Vestal was a disappointing exploit."

"Did he come back?"

"No, thank the gods. He likes only virgins."

Rhea's pain summoned fresh memories of That Man. The shame, fear, and despair rose like bile in my throat. Rhea needed my help. I would not deny her. I refused to condemn a blameless woman.

"I'll help."

Rhea and her mother shared a hopeful glance.

"Your handmaid says you're from Gaul and will not stay long in Rome," Rhea said.

Her meaning was clear. A stranger from Gaul posed no threat, possessed no connections, and spread no rumors.

"I've little reason to remain." Not anymore.

Rhea blew her nose again. "Can you…return my monthly blood?"

"Yes."

Romana hugged her daughter, kissed her forehead, then turned to me. "Rhea visits our family home tomorrow. The remedy must be applied there, far from prying eyes."

Rhea touched her stomach. "Will there be much pain?"

"There will be some cramping. Perhaps lower back pain. The remedy isn't immediate. A few days may pass before your blood flows."

"I see from your fine garments and poised demeanor you're a woman of privilege," said Romana.

"My father is a vintner in Gaul."

She nodded, my equestrian class suitable for helping her daughter. "Who is your host? Perhaps we're acquainted."

"Gaius Theon."

"Ah, yes, I know Theon and Annona." Romana's mouth pressed into a polite smile. "Locusta, at sunset tonight, go to the House of the Vestals. Rhea's servant will wait in the building across the street. Give her the tonic."

Romana was obviously a woman used to telling people what to do.

"I must be with Rhea to make certain there are no complications," I said. "If the blood flow is too heavy, I can give her a remedy."

Romana waved her hand. "Impossible. A newcomer will arouse suspicion. If my daughter requires assistance, I'll send for you."

"But—"

Romana held up her hand. "If anyone—my husband, servants, a friend—suspects the slightest deviation from Rhea's customary visit, there will be talk."

She was more afraid of gossip than her daughter's life.

I did not mince words. "Rhea could bleed to death."

"I'd rather bleed to death," whispered Rhea, "in my mother's arms than be buried alive."

Rhea bore her burden with dignity. Was a testament to her namesake. Named after Romulus's and Remus's mother—a woman seduced by Mars—Rhea's misfortune bore cruel similarities to the first Vestal priestess' tale. Unfortunately, no Roman today would believe a god fathered Rhea's child.

I spoke directly to Rhea, after all, it was her life at stake. "You must send word if you weaken."

"I will." Rhea pushed open the carpentum door. "You have my gratitude."

I took her hand. "Please, if anything doesn't feel right, if you're faint, sick, or think the blood comes too fast let me know."

"I understand." She sniffed, put on a brave smile.

I stepped down from the carpentum, noticed a man lurking in a shadowed alcove.

Roman walls have ears. And eyes.

I hurried back into the courtyard, then glanced back. The

man hoisted himself into the driver's seat, flicked the reins, and drove away.

"Did you agree?" Pricilla looped her arm through mine as we walked.

"Of course, I did. How could I not? The man raped a Vestal Virgin."

"What fee did you charge?"

I stopped before the water-spewing Neptune. "Why did you offer my services? You're more skilled."

Pricilla sat on the fountain's edge and swished water through her fingers. "You're an equestrian with friends in the senate. I'm a slave without status. Who would trust me? Or believe I knew the healing arts? Besides, no patrician would agree to be treated by a common handmaid. Besides," she flicked water at me, "your skill equals mine now. Maybe a drop or two better." She shook the water from her hand.

"No, I'm not."

"You made a new potion."

"Making one new potion doesn't make me better."

"Yes, it does. I never made a new one. I only make those taught to me. I never made notes on dosages or effects or tried new combinations."

"But—"

"The authority of those who teach is often an obstacle to those who want to learn. Isn't that what your father says?"

Father often quoted the long-deceased statesman, Marcus Tullius Cicero.

"You're not an obstacle, Pricilla. You're my mentor."

She patted my arm. "Fine, well this mentor wants to know what you charged those women."

"I never thought to charge a fee. We never did at home."

Pricilla exhaled her disappointment. "Charity is expected

of the domina. It's your duty to help others less fortunate. But in Rome you don't enjoy the same status. Here you are…"

"Nobody."

"Exactly. Oh well, at least these women owe you a favor. That's often worth more than coin."

I chewed on my lip. I didn't need favors. I needed to go home.

TWENTY-EIGHT

I had helped many people of distinguished birthright before. In Gaul. I had extracted essences and mixed ingredients with care and accuracy. My hands never trembled then.

Today they shook.

Mugwort and pennyroyal spread on the table, I noted any tiny blemishes on the leaves, any inconsistencies of the petals. Much was at stake. I would not choose an inferior plant. Perfect medicines required perfect plants.

I laid my hand on my stomach. The dosage Pricilla gave me That Night had been incorrect. Too strong. I had bled for too long a time. The rhythm of my monthly courses had changed. Although neither Pricilla nor I spoke of it, I feared I might be infertile.

I thought of Rhea. A Vestal Virgin. Priestess of Vesta. Keeper of the Sacred Flame. Guardian of Blessed Vessels and Imperial Wills.

After completion of her thirty-year service, Rhea would have her pick of suitors. Wedding a Vestal Virgin was an honor. I must not damage Rhea's ability to bear children.

I leaned over and inhaled, my fingertips grazing the leaf's edge...

The sun moved across the sky before my back straightened again.

"Why did you add wine, pears, and honey?" asked Pricilla watching me mix everything together.

"Vestals begin their service when they are ten-years-old. They know only luxury. This sweet beverage is a poor substitute for the discomfort Rhea will endure." My fingers glided over the curved spout of the alembic. How many essences had it rarified since I purchased it?

"A sweet disguise for a sour deed," Pricilla said.

"There's one more sour deed to accomplish." I departed the room in search of Lucius.

It wasn't too difficult. I knew his favorite places.

I found him lounging under the portico, wine goblet in his hand.

I sat beside him, set a hand on his knee. "I have an errand and need the carpentum."

Unlike young women, masters like Lucius went anywhere in the city anytime they pleased. Without Lucius's consent, I could not go to the Forum to meet Rhea's servant.

"What kind of mischief do you intend?" Lucius set down the goblet and laced his fingers behind his head. His eyes sparkled with delight over the power he wielded.

"I have an appointment."

"With whom?" He lifted his chin, looked down his nose, but his mouth twitched with interest.

"It's a secret."

"Ah, it's an intrigue then." Lucius sat up, swung his legs over the sofa.

"No." I laughed as though the very thought was absurd.

His brows lifted. "Do you have a lover?"

"Of course not." I pushed his shoulder.

"I don't believe you. And if you won't be honest with me then I have no choice but to refuse to let you have the carpentum."

I concealed my irritation with fluttering eyelashes. "Then I confess. I'm meeting my lover."

Lucius beamed. "Oh, that I yield to a woman. Yes, you have my permission." He held up one finger. "But there's a fee."

"Coin?"

Lucius balked. "Please, I would never stoop so low. I trade in favors."

"What possible favor would you want from me?"

"None. That's why I require two favors. First, I insist on driving the carpentum. Second, I need another dose of the love elixir."

"Abelia no longer loves you?"

"Don't be a fool. She's devoted to me. I want to entice another lovely vixen."

My mouth hung open.

"Don't look so shocked, Locusta, it's a most unbecoming look for you."

"I thought you loved Abelia."

"I do. I also love others." Lucius examined his nails. "Father has two mistresses and several lovers. I'm determined to have more."

"It's not a competition."

"Everything in Rome is a competition." He looked up. "More of the love elixir and I drive. Those are my terms."

"You ask two favors for my one."

"The happy privilege of status and gender."

I stood. "Fine. Let me get my basket."

"Excellent." Lucius rubbed his hands.

On the trip to the Forum, Lucius was relentless. He promised introductions to eligible bachelors if I would tell him who I was meeting. I would not be cajoled.

"There's nothing more intriguing than a woman with a secret," he nudged my side.

"Is that all it takes to intrigue you? How dull."

"Nothing about me is dull." He reached for the basket on my lap. "What's in there?"

I gave his hand a light slap. "Women's things."

His brow quirked. "I like women's things. Show me. Is it a love letter? Homemade bread? Beads? A stone phallus?"

"It's a love letter wrapped around a stone phallus I broke off from one of the statues in your father's garden."

Marcus burst out laughing. "Now I'm really intrigued. Are you seeing a man or a woman?"

"Both." I winked.

"Ooooh, I'd pay to watch that."

I patted his leg. "Stop here."

The House of the Vestals was ahead.

"My interest increases," said Lucius. "What scandal did our little winemaker embroil herself in?"

I searched the street. Saw no one who looked like a Vestal's servant.

"What's the secret signal?" asked Lucius.

I frowned. "Signal?"

"Next time, my little conspirator, you must have a sign. I'm not going to wait much longer."

"What do you suggest, oh Master of Guile?"

Lucius stuck his thumb and middle finger in his mouth. His whistle was loud and high-pitched.

I looked around. Lucius too.

"Your lover stood you up," he said.

Perhaps the Vestal changed her mind. Perhaps her monthly blood arrived. Perhaps—

A figure, one cloaked from head to sandal in a thick mantle, stepped from a dark cover.

"The intrigue continues," Lucius said.

I stepped down from the carpentum and crossed the street. "Are you…"

"State your name," said the young woman.

"Locusta."

"I'm Rhea's servant. You have something for me?"

I drew a small flagon from the basket. "She must not drink the entire contents tonight. There's enough for two days. Eight doses each day. I must know immediately if…"

If the Vestal Virgin bled to death?

"Summon me if she needs help," I said.

She nodded and the container vanished under her mantle. "Go," she whispered and stepped back into the shadows.

I returned to the carpentum. When I looked back Rhea's slave was gone, had disappeared into the rosy-hued twilight.

"Pedaling love elixirs?" Lucius picked up the reins. "How industrious of you. You're a merchant of love."

I smiled sweetly. Let Lucius think what he wanted.

"I'll expect my share of the love elixir later." He laughed out loud, then urged the horses faster through the streets.

THREE DAYS PASSED. No word came from Rhea or Romana. Was my tonic a success? A failure?

I stayed home and pled a headache when Annona invited me to the gladiator games. I didn't want to miss a note or visit in my absence.

On the fourth day, one of Lucius's personal slaves stood

outside my room. "This box was delivered before dawn. It bears your name."

I took the box, closed the drapes.

"It must be important," said Pricilla. "Look, the latches are sealed with wax." She used a sharp blade to slice it open.

I lifted the lid.

And gasped.

Coins filled the box. Gold, silver, brass, copper—a cache of denominations.

I plunged my hand into the shiny pile. "There's more than enough here to pay the taxes." I glanced at Pricilla. "The tonic was a success."

"You're making friends in high places." Pricilla raked her fingers across the coins. "Such a sweet melody. And not a scrap of parchment to identify the sender."

"Romana knows better than to leave evidence of the deed." I shut the lid, suddenly wary of the greedy eyes and large ears going about their household tasks. "We must hide the box until I can find a way to send it home."

That evening, during the evening meal, I told Gaius Theon my purchase of brass figurines required delivery to Uncle Amando. He assured prompt delivery of the package. The next morning Pricilla and I wrapped the coins tightly in soft linen. No one would suspect the package contained anything but trinkets.

UNCLE AMANDO VISITED Rome two months later. An important senator had demanded his newly-purchased race horses be accompanied by the seller. My uncle claimed this was a common practice, the buyer's method of exposing an unscrupulous breeder and a good way for him to meet prospective clients.

Uncle Amando did not stay at Gaius Theon's villa, although he did dine with us on several occasions.

"Walk with me, Locusta," Uncle Amando said one late afternoon before dinner.

"Is everyone well?"

"Everyone is healthy and much the same. Camilla is frantic for a husband. Your aunt is anxious about finding one. Varinius's woman is ripe with another bastard child. One would never suspect beneath his awkward nature is such a proliferate breeder. His servant is a sharp young woman though, a natural administrator. The overseer often confers with her."

"Her overreaching doesn't concern you?"

"By appearances she loves Varinius."

I wondered if she loved her new status more. It would not be the first time an equestrian's heirs were begot from a favorite servant.

"Has Father granted her freedom?"

Uncle Amando frowned. "You father's mind is no longer capable of such tasks. I expect Varinius will when the opportunity presents itself. Or when his mistress tells him to."

The opportunity being Father's death.

Uncle Amando paused to admire a statue of Ceres. "I received your package."

"All the taxes are paid?"

"Yes, but I'm curious, how did you come upon such a sum?"

I expected this question. Had practiced my answer. "My knowledge of herbs helped a friend."

Uncle Amando's eyes widened. "I would say it was a

most grateful and wealthy friend. I'm glad you're enjoying Roman society."

His comment set my heart pounding. "I'm coming home with you, aren't I?"

"Your father and I believe you must stay another year. Make more friends, Locusta."

This was a lie. Uncle Amando ought to have chosen his words more wisely. How could Father not be of sufficient mind for administrative tasks yet be able to decide my welfare?

"You want me to find a husband." It was best not to call my uncle a liar.

"Your father and I insist upon it."

"Gaius Theon is not overly fond of me. He thinks—"

"Theon wants you to stay. He says Lucius is quite adamant about extending your visit." Uncle Amando touched my shoulder. "Is there a betrothal in the future?"

"Lucius is already promised to another."

"I thought…" His brow furrowed. "Not Lucius?"

"Of course not," I snapped. How could he possibly think a country girl from Gaul of equestrian status could wed the senator's son? "I have no political connections."

Uncle Amando's brows lifted. "It's not that impossible." He laughed with the practiced ease of the elite. "No matter, I received a dinner invitation to a well-connected noble family. You'll be my guest. I want you to capture the attention of every worthy bachelor in the room."

I returned his false smile with my own. "Nothing would give me greater pleasure."

TWENTY-NINE

A trail of rose petals led the way to the dinner party. From the vestibulum, through the entrance hall, past the atrium, and up the wide marble steps. The flowery path released its sweet fragrance with every step.

"Are we dining on the roof?" Uncle Amando asked as we followed the trail up another flight of stairs.

"It's fashionable to dine in the coenaculum on the upper terrace. The breeze is cooler and the view of Rome better," I explained.

Above, the pulse of drums and cymbala mixed with the melodies of lyre, lute, and cithar. The music floated down in a harmonic welcome.

"Such splendor," Uncle Amando said when we reached the top.

A marble Venus in a provocative posture of repose greeted the guests. A naked and forever-erect Apollo played his lyre nearby. Sea nymph, Thetis, with her unclad appeal to Jupiter, rose from the floor like an enticing beacon. Every statue was ripe with innuendo.

Exotic trees in carved pots lined the coenaculum's

perimeter, and off to one side a grape-laden arbor sheltered a statue of Bacchus riding a leopard.

The rooftop glowed with opulence and the oil lamps cast a burnished radiance on the gem-clad guests. The space hummed with conversation. Paunchy senators. Important patricians. Wives aglitter with gold-threaded garments. Nude courtesans. Everyone mingled and laughed.

A servant dressed as Mercury offered us a platter heaped with stuffed mushrooms, bacon-wrapped asparagus, and marinated olives.

"Shall we find our hosts?" Uncle Amando plopped a mushroom in his mouth and headed into the crowd.

I saw several familiar faces. Said hello to women I had met at the baths or Annona's parties.

"You've made many valuable friends." Uncle Amando snatched another mushroom off the platter.

"A few." I nibbled on an asparagus spear.

Uncle Amando looked impressed. "Sadly, I'm not a friend, merely the humble supplier of their race horses. My invitation was a courtesy, nevertheless, I might as well take advantage of it. I'll make sure everyone knows I sell the fastest horses."

A tall, slim man emerged from a laughing clique of senators to embrace my uncle. "Amando, you do me honor with your presence."

"The honor is mine, Gellius Septimus, but I confess I made bold with your invitation and brought my niece, Locusta."

An elegantly attired woman appeared at Septimius's elbow. Her smile was wide but there were dark shadows under her sad eyes. She looked like she hadn't slept for many days.

"Unknown faces. How grand! How clever to invite new acquaintances. Welcome to our home. I'm Eugenia."

After her husband made the introductions, Eugenia took my hand. "Locusta. Such a distinctive name. Where do you call home, Locusta?" She drew me away from the men.

"Gaul."

Eugenia's eyebrows lifted. "I hear it's a lovely place. You're staying with Gaius Theon and Annona?"

"Yes. You know Annona?"

"She's a friend." Eugenia smiled brightly, her head moving from side to side as though surveying her party's success. "There's a small matter I wish to speak of in private. Later. For now, allow me to play the gracious hostess."

Eugenia introduced me to her friends and made me feel welcome. The women chatted about their children's antics and pondered the suitability of Sappho's poems as worthy reading for their daughters. They discussed the best tutors for their sons and best artists for their frescos. They gossiped about the charioteer caught frolicking naked with a wealthy widow.

They did not discuss Emperor Claudius or his wife Agrippina. Was it too politically dangerous?

After a seven-course dinner under the stars, beating drums announced the evening's entertainment. Six male dwarves in tiger-skin tunics scampered around the tables and waved long airy scarves in the air. A clash of cymbals signaled another troupe. Six belly dancers shimmied out from behind a drape. They undulated around tables while the dwarves pantomimed obscene sexual acts. The men hooted and hollered. Their wives resumed their conversations.

Eugenia took a seat beside me. "Gyrating hips may enthrall lesser men for hours; however, this distinguished group thrives on gaming pleasures. No doubt they'll soon place wagers on the dwarves' strength." Eugenia set a hand on my arm. "Would you like to see the rest of the villa?"

An esteemed patrician wanted to show me her house? How odd.

"I would like that," I said.

Eugenia took my hand as though I was an old friend, and together we made our way across the lively terrace.

Eugenia chatted about the hot weather. It was a safe topic. Too safe. I wondered at her intention. Her pace quickened as we descended the stairs and crossed the atrium.

"My cousin, Romana, speaks highly of you." Eugenia paused before an arched doorway, its thick drapes closing off the room.

The Vestal Virgin's mother. Had Romana confided in her?

"She is too kind," I said.

"Romana has many fine qualities; false kindness is not one of them. She praised your knowledge of herbs. She claims you saved her slave's life."

"I did." My response was quick and sure.

"I'm in need of your services." Eugenia lifted the heavy fabric, ducked under the swag. "Follow me."

THIRTY

Eugenia entered the room and I followed.

My eyes took a moment to adjust to the dim glow of light from the two tall oil lamps. Then I saw her.

The frail, petite figure almost disappeared among the blankets and pillows.

"Domina." A sleepy-eyed servant sprung from a chair when we entered. "She's restless tonight."

"This is my mother." Eugenia kissed the woman's cheek. "Mother, I brought the herbalist Romana spoke of. Fortune brings her this very night to our doorstep." She beckoned me forward. "Mother is very sick. Her pain increases each day. We went to the shrine of Asclepieia, but the god of medicine was mute. Our physician can do nothing for her, he says Mother has an old woman's illness."

The old woman opened her eyes. "Daughter..." Pain creased her face.

I could not heal this woman. Her breathing was shallow, her body wasted. There were no herbs to cure old age.

"You bring a child," the woman rasped between dry lips. "How can one so young possess such knowledge?"

"She might be young, but she's no child. She comes with Romana's highest recommendation."

The old woman closed her eyes. "What's your name, child?"

I took the woman's hand, her flesh as thin as onionskin. "Locusta."

"Tell me, Locusta, can you cure my ailment?"

"I cannot."

The old woman's eyes fluttered, her smile multiplying her numerous wrinkles. "Good. You're not a charlatan then. I've known too many of those. Can you relieve my suffering?"

Many plants alleviate pain, but without identifying its source I could not answer with certainty. "I don't know. Where does it hurt?"

The old woman dragged her hand to her chest. "My breast is red and swollen. The left side of my body is sore to the touch. My head throbs. My joints ache." She took several ragged breaths. "Each day brings more pain."

The doctor had diagnosed her correctly. It was the malady of old women. An illness of the breasts, an infection that grew like a weed and spread roots of pain throughout the body.

"I can make a drink to ease your suffering," I said.

Her weak fingers gave mine a feeble squeeze. "I want this pain gone forever."

"There's no such tonic."

"I want the pain gone forever," she repeated, her gaze sharp with meaning. "No more pain."

I glanced at Eugenia. Did she understand her dying mother's wish?

"Your mother wishes to…"

"Yes. That's why you're here. Mother speaks of little else.

I can't bear to see her suffer. I will not permit her to endure all this agony any longer." Eugenia's voice faltered, and she buried her head in her mother's shoulder. "Mama...sweet, self-less mama. You have no equal." Her body shook with sobs.

The old woman's eyes sought mine as she consoled her daughter with whispered endearments.

I averted my eyes, felt like an intruder during their tender moment.

Eugenia wiped away her tears and turned to me. "I beg you. Mother begs you. Release her from this pain."

"Your mother is courageous, but I can't help her."

"You mean, will not."

I looked down. How could Eugenia ask this of me? People in pain say anything to end their suffering.

"You will allow the most noble of mothers to linger in pain for weeks?" Eugenia's voice was as brittle as a dry leaf. "You will do nothing to alleviate the torment of my beloved mother? What if she was your mother? Could you stand idle and watch her moan and writhe in agony...day after day? Could you!?"

"Locusta." The old woman's voice was soft but commanding. "I lived many joyous years. Held great-grand-children in my arms. I'm old and weary. My wish is only to say a proper farewell to my family...without pain...to touch them one last time...to offer words of wisdom. I don't want their last memories to be of my anguished moans. Please help me."

I lifted my head despite my heavy heart. "When?"

The old woman looked to her daughter. "Eugenia?"

"Yes, Mama?"

"Gather the family tomorrow."

A few more words bound me to the deadly deed.

I returned to the party alone, my thoughts occupied with ingredients and dosages. And death.

"Did you enjoy yourself?" asked Uncle Amando as we waited for our carpentum.

"I did. But did you notice that not a single guest spoke ill of Emperor Claudius. It was as if they avoided all talk of politics."

"You're a shrewd observer of the Roman elite." Uncle Amando helped me into the carpentum.

I offered an insipid smile.

"These people are loyal to the emperor. They would never say anything against him. At least not in public."

My bed remained unused that night. Pricilla and I deliberated over ingredients and debated quantity. I wanted a gentle pain reliever that brought a peaceful end.

"I wish we could test the potency on a goat," Pricilla said.

"Impossible. Someone might see us and tell Gaius Theon."

"Too bad rabbits are immune to the belladonna's effects," said Pricilla.

"We have no choice but to rely on knowledge and assumption."

Dawn's red light came on swift clouds, morning and death biting at its heels.

I scooped a bit of the potent powder into a dish. Pricilla and I had agreed to use the plant of Atropos, the Greek name for the goddess of destiny and fate. It was best suited for the deed. The eldest sister of the three Moirai, Atropos had given the deadly plant its name. Much like the three Sisters of Fate, each part of the plant had its own fatal role. Powder from the leaves eased pain. The roots brought pleasant thoughts. The shiny berries produced dreams of flying. The old woman would feel wonderful and free as she soared to the end of her life.

Preparations complete, I fell into an exhausted sleep. It was not until early afternoon when Pricilla woke me.

"Eat these." Pricilla held out her hand.

"Fennel seeds?"

"For courage. Gladiators eat them before going into the arena."

"Do you have seeds for endurance, as well?"

"Not seeds but—"

"I must be of clear mind." I declined her offer of a reviving stimulant. "An afternoon of sorrow lays ahead."

"A carpentum arrived for you," said Annona. "Where are you going?"

"Gellius Eugenia's villa." I draped my palla over my shoulders.

"Whatever for?"

"She's interested in growing a flower garden. I offered to help chose the best varieties."

Annona's eyes lifted to the ceiling. "Women of my station should really avoid such tedious pursuits." She shook her head. "Each to his own diversion, I suppose." She picked up her wine goblet and dismissed me with a wave.

During the too-short trip, I hugged the basket of death close and readied my mind for the task.

My arrival at Gellius Septimius's villa bore no resemblance to the evening before. I descended from the carpentum, stepped on scattered leaves, last night's red rose petals now curled into purple flakes. The fragrant party path had become a trail of decay.

A servant escorted me into the old woman's room. Eugenia, swathed in bright silk and adorned with earrings, rings, necklaces, and bracelets sat by the bedside. Dark shadows rimmed her eyes.

The old woman was propped against a mound of pillows. Her gray hair, piled high in an elegant coiffure, was woven with ribbons and flowers. A light dusting of ochre powder added the bloom of vigor to her face. The jeweled brooch that secured her silk stola glittered in the single ray of light falling across the bed.

The dying woman burst into a smile at my arrival and beckoned me with ring-heavy fingers.

"Am I not the vision of health?" she asked.

"I hardly recognize you." I lifted her hand to admire the gems.

"It's best to die with dignity and grace. I want my family's last visit be one worth the remembering."

"Are you certain you want this?"

"My mind is fixed."

I added the powder to her wine goblet and offered her the cup.

"The pain will decrease?" She took a small sip.

I nodded.

"When will it be over?"

"When you give your consent."

A few moments passed before her breathing became less labored. The belladonna was taking effect.

"Summon the family." Eugenia spoke to the servant.

That afternoon, the old woman enjoyed the company of her children, grandchildren, and great-grandchildren.

A granddaughter placed her newborn in the old woman's thin arms. The cooing and nuzzling that followed brought tears to everyone's eyes. The youngest granddaughter sang a song. A grandson recited a Greek poem. Another grandson played a favorite melody on the lyre.

The old woman offered advice. She hugged and kissed each one. She whispered kind words.

When her breath grew labored, I offered another sip from the cup, and as the sun slunk over the hills of Rome the old woman declared her fatigue.

The family departed, unaware the matriarch wished to die before day's end. Only Eugenia and her brother remained.

"You have my gratitude, Locusta. I will die content."

I wiped away a tear. "You're a brave woman."

"No, I'm not. If I were truly brave, I would bear this pain." She gestured to the cup. "It's time."

I held the cup to her lips.

With both her son and daughter at her side, the old woman gulped down the tainted wine.

Eugenia stroked her brow. "I love you, Mama."

"Mmmm. I love you." The old woman closed her eyes. "I'm proud of you both. What fine loving children I have…no greater joy…son and daughter…my light…flying... soaring...above the fields." The old woman's words shriveled into a whisper.

I dipped a twisted cloth into a mixture of crushed berries.

"Juno!" The old woman suddenly called out. "Goddess! I have served you well. Fly with me."

The old woman sucked greedily on the berry mixture.

Eugenia and I exchanged a glance of understanding.

"The room grows dim. Who's here?" asked the old woman.

"It's evening, Mama. Your loving children sit beside you." Eugenia clutched her mother's hand.

"Oh, beautiful Goddess Vesta. Yes, of course. You have been with me all my life. Vesta…"

"She does not recognize me?" Eugenia asked.

"Hallucinations are common."

"Vesta, goddess…" the old woman mumbled.

A few more drops of the berry mixture and her breath grew labored, her body trembled. And then she breathed no more.

Eugenia tucked a blanket around her mother, kissed her cheeks, her tears falling on her mother's forehead.

"The deed is done." Eugenia collapsed into the arms of her weeping brother.

I picked up my basket of herbs and left them to their grief. A servant escorted me down the maze of halls and through the atrium. My eyes blurred with tears and my heart ached. I paid little attention to the men standing in the corner. Until I heard a familiar voice.

"Oh!" I dropped the basket.

THIRTY-ONE

That voice! Marcus's voice.

"Locusta!" A smile lit up his face.

"Marcus!" I wanted to fly into his arms, instead I felt rooted to the floor, unsure of what to do or say.

"Old friends?" asked Gellius Septimus.

"I had the pleasure of this woman's acquaintance several years ago while on campaign through Gaul. My former manservant, Saul—you know him—required medical attention, and Locusta graciously provided relief." His eyes twinkled. "If our business is concluded, patron, I would like to see my friend safely home."

"Of course, but first I have a question for Locusta." Gellius Septimus turned to me, his face tight with unexpressed grief. "How is my wife's mother? Is she feeling better now?"

"She died peacefully."

Gellius Septimus closed his eyes and exhaled his relief. "I'm glad you were able to ease her pain. The woman suffered so. Now, if you'll excuse me, my wife needs me."

He turned to go then stopped, curved his neck toward Marcus. "You will tell me the moment it's done."

"Yes, patron."

Gellius Septimus hurried away, leaving Marcus and I alone.

"A happy sight to find you in Rome." Marcus crossed the atrium, picked up my basket. "I suppose you're married now. What's the name of the lucky noble who calls you wife?"

"I am wife to no one." I fidgeted with my cloak.

His brows lifted. "Not married?" He took my hand. "You're never far from my thoughts. Do you still think of me?"

"Yes." A familiar heat warmed my body.

"I'm curious." Marcus traced the side of my face. "How does the daughter of a vintner with no political connections come to be in the home of the esteemed senator Gellius Septimus?"

I tilted my face, reveled in his touch, wanted his fingers on my lips. "Uncle Amando and I attended their dinner party last night. Eugenia knew of my herbal skills and asked me to help her ailing mother."

Marcus caresses moved down my neck. "You move in lofty political circles. Does your family have a villa in Rome?"

"I'm the guest of Gaius Theon."

"Ah, then you move in dangerous political circles."

"Politics is no concern of mine."

Marcus laughed, his hand dropping to his side. "That's not possible. Politics is the very breath of Rome."

"I breathe the air of gods and goddess. Senatorial gossip is foul wind I avoid." I put my arm through his. "Will you escort me home?"

"No errand will give me greater pleasure."

Marcus led me from the atrium, patted the guard dog with affection on the way out.

"I'm a different girl than the one you knew," I said.

"Yes, more beautiful."

I blushed, set my hand on his arm. "I made a mistake then. I should have gone with you."

"Gone with me? Followed me from camp to camp like a commoner?" Marcus shook his head. "No. I would not have allowed it."

"I don't need wealth. Or a grand home. I need you." Perhaps this desperation to live and love came from having watched the old woman die.

Marcus guffawed. "The rigors and conditions of camp will disgust you. You won't bathe for days, maybe weeks. The people we conquer are pagan barbarians. It's no place for a woman like yourself."

Marcus lifted me into a wagon and I searched his face for deceit. For an excuse. I found neither.

I drew the mantle over my head to hide the pain of his rejection.

"The truth angers you." Marcus picked up the reins.

"I'm sure to be married the next time we meet." I sniffed, fought to control the deluge of emotions that clogged my throat. And yet I felt hollow too. As if all the grief and death I witnessed over the past few hours had tunneled a bottomless pit into my soul. And then seeing Marcus...

I was overwhelmed and overwrought.

The wagon stopped at the end of the driveway. "I can take you home. Or I can take you with me on my secret errand."

The old woman's death. Marcus's rejection...

"Take me to Gaius Theon's villa. He lives on Caelian Hill." My voice sounded small and flat. "Without delay."

Marcus stared at me. "No curiosity at all? No questions about the nature of my secret task?"

"I spent the afternoon administering herbs to a dying woman. I'm weary." And heart-broken.

"My task also involves dying. A man. Perhaps you heard of him? He's a notorious troublemaker."

"I saw enough of death today."

"The commoners claim the man is a bringer of life ever-lasting."

"Life everlasting? Impossible. Does he pretend to be a god?"

The city was rife with soothsayers and magicians from conquered lands who made outrageous claims of immortality.

"Quite the opposite," said Marcus. "He's the humblest man I've ever met. Nevertheless, there are many politicians who believe he promotes radical beliefs that inflame the poor. They want him to die."

"Is this what Gellius Septimus wants?"

"He wants a report on his health. That's all." Marcus turned right onto the road. Away from Gaius Theon's villa. "I believe any man bringing a message of peace and comfort to commoners deserves to live."

"Why do senators want his death?"

"They're worried about the effect this man has on their clientalia, those merchants and freedmen they lord over. The nobles believe he creates unrest and disloyalty with his fantastic promises of an abundant life."

I scowled. "He promises them power and wealth?"

"Not at all. He simply offers them an afterlife of abun-dance and joy."

"Absurd. Our gods say otherwise."

"He claims a rich man is not likely to be granted access to the kingdom of paradise."

"A god for the poor?" I laughed. "What's this rebel's name?"

"Simon Peter." Marcus slowed the horses as we rounded a corner. "Gossip suggests Peter usurped the former elder's position as Sacerdotal Chair with god-given magic."

"Ah, this Simon Peter is a magician."

"So it appears. The previous elder, a man named Magus, also practiced magic when he levitated over the Forum. Simon Peter claimed this was a false act and called upon his god, who then caused Magus to fall to the ground."

"A man levitated over the Forum?" I snickered. "Are there any witnesses?"

"This is Rome. Anyone will swear they saw anything if enough coin is involved."

"Did Magus die?"

"He lived but the fall broke his legs, which gave Simon Peter the perfect opportunity to seize his position."

Men and their quest for power!

"It appears Simon Peter is the better magician," I said.

"Perhaps." He shrugged.

I studied the profile of Marcus's face. His straight nose, full lips, and jutting chin. A strong face. A face that did not fear battle and blood. The face of a man I didn't really know. "Do you believe in tales of magic?"

"I don't judge what I have not seen with my own two eyes." At the crossroads, Marcus halted the horses. "Homeward?"

"You've piqued my interest. Which was your intent all along."

"You know me to well." He smiled.

"We've been heading in the opposite direction of Gaius Theon's villa since we left."

"I can turn left here. Take you home if you want."

"After teasing me about a magician that threatens patricians? Not a chance. I want to meet him."

On the way to visit Simon Peter, Marcus shared stories of his latest adventures. They were light-hearted, amusing tales that lifted my spirits.

"Which hill does Simon Peter live on?" I asked.

"Simon Peter refuses to live near the villas of the elite. He lives among the poor."

"Then he's probably fallen victim to one of their illnesses."

"Sickness targets the poor?"

"Sometimes," I said.

The poor were often malnourished, their meat old, their vegetables rotten, and their grains rancid. The quality of one's food, I had begun to believe, contributed to a person's overall health.

We stopped in front of a three-story insulae. The ground floor was constructed of mud-brick, the two upper levels erected from inferior timber.

"The crusader for the poor lives here?" I drew the hood over my head.

"Simon Peter will have it no other way."

I followed Marcus into the building.

The room was dark. A single lamp cast a dim glow on the gathered crowd. The air was foul with sweat and filth.

Men in dingy wool tunics and worn sandals quickly shuffled back to let us pass. A centurion signaled trouble. They knew all too well that prison, beatings, and crucifixion were the penalties for a perceived slight or defiant action.

The four men who stood at Simon Peter's bedside took one look at Marcus and stepped aside.

"Welcome, centurion." Simon Peter spoke from his prone

position, feet extending well past the bed. "Have you come to verify rumors of my illness?"

"Your ill health is of no consequence to anyone of importance. Except, perhaps the healer I brought." Marcus drew me forward.

Close up, I saw that Simon Peter's pale skin had a yellow hue.

"Tell me your ailments," I said.

Simon Peter turned his head, his sparse eyebrows lifting in surprise. "That's not a physician's voice. Reveal yourself."

I pushed back the hood. Simon Peter gazed at me, his bright, keen eyes searching my face with such intensity it felt like he took measure of my soul.

"Fever. Headache," he said.

I was surprised. He did not comment on my sex or youth. How odd.

"Do you get sudden chills?"

"Yes."

"Is it followed by fever and sweating?"

Simon Peter nodded.

I reached out, laid fingertips on his wrist. "Do you have pain in your joints?"

"More every day." Peter coughed, the rasp weak and telling.

"How's your appetite?"

Simon Peter frowned. "I have none."

"Is your business done near ponds or still water?"

"I baptize new believers in ponds, streams, and fountains." Simon Peter scratched his short gray beard. "Do I have semitertian fever?"

"Your symptoms match those of the illness." I looked at Marcus. "Foul water often brings on this fever. It's not too late though. I can cure him."

Peter clasped my hand. "You are sent by God."

"The centurion brought me to your bedside, not one of the gods."

Peter gripped tighter, his focus fixed. "There's only one true God. Roman gods are impostors."

I smiled kindly at his preposterous statement, patted Simon Peter's hand, and directed my words at Marcus. "I don't have the necessary herbs with me."

Simon Peter coughed again. "You will return to heal me?"

"That's for the centurion to decide."

Simon Peter squeezed my fingers, his grasp surprisingly strong for a sick old man. "Jesus, the son of God, said I would know the time of my death when I would be dressed by another, my arms outstretched, and I would go where I do not want to go."

The son of God? Peter believed a demigod spoke to him!

I suppressed a smile. Roman and Greek gods sired many children by earthly woman. Hercules. Aeneas. Dionysus. Orpheus. Theseus. Perseus. Achilles. The list of demigods was long. I never heard of Jesus.

"I'll return with the healer," Marcus said.

"Good noble woman, I await your tonics. The Lord will bestow the healing." Simon Peter's eyes grew heavy, the effort of talking had made him weary. He closed his eyes, and I do believe he fell asleep.

THIRTY-TWO

M arcus drew my hood over my head, hiding my face in the shadowed depths, and guided me silently through the crowd and out into the cool night.

"How near is Simon Peter to death?" Marcus lifted me into the carpentum.

"If he doesn't receive treatment he may not recover. The old are less resilient than the young."

Marcus's brow wrinkled. "That bad? What do you know about this illness?"

"Semitertian fever strikes most during hot weather. People living near ponds or lakes are more at risk. Pricilla and I believe the insects that hover over the still water cause the sickness."

"Insects are too tiny to bring such great harm. Wasps and mosquitoes are small, easily crushable." He twisted his thumb into his palm. "Their bites and stings are only a minor annoyance."

"This is not an army or a battle where size and strength and sheer numbers matter. Illness and disease have their own way of doing battle. They must be tiny enough to slip undetected into a person's body. The tiniest substances have the greatest impact. And I have proof. The poison in a bullfrog's skin kills a man. A certain berry causes vomiting. Several mushroom varieties are fatal. Why does one wound heal and another fester and cause death? Because of what we cannot see."

"You make bugs and berries to be more dangerous than the Roman army."

"I think they are."

"You might be right."

I shivered in the damp night air. "Why do you want to help Simon Peter if your patron prefers that he dies?"

Marcus's jaw moved as though he chewed on a dilemma. "I owe Septimus considerable gratitude. It was his connections that got me my military commission. And it was his recommendation that secured my centurion rank. During my servitude to his son, I learned to read and studied Ovid, Virgil, Horace, and Cicero. I also learned to think." His eyes slid toward mine.

"About what?"

"About things that others take for granted or don't question. I decided to come to my own opinions through reasoning and analysis. I owe Septimus my education and my career. I do not owe him my obedience to his opinions."

"What's your opinion about Simon Peter?"

"The senators are wrong about him," said Marcus. "He's not a threat. Yes, he's an elder and a leader for the poor, but he has no desire to overthrow senators or seek political power. His message is simple. He comforts the needy, the outcasts, and the suffering."

"You make him sound harmless. Remember Spartacus led a rebellion of slaves."

"Spartacus fought for freedom. Simon Peter offers a new

religion, a forgiving god, nothing more. He claims his god accepts, even welcomes the poor. His god offers mercy and eternal life." His voice was matter-of-fact, as though he spoke about the weather.

"I can see why the poor follow him." I shrugged. "Roman or Greek gods make no such promises."

"Exactly, which is another reason why the elite consider Simon Peter dangerous. His god offers them what Roman gods do not." Marcus's hand covered mine. "My centuria leaves in two days."

So soon?

My heart sank, all excitement about seeing Marcus again pulled under by a lake of despair. "Will I ever see you again?"

Marcus nudged my shoulder with his. "Fate already granted two favorable encounters. Both that required your herbal expertise. Perhaps the third meeting will be the same."

"By the time your military service concludes I'll be a wedded woman grown fat with many children."

"The soothsayer said—"

"The soothsayer! The soothsayer! He said you would find love with a woman of courage with skills that far surpassed your own, a woman revered and feared because of her skill. I'm not that woman, Marcus."

Marcus stopped the carpentum under a Linden tree on a desolate road that wound its way past the elites' villas on Caelian Hill.

His arms encircled my waist, drew me close. His mouth found mine and we kissed. It was a kiss of passion, yearning, hope, and despair. A kiss that left us greedy for more. A kiss offering nothing. And everything.

Marcus pushed back the hood of my cloak and ran his hand over my hair. "You haunt my dreams, Locusta. I lay in my tent on the battlefield and thought of you. I woke each dawn, my body eager to fill you. I wondered if you married. Took a lover. I wondered, who makes love to my woman? And then I come to Rome to find you unwed and more beautiful and...and in the home of my patron, Gellius Septimus. It's as if the gods— "

I silenced his words with hungry lips and eager tongue. His centurion uniform prevented further intimacies.

Marcus broke the kiss and cupped my face with his hand. His thumb traced my lips. "If I were a lesser man, I would ravage you right now."

"Do it." I pressed his hand to my breast.

"No. I will not use you to serve my lust."

"Take me here. Now." I pushed his hand beneath my stola. "Take me with you on campaign."

He groaned and pressed his lips to mine, held my breast, caressed my nipple.

"Take...me...with...you," I said between kisses.

Somewhere a nightingale sang, and an owl hooted. I did not hear the night's music. I listened only to the song of Marcus's quickening breaths and his promises of love.

His eyes dreamy, Marcus pulled away and picked up the reins. "This does neither of us any good. I'll come to you when I can provide the life you deserve."

The horses walked onward.

I crossed my arms. "What if I'm already wed and happy when your commission ends?"

"I'll laugh at my foolishness for believing in the words of an old soothsayer." Marcus urged the horses faster. "You must go to the baths tomorrow."

"What? Why?"

"You need an excuse to leave the villa, right? Bring the

medicine for Simon Peter. I'll wait across from the women's entrance."

His plan was simple, but a lot could go wrong. I wasn't free to go where and when I pleased.

We turned into the shaded lane toward Gaius Theon's villa, the grounds so heavy with fog the statues were obscured.

"I don't recognize this carpentum." Lucius's slurred voice came from the shadowed depths of the front portico. "Make yourself known."

"It's Lucius," I whispered. "He's drunk."

"Good evening, Lucius. I am Marcus. Gaius Septimus requested I escort Locusta home." Marcus leapt down and offered me a gallant hand.

I stepped from the carpentum. Did my rumbled clothing and flushed face betray my evening activities?

Lucius stumbled toward us, a small amphora of wine dangling from his hand. "My, my, Locusta, you manage to charm everyone you meet. What feminine wiles enticed this Goliath to take you home?" Lucius made an arrogant show of sizing up Marcus before he waved him away as though he were a mere servant. "How is Eugenia? What flowers did you decide on?" He latched onto my arm, more for balance than gallantry. "It's late, my sweet." With a belch, he veered toward the doorway.

I was tempted to turn around, to watch Marcus depart, but refrained. I was worried it might arouse Lucius's suspicion. Rome was a pit of vipers, and though Lucius was a young serpent, he already had a venomous bite.

Lucius swung his arm over my shoulder to steady himself, and together we lumbered through the atrium while he slurred nonsense. This senator. That wife. A ravaged virgin. A grateful servant.

I detangled myself from his clutches by the bedchamber, where he gave me a wine-wet kiss on the cheek and stumbled away.

I went straight to Pricilla's cot. "Wake up. I must prepare a healing tonic for the still-water illness."

"Now?" Pricilla yawned and burrowed into the blanket. "Wait until morning."

"I must do it now." I lit the lamps, set the herbal coffer on the table, and recounted the evening's events. The old woman's peaceful death. Seeing Marcus. Our secret trip to the rebel religious leader, Simon Peter.

Pricilla sniffed and wrinkled her nose. "You smell like cheap olive oil and unwashed bodies."

"Simon Peter lives among the poor, and his room reeked with the despair and poverty of the followers who kept vigil at his bedside."

"Why are you helping this man? The poor can do nothing for you. Neither can Marcus." Pricilla rubbed her eyes.

"He loves me and says I'm always in his thoughts."

Pricilla frowned. "Forget about him. You're destined for a grander life than what he can provide." Pricilla rifled through the coffer. "Was Simon Peter's skin and eyes yellow?"

"Yes. The illness is advanced, and though he is tall and strong-looking, his advanced age will hinder his chance of recovery." I shook bits of dried wormwood into my palm.

Pricilla poked at the pieces. "Fresh is best. I know a magician who grows sweet wormwood in his garden, but he'll demand payment."

I withdrew a coin purse from the bottom of my clothing chest and tossed it to Pricilla. "Take all you need but don't pay more than necessary."

"If the magician was not so old and ugly, I wouldn't have to pay him at all."

IN THE PRE-DAWN DARKNESS, Pricilla departed for the magician's home to purchase fresh wormwood. By the time she returned, the sun crested the sky.

Pricilla, her face rosy from the long walk, set down her basket and withdrew a thick bundle of green feathery leaves.

"I bought enough for drying and for growing our own." Pricilla pulled out a bulging papyrus-wrapped package. "This little bundle cost a few extra coins. The magician swears it cures still-water illness in his land." She untied the string and unwrapped the package to reveal finely ground leaf.

I put my nose to it. "Pungent."

"He swears that grinding it this way releases its full potency and will cure diarrhea, coughs, and boils." Using the knife's edge, she drew off a small measure. "This amount must be added to an amphora of boiling water. The magician said it usually works in a day, unless the illness is advanced, then it takes several."

"A dose equal in size to a date fruit." I poked at the small pile of dark green crumbs before scooping the semitertian remedy into a small clay jar. "I hope this heals Simon Peter."

Pricilla put her hands on her hips. "You don't care about Simon Peter. You care about pleasing Marcus."

"What does my intent matter as long as the outcome is good?"

"One day it may matter a great deal."

I rolled my eyes and strode from the room in search of Annona.

I concealed the clay jar in the folds of a thick palla. Annona was none the wiser as we headed toward the baths.

The sway of the carpentum, the warm day, and the sleepless night weighed down my eyelids, yet I dare not dose off.

Usually, Annona was talkative, her gossip indiscreet. Today, her words were guarded, her tone contrived and cautious. Instead of tales of debauchery she prattled about household matters. She never asked about my visit to Gaius Septimus's villa.

Did she expect me to talk about it? My invitation to an esteemed senator's house was rather odd.

"Are you looking for something? Or someone?" asked Annona.

I turned my head away from the window. "Why do you ask?"

"You appear distracted today." Her voice was as sweet as honey and thick with suspicion.

"I'm thinking of home," I lied.

Annona patted my hand. "You've been gone a long time."

We arrived at the woman's entrance and climbed down from the carpentum. I looked up and down the street for Marcus. A few luxurious carpenti, several litters, and some old carts lined the street. None driven by a handsome centurion.

"Don't wait for me, Annona. I want to do a bit of reading in the library before bathing." It was the only room she never went into.

Annona scrunched her face. "Reading? I find it so tedious but if you enjoy it…" She shrugged, flashed an ingratiating smile. "You know where to find me."

I waited until she went into the dressing room, then went back outside.

THIRTY-THREE

I looked left and right. Saw no sign of Marcus. I was about to turn around when I noticed a man hunched low in a battered vegetable cart waved.

I squinted, but a hood obscured the driver's face. I shielded my eyes from the sun's glare and stared.

Marcus lifted his head.

I crossed the street and climbed into the wagon.

"Cover your clothes." Marcus patted the moth-eaten rag heap on the seat. "Quickly."

I picked up the mildewed old cloak. "I need a disguise?"

"A visit from a wealthy woman will arouse suspicion. The servants will return to their master's home with stories about a beautiful raven-haired woman who cures the poor. We don't want gossip to reach unsympathetic ears."

"Why must I look like a filthy wretch?"

"Everyone pays attention to the beautiful and wealthy. No one notices the poor." Marcus made no attempt to hurry the sluggish burro pulling the cart. "When we arrive, stoop and walk with the hitched gait of the old. Keep your face hidden. If you must speak, alter your voice."

"Is this fraud really necessary?"

Marcus sank into his cloak. "You come to cure a man many senators believe is dangerous. Men like Gaius Theon, Gellius Septimus, and even Emperor Claudius."

I drew the foul-smelling hood over my face and slumped down. Marcus was right. A shabbily-dressed couple in an old cart drew no attention. We were lost amid the throng, poverty cloaking us with invisibility. It was a strange experience, one that made me feel insignificant and dull. I had always traveled in fine carpenti driven by well-dressed servants and accustomed to the envious stares of commoners.

Marcus stopped the wagon just outside Simon Peter's home. The crowd had increased since last night. Women, children, and men gathered around the doorway and leaned against the walls. A few women wept. Men huddled together and whispered.

"Remember, your bones are weary and weak," Marcus said.

I got out slowly, carefully, and clutched Marcus's arm as we moved through the crowd.

In our frayed cloaks, our arrival drew only a few disinterested glances. We kept our heads down, Marcus bending low and shuffling like an old man as we made our way through the doorway and into a hallway crowded with Simon Peter's tear-stained and grave-faced followers.

"You returned," said Simon Peter.

His yellow skin and high fever told me everything. The still-water illness had worsened.

"The centurion keeps his promises." I pulled a clay vessel from beneath the grubby cloak and looked at the young man kneeling by the bed. "I need a goblet of wine."

I checked Simon Peter's pulse, listened to him breathe, and spoke encouraging words.

The young man returned.

"Mix this much and no more." I showed both Simon Peter and the young man the amount. "You'll feel better by evening."

I stirred the wormwood into the wine and held the cup to Simon Peter's lips.

He took a tentative sip. "You're a wealthy healer but you can still see the kingdom of heaven."

The fever had addled his brain.

"Yes," I said. "Drink more... more... very good."

After he consumed every drop, Marcus and I departed.

"An odd man." I stayed close to Marcus as we threaded our way through the crowd in the hall.

We emerged from the building, and once again, no one paid any attention as we climbed into the old wagon and set off down the street.

Marcus turned his head, his face shadowed by the hood. "I leave Rome in a few days. I don't know when I'll return."

If ever. The possibility hung in the air like a putrid stench.

"Let me come with you," I said.

"I have nothing but a horse, a suit of armor, and years of unfilled service to offer."

"I don't care." I ripped off the horrid cloak.

"Spoken like a woman who never wanted for anything." Marcus put a finger through a moth-eaten hole in the cloak. "I refuse to subject you to such deplorable conditions."

I huffed out my irritation. He was right of course. And it showed concern for my wellbeing. But I wasn't some spoiled young woman in need of luxury. I had a skill. One that would be useful on the battlefield.

"I could assist the phys—"

"No, I won't have it. Don't ask me again." His voice was

gruff. "Please, Locusta." His tone melted, grew soft. "Don't make me do something I know is wrong for you."

"How do you know what's wrong for me? That's my decision." I was tired of people like Uncle Amando and Lucius and Gaius Theon telling what was best.

Marcus pushed back his hood. His face was grim, his eyes sad.

"You think you want to travel from camp to camp with me? Let me tell you what will happen. It will be fun for a month. Maybe two. But then you will grow to hate it—the tents, the blood and battles, the heat and cold, the hardships. Your love for me will turn to anger until you finally come to despise the hard life you have." He swallowed. "I cannot bear your hate, my love."

I said nothing and we traveled the rest of the way in silence. My eyes welled with hot tears. Seeing Marcus again was torture. To love him and not be able to be with him wrenched my heart.

Marcus stopped across from the women's entrance of the baths.

I climbed down.

"Locusta..."

"I don't care if you never return!" I marched away and ran up the steps before realizing how immature I acted. I turned to wave goodbye, to look at his face once more.

The wagon was already halfway down the street.

My body tensed and a strangled cry erupted from my lips. Marcus was gone.

I trudged through the women's entrance, the weight of an impossible love stealing my energy and sucking all hope for a happy future.

I found Annona in the heated pool.

"Must have been a very good book," she said.

"Several in fact." I did my best not to look guilty. "It's so easy to get lost in a book."

"You missed all the gossip about the marital trouble between our emperor and empress," she whispered and turned to the wrinkled matron who had every woman's ear.

I paid no attention to their gossip. My heart ached for a man I would never have.

"Locusta, do you believe the rumor about Agrippina and her son Nero?" asked Annona. "Do you think they're lovers?"

I shrugged. Who cared?

THIRTY-FOUR

"You must stay in Rome." Uncle Amando's voice rose over the course of our too familiar conversation. The same one we had every time he visited.

"I want to go home." I clutched his mantle. "I miss Father and Camilla. I'm an aunt to Varinius's three children and have never set eyes on two of them."

"Your opportunities are here. There's nothing for you in Gaul. You'll stay in Rome until you find a husband."

I did not tell Uncle Amando that my husband-less state was my own fault. Annona had invited a string of suitors to dinner. I didn't like any of them.

At first, Annona and Gaius Theon were dismayed by my lack of interest. Then I think they began to believe the rumors about my preference for women. However, more swift of foot than the rumors I bedded Pricilla were those of my herbal skills. I blamed Annona. She woke with a horrible hangover one morning and told Gaius Theon she could not attend an important horse racing event. Their argument was so vile the servants hid. I made her a tonic that she swore made her feel better than she had in weeks.

It didn't take long for Annona's friends to seek my services for a variety of ills. Dried yellow tops of hypericum for women who suffered from chronic sadness. Lavandula treatments to cure an anxious bride with insomnia. A special mixture of visnaga to soothe an old man with breathing problems.

"Lucius and I decided to allot you the south corner of the garden," Annona said one afternoon after listening to her friend extol my herbal virtues.

I kissed her cheek. "I'm in your debt and I fear I've imposed on your hospitality for too long. And now this! How will I ever repay your kindnesses?"

Annona's smile bore all the likeness of truth, but her eyes shone with dishonesty. "Think nothing of it. A small courtesy. The ground lay fallow, anyway."

Pricilla and I went to the market the next day. I purchased plants sold in back alley stalls from vendors as exotic as their merchandise. I bought seeds from a woman with skin as dark as ebony and roots from a man with almond-shaped eyes. But it was the merchants who spoke in a foreign tongue and haggled with thick accents that traded the rarest plants.

"AM I IN AN APOTHECARY SHOP?" Lucius swept his hand over the profusion of flasks, urns, and vessels cluttering the tabletop.

I plucked a dried petal from his hair and pointed to the bundle of dried herbs over his head. "Herbalists need more than a plot of dirt."

"I'll have another table brought to your room." Lucius held out an open palm.

I laid the petal in his hand.

Lucius snatched my wrist and pulled me close.

"Not the payment I have in mind." His lips crashed onto mine, his tongue pushed past my lips.

I let him kiss me. It was a small fee. Yet when his hand wandered to my breast, I pushed him away.

"A kiss for a table. Nothing more." I wagged my finger at him.

"There will come a time you need more than a table."

I tapped my finger on my chin in mock deliberation. "Mmmm, will you settle for a peek at my breasts?"

He snickered. "You've become quite a problem for Mother."

"Why?"

"She doesn't approve of our friendship. Fortunately, your reputation as a healer makes you—and therefore her—a welcome dinner guest. You, my pretty herbalist, prove to be a socially advantageous acquisition for Mother. And that makes her uneasy."

"Because her friends like me?"

"Because her friends need you, or at least your remedies." Lucius twirled a stem between his fingers. "Do Mother's friends pay you?"

"Not in coin."

"Mmm, yes, future favors are the preferred fee of the Roman elite."

I frowned, snatched the stem from his fingers. "Favors don't buy supplies at the market."

"Trust me, favors are more valuable than gold or silver."

"The advice of a politician," I rolled my eyes.

Lucius placed his fist over his heart and dipped his head in mockery. "Manus manum lavat."

One hand washes the other.

"That old saying? Well, politicians may wash one another's hands, but they do it with dirty water," I said. "Besides when have you ever seen a senator haggling over a flower at the market?"

Lucius burst out laughing.

THE DAYS FELL into a regular pattern. In the morning I tended to my herbs and went to the baths. In the afternoon I want to gladiator contests, wild beast games, and chariot races with Annona and her friends. Not a day passed that I didn't think about Marcus. I made offerings to the gods for his safety and health, even though I knew we would never meet again.

Some days were interesting. Others frustrating. One afternoon a promiscuous charioteer asked me to treat a skin infection on his phallus. The stubborn man refused to name his lovers, even after I explained he spread the infection with every tryst.

Although I accompanied Annona to the games and contests, I preferred to spend time concocting and testing new mixtures. The household servants brought me mice. They were imperfect test subjects, but they were always in supply. When Pricilla let it be known I tested a new love elixir, a few servants asked to be volunteers.

On rain-soaked days I spent the day in my chambers content with my herbs and potions. It was on such a wet day while I macerated a plant with olive oil that Pricilla made an announcement.

"The student surpasses the master," she said with motherly pride. "Your skill with dose and mixture now exceeds my own. I might be jealous if we weren't such good friends."

"You think too highly of my skills."

Pricilla hugged me. "I speak the truth, Locusta. Your talents and dedication amaze me."

My heart swelled. Her compliment meant more than she realized.

Pricilla pulled up a chair next to me. "I expect your skills will increase even more since your time isn't taken up with a husband and children."

I frowned, her compliment wilting my delighted bloom. In a way it was my fault I wasn't married. I was too discriminating.

"You would've made an excellent Vestal Virgin." Pricilla gave me a playful nudge. "Tending the sacred fire, preparing the flour…"

In the past few months, Pricilla and I were apt to snip at one another. I did not approve of her affair with a certain married woman and she scoffed at my warnings.

I rubbed my chin and lifted my eyes to the ceiling. "Vestals do have the best seats at the games."

"You don't like the games." Pricilla's playful grin bent into an earnest one. "Have you thought about my request?"

Her request was manumission, freedom.

Uncle Amando had made me Pricilla's legal master. Which meant I could grant her freedom. My heart wanted to. My mind did not. I needed her! I trusted her opinions, valued her suggestions, and relied on her friendship.

Besides, granting Pricilla's freedom came with responsibilities. I refused to send my best friend into the world without enough coin to start a business. I scarcely had enough silver to pay an assistant's wage.

"I have, but…" I looked away, embarrassed.

"I understand." Pricilla tied a string around a bouquet of herbs and suspended the bundle from a hook. "Every week brings new clients and more coin to your purse."

"Taxes are due again."

"Your uncle and brother's wife manage the vineyard. The money you earn is yours alone.

"Soon. I promise."

THE HALLWAY RESONATED with the sound of marching feet.

"Locusta!" Annona raced into my room. "Locusta! Hurry, my girl! Hurry—she's—"

"Good day, Locusta."

Glittering with gems and shimmering with opulent garments, a woman of arresting beauty swept into my room.

I had never met the woman but knew her at once. The full lips, large eyes, high cheeks, and straight nose had been carved into marble for everyone in Rome to admire. Great-granddaughter of Augustus. Sister of Caligula. Wife of Claudius. Empress Agrippina.

I dropped to my knees and lowered my head.

"Empress." Sharp thorns punctured my skin, but I dare not drop the hawthorn clutched in my hand.

"Arise, young herbalist." Empress Agrippina's voice was honey-sweet, yet laden with command. "Annona dear, I wish to speak to your young charge alone. See no one disturbs us and keep the drapery open when you leave. My visit is not a secret."

My gaze flitted into the hallway where a line of Praetorian guards stood at attention.

Annona backed out of the room, stooping all the while. She tripped over her stola as she fled down the great hall past the grim-faced palace guards.

"Come, child." Agrippina perched on a cushioned bench and pointed to the floor beside her.

I scurried over to kneel before her and gazed at Rome's most talked about woman. I noted every noble detail, from the rows of obedient curls coiled at the nape of her neck to the jeweled wreath adorning her royal tresses. Her clothing was scandalous, the snug-fitting stola crisscrossed with golden cords that hugged her curves. It was an intimidating display of her sensuality. The immodest style accentuated her small breasts and the sheer layers of gossamer silk flaunted her erect brown nipples.

Agrippina lifted my chin, turned my face from side to side. She smiled, her double canines showing. "The gossip is true. You're as young as you are beautiful. How is it Lucius has not bedded you yet?"

My mouth dropped open.

Her jeweled finger touched the tip of my nose. "My ear has been tickled with rumors of your herbal skills."

I looked into her sharp, bright eyes. A cool woman of infinite power and resourcefulness stared back. My fist tightened in panic, the thorns piercing my palm.

"I have only minor skill," I whispered.

"Modesty is a charming trait in a young woman but altogether unwise in your profession."

"I—"

"Save the apology and humility. Whether you like it or not, you earned yourself a reputation as a skilled pharmacist."

"As you say, empress."

"Tell me, Locusta, is there someone you love, someone for whom you would do anything? A lover, perhaps?"

"I love someone, and he loves me, but we can't be together." What did she want? Why did she care if I loved someone?

"Love is heartache," she simpered. "I'm sorry for your misfortune but perhaps you will understand my own torment regarding love better because of it." She pressed her hands to her bosom.

I blinked, unsure of her innuendo. Could it be Empress Agrippina required one of my love elixirs? I kept my face free of emotion.

"The emperor is in great pain," whispered Agrippina. Her eyes flicked toward the Praetorian Guards in the hall. "Every day his condition grows worse. Claudius shows a brave face to the senators—to the world—but speaks plainly to me—his devoted wife—of his agony. The emperor swore me to secrecy...except now you know, too."

My heart pounded harder and faster than a four-horse chariot team.

"This is our secret. His pain. His suffering." She slipped a handkerchief from her stola and dabbed at her eyes. "I cannot bear to see my husband suffer."

"Do you want me to ease his misery?"

"Yes." She wiped her eyes, even though there was not a single tear.

How odd. Emperor Claudius had a personal physician, a man named Xenophon, whose extensive knowledge of herbs was well known.

"What ailments does he suffer from?"

Agrippina sniffed loudly. "Crippling and agonizing pain throughout his body."

"There's an ointment for those general aches plaguing older folk." I breathed a sigh of relief. The malicious gossip about Empress Agrippina was wrong. This loving wife merely wished her husband free from pain.

"Ah yes, except those remedies only lessen his pain." Agrippina's hand felt heavy on my shoulder. "You must end his agony."

End.

There was no mistaking the emphasis placed on the word. End. Spoken with cruelty. With evil. With ruthless intensity.

"I…" My tongue thickened with fear.

"Look at your empress when speaking."

I lifted my head.

Agrippina wanted me to poison the Emperor of Rome!

THIRTY-FIVE

Empress Agrippina was commanding me—for one did not refuse an empress—to murder the most powerful man in the world.

"I cannot," I mumbled.

Empress Agrippina's face changed in an instant. Her eyes hardened into black marble. Her chin jutted and her nostrils flared.

"I misjudged you," she growled. "How unfortunate I entrusted my secret to one so...naïve." The double canines that were so charming moments ago now exposed her vicious ambition. She glanced down the hallway. "Such a pity, the guards detest stabbing a beautiful woman for treason."

My heart missed a beat, then pounded double time in my throat.

Empress Agrippina had divulged a secret desire. I declined. She had no choice but to kill me. But I did have a choice.

"Swift or slow?" I chose life.

Empress Agrippina's eyebrows lifted and her pupils

dilated with pleasure. "It makes no difference as long as I administer the emperor's pain relief."

No one would suspect the emperor's own wife of poisoning him.

"Food tasters?" I asked.

Empress Agrippina cupped her palms. "It won't be necessary when the food comes from the hands of his loving and obedient wife." She dabbed at her tearless eyes. It was a convincing charade for any guard with wandering eyes. "In three days, a carpentum will deliver you to the palace. Alone. The emperor's misery is our secret."

"I understand."

"You'll stay until the emperor is relieved of his suffering." Her slim fingers reached into her bosom and withdrew a silk satchel. "For your troubles." She pushed it into my hands, pressed my fingers on it.

I lowered my head.

Empress Agrippina left the room. When the heavy thud of the Praetorian Guards' footsteps faded, I lifted my head. The empress and her retinue were gone.

I uncurled my fingers and dropped the thorns I had clutched during her visit. With shaking hands, I spilled the purse's contents onto my bloody palm. Gold coins. Emeralds. Rubies. I had never held such wealth before.

I made a fist. No one must see these gems. No one must know. Not even Pricilla. To reveal Empress Agrippina's secret meant death. For me. For anyone who knew.

Voices echoed down the hall. I stood, shoved the blood-stained pouch into my bosom, and hurried to the window.

"Locusta." Annona rushed into the room.

I focused on the drapes billowing in the breeze and willed myself not to cry.

Annona touched my shoulder. "What did the empress

want?"

I spun around. "Oh, you startled me. The empress needs a tonic for Britannicus's face." I shrugged. "He has unsightly pustules."

Annona's eyes widened. "What an honor. Don't look so stricken, my dear. Agrippina won't kill you if your potions don't clear her son's face."

A single tear escaped.

Annona brushed it away. "You've become like a daughter to me, Locusta. How silly you should fret about the empress's request. Come, let's celebrate with a cup of our finest vintage."

Annona drew me from the window and shepherded me past the sharp eyes of Pricilla who stood in the doorway.

"You lie," Pricilla said later that evening.

I looked away.

"Empress Agrippina does not make personal visits for such a simple tonic," said Pricilla. "She would send one of her confidantes or servants."

"Maybe she's embarrassed her son has pimples." I rearranged the herb table to avoid her skeptical stare.

"She came for your love elixir, didn't she?"

I moved the alembic from one side of the table to the other. "I told you, the empress wants a tonic for Brittanicus's skin."

"You never keep anything from me. Why now? What do I care who a spoiled empress spreads her legs for?"

"I sent you on an errand. Why do you hover about like a mosquito?" I banged down a clay vessel.

"I'm no fool. You send me away to prepare the tonic in

secret."

I loved Pricilla too much to tell her the truth. Her love of gossip made her vulnerable. One slip of the tongue and we would both be executed.

"Do I ask for details of your late-night visits to the far side of the villa?" I looked her in the eye, smacked the table. "I do not. Not every secret needs to be shared. Do I ask why the belladonna is in short supply after one of your midnight excursions? Or why you sleep so soundly the next day?"

"I'm careful. I don't take it orally." Pricilla flashed a mischievous grin. "Mixed with oils and inserted into certain orifices the narcotic is safe and oh, so pleasurable."

Pricilla had made many friends in Rome. Not all of them reputable. She thrived in the hustle and bustle of the city where citizens quenched lustful appetites without criticism. Where men and women indulged in an unending diversity of pleasures. Pricilla had no desire to return to the quiet life of my family's vineyards.

"Allow me this one secret," I said.

"If I overstep myself..." She gnawed on her lip.

Her sudden submissiveness tugged at my heart. She didn't want to argue. She needed us to stay the best of friends. She wanted so badly for me to grant her freedom.

I wrapped my arms around Pricilla. "I'm sorry. This business with Agrippina is nerve-wracking. Imagine me, a girl from Gaul making the emperor's son a potion for his face." I kissed her cheek and pressed coins into her hands. "I need your help. Find me linen as thin as a spider's web."

"This fool's errand will take all afternoon." Pricilla shrugged. "Fine. You keep your secrets and I'll keep mine."

Pricilla did not return until dinnertime. Plenty of time to prepare the mushrooms.

Mushrooms to murder an emperor.

THIRTY-SIX

The time had come.

I gave Pricilla a long hug goodbye.

Pricilla gave me an odd look, almost as if she knew this was no ordinary leave-taking. "Pimples? Are you sure?"

"Horrible pimples." I swallowed.

Annona waited in the atrium. "I expect a full accounting of the palaces' splendor when you return." She beamed with pride, my personal audience with the empress increasing my status and, by association, her own.

Pricilla and Annona followed me to the ostium, where a servant opened the door to a swirl of dry leaves scrapping across the floor. I lowered my head into the wind of the gathering storm and entered the imperial carpentum.

My stomach churned, a whirlwind of emotions gathering speed with every turn of the wheel. The trip to the palace was too brief. The carpentum arrived before I could master the maelstrom of worries spinning in my mind.

I alighted from the carpentum. Frigid gusts blew through my wool cloak. Dead leaves whipped around the entrance and treetops bowed over in the wind. The sky, ominous with gray clouds, waited for the gods to decree a downpour.

A servant ushered me through the gate and into the palace. With the speed of a gazelle, he walked by marble statues, silver fountains, soaring columns, gilded furniture, jewel encrusted mosaics, and jade urns. The magnificence of the palace was a blur.

I went down numerous corridors, across atriums, and past multiple chambers and alcoves and courtyards. There was no time to admire Egyptian art or appreciate Babylonian statuary. I arrived at Agrippina's chambers breathless and disoriented.

The room was warm. Several braziers provided a cocoon of heat. The empress, draped in a breast-baring tunic, lounged on a sofa piled high with fur pillows.

She dismissed four handmaids with a flap of her hand. "Oh, Locusta, your visit brings me such joy." She patted the cushion at her feet.

I sat, mindful of this lowly position, and tugged off my cloak.

"What did you bring?" she asked.

With trembling hands, I pulled two packages from under my stola, unwrapped both. "The emperor's fondness for truffles and mushrooms is well known."

"Mushrooms?" Agrippina lifted an eyebrow.

"There are many kinds of mushrooms, and to the untrained eye, the varieties look alike." I lifted the package. "This contains a fine powder ground from a deadly fungus. A few spoonfuls sprinkled over these edible mushrooms are all that's necessary." I opened the second container, showed her the contents.

Agrippina bent down, poked the truffles with her finger. "They smell divine."

"They've been marinated with tarragon-infused olive oil."

The empress clapped her hands and a handmaid appeared. "Bring the most beautiful dish in the palace."

Agrippina waited for the servant to leave. "If it fails?" She sniffed the truffles again.

"I brought something else."

The empress threw her head against the pillow and sighed. Not a sigh of worry or distress, a sigh of boredom.

I wondered what her motives were. Women were not permitted to become rulers. Her son, Nero, was only sixteen. Emperor Claudius's son, Britannicus was three years younger. Neither son was old enough to rule the greatest empire in the world.

I recalled snippets of chatter from Annona and her friends. Odd tidbits of incestuous love and inappropriate behavior between Agrippina and Nero. At the time, the gossip seemed preposterous and far-fetched. Now I wondered if it was true.

Too intimidated to stand or speak or even shift from my seated position on the floor, I waited for the handmaid to return. The empress rested, my presence forgotten.

The handmaid returned with a golden plate. "Empress."

Agrippina opened her eyes. "Get out."

The handmaid looked from Agrippina to me, thrust the platter into my hands and dashed from the room.

"The emperor loves the beauty of symmetry." Agrippina rolled onto her side and pointed to the plate.

I smiled, unsure how to respond.

"What are you waiting for? Prepare the mushrooms."

I took the plate and ingredients to a nearby table and cut the non-toxic mushrooms into thin slices. Next, I layered them in an overlapping spiral pattern. When finished, the mushrooms looked like a flower, its tan petals in full bloom.

Agrippina looked on in interest, her eyes brightening when I sprinkled toxic powder over the plate. The mushroom dust absorbed into the shiny slices. Undetectable. Untraceable. Fatal.

"Wait outside my chambers." Agrippina pointed to the door.

I sat on a bench in the hall as fear and anxiety burned like hot coals in my stomach. I watched the afternoon shadows lengthen, watched servants come and go. Watched them light the tall lamps abutting the walls.

I waited. And waited.

An eternity passed before Agrippina and her attendants emerged from the chambers. The empress looked like a gilded Aphrodite. Her hair hung in sparkling spirals down her back. She dazzled with gold-dusted skin and jewelry. Strands of gems dangled from her ears. Her shimmering gown hugged every curve with cords of silver crisscrossing her body. Ruby-incrusted sandals peeked from beneath a stola that trailed on the floor.

Holding the plate of mushrooms, Empress Agrippina glided past, my presence unacknowledged.

I am not certain how long I sat and waited. Fear and anxiety are poor timekeepers. I knew nothing of palace protocols, yet suspected Agrippina's snub boded ill. I was about to rise from the bench and find a way out through the palace labyrinth when a gray-bearded man rounded the corner.

"Locusta?"

"Yes?"

"Come with me, my unfortunate girl." The man beckoned me forward. "I'm Xenophon, the emperor's physician. And tonight, you're my lusty young nymph."

I shook my head. "There must be a mistake."

"Play the part, Locusta," he said. "You make history tonight."

THIRTY-SEVEN

Xenophon hurried me through the maze of corridors, down circular stairways, across marbled courtyards, through a vast atrium, and into a grand dining hall, the likes of which left me amazed.

There were hundreds of tables and couches and people. Too many to count. Quick-footed servants filled bowls, served food, and poured wine. Musicians wandered the room serenading the guests. Women clad in little more than a jewel in their navel danced on tabletops and shimmied around guests.

Xenophon's mouth hovered over my ear. "If you want to live, play along." He sprawled on a couch and patted the cushion beside him.

I reclined, my back against his stomach, my fear so great I obeyed without question.

"What vixen do you bring tonight?" asked a man with an enormous belly.

Xenophon nuzzled my neck. "A young one. A follower of Bacchus who will suck me dry before morning." He grabbed my breast.

If you want to live, play along.

I plucked a chunk of meat from a platter and fed it to Xenophon.

"Look to your right," he whispered in my ear. "Do you see the empress?"

I did.

Agrippina held the golden plate of lethal mushrooms before a wrinkled old man.

Emperor Claudius had aged since I last saw him, since he had refused my plea to extend the taxes, since he had dismissed me with a harsh rebuke. Dark shadows now rimmed his eyes, his skin a sickly hue, his weak chin disappearing into a thick fold of flesh.

"The emperor looks ill," I whispered to Xenophon.

"He is," he mumbled.

Agrippina pushed the plate at Emperor Claudius, then moved it away. She shook her breasts in his face and retreated. A plate of mushroom. Her bosom. Back and forth she taunted him. The guests hooted and clapped. The emperor leered and licked his lips.

"Give me the mushrooms, woman, before I put you over my knee," said Emperor Claudius loud enough everyone heard.

"Promises. Promises." Empress Agrippina kissed him on the lips.

"Claudius. Claudius." The guests began to chant and stomp their feet. "Claudius. Claudius."

Emperor Claudius reached for the plate.

"I cannot refuse my emperor." With a flourish, Agrippina set the platter before him.

A greedy-fingered Emperor Claudius stuffed the mushrooms into his mouth.

Everyone clapped their hands.

After devouring the last slice, the emperor quaffed a large goblet of wine. "Perfect." He smacked his lips and belched to roars of approval.

"How much longer?" asked Xenophon.

"Soon." I didn't know. Not really. The mice I usually used to determine potency had died almost instantly. A goat would have been a much better test subject. But that would have aroused suspicion.

"How soon?" Xenophon poked my back. "A moment, an evening? Overnight?"

"Everyone is different." I spoke with the haughtiness of an expert, although my stomach clenched with panic. What if I didn't use enough of the lethal mushroom powder? What if those particular mushrooms were deficient?

Six burly servants entered the room bearing a roasted sow on a golden platter. The dinner guests stomped and shouted as the men lowered the succulent beast to the table. They shouted even louder when a knife-brandishing servant tossed his blade into the air. He splayed wide the beast's belly and a great fish slid out. Another servant opened the sow's mouth and oysters spilled onto the platter beneath.

Emperor Claudius banged his knife on the table. "More! More!"

The servant carved off slices of pork.

I looked at the emperor. He winced. Blinked. Grimaced. Then he shuddered and his face blanched.

Emperor Claudius whispered in Agrippina's ear. She patted his shoulder. Kissed his cheek.

"It's happening." Xenophon's breath was hot on my neck.

Emperor Claudius doubled over, clutched his stomach with one hand, banged on the table with the other.

"Xenophon!" Agrippina cried out. "Help the emperor!"

All conversation ceased, everyone's attention fixed on the spectacle.

Xenophon nudged me. "Let the play begin."

He pushed me from the couch and ran to Emperor Claudius. With the ease and authority of one who had performed such kindness many times before, Xenophon wrapped his arm around the emperor's waist and helped him stand. Together, they lumbered to the doorway.

Xenophon turned his head and stared at me. His head dipped. It was my cue to follow.

The horrified silence of a moment ago vanished. A hundred conversations began at once. No one noticed as I made my way through the tangle of nobles and servants and tables.

I hurried down the corridor, keeping well behind Xenophon, who struggled to support the staggering Emperor Claudius. At their heels, Agrippina wailed so loudly the walls echoed. I followed them through the palace until they disappeared into a room. Claudius's private chambers.

From the doorway, I watched Xenophon lay the moaning emperor on the bed.

"W-w-w-wine…" Claudius, his face ashen and contorted with pain, lifted a shaking hand.

Agrippina poured a goblet from a nearby amphora. "My love, my love, what's wrong?"

"P-p-p-poison." Emperor Claudius gagged, convulsed, and splattered vomit all over Agrippina's gown.

She winced and sat beside him on the bed. "Halotus tested everything, my love. You're having one of your spells. It will soon pass."

Emperor Claudius's arm flung out and struck Agrippina full in the face. Then he fell back in a faint.

Xenophon touched the emperor's neck. "Enter, Mistress

of Poison, and see your reprehensible handiwork. Claudius yet lives."

I flew to the bedside on quick feet, placed a light hand on the emperor's chest. I lifted his eyelid. "He's unconscious. The poison has taken hold."

"He lives," hissed Agrippina, nostrils flaring, fists clenched.

"His breathing is shallow and labored," I said. "The emperor is a strong man with a hearty constitution."

"Finish the deed." Agrippina wiped the vomit off her dress with the emperor's tunic.

"I need my bag of herbs," I said. "They're in your room."

Agrippina pointed to a curtained archway. "Our chambers are connected. Two short knocks. Two long. The handmaid will unlock the door from the other side."

I fled down a narrow corridor until reaching an iron-latticed door. A young woman granted access the moment I completed the coded knock.

My basket and palla were exactly as I had left them hours ago. I grabbed the basket and raced back down the passageway.

An awful sight met me when I returned.

THIRTY-EIGHT

E mperor Claudius sat up! Alive! And he retched into an urn!

Agrippina patted the emperor's back. She mouthed comforting words to her husband, but her venomous eyes glared at me.

I withdrew a long feather from my bag, sprinkled the mushroom powder over it. I made certain the fine dust clung to the plume. Without a word, I showed it to Xenophon. He snatched it from my hand.

"Emperor, it's good to purge," said Xenophon. "You must empty your stomach of all food. Allow me to speed the process."

"No need. I feel better already." Emperor Claudius lifted his face, wet with spittle and sweat. "Who's she?"

"A servant. Don't you recognize her?" said Xenophon. "You're not fully recovered. You need to purge again. Open our mouth, this feather will stimulate your gag reflex." Xenophon lowered the poison-dipped feather over the emperor's mouth.

The emperor parted his lips.

Xenophon jammed the feather down his throat.

Emperor Claudius gagged and choked. Heaved once. Twice more. His head swayed from side to side without muscle control.

"My feet. My feet are numb..." Emperor Claudius fell back on the bed. "M-m-m..." His lids fluttered. His arm jerked.

And then he was still.

Xenophon touched Emperor Claudius's neck, put his hand over his heart. "He's dead."

I killed the emperor.

"Noooooooo!" Agrippina threw herself over the emperor. Her scream rose in a deafening crescendo. Her high-pitched wailing so authentic it chilled my heart.

Xenophon pointed the feather at me. "Go."

I snatched the quill, stuffed it into my basket, and hurried past the servants gathered in the doorway.

Empress Agrippina's howls grew louder. Each new wail summoned attendants, devotees, and palace guards like a Siren's song.

Xenophon told me to go. Go where?

Atriums. Courtyards. Corridors. Rooms. Halls. Vestibules. Gardens. The palace was a labyrinth. I was no Theseus. But I knew who the evil Minotaur was. Agrippina. My fate grew more evident with each turn.

Even if I did find the way out, no carpentum waited to take me home. My arrival, so skillfully planned and executed by the empress, lacked a quick and safe exit. I gagged on my panic. Felt fear's bile coat my throat. There was no way out and I had just poisoned the most powerful man in the world.

I paused before three vast hallways. None of them looked familiar.

The rhythmic stomps behind me rooted my feet to the floor. They came closer…

I turned around. Six Praetorian Guards led by a curly-headed young man walked towards me.

The youth held out my wool cloak. "Does this belong to you?"

I stepped forward, hand outstretched, before realizing my mistake.

He smirked, dropped the cloak. Six guards surrounded me.

The first blow came from behind, the force knocking me to the ground. A kick to the stomach stole my breath. Another kick sent spikes of pain up my spine. I covered my head with my arms. Curled into a ball.

Hands grabbed my legs, arms, hair. A knee smashed my face against the marble floor. The guards laughed. Another kick. A hundred blows. A heavy weight fell on top of me, wrapped cold hands around my throat.

My memory of that night ends there.

FLOWERS & FORTUNE

THIRTY-NINE

C old. Putrid. Filth. Silence.
Except for the thump of my heart.
Except for the rattle of my breath.
I was alive…

MY EYELIDS REFUSED TO OPEN. Sealed shut by pain. Crusted with despair. Nose and fingers perceived what my eyes could not. Rough rock. Foul-smelling hay. Sticky sludge. Dried blood and scuffling rats.

BREATHING WAS TORTURE, each shallow inhalation a sharp pain. A rodent scampered across my leg, my instinctive shriek stabbing my gut.

I moved as little as possible, my anguished thoughts mired in regret and sorrow.

And rage.

I do not remember the length of time I spent in this lifeless state. Sleep and wakefulness fused into a single memory. Hours. Days. It mattered not. Time lost all meaning.

"Locusta."

Warm water washed my eyes.

"Locusta."

A gentle hand caressed my forehead. Liquid touched my lips.

"Drink. Please drink."

I licked my lips. Nothing had ever tasted so sweet.

"Open your eyes."

A gray shadow appeared, indistinct and hovering. I knew that shadow. "P...P..."

Pricilla tilted a cup to my mouth. "I'm here now."

Tears sprung from my eyes. "I killed—"

"Shhh. Agrippina arrested you for crimes against Rome."

"I...I..."

"Drink. The tonic will speed healing and reduce your pain. You must eat."

Pricilla thrust bread into my hands. My grateful fingers curled around it.

I nibbled, hunger returning.

Pricilla lifted the cup. "Drink more. You'll sleep well tonight. I must go. I promise to return tomorrow."

Pricilla did not return the following day. Or for many days after. When she arrived again, I scarcely recognized her.

"You're sitting up today." Pricilla wore a fur-lined cloak, and her braided hair peeked from beneath a silk palla. She set a basket down, withdrew an amphora of wine, a jug of water, dried meat, and parsnips. "You look better."

"You left me."

"No, I've been here every day for a week."

"Lies."

"The potion causes forgetfulness."

"I—"

"Your body must heal. Sleep is the best curative."

My eyes swept over the dank cell. The vomit, urine, and excrement was gone, the ground strewn with fresh hay. A flood of gratitude burst forth as tears.

"Where am I? What's to become of me? Why do you disguise yourself with wealth?" I pointed to the gaudy jewels on her fingers.

Pricilla lifted one finger to her lips before pointing to the ceiling. "Shhhh. No good comes when an empress as ambitious as Agrippina visits a young woman of little consequence. I knew there was only one reason for her visit."

"You suspected?"

"I did. No doubt Agrippina heard of your healing skills, and assumed your herbal knowledge extended to poisoning."

Smooth fingers smoothed my brow. "After you left that afternoon, I gathered our possessions and fled the villa. The next morning my fear was confirmed. Every tongue in Rome wagged with the news of the emperor's unexpected death."

"Where am I?"

"Oh, Locusta, I searched for days! At first, I feared Agrippina threw you in the dungeons of Tullianum. Then I heard wealthy citizens are never sent to the prisons for the poor, so I snuck into Gaius Theon's villa and spoke to one of his servants. He told me you were under house arrest, but he didn't know where. It took several coins in many palms before I found you."

"Am in someone's home?"

My cell was deep underground, great blocks of stone on every side, the only opening a small square cut into the rock ceiling. Pricilla had to descend into my cell be means of a rope ladder.

"Agrippina ordered you sent to one of Claudius's villas," she said.

"A villa?"

"Above is the villa, several dungeons are beneath. Evidently, you're not so wealthy that you enjoy the privileges of house arrest nor so poor to be shackled in manacles. Even so, the conditions are deplorable."

I pointed to her costly cloak. "You found the hidden coins."

"I took every chest and coffer with me. I didn't find your hidden cache under the false bottom until days later." Pricilla stroked the fur. "I must appear a patrician or the guards won't grant me access. I told them I was your cousin."

"I'm glad you found the coins. They're yours now. You're free. There's enough money for you to open an apothecary shop and live a dignified life."

"Perhaps, but first I must attend to my best friend." Pricilla pointed at the ceiling. "The guards are poor; a few coins and a vial of love elixir were persuasive gifts."

I nodded and gnawed hungrily on a bit of dried meat.

"Are your ribs healing?" Pricilla lifted my soiled stola. "Does it still hurt to breathe?"

"Not if my breaths are shallow." I ran a hand through my matted hair. "Why didn't Agrippina kill me?"

"Who knows what goes through that vile woman's mind?" Pricilla pulled a comb from a basket and began to unsnarl my filthy strands. "Tomorrow I'll bring water for washing."

"Will Agrippina have me tortured?"

"Don't talk like that. Don't even think it."

"But—"

"Her son Nero is emperor now." Pricilla crushed a bug between her fingernails.

"Nero? He's not a man. Why, he can't be more than—"

"Sixteen. Gossip at the market claims Nero is a political puppet."

"For Agrippina?"

"That's the rumor. Others, however, believe Nero is not as easily led. He may be young, but he's no stranger to Roman politics."

"What about Theon and Annona?"

Pricilla snorted. "They hang their heads in shame. Only…only…"

"What is it?"

"The female servant whose bed I share on occasion once mentioned that Lucius and Nero are friends—or perhaps acquaintances—or were once childhood friends. I didn't pay attention at the time."

"Why do I care?"

"Well, maybe it means nothing. Maybe everything." Pricilla withdrew a small satchel from the basket. "Herbs. Keep them hidden. Do the guards harm you?"

I shook my head.

"I'll come back tomorrow." She walked under the aperture in the ceiling. "Lower the ladder!"

"Pricilla."

"Yes?" She did not turn around.

"I'm at Agrippina's mercy, aren't I?"

"I don't know. I hope not."

The rope ladder fell through the ceiling, and Pricilla climbed up and disappeared from sight.

The door banged closed, the metallic squeal of the locking mechanism inspiring new terrors. Whether by torture or abandonment, my death was certain.

FORTY

Days became weeks.
Weeks became months.

I lost count.

The air grew cold, winter weather froze the ground of my subterranean prison. Hay provided little warmth.

Pricilla did not come every day. A week might pass before the rope ladder unfurled from the ceiling.

The guards were fickle and mean-spirited. They often refused to allow Pricilla to bring anything but the smallest rations of water and food.

My love and respect for Pricilla increased tenfold. Her chores were more distasteful than when she had been my servant. Like a trained dog, I defecated and urinated in one corner and buried the stench under hay. Weakened by my injuries, I watched in shame as she swept dirtied straw into a sack. Pricilla never complained, always distracted me with gossip as she wiped grime from my body. Without a proper bath, the stench of filth permeated my skin.

I looked forward to her visits, her reports of scandals and intrigues offered a break from the boredom.

My body grew thinner and my spirit weaker each week. Despair clung to me like a funeral shroud.

I expected to die in this dungeon.

To pass long hours and to keep my mind alert, I imagined myself at my herbal table. I pictured each leaf, root, and flower. I recalled their individual properties and potencies. I mixed concoctions in my mind. Healing potions. Toxic drinks.

Pricilla smuggled in more herbs, concealed them in a secret pocket or stuffed them in her bodice. I tested new blends on myself. Or on mice. One mouse was so agitated after a dose it slammed into the wall.

When I wasn't observing mice or my own symptoms, I thought of Agrippina. I cursed my gullibility. I wondered if Nero was the young man who laughed while the Praetorian Guards broke my ribs and beat me senseless.

The memory of that fateful night festered like a sore. Each false statement. Every furtive look. How had I not recognized my role as the expendable pawn? Could I have prevented it?

By day, I tortured myself with these questions. Cursed my stupidity. Railed against Roman aristocracy. Wept over my fate. I cried until tears no longer came, until winter's coldness seeped into the marrow of my bones, penetrated my heart, and hate enveloped my soul.

By night, this hate nurtured my nightmares.

One night, in the midst of a vengeful dream, the loud squeal of metal wheels woke me. I lifted my eyelids and squinted. A torch's glow shone from the opening above. The rope ladder unfurled. A figure holding a lantern descended.

"Locusta?"

I scampered into the far corner like a whipped mongrel

and blinked. The lantern moved forward, the person still shrouded in darkness.

"Locusta? Where are you?"

I knew the voice.

I wedged myself into the corner, afraid and ashamed to be seen.

The lantern's glow fell on my face.

"Oh!" His feet shuffled back. "By all the gods, answer me, are you Locusta?"

"Yes."

He moved closer, the lamplight illuminating both our faces.

"My sweet Locusta, you look terrible," he said.

"The guards don't allow trips to the baths."

Lucius burst out laughing, the sound echoing off the walls. "Come with me."

"What?" I must have misheard.

"I arranged a meeting with Emperor Nero. You have a few moments to convince him you're the most skilled woman for the task at hand." Lucius wrinkled his nose and grimaced.

"I'll convince him of nothing."

"Not in your present state. Come on, get up. Nero signed a writ of release for one day. You must stay in my constant company, and I have permission to kill you if you attempt escape."

"No."

"Don't be a fool. Do you want to die here?" Lucius wrapped a scarf around his nose.

"The emperor will send me back. Or kill me."

"Maybe not. I expounded your charms of late. Make it worth Nero's while to keep you alive and comfortable."

I stood, my legs shaking, and shuffled across the cell.

"You first." He pushed the ladder at me.

I wrapped my hand around the rope and climbed. Scrabbled up and over. If not for Lucius's hand guiding my unsteady foot to each rung, I might never have made it.

My heart banged in my chest and a thin film of sweat covered my body. I stood, my toes curling as though they could clutch the floor. I stared down at the dungeon below and for the first time fresh hope swelled in my bosom.

I followed Lucius through the subterranean passages, up three flights of stairs, and under an iron opening into an alley. I gulped the fresh air, each breath a vow to do whatever was necessary to stay free.

Lucius opened the door of the carpentum waiting nearby.

Pillows. Blankets. The spice of perfume. These once unappreciated luxuries now moved me to tears.

Lucius sat opposite me, his head by the open window.

I did not apologize for my stench, and although my teeth chattered from the cold Lucius did not offer a blanket.

"Where are you taking me?"

"I keep a small apartment."

"I need my ser—Pricilla." I remembered she was a free woman.

"I'll send for her." Through narrowed eyes, Lucius regarded my wasted form. "You're not the same young woman from four months ago. I thought perhaps your skill and beauty might convince Nero, but is seems prison has… " He looked away.

"My skill with herbs has increased. And as for my beauty, it's hidden beneath layers of filthy rags." And hate. But there was no reason to tell Lucius this.

"I hope so." He did not sound convinced.

Lucius's uncertainty angered me. If he doubted my ability to charm Nero why not end this scheme and return me to prison.

"Do I look that bad?"

"It's more than your appearance that changed, Locusta. There's something different about you."

Appearing strong, unaffected, and courageous was my only course of action. "Nothing a bath and some food won't fix." I forced a laugh, the sound odd to my ears. "Nero will be captivated, I promise you. Now tell me, dear savior, in the months during my captivity, how many maidens have you seduced? Did you exceed your father's conquests?"

Lucius chuckled. "Indeed. It seems the more girls I seduce, the more others want me."

"Ah, your reputation as a skilled lover grows."

Lucius pulled the scarf down, eager to gloat about his conquests. "They come to me now. I have suckled on the breasts of every pretty servant in the villa. Made love to Mother's grateful friends. These older women—what they lack in youth, they replace with creativity and fortitude."

"You rival Bacchus."

"I had sex with four in one day. And just last week, two immodest sisters wrung every drop from my body."

"Prostitutes?"

"No. I enjoy prostitutes only on rare occasions. It's more gratifying to deflower a virgin or slide into a matron's bed while her husband is conducting business at the Forum."

"Sounds like you don't need my love elixir anymore."

"Not so. Your potion enhances the act, prolongs the pleasures. I use it often."

My mouth twitched. "Pricilla makes the elixir?"

"Yes, but even with all my cajoling—and coin—she fails to duplicate your combination."

"I'll make a batch tomorrow."

"I'd like that." Lucius's eyes twinkled. "There are three sisters I plan on seducing."

I laughed with him, although it was for a different reason. In the past, I had only tolerated Lucius. Now I realized the real value of his friendship.

The carpentum stopped.

Lucius gave me a careful smile. "Let's hope a bath washes away the prisoner to reveal the beautiful maiden of Gaul."

"Where are we?"

"My favorite brothel."

FORTY-ONE

This particular house of prostitution was renowned for its illustrious clientele. Whether one was a senator, patrician, or equestrian, the owner provided a wide assortment of amusements. Young boys. Younger girls. Experienced whores. A person possessing parts of both man and woman. Lucius said the individual was in great demand, appointments already booked a year in advance.

I followed a toothless old woman through a series of dark rooms before she pulled back the drapery of a private bathing chamber. It was a spacious room with three pools, animal pelt sofas, and murals of men and women engaged in imaginative sexual acts. When I turned around to ask for an attendant she was gone.

"You're on your own," said Lucius. "I'm just here to make sure you don't escape."

Behind him, a young slave girl in a sheer tunic carried in a golden mug and carafe of wine. Eight years old at most, the girl's kohl-rimmed eyes and ochre-stained lips gave her the appearance of a stunted nymph. Though her head was adorned with bouncing curls and her ears festooned with swinging rubies she looked exhausted. World-weariness marred her young face. After the waif filled Lucius's goblet he reclined on the sofa.

"Food is arriving shortly." Lucius lifted his wine in mock salute.

I tugged the filthy rag over my head, kicked it aside. "Burn this."

Lucius did not take his eyes off me as I entered the first bath. Let him gawk. I sank into the heated pool, the warm water penetrating the bone-chilling cold of imprisonment.

"You're too thin for my taste," Lucius said. "How disappointing, since I used to dream of ravaging you every night."

"You mock me, good Lucius." I submerged my entire body into the bath's heat. The plunge gave me time to compose myself and disguise my fear. I needed Lucius to feel confident that he had made the right decision to bring me to Nero. And I might need more of his help.

Though reluctant to leave the watery heaven, I emerged from the pool and went to a table set with herb-infused olive oils and fresh strigils. Rivulets of water ran down my body and pooled at my feet as I sniffed each flagon.

I set one foot on the bench, poured the rosemary-infused olive oil over my hands and massaged it into my skin.

Lucius watched with increasing interest, his gaze never wavering as my hands slid over my legs, stomach, and breasts. Oil seeped into my thirsty skin, months of neglect had left it dry and chafed.

I repeated the process, deliberate with my movements, intent on making Lucius more than a friend. I needed an enthusiastic ally. I scraped off the oil, each stroke removing another layer of filth. Each scrape shedding a layer of my former self. The trusting young woman was gone. I would never be so foolish again.

When the filth of my naiveté was scraped clean, I rubbed clay into my hair. I paused to smile at Lucius. His eyes sparkled with lust.

I tossed a jaunty grin over my shoulders and descended into the depths of the hot bath, my sigh of pleasure genuine. Fooled by my composed demeanor, Lucius chattered about his sexual conquests while I washed my hair.

"I need a comb." I was relieved to see the waif return with a plate heaped with mouthwatering delights.

Without a word, the slave girl set the meal down, brought me a comb, and retreated through the entry.

"Sing for me so I can tell everyone how I saved a Siren from prison." Lucius smiled mischievously.

"Am I a Siren? Luring you to your death?" I began unsnarling knots.

"You'll never have such power, but I wish to hear you sing just the same."

"I'll humor my savior." I tossed back a lock of hair and thrust out my bosom.

"Once he hears to his heart's content,
Sails on, a wiser man,
We know all the pains that the Greeks and Trojans
    once endured,
On the spreading plain of Troy
when the gods will it so—
All that comes to pass on the fertile earth, we know it
    all."

I splashed him with water, this charade of lightness growing easier with every passing moment.

Lucius chuckled. "I'm glad your brief stay in that

damnable cell didn't smother your spirit, my poisonous Siren."

I lifted one shoulder, pouted prettily, and sniffed the air. "Do I smell lamb?"

"Are you hungry?"

"Ravenous! But I have little desire to leave this warm bliss."

Lucius peeled himself off the couch and set the plate at the pool's edge.

I opened my mouth and closed my eyes.

A bit of honey-drenched lamb touched my lips. I wanted to inhale it. Gobble it down. Instead, I nibbled at it. Each succulent morsel he fed me was accompanied by my grateful groans.

"I'll feed you the whole lamb if you continue to moan like that."

I pointed to the goblet. "Wine."

Lucius tipped his goblet to my lips. I left not a drop.

Hunger sated, thirst quenched, and body scrubbed clean, I rose from the pool like Aphrodite born anew. "Thank you. I won't ever be able to repay you."

Lucius came up behind me, moved my hair to the side and kissed the back of my neck. "Oh, but you can."

I took his hands and moved them over my breasts. "Take what you will."

Lucius was more tender than I expected and more skilled than I imagined. His arrogant boastings proved true. Gentle fingers probed and caressed with a thoughtful slowness that was surprisingly pleasurable.

I suppose he felt some satisfaction in seducing me, but it was I who felt the most satisfied with my ability to mask the horrors of captivity. I would do anything to gain my freedom.

"Sleep, my pretty poisoner. Dream away the dark

reminders of your imprisonment." Lucius stroked my hair. "Dress like a goddess tomorrow. Entrance Nero. Entice him. If he's not convinced of your skills he'll send you back to prison, and there will be nothing more I can do for you."

"I will not return to prison." I placed Lucius's finger in my mouth and sucked.

Lucius's age granted him unquenchable desire. With each coupling our bond strengthened. But soon the pleasures of food, drink, sex, and down quilts summoned a deep slumber.

I awoke the next day confused. Was this a dream? Then I remembered. Lucius had obtained a writ of release for one day. A day I had to meet Emperor Nero and convince him of my skills.

I rolled over.

Pricilla sat in a chair by my bed. "Lucius said you needed me."

I held out my arms and we both wept. Relief, happiness, fear, worry—all our emotions released in a rush of tears.

"Enough of that." Pricilla wiped her eyes. "You're not free yet." She opened a satchel. "We must prepare for your audience with Emperor Nero."

"How did Lucius find you?"

"He has friends in both high and low places. Now, acquaint yourself with the contents inside. Emperor Nero might require a demonstration."

I lifted the sheets, found a clean but too thin body underneath. "I have no clothes."

Pricilla pulled gossamer gauze from a pile on the table. "The workers were kind enough to provide a few bits of material."

I held it up. "It's see-through."

"We're in a brothel."

"I can't go dressed as a whore."

"Why not? Men are reduced to idiots when confronted by a naked woman." Pricilla wrapped the gauze around me. "There must be something suitable I can make from this pile of threads."

The day passed quickly. A servant filed, shaped, and buffed my nails. My skin was moistened with fragrant lotions. My feet smoothed with pumice and softened with perfumed oils. Pricilla treated my curls with olive oil and brushed the locks until they cascaded down my back in shiny spirals.

"No severe hairstyle tonight." Pricilla gathered a few strands and secured them with silver pins. "Nero is a young man, his taste for depravity and wickedness already the talk of the market. Your herbal skill and body are your only weapons."

"Weapons? Am I going into battle?"

"You battle for your freedom and your life."

My chest clenched. "What if Agrippina is there?"

"Let's hope it's a private meeting." Pricilla sat down beside me. "You have one chance to succeed. And the best way is to appeal to Nero's desires. What do you know about him?"

"Very little. But with a mother like Agrippina he's bound to have learned ambition. He must know she had me murder Emperor Claudius so he could ascend the throne. That makes him complicit. His lust for power is more of an aphrodisiac than I could ever make."

Pricilla exhaled her frustration. "Don't think like that. You must promise him tonics to satisfy all his desires. Anything less will doom you to a lifetime locked in a dungeon under Rome."

"I will not return to that pit. I'll do whatever it takes." I slid two tunics over my body. "I still feel naked."

"I have an idea." Pricilla wrapped two more filmy swaths of cloth around my body. She stepped back. "Not bad. But even my artistry cannot hide your wasted body. Mmmm…" She coiled silvery ropes around my torso to emphasize the one feature that had not changed since my imprisonment—my breasts. "Shoulders back. You're a goddess, a thin one, but a goddess nevertheless." She kissed my cheek. "I'll make offerings to the gods for Emperor Nero to grant your freedom."

"Tonight, Nero is my god."

Pricilla chuckled. "Pay proper homage to him, and when you convince him of your skill—and you will—I want to be your assistant."

"Impossible." I shook my head. "I insist we be partners."

"No thank you. I don't want that responsibility." Pricilla handed me a fur-trimmed cloak. "I bought this with your coin. You'll need it tonight."

We hugged, uncertain fates making for a heartfelt embrace.

With all the flourish and bravado I could muster, I entered Lucius's carpentum.

Lucius's brows lifted. "I'm glad to see four months in a dungeon didn't diminish your beauty." Lucius buried his face in my neck. "You smell divine. Kiss me."

I did not intend to kiss Lucius ever again.

"Later." I stroked his face. "If we kiss my lips will lose this glossy pout."

Lucius settled back in the seat. "Later tonight?"

I slid my hand up his thigh. "Whatever you desire." My false words came easily. They left no mark on my conscience, no trace on my heart.

"My desires are naughty," said Lucius. "But for now, I'll

just have to be content with telling you all the latest imperial gossip."

I listened with rapt attention. Gossip was important. I understood this now. Knowing which senator bedded another's wife or knowing the names of senators disgusted by Agrippina's motherly attentions might one day prove beneficial.

I learned that Nero's marriage to his stepsister, Claudia Octavia, was a disaster. That the Praetorian Guard commander, Afranius Burrus, hired the notable statesman and philosopher Seneca to be Nero's tutor. That senators had faith in Nero's leadership after his rousing speech which promised the restoration of principles as set forth by Augustus.

"Lastly, and of the least interest, is my wedding to Sarra in the spring," Lucius said.

"You're too young. Not yet seventeen."

"Nero married Claudia at fifteen."

"Agrippina expects him to produce male heirs. Enough to keep the Julio-Claudian dynasty in power for a thousand years."

Lucius bellowed with laughter. "Not likely to happen. Nero hates the girl. He told me she was ugly and wept during the consummation of their marriage. Cold as a marble statue. Those were Nero's words."

"He shares confidences with you? Nero is your friend?"

"No one is friends with Nero." Lucius stroked my cheek.

I was about to ask another question when the carpentum stopped and a member of the Praetorian Guard whisked open the door.

Head held high and shoulders back, I descended with the haughty air of nobility. "Lucius?" I turned around when I realized he was not behind me.

"I'm not permitted to attend." He blew a kiss. "May the gods look upon you with favor."

His salutation reminded me of the gladiators in the arena. Nos morituri te salutant.

We who are about to die, salute you.

I put little faith in gods anymore. Preferred to rely on my wits and charm. And so with firm resolve, I walked into the palace.

FORTY-TWO

Nero's face was slack with boredom. His body slouched on the throne. The young emperor with a head of blonde curls regarded me with disinterest, his arms draped over the chair with the relaxed posture of one untroubled by the rigors of his exalted position.

My fingers squeezed around the handle of the herb basket as I strode across the room. I knelt down, touched my forehead to the marble floor.

"Arise, Locusta, and tell the emperor why you must live." He yawned and scratched his chest.

"Your mother doesn't like me." It was a bold statement, nevertheless the occasion called for risk. As a young man and ruler of the world, I hoped he would want to prove he was not shackled to his overbearing mother.

The corner of Nero's mouth twitched. "My mother is the best of mothers. I decreed it on the first day of my reign." His lips settled into a scowl.

"You're correct. A worthier mother cannot be found in all the world. I don't dispute this fact." I held out the basket.

"Will you permit me to show you the herbs I have brought for your inspection?"

Nero slid forward, deep-set eyes keen with curiosity. "Proceed."

I set several vials on the floor and arranged various berries and leaves in a row. Nero sighed, suddenly uninterested. I panicked. A bored emperor would return me to prison!

I removed my fur cloak with a flourish. Nero's eyes widened, his attentions not on my herbal offerings but on my fleshly ones. His gaze wandered over my body, the effect of the sheer fabric tantalizing and provocative.

With a practiced move, I bent down, picked up two vials, and held each in my hand. "The contents in this one will kill a giant with a single swallow. The other is a slow-acting poison designed to mimic illness. This vial will—"

"Enough. Words are hollow." Nero summoned a servant standing by a doorway. "Drink."

The slave turned to run, but two guards grabbed him and dragged him forward.

"Nooo. Please, emperor, I beg you," he pleaded. "I'm more useful to you alive."

"Give him the first vial," said Nero.

The weeping servant clamped his mouth closed, swung his head back and forth.

"You will die with honor and for the glory of Rome." Nero crossed his arms. "Open your mouth or I'll slice off your feet and watch you bleed to death on the floor. Honor me, good man, with your death!"

The servant parted his quivering lips. My hand trembled as I poured the contents into his mouth. Our eyes met. We were not so different. Neither of us had any choice. We must obey the emperor.

The guard held the servant's jaw closed.

"Swallow," growled Nero.

He did.

His face changed from pink to red to purple. His body grew slack, and when the guards released their hold, he dropped to the floor.

Nero squinted. "Is he dead?"

A guard checked for signs of life. "He is, emperor."

Nero's lips twisted and he wrinkled his nose. "Too swift for my liking."

"I can show you another," I said. "I specialize in poisons. Swift or slow. Agony or euphoria. My desire is only to please you and serve the glory of Rome."

Nero licked his lips. "Lucius speaks of one potion in particular."

"A poison?"

"A love elixir."

"It's very potent." I removed the clay vessel from the basket.

Nero pointed. "Drink it."

I anticipated his request. No emperor would be foolish enough to eat or drink my tonics without assurance of its safety.

I did not hesitate, and although I had only ever swallowed the smallest bit of the potent elixir, I uncorked the stopper and swallowed half of it.

Nero watched me for several moments before heaving his body from the gilded throne. He stepped down from the dais and nudged the leaves and berries on the floor with his toes.

The love elixir was fast-acting, already my body grew warm. It was difficult to stay steady. The walls undulated. My breath quickened, heat spread through my loins. I swayed.

"Having difficulty standing?" Nero asked, his eyes fixed on my heaving bosom.

"This is a tonic for flying not standing."

Nero laughed, took the vessel from my hand, gulped down the rest, and returned to his throne. With closed eyes, he held out both hands and spread his thighs. "Come."

I mounted the dais and stood before him.

"Closer." His eyes still closed, he beckoned me forward.

There was nowhere to go but to stand between his legs. Nero stroked my arm. Pleasure quivered up my limb. His hand moved upwards, over my shoulder, grazed my chin, then moved downward. Over my neck. My breasts. He fondled my eager nipples. It felt exquisite. Intense and warm. I moaned.

Nero opened his eyes. "This is fucking amazing."

He pulled me closer, tugged at my flimsy stola. In frustration, he drew a dagger from his tunic. I watched, enthralled as he sliced. Cords and fabric fluttered to the floor.

Nero grabbed my buttocks, lifted them over his lap, and set me down. He kissed me, parted my lips with his tongue. He tasted of wine and desire. Every inch of my skin demanded to be stroked and caressed. My loins ached, my mind fixed on a single intent. Pleasure.

The love elixir was more potent than I realized. Once consumed, a person's sensual desires became a tempest. All reason vanished into the gale, inhibitions swept away on the winds of lust. Consumed by a torrent of sensation, control and prudence was impossible. I had fallen victim to a carnal craving of my own making.

Nero and I ended up in his private chambers. I have a vague memory of our dashing naked down a long hall, of our falling into his bed. He was a curious lover, howling like a wolf at times, whooping and squealing with disturbing loudness. As though he wanted everyone in the palace to hear.

The sexual euphoria lasted longer than expected. It rendered me powerless to do anything but beg for more of him and he of me.

As the sun rose skyward, the feeling subsided, the heightened sensations of touch no longer arousing. My head throbbed and waves of nausea made my mouth water.

I rolled on my side. Nero lay flat on his back, his hands behind his head. No longer under the influence of the elixir, he lost his erotic appeal. Nero's muscles were few, his stomach soft, his appendage limp.

"I want more," he said. "And bring a friend. Male. Female. It doesn't matter."

"I don't have any more." It was the truth.

"Can you make more?"

"How much do you want?"

"A year's supply." He flung off a fur blanket.

I sat up. Stared at him. Did he really say a year's supply?

"The love elixir loses potency in a matter of days." It wasn't a lie. It wasn't the truth. I didn't really know how long it remained potent. It sold as fast as I could make it.

"Make enough for a week then." Nero rolled off the bed. "I have another task for you." He wiggled my toe. "Poison Britannicus."

Not again!

"Make it look like he has the falling sickness. You know the one, the same as Julius Caesar." He traipsed to a wide window, looked out. "Bring me more of the love elixir by nightfall." He glanced over his shoulder. "A guard will escort you to one of my villas. You answer only to me." He turned, extended his arm.

I jumped from the bed, kneeled before him, and kissed his hand.

"My mother may not like you, but I do." Nero stuck his finger in my mouth.

I sucked on his finger.

"Mmmm..." He took my head and moved it to his now rigid cock. "I'll put your skills to good use."

"You have my eternal gratitude." I took him in my mouth.

The ruler of the entire world commanded me to make his ambitions a reality, his delusions authentic, and his passions sustainable.

After he filled my mouth with his brine, a guard secreted me away to his villa across town. The decadent world of the Roman elite laid wide open before me.

FORTY-THREE

"You trade one prison for another." Pricilla swept her arms about the atrium.

"Everyone lives in a prison of their own making. At least mine is built of marble." I pressed coins into her hands. "Go to the market. We need fabric, herbs, and food."

"One misstep, Locusta, and he'll throw you back in prison. Or worse! He might toss you into the ring to fight the wild beasts with nothing but a sprig of parsley to defend yourself."

"What do you want me to do?"

Pricilla's voice dropped to a whisper. "Nero's a child, an immature and indulged adolescent. It's only a matter of time before senators conspire to murder him. And once again, you'll be an enemy of Rome."

I flopped down on a silk-cushioned couch. "Then I leave it to your wise ears to tell me when rumors require my escape."

Pricilla closed her hands around the coins. "I'm glad you're clever enough to realize the precarious nature of your imperial service."

Pricilla's gentle chide was unnecessary. Foolish arrogance would get me killed. Nothing less than cautious humility was required to survive this notorious appointment.

"Rome is a den of hungry lions." Pricilla's hand clawed the air. "You're a mouse."

"I'm unworthy prey for such noble beasts."

"It's not funny, Locusta."

"In Aesop's tale, the mouse frees the lion from a net of ropes." I arranged the pillow behind me. "I'm that little mouse, too insignificant to murder and only helpful when the Lion King needs my services."

Pricilla's brow furrowed. "It's a child's tale."

"About Roman politics, but let's not argue."

Pricilla sighed. "I'm not arguing. I'm merely warning you. Besides, how can I not be happy? The gods answered my prayers." She looked up, lowered her voice, "just not how I expected."

"The only thing I'll be expecting is delicious food and luxurious comfort." I stretched out on the couch, reveled in its plushness and longed for a nap. "Let's celebrate our freedom tonight."

After Pricilla—with her own servant in tow—left for the market, I explored the villa.

Nero had a fondness for beating unsuspecting tavern patrons and engaging in debauchery at the brothels. Which made me curious. Why did Nero need a second villa? Was it a safe place to engage in all of his other wicked exploits?

This domus was smaller than most noblemen's, and yet its extravagant luxuries made up for its size. Intricate Greek-inspired murals and towering statues decorated the reception room. The bedrooms were plush, the frescoed alcoves adorned with ancestor masks. There were two proper bath-rooms. Inside a colonnaded courtyard, water spewed from an elaborate fountain in the middle of an azure pool where rearing centaurs squirted water through enormous marble phalluses.

I walked around the flowering peristyle and peered into an open-fronted exedra. There was a sculpture of Theseus slaying the Minotaur, a Sphinx mosaic, and a man-sized urn emblazoned with Odysseus's journey. Nero certainly loved Greek art.

I wandered into a grand bedroom. Was it in this room that Nero romped with his mistress, the former servant, Claudia Acte?

Footsteps thudded in the hall. I went to see who was paying me a visit.

"You're not on the emperor's payroll to play the noble wife." A bald-headed man lumbered towards me.

The stranger's fleshy face, sagging jowls, and ponderous figure suggested a life of excess. And although it was a chilly kalends of February, beads of sweat spotted his forehead and his eyes were red-rimmed and puffy.

The man dabbed at his face with a handkerchief. "I come on an unsavory errand."

"I'm at a disadvantage, sir. I haven't the pleasure of a proper introduction."

"Lucius Annaeus Seneca." He touched his hand to his heart.

Imperial advisor to Emperors Caligula, Claudius, and now Nero. Seneca was renowned for his philosophical treatises and tragic plays.

"It's an honor to meet—"

"Of course, it is." Seneca dabbed at his nose. "The emperor makes inquiries about your preparations. Are they complete?"

"I only just arriv—"

"Immediate results are expected." His steely eyes narrowed and sniffed in disapproval at my less than elegant clothing.

"If you're indeed as skilled as the gossip claims then you'll find more interest in another part of the house." With that, the celebrated stoic turned on his heel and plodded down the corridor. "Did Oedipus make you weep?"

"Yes, much more than the Furies of Hercu—."

"Your family's lineage is undistinguished." Another sniff, this one accompanied by a cough.

"The Parisii clan is a respected wine—"

"Nero did not summon you without thoroughly investigating your relatives and political ties. I know more about your family than you." Seneca dabbed at his leaking nose again.

The man was arrogant, but I needed his friendship, or at least, less of his disdain.

"Do your symptoms increase after a rain?"

One bushy eyebrow lifted. "Indeed. Why do you ask?"

"Rain releases plant spores into the air and this aggravates your malady."

"I have no symptoms when I summer in Corsica."

"The climate is dry there, yes?"

"Your education includes more than poison?" Seneca paused beneath a great archway and flicked his thumb toward the backyard. "Goats and chickens to your right. Garden to the left." He cocked his head, scratched his chin. "You don't have much time. Britannicus's fourteenth birthday in a few days marks his adult status and rightful claim to the throne."

"Does Agrippina know—"

"Despite what you may have heard, Nero is not Agrippina's puppet."

"I thought—"

"Agrippina cannot control Nero. She thinks Britannicus will be easier to manipulate. That woman's lust for power is insatiable."

"So it appears."

"You can make Britannicus's death appear natural, right?" Seneca blew his nose, a trumpet of mucus echoing in the marbled hall.

"It's easily done." I spoke with more confidence than I felt.

"I'm instructed to deliver the dose to Britannicus's tutor." Seneca held out an open palm. "Immediately. Nero is not a patient man."

"I work in private."

Seneca chuckled. "As do my mistresses. I'll wait in the dining room."

"That room is cold, one side is completely open to the elements."

Both bushy eyebrows lifted. "You presume to tell me about a villa I visit often?" He tapped his foot on the floor. "Pipes beneath heat the floor." He waved me away. "Now go, get about your business. Waiting on a woman is quite beneath me." Seneca turned down the corridor.

I returned to the room Pricilla and I had already dubbed our herbal sanctum.

The sun was low in the sky when I finished preparing the lethal mixture. During that time, Pricilla returned from the market to find me hunched over a table spread with leaves and berries.

"This herbal combination concerns me," Pricilla said. "Is it potent enough?"

"It's a slow-acting poison," I said. "The toxins will take several days to reach full effect. No one will suspect foul play."

"Several days? How many is several?"

"Two. Three? Nero insists Britannicus's death appear natural." I fitted the stopper into the clay container and went to the dining room where I found Seneca snoring on the sofa. "Ahem."

Seneca lifted one eyelid. "So soon?"

I lifted up two small vessels.

Seneca sat up with a groaning yawn. "Two?"

"This one opens nasal passages and will clear your head. This one," I pointed to the marking, "is for Britannicus."

A slow smile spread across the old tutor's face. "A punishment to some, to some a gift, and to many, a favor."

"His death will appear perfectly natural," I said after explaining how to administer the poison.

"Are you certain?" Seneca arched an eyebrow.

"Absolutely."

Unfortunately, Britannicus did not die.

FORTY-FOUR

A one-horse chariot careened full speed through the garden three days later. The driver toppled statues, crushed flowers, and trampled bushes.

Pricilla and I were cutting herbs when the thundering hooves sent us scrambling towards the villa.

"It's him!" Pricilla dropped to the ground prostrate, her head to the dirt.

I stood tall, despite Pricilla tugging the hem of my tunic.

Nero leapt from the chariot, dagger in hand, and raced toward me.

"Vile whore! I'll kill you!" He lunged at me and his dagger slashed my tunic.

I staggered back as blood seeped through the gash on my stomach. I set my hand over the wound.

Nero grabbed my arm and twisted, trapping me in his arms, and put his dagger at my throat. "Your putrid blood will pool at my feet and I will laugh as you die."

I smiled. I couldn't help myself.

That morning, I had ingested a rare herb to test its calming properties. The plant, I realized, produced another effect as well, for as the light reflected off the blade I thought only of the sun's beauty.

Nero's arm tensed around me, the knife's sharpness an exquisite sting. Instead of panicking, my body relaxed into his. He noted this, mistook my calm for courage.

"Speak," he snarled into my ear.

"Slow…acting," I said, enjoying the buzz of his voice. "That was your request. I honored it. The toxin will cause Britannicus to die a seemingly natural death." My words were unhurried, each syllable oddly emphasized.

The point of Nero's blade pinched my skin. "He must die tomorrow. If not, I'll kill you."

My hand crawled up his arm and over his knife-gripping fingers. "I'll make certain his death will be as swift as a dagger."

I felt the sharp sting as Nero bit my earlobe. Even as I cringed, the pain felt extraordinarily seductive. Pleasure derived from pain. I decided to include the combination in the love elixir.

Nero shoved me to the ground, and I rolled over on my back. He stood over me, his dagger aimed at my heart. "Britannicus and other nobles attend an important dinner tomorrow where he will be pronounced an adult and contender for my throne. Poison him then. A litter will come for you in the afternoon." Nero's head swept from right to left. "Your negligence caused my anger. I'll deduct coin from your wages to cover the damages to my property."

Nero stalked away, bounded into the chariot, and with a slash of the whip circled the gardens twice more, hooves and wheels destroying more of his garden.

I stood, brushed the dirt from my tunic and pulled a wide-eyed Pricilla to her feet.

"Did he say he's paying you a wage?" asked Pricilla.

"If he doesn't kill me first."

Pricilla and I spent the remainder of the day discussing the most lethal plants for killing Britannicus. The essences of hemlock and poppy ought to be the perfect mixture. Hemlock for a speedy death. Poppy for sedation.

I paced the atrium. "The mushrooms used on Claudius were not all that potent. The toxins for Britannicus proved weak as well. Failure means my death. I can leave nothing to chance."

"Test it on a servant," said Pricilla.

I grimaced, her suggestion repellent. "There must be an animal we can use instead. A goat, perhaps?"

We found an old goat in the stable. He was the perfect test subject, too old to eat and too ornery to sacrifice. The hungry billy gobbled the deadly alfalfa blend from my hands while Pricilla looked on.

One… two… three… the goat bleated and convulsed several times before dropping to the ground.

Pricilla and I exchanged an optimistic glance.

"The goat weighs less than Britannicus," Pricilla said.

I prodded the goat with my foot, made certain the animal was dead and not in a drug-induced slumber. "I hope it works as quickly on the boy."

TRUE TO HIS WORD, Nero sent a litter, and I crossed the city in imperial style. As I reclined behind gold-threaded drapes and silk pillows, the poor rabble parted to give the litter wide berth.

My swift change in fortune was complete. Like the coin in my hand—Nero on one side, his adopted-father Claudius on the other—my circumstances had flipped. No longer an innocent, I understood politics well enough to know a mere spin of a coin might transform my circumstances yet again.

But I was lucky. Unlike the slaves bearing the litter, my equestrian status granted many privileges. The chance that a poor litter bearer would change his lot in life was low. And yet my position was equally tenuous. My life rested on the whims of a capricious young emperor. Was I really so different from the poor souls who carried me?

I had to forge a strong alliance with Nero. I would not let him down. I would become indispensable to him.

The sun had just touched the horizon when I arrived at the palace. Seneca waited in an alcove.

"Are you hiding?" I whispered.

He balked. "I? Hide? Never. The atrium is crowded with too many sycophants and spies." He strode past two purple-sashed senators in heated discourse and shook his head. "It's the superfluous things for which men sweat."

"What do you mean?"

"It's the unnecessary things in life that wear our togas threadbare, that force us to grow old in camp, that dash us upon foreign shores."

What one deemed superfluous, was another's necessity. But I did not contradict the renowned philosopher.

We continued through a gallery of corridors and empty rooms to avoid the vast peristyle adjoining the coenacula where dinner had begun. We walked near the walls—Roman walls have ears—and kept to the shadows.

Seneca slipped behind a draped-off room adjacent the dining room. "You can see the entire dining room from here."

I looked around. "I see nothing." I could, however, hear the guests' boisterous conversation through the thin walls.

"You're such an innocent." From beneath his toga folds, Seneca withdrew a thin blade. He slipped its tip between the seams of two wide stones and slide it back and forth until a concrete sliver wedged between the masonry loosened. He tugged the piece out and placed it in my hand. "A word of caution, Agrippina is present."

My breath caught in my throat.

"She's losing favor with Nero." Seneca set his hand on my shoulder. "Still, it's best she's not aware of your new imperial function." He held out his hand, wiggled his fingers. "The poison."

I pulled the vial from under my cloak. "Pour the contents into Britannicus's water pitcher."

Food tasters tested food and wine. They never tested the water used to dilute the wine.

Seneca plucked the vial from my hands and left without another word.

I removed a leaf from my satchel, stuck it in my mouth, and chewed. The plant would calm me, although I disliked how it made my ears buzz. I pushed a stool next to the hole, sat down, and put my eye over the hole.

FORTY-FIVE

The marble table was laid with gold goblets, onyx bowls, and silver platters heaped with food. Nobles reclined on fur-covered sofas. Agrippina, wearing a provocative silver stola, batted her eyelids as Nero recited poetry.

> "...and the Tigris too,
> Which traverses Persia,
> but then forsakes it,
> Vanishes, and runs in a long
> subterranean cleft,
> Eventually returning its sorely
> missed flow
> Only to peoples who set no
> store by it."

Nero's guests clapped politely, then exchanged puzzled looks when he called for his lyre. Nero enjoyed playing the entertainer. It was shocking behavior for an emperor.

My quarry, Britannicus, was a fresh-faced boy lounging beside Agrippina. Pleasant-looking and with an easy demeanor, he conducted himself with dignity. I was not fooled. He might be as corrupt as Nero, although tonight he appeared the innocent lamb.

A line of loincloth-clad servants stood behind each guest. They replenished wine, served food, and removed plates.

Platter after platter arrived. Lobster, goose, capon, vegetables, and exotic fruits, each displayed to spectacular effect. The guests feasted, their voices louder with each refilled goblet.

A troupe of clowns cartwheeled into the room. Their claps and shouts announced the arrival of the evening's entertainment.

A serious-faced man entered the room. Water pitcher in his hand, he took his place behind Britannicus. Only a few moments passed before Britannicus pointed to his goblet. Whoever the man was, the heir-apparent trusted him, because they exchanged a friendly smile while he poured the tainted water.

Britannicus lifted the goblet to his lips, paused to snicker at the clowns whose ridiculous antics elicited cackles of mirth from everyone.

I held my breath when Britannicus drank. Music and laughter surrounded him. Clowns danced. Guests clapped to the tempo of the drums. Nero and Agrippina waved their arms about. The tambourine's rattle and tintinnabulum's bells rose to a crescendo.

And then it happened.

Britannicus's hand flew to his throat. His arm flailed. His goblet crashed to the ground. The boy's face bloomed bright red. His pupils shriveled. His eyes bugged out with terror. Britannicus clawed at his throat and collapsed on the floor. His limbs jerked violently, and his face was a mask of terror.

Agrippina gaped, the uncertainty in her eyes turning to

horror as saliva spewed from Britannicus's mouth. Her blood-curdling scream silenced the music.

The clowns grew still. The nobles stopped laughing.

Britannicus, the true heir to the throne, gurgled and gasped, convulsions wracking his body.

"Play on!" Nero hurled a plate at a clown's head. "Britannicus has the falling sickness—the same malady as the great Julius Caesar. It's a momentary fit that will pass."

The clowns lifted their instruments, about to play, when a noble leaned over Britannicus and touched his neck. "He's dead."

Pandemonium erupted.

I pushed back from the wall. My mouth tasted of bile and I gagged, vomited into a nearby urn in an attempt to expel the horror I witnessed. The death I caused. The agony I inflicted. Locusta of Gaul, daughter of a vintner, was a murderer. My retching gave way to dry heaves.

I murdered a boy. The rightful emperor.

Claudius was old and sick when the mushrooms took his life. Britannicus a mere child. I heaved into the urn again.

Perhaps Nero knew something about Britannicus. Perhaps something about his inability to rule Rome. Nero must have a valid reason for killing his stepbrother.

I vomited a third time. My justification offered no comfort. My body knew what my heart refused to believe.

I poisoned a child because Nero commanded it. And to save myself.

A hand touched my shoulder.

I jerked upright.

"Success is not always sweet." Seneca's words were a bee sting. "Quickly now, you must leave while the palace is in confusion."

I wrapped myself in the mantle, drew it over my head, and followed Seneca from the room. A few steps later, a coughing fit seized Seneca. He stopped in the hallway, hacking, one hand against the wall.

"You!"

I turned my head. Agrippina stared back.

Agrippina's grief was genuine, although I suspected her anguish was over the loss of a future imperial puppet and not the death of her stepson.

I looked her full in the face and summoned every scrap of courage.

"You poisoned him." Agrippina's accusation was the hiss of a cornered cat.

With pretended boldness, I lifted my chin and my eyes bore into hers.

Agrippina blanched at my effrontery, a new dread realized in her tear-soaked face. "Futete!"

Fuck you too, you, vile woman.

"An untimely meeting." Seneca hustled me away. "Pay no heed to her vile language, she fears you, Locusta."

"Why?" My voice trembled.

Seneca arched an eyebrow. "Nero killed his stepbrother against his advisors' recommendations. Whose death will he order next?"

Seneca's words hung in the air like a toxic mist. How many will Nero want me to poison? Who else in his family did he deem a threat? Surely not his own doting mother.

That night as I lay under blankets not my own, on a bed belonging to the emperor, and in a villa purchased by his ancestors, a terrible dream had me jolting upright in terror, my heart galloping like a runaway horse.

I dreamt an avalanche of coins rained down from the sky.

Mother cursed me, and Father gave me a bouquet of rose-mary, sage, and basil. The coins continued to fall. Soon they covered my shoulders. I was being buried alive. I shouted for help, but Pricilla and Lucius, copulating like dogs, did not hear my cries. I awoke in the morning gasping for air, a metallic taste on my tongue.

FORTY-SIX

"Pack your bags," said an advisor of Nero.

My chest tightened. "Why?"

"The emperor is moving you."

To prison?

I swallowed, put my shaking hands in my lap. "Where?"

"You'll see."

I moved to a new domus, a grand residence not far from the palace. It was elegant and lavish. And it was mine. A gift from Nero. It had marble floors, proper bathrooms, sumptuous sofas, and fine-crafted furniture. The villa was goddess-worthy. Rich washes of color covered the ceiling of each room, deep reds, vivid blues, and golden yellows enhancing the frescoes of temples, gods, and animals painted on almost every wall. Resplendent with statuary and urns, the villa had running water, a rooftop solarium, and a large garden. Cool, warm, and hot pools overlooked the city below. Rome stretched out before me like a gift.

The day after moving to the villa, a carpentum arrived and two palace guards hauled in a cedar chest adorned with the emperor's seal.

"They forgot the key." I pointed to the lock.

"Maybe it will come later," said Pricilla.

It did. Delivered by three Praetorian guardsmen.

I raked my hands through a mountain of gold, silver, copper, and brass. "How much is here?"

"I can't count that high." Pricilla grabbed a fistful of coins. "You're a wealthy woman."

The following day I received another chest. This one was filled with necklaces, earrings, bracelets, and anklets, all made from garnet, pearls, lapis lazuli, peridot, and silver.

On the third day, a palace servant delivered a tiny box. Nestled inside was a ring with a likeness of Nero etched into the stone. I slipped the carnelian, the stone of healing, on my finger.

On the fourth day, a servant brought a puppy. "His name is Lupus. Nero says the pup was whelped from his favorite guard dog."

I nuzzled the pup and he licked my cheek.

Gifts arrived every month. A pearl-encrusted bench. A statue of Nero as the Roman god Jupiter. Silks and fine linens.

Each gift came with a request. A flask of the love elixir. An ointment for a skin rash. A cleansing enema. Essential oil for a cold. A tincture for a headache. These tonics caused me no remorse. Nero's lethal requests, however, sent stabs of shame through my heart.

Months slipped by. I watched gladiator games, attended dinner parties, and created new concoctions. I tested the pleasure elixirs myself. Attuned to the medicinal nuances, I required only small quantities. Pricilla offered larger doses to the servants. Eager to test new love elixirs, there was no shortage of willing participants for tonics that brought bliss.

Testing deadly compounds was problematic. Pricilla and I

used goats for the unpleasant task. Quick deaths were easy to watch. Slower-acting poisons more difficult. To watch an animal flail about or bellow in pain struck my heart and reminded me of Britannicus's violent end.

Quick or prolonged, I watched each death. Recorded the time, manner, and symptoms. I had to. It helped me perfect the lethal doses.

"Another goat." Pricilla nudged the animal with her sandaled foot. "Are you certain we can't eat it or give it to a servant?"

"The beast's body is infused with poison. I wouldn't risk it."

"Such a waste." Pricilla tapped her lips. "I have an idea. Why don't we test on sick people and prisoners?"

"The ill often get better," I said.

"What about prisoners? They might prefer death over years shackled in manacles as they stand in their piss and shit."

"Some prisoners have family or friends who visit, like you visited me."

"Nobody can visit prisoners in the Tullianum dungeon. Let them choose. A lethal dose or years of torment until they die."

"That would be almost merciful," I said.

"Don't tell Nero that."

That same month, I asked Nero for permission to test my lethal compounds on prisoners. The sadistic emperor, known for throwing Christians to the lions, clapped his hands. "Love it! Let their life serve the glory of Rome."

Or the whims of the emperor.

We went the next week and asked for volunteers.

Prisoners whose chains were grafted into their skins, who inhaled the stench of their own defecations and vomit, who had long since lost hope for release or trial, were the most willing participants. They gulped deadly drafts without hesitation. Many thanked us for putting an end to their suffering.

I hated these trips. I had bad dreams for nights after. Those I had killed spoke to me from the river of the damned. Join us. They beckoned to me.

Only one thing shook those nightmares from my mind. I created new tonics. Lost myself in herbs and leaves and roots.

I heal people. I serve the glory of Rome. I only poison those I'm ordered to.

The herbal arts took time and dedication to learn and perfect. There were always questions. Did a fresh leaf have increased potency? What part of a stalk was more effective? Did wild or cultivated herbs yield the most toxicity? What time of year increased its potency? Every plant held distinctive secrets. Had unique needs for thriving.

It was on an unseasonably cold day, while I grumbled about the short growing season, that a wondrous idea came to me.

"Brrrr, unusual weather." Pricilla draped a thick shawl over my shoulders.

I studied the wilted berry in my palm. The cold had killed it. "What if Nero demands a tonic that requires an ingredient that's out of season? What then?" From the portico, I stared across the gardens to the ominous clouds blanketing the sky.

"The emperor isn't stupid. He knows plants don't grow all year long."

"Nero is a self-absorbed monarch. I don't dare tell him an herb is dormant in winter or I can't find toads in the cold."

"You think he'll kill you?"

"I know he will." I set down the berry. "But I may have a solution."

FORTY-SEVEN

I led Pricilla to a large south-facing room off the peristyle.

"I don't understand," she said.

"Remove the roof, cover it with cloth, and fill the room with dirt. It can be heated with braziers during cool winter months so our most essential plants will grow throughout the year."

"An indoor garden!" Pricilla rubbed her hands together. "Can we breed toads as well?"

"I don't see why not."

We sketched ideas for our indoor garden the rest of the day.

I CHEWED ON CALMING LEAVES. They soothed my troubled spirit. I spent too many anxious days pacing the marble halls until I received word that a toxin had produced the desired result.

Seldom did a week pass that I did not prepare a tonic for the emperor. Nero had an insatiable and perverted sexual appetite. His repeated demands for the love elixir soon depleted my herbal supplies.

Nero also insisted I keep a cache of tonics at the palace. I stored the poisons, aphrodisiacs, medications, and narcotics in a specially designed chest. Rows of tiny drawers held seeds and powders. Shelves were lined with miniature clay vessels. I labeled every packet and container, but never gave Nero more than a month's supply.

On several occasions, a frightened guard or servant demanded I come to the palace at once. It was always the same. Nero overindulged.

"He's late for a senate meeting," Seneca said. "I found him in bed with five women. One, I believe, possesses the parts of both male and female—although I can't be certain. Do something, Locusta! The senators are waiting for him."

I was prepared. Each narcotic Nero overdosed on, I had a remedy to counteract its effects.

"Can't you persuade him that governing the empire is more important than fucking everyone that strikes his fancy?" I asked.

Seneca stepped towards me. "Can't you make a tonic that makes him more rational? More judicious?"

"If he asked, I would."

NERO'S lustful appetites grew more uncontrolled each year.

One rainy night while the citizens of Rome slumbered, a servant banged on my villa door. "The emperor demands you come to the palace!"

I suspected Nero wanted a love elixir or tonic to sooth his spirits because his poison requests always required strategic planning.

Nero was ranting when I arrived. Octavia, his wife, cowered in the corner, arms over her head.

"Locusta, search this ungrateful wife's chamber! I fuck her daily—a repugnant task—and no child grows in her womb!"

I glanced at Octavia, noted the blood trickling down her leg and the bright red droplets at her feet.

The room was in shambles. Broken urns and pottery were scattered on the floor, her clothes strewn about. Necklaces, bracelets, anklets, broaches, and rings were dumped on the bed, her cosmetics heaped in a pile.

"What do you want me to find?" I asked.

"How do I know? You're the herbalist!"

I searched the chamber while Octavia wept. I looked for evidence she was using something to make her womb cold. Apricot kernels, wild carrot, water pepper, neem oil, pomegranate. I found none of these things.

"There's nothing here," I said.

"Give the bitch a tonic to make her womb fertile."

Raspberry leaves, red clover, alfalfa, nettles, and oat straw may create a hospitable womb, but if the rumors were true then Nero lavished his sexual attentions on his former servant, Claudia Acte, not Octavia.

"Herbs don't always—"

"I command you!" Nero picked up a gilded chair and heaved it against the wall.

"I'll need to return to my villa to get the proper—"

"Go! Come back tomorrow! I want this useless cunt with child by month's end!"

I concocted several mixtures for Octavia. She remained barren. I visited her many times, asked questions about her monthly courses, blood flow, and cramps. She was a gentle woman, and any mention of her husband's name made her tremble with fear.

"He tried to strangle me," she said. "Not once. Several times."

My eyes widened, but I dare not say anything.

"He visits once a month and makes me…I endure…. unspeakable acts…not intercourse…other things. He says I should be honored to serve his needs this way. Honored? He's not normal, Locusta," she whispered.

"I heard the rumors."

"They're all true." Her eyes darted about the room and she sidled close. "One night he tied me to the bed and came at me wearing tiger skin. He played the tiger. And he roared and bit and scratched and I screamed and…" She touched her womb. "My womb closes at the thought of bringing forth life from his monstrous seed."

The empress's fate was worse than my own. Nero dared not divorce her. Octavia's political ties were far too important.

"Nero takes anything he wants." Lucius lounged on a sofa and sipped fruited wine.

The passing years sealed our friendship, misbegotten as it was. I came to anticipate Lucius's weekly visits. He shared political news and gossip, essential information in my line of work.

Lucius, like Nero, enjoyed the love elixir's heady effects. I enjoyed the referrals.

The wealthy citizens of Rome were a capricious and narcissistic lot, my potions were always in demand. Lascivious lovers desired the seductive sensations provided by the love elixir. Anxious senators called for calming tonics. Frustrated mothers required relief from female ailments. Rome's elite paid dearly for my services.

"Why shouldn't he? Nero is the leader of the world," I argued.

Lucius scowled. "His flagrant disregard for all that is decent angers the patricians. Have you heard that Nero is smitten with Poppaea Sabina? And she, the noble harlot, plans to divorce her husband."

"Nero is married to Octavia."

"Not if you poison her," Lucius laughed.

I pounced from the sofa, hand aimed to smack him across the face.

Lucius grabbed my wrist, pulled me close. "Your venom is misplaced."

"Let me go." I struggled to escape his grasp, but Lucius no longer had the body of an adolescent. He was as muscular and chiseled as a statue of Adonis.

"Make love to me." He squeezed my wrist.

"No. You insulted me."

"How? By speaking the truth? You're a hired killer. The emperor's assassin."

I twisted away. He held tight.

"Should I disobey Nero?" I asked.

"Not if you want to live."

"Then why taunt me if my fate is sealed?"

Lucius kissed me hard, his tongue thrusting against my clamped lips.

He pulled back and released me. "I love you, Locusta."

"I love you like a brother." I stroked his head. I knew Lucius well. He liked best what he could not have.

"How horrible. Although it never stopped some emperors." He leered.

I tugged on his earlobe. "Tell me about Nero and Poppaea Sabina."

"Well, Agrippina despises her."

"Of course she does, the affair offers no political advantages. In fact, quite the opposite. Poppaea Sabina's husband is Nero's friend."

"You mean was his friend. Ortho best keep a long blade at the ready. He may be next on Nero's execution list. Which brings us to our emperor's advisors. Seneca's and Burrus's influences have been reduced to such an extent they now only minimize Nero's outrageous actions."

"Not Seneca." I liked the old stoic, enjoyed his witticisms.

"Nero accused him of bedding his mother," he laughed. "Naturally, the wily old philosopher proved him wrong." Lucius scratched his chin. "Is it true Nero keeps a larder full of your tonics?"

I looked away. I trusted no one, not even Lucius.

Lucius took my hand, kissed my fingertips. "How many contenders for the throne and out-of-favor senators have succumbed to your poisons?"

"You know I can't tell you."

"Will not? Or too ashamed to admit?"

I yanked my hand away, crossed the room, and clutched the drapery hanging from the doorway. It granted a fine view of the gardens, verdant and colorful with trees, shrubs, and herbs. Plants of lust and death. Plants of pain and pleasure.

"What's with all the questions?"

"There are whispers, murmurs almost inaudible to the ear, of Nero's desire to commit matricide."

I turned from my Garden of Death. "Even Nero is not so vile as to kill his own mother."

FORTY-EIGHT

Nero attempted to poison Agrippina with herbs from his private cache, the herbs I replenished monthly.

Both attempts to poison his mother failed.

Nero blamed me. He claimed my herbs were impotent and placed me under house arrest. Praetorian Guards stood at each door of my villa. I was not permitted to leave. My regular clientele, however, was permitted entrance.

I lived in fear, terrified Nero might give the order to a guardsman to sink his blade through my heart or drag me to prison in chains.

Pricilla was a great comfort. She spoke reassuring words and held me in her arms whenever I burst into tears.

Two weeks later, the guards were gone. The day after that, the imperial litter took me to the palace.

I expected to die. To drink my own poison.

"Your herbs are useless." Nero kicked at the herb chest. "Mother suffered only from an upset stomach."

"I applaud your efforts, emperor, unfortunately many herbs lose potency, or require a specific quantity, or work best in conjunction with another—"

"Enough!" Nero stalked from the room.

I waited alone in the room for hours, pondered my fate. Death, imprisonment, dismissal, or a promotion were all possibilities.

A servant arrived to escort me home. Perhaps Nero realized the art of poisoning was not so easily mastered.

"TAKE AWAY THE PAIN, LOCUSTA." Nero lay flat on his back amid a mountain of pillows. "Empty my mind of these tortuous thoughts."

I mixed a strong narcotic into his wine, tilted the goblet to his lips.

"I loved her. I did." Nero's eyes, swollen and red with tears, burned with a torment no remedy in the world could cure. "More. Give me more."

Nero tore the chalice from my hands and drank greedily.

"No one loved Mother more than I. Our bond was unique. A gift from Jupiter." He grabbed my hand. "Do you believe the gossip, Locusta?"

There was no shortage of rumors about Nero's latest deeds. His antics kept Roman tongues wagging, especially after he expelled Agrippina from the palace.

After his failed attempts to poison her, Nero tried other methods. One elaborate attempt included rigging the ceiling above her chambers to collapse as she slept. As fate had it, the falling debris missed Agrippina by only a few unciae.

Nero's next attempt had been equally disastrous. After dining with his mother at the seaside resort of Baiae, Nero had sent Agrippina home on a booby-trapped boat. As the vessel sank into the sea, she leapt overboard and swam to shore, which was not far from one of her villas. Nero had been enraged. He took out his fury on the unlucky messenger who reported Agrippina's miraculous survival by throwing him into the Tullianum dungeon on false assassination charges.

Agrippina managed to thwart or survive every murder attempt. Nero finally ordered his most loyal soldiers to kill her.

They stabbed Agrippina. Left the dagger by her body to look like suicide. It was a violent end for a wicked woman. Even though I was happy to hear she was dead, I was glad I had no hand in her death.

"I pay little attention to gossip," I said to Nero. "Anyone who knows you will attest to your devotion to her."

"You understand me, Locusta. I still love her." With each passing moment, Nero succumbed to the opium haze. The narcotic loosened his tongue and a torrent of emotion gushed forth, a perverted son's confession I hated to hear. "What a swimmer she was—those legs of hers—wrapped around me—oh, her scent, her breasts, small and pert—I did suckle on them—stabbed those wondrous breasts—no one controls me—tells me I cannot or shall not—Mother! Juno worships at your royal feet—slanderous bitch, spreading lies—planning to usurp my right! To Hades, wanton Mother—I love you! I love you—forgive me…forgive your son who loves you too well, knows you better than yourself…" His grip relaxed and he moaned. "Send for Poppaea Sabina." Nero's head rolled to the side.

WITHOUT NERO'S domineering mother to restrain him, the twenty-one-year-old emperor ran rampant. He favored orgies of the basest kind. Indulged in sex acts too strange to be true.

Senators believed Nero was dangerous and subversive. The commoners celebrated his policy reforms. Nero decreed it illegal to kill gladiators for sport, halted gruesome public executions, and stopped dubious tax collecting procedures. The poor loved him. The free chariot races, musical contests, and wild beast entertainment became a hallmark of Nero's generosity. Freedmen loved that he supported their rights. Commoners loved that he cut taxes.

Although adored by the commoners, the complexities of politics and tedium of governing bored Nero. He spent too much time singing, playing the lyre, chariot racing, or bedding whatever male or female caught his eye.

Between Nero's infamous orgies and extravagant state dinners, it was a wonder he made the time to respond to reports of trouble in Britannia. He almost had to call back his forces in Londinium, a trading town of little consequence in a godless land.

I did not usually concern myself with the exploits of the Roman legions, but I knew Marcus was fighting there. A fact I might never have known had it not been for a conversation with Seneca.

"Does Nero forbid you to wed?" he asked after we had concluded our business for the afternoon.

I rolled up the scroll, a list of my expenditures. "That's a strange question."

"I find it odd that a woman of your beauty and skill is not wed and minding a brood of children."

"The man I love is a centurion." I tied a knot around the scroll. "He promised to wed me after his commission is completed."

"Your centurion fights in Londinium." Seneca told me a week later.

I made sacrifices to Vesta and Juno for a safe retreat. It

was an unlikely military strategy for the mighty Roman legion.

I did not allow myself the luxury of wondering about Marcus until I went to bed. What would he think of my new profession? Would he be proud that I served the emperor for the glory of Rome?

Or had he forgotten me?

FORTY-NINE

Emperor Nero's demands were frequent. Implementing his wicked schemes required preparation and imagination. Emboldened by his mother's death, Nero indulged every debauched proclivity. He gorged on food, women, and young men. He murdered sexual rivals and executed political conspirators.

The years kept me busy. Together Pricilla and I procured exotic herbs, concocted new potions, and perfected dosages.

Poisons were abundant, the methods to administer them equally numerous. The world supplied a surplus of toxic plants and animals. We often discovered unusual leaves, berries, and venoms in roundabout ways. A trusted confidant whispered the location of an unscrupulous back alley merchant. An address was slipped into my hand as I walked through a crowd. Leather encased samples were left at my door. Messengers delivered clay pots.

As Rome's dominance expanded, so too did their roads advance into new-conquered lands. Roman control unwittingly laid a brick foundation for the transport of new poisons.

Exotic deadly plants and creatures arrived from Aegyptus, Carthage, Judea, and Britannia. Magicians and healers carried toxins with the power to kill the very oppressors whose roads they traveled. It was The Defeated's unwitting retaliation against their Conquerors.

And yet most poisons grew in my garden.

"Nero ordered soldiers to rape and sodomize Octavia's handmaids until they confessed her infidelities," Pricilla said one day after returning from the market with the latest gossip.

Three years after he had murdered his mother, Nero banished the barren Octavia to the island of Pandateria and wed his pregnant mistress, Poppaea Sabina.

"Octavia was never unfaithful," I said.

"I agree. The empress is a testament to wifely devotion. Her handmaids claimed her womanly parts were purer than Nero's mouth."

"That I believe."

So did the commoners. They were outraged and demanded the return of their beloved empress.

This angered Nero and Poppaea Sabina. They were determined to get rid of her.

No sooner were statues of Empress Octavia re-erected in the squares then Nero ordered his estranged wife tied up and her wrists slit to mimic suicide.

But Nero wasn't done proving his love to Poppaea Sabina. During a formal dinner, he presented Octavia's head on a silver platter.

Those in attendance reported Poppaea Sabina laughed so hard, tears ran down her cheeks.

"Do something," Nero shouted.

"I'm not a physician. I know about plants." I stared down at the sickly babe, Nero's first child, a girl.

Poppaea Sabina wept on the sofa while a terrified wet nurse held the weak baby in her arms. I pitied the wet nurse, if the child failed to thrive Nero would kill her.

Although the spotted thistle, anise, and alfalfa I had given the nurse made her breasts heavy with milk, the babe weakened. I examined a cup of her milk. It was thick and creamy.

"I am the Pontifex Maximus! The world obeys ME!" The emperor pounded his chest, then wrapped Poppaea Sabina in his arms.

I made a show of sorting through my supplies and refrained from reminding Nero that herbal remedies did not cure every illness. Babies often died before their first birthday. Of the six children my Aunt Diana gave birth to, only four survived.

"Perhaps," I said. "if the babe slept in the arms of a handmaid who roused her during the night… "

"We tried that," wailed Poppaea. The nursemaid even coats her nipples with honey to entice my daughter to suckle." She pointed to the nurse. "Her milk is bad."

"My own child is thriving and fed after the emperor's baby." Tears rolled down the nurse's cheeks, her voice a choked whisper.

"Did you speak to Dioscorides?" I examined the babe's eyes. They were dull.

"He doesn't understand babies." Nero threw a vase across the chamber. "He knows only battle wounds and ailments."

"Dioscorides has traveled far and collected many uncommon plants, I'll ask—"

"That bastard, Dioscorides! He's more interested in writing his book and drawing pictures!"

Poppaea sobbed into her husband's shoulder. "Help us, Locusta."

I clutched my herbal satchel. "I'll make an offering to the gods for your daughter's health."

"Get out," Nero screamed.

I rushed out, uncertain whether his command was directed at the unfortunate wet nurse or me.

I fled from the palace feeling despondent and useless. For all my remedies, I could not save the emperor's newborn daughter.

News of the babe's death came four days later. I learned of it on the very day Uncle Amando and Aunt Diana paid a surprise visit.

They brought sad news. My father, his mind long since gone, had eluded his attendant and wandered away. Vineyard workers found Father's dead body in a dry creek bed several days later.

I wept the rest of the day. I wept for Father's passing and for the malady that clouded his mind in his final years. I cried because I had been a neglectful daughter.

I sobbed until Pricilla brought me a calming herb. I chewed it gratefully.

"Whose lovely villa is this?" Aunt Diana asked the next day as we lounged under the portico and nibbled fruit.

"Mine."

"All this? How is that possible?"

"I work for Nero."

"The emperor?" Aunt Diana's jaw dropped. "Are you his mistress?"

"No. I have a skill he finds useful."

Aunt Diana swept her arm about. "A skill? What kind of skill warrants such gratitude?"

"My herbal knowledge."

Aunt Diana laughed. "Oh, Locusta, you have no reason to be embarrassed at being the emperor's mistress."

"Nero married Poppaea Sabina after he banished Octavia. Poppaea was his mistress, not me."

"I'm sure the emperor has many mistresses." She winked.

"Nero loves Poppaea Sabina so much he condemned the barren Octavia to an island prison on false charges of adultery until he had her head chopped off and brought to Poppaea Sabina as a gift. I am not Nero's mistress."

"But herbs? He gives you this beautiful villa because your little concoctions help a headache?"

"My knowledge is more extensive than that." I must have given her an exasperated look because she flinched.

Aunt Diana pursed her lips. "When you left Gaul, you were an innocent girl. You've changed in the last ten years."

"I hope so."

Her eyes narrowed. "You're still beautiful but your eyes lost their innocence. They're as mistrustful as a thief."

"I'm not a thief."

"You live in a luxurious villa with many servants. You're bedecked in the finest clothing, every finger glitters with costly gems." She leaned close. "Gaius Theon thinks you're Nero's personal poisoner—that you supply nobles with love tonics and death brews. Theon told him this is preposterous and explained that you know a little but certainly not enough to… hurt anyone."

"You would rather I was the emperor's whore than a skilled pharmacist?"

"Pharmacist?! What a clever and deceptive title. Is that what you call yourself?"

I folded my hands together. "Yes."

"I didn't realize shopkeepers enjoyed such wealth. Is your shop in the Forum?"

Aunt Diana refused to believe what she knew in her heart to be true. Refused to acknowledge my profession.

"I have no shop. Nero summons me to his palace. Senators and patricians come to my villa. I make a variety of tonics. Many are healing remedies. I help more people than I...than I harm."

"It's true then?" Her face drained of all color. "You're a murderer."

"For the emperor. I serve the glory of Rome."

She sat back, wrapped her arms around herself as though my mere presence could harm her. "We heard the rumors. I didn't believe them. How is our innocent Locusta—who's like a daughter to me—engaged in such an unscrupulous occupation? When we saw the luxury of your villa, we hoped —well, there's more honor being Nero's mistress than his poisoner."

Any mistress of Nero's was likely to end up dead. My occupation was a bit safer.

I touched Aunt Diana's hand. She jerked away as though my skin was toxic.

"I have no choice. One doesn't disobey the emperor. If Nero can murder his own mother, he won't hesitate to kill a poisoner for disobedience."

Aunt Diana buried her face in her hands. "I blame myself. I sent you here. I was certain you would find a wealthy husband. Vicious Romans! They didn't see your charm, only the allure of your skills, and they perverted them to do their wickedness."

UNCLE AMANDO and Aunt Diana stayed for a month. They witnessed the midnight meetings with customers cloaked in disguise. They watched me pulverize petals and concoct potions.

"Come back with us." Aunt Diana's eyes welled with tears. "Return to Gaul. Leave this world of perversion behind."

Aunt Diana did not understand. Escape was impossible. One did not escape an imperial appointment. Nor did I want to. I welcomed the request for poisons, love elixirs, and hallucinogens. They provided the coin to purchase exotic plants. Plants to ease suffering or cure a common ailment. I served the most influential and powerful people in the world. I made a difference in people's lives.

Moreover, buried in my heart, I nurtured the absurd hope of Marcus's return.

I sniffed a bouquet of poppies. A senator wanted my special blend for his next party. "I can never leave Rome. I know too much. Nero would see it as an act of treachery. He would call me an enemy of Rome and send his guards to kill me."

"We can hide you in the north. Maybe you'll find someone to marry you."

I set the poppies on the worktable. "Nero severed his first wife's head. He sent soldiers to slay his own mother. He ordered me to poison Burrus, his Praetorian Prefect, after an argument. If I leave, I die."

"You'll change your name. We'll take you far away."

"He'll find me."

Aunt Diana and Uncle Amando left the next day.

Aunt Diana thrust her head out the carpentum's window. "Is this the legacy you wish to be remembered by?"

My legacy.

I had none. My name would disappear. My concoctions forgotten. Any good I ever did ignored.

I pretended not to hear the question, waved goodbye, and walked back into my villa of venom.

Aunt Diana's words haunted me for months. Like a seed, her suggestion of fleeing Rome germinated in my thoughts and took root.

Dare I make a new life for myself?

Britannia was populated by heathens. Greece was too close. Nero went there often. Egypt had the celebrated Library of Alexandria. Jerusalem was far away, but their medical knowledge was more advanced. Rome had ports in India, but it was an unusual place with strange customs.

I rejected every location.

Once Roman soldiers occupied a land, there was no hiding from Nero's all-seeing spies. I would not dare venture into barbaric lands. Better to remain with the enemies I knew than trust my life with savages.

My legacy?

Surely, history had no use for a poisoner. I had no children. The life-expelling herbs Pricilla administered long ago fouled my womb. My monthly blood came irregularly, the occasional lovers I took never produced a child.

My legacy!

My herbal knowledge was destined to perish, consumed in my funeral pyre. It was a sobering thought.

And then I had an idea.

FIFTY

I rushed into the indoor garden. "Pricilla, I want to establish a school of herbal learning for women. Only women."

Pricilla looked up from a workbench spread with clippings. "A fine idea but why exclude men?"

"Because it's women who tend sick family members and care for children."

"A school?" Pricilla asked. "Not a real school. You want an apprentice."

"One apprentice is not enough, I want a school. With many students. Our knowledge must be shared. Here. In this villa. It's large enough, the gardens easily accessible, and there's plenty of room to provide sleeping accommodations."

"How much will you charge for tuition?"

"I don't need money. Nero is generous to a fault."

Locusta grimaced, shook her head. "A free school has no credibility."

"Fine, then you decide. Keep a portion for administrative duties. Give the rest to the needy." For the first time in years, I was giddy with anticipation. "Find ten girls of low means—prostitutes or freed slaves—and give them scholarships."

"Why?"

"Those women are the most in need of an income-earning skill."

PRICILLA SPREAD the word about my Herbal Academy. In days, young women knocked at my door. Daughters of shopkeepers, especially those with limited marriage prospects, were eager to better their circumstances. A few girls from noble families also enrolled.

By month's end, twenty girls were learning to masticate plants, draw out powerful essences, and make tinctures and tonics.

More came the next month. I limited enrollment to forty. Pricilla and I couldn't handle more than that.

The wealthy paid tuition. The poor students did household tasks to earn their education and offset the cost of food and supplies. Both had gardening chores.

I had a household of young women. Which meant I needed rules.

The first rule. Servants and students could not fornicate with one another. This was a school, not a brothel.

As for Pricilla—who enjoyed men and women with equal abandon—I asked her not to make love to any of the students. Pricilla pouted and begged, but finally agreed when I reminded her that favoring one student over another created an unfair advantage.

The second rule. Students wore identical stolae. In this way, girls could not mock the clothes of a freed slave, covet the finery of the wealthy, or ridicule the frippery of a prostitute.

The third rule. The girls must use kind words. Girls who slandered or humiliated others had to shovel fertilizer for a week.

For the first time in years, I felt pride in my occupation. Once educated, these young women would have the skills to comfort ailing parents and provide relief to those with semi-tertian fever. The illness raged during the summer months and brought a host of breathing maladies. The poor living in the cramped quarters of the insulae suffered the worst.

Even with my rules, a household of energetic young women was not without problems. During school hours, male servants found reasons to linger about the villa. Love elixir days were the worst. Pricilla and I were extra vigilant. Sometimes we were not watchful enough.

One morning, intoxicated from the love elixir they had just learned to mix, Helene stumbled from the room in a daze. When she did not return, I went after her.

I found Helene straddling my guard in the entrance hall.

It saddened me to dismiss Helene. She was a bright girl with intellectual promise.

That evening, Pricilla and I argued about my discipline methods.

"Helene's gift for memorization and illustrations are beyond compare." said Pricilla.

"She was humping the guard like a dog in heat. They didn't even notice me until I was practically standing over them."

"She was under the sway of the love elixir. Dismiss Daniel. Not her!"

"I need the guard," I said.

"Helene was sold into prostitution when she was only six years old."

"Her tragic childhood doesn't change my decision."

Pricilla took my hand and guided me to the sofa. "Does her face look familiar to you?"

"No, should it?"

"That's a great pity, because your face has been etched in Helene's mind since she first saw you many years ago…in a brothel."

I gasped. That face. Those eyes. How had I not recognized her?

The world-weary little girl. My first hour of freedom from the dungeon. The brothel Lucius had brought me to for a bath. It all came back.

"Helene watched you and Lucius that night. She hid behind drapes, intrigued by the woman rescued from the depths of hell by a handsome noble. Your haughty demeanor and flirtatious behavior made an impression."

"Oh, Pricilla, I had no idea."

"Helene asked everyone at the brothel who you were. Why you were there. Then she heard you poisoned Emperor Claudius. Helene told me you gave her hope. She learned that in order to survive she needed to be smart and she needed a skill."

"Did she become a prostitute?"

"Yes, but she also learned how to memorize and draw. She told me those were the only activities she could pursue without censure or question." Pricilla wrapped an arm around my waist. "Helene was our first student. Her aptitude far exceeds the others."

"I will not bend the rules."

"Helene and Daniel have been flirting for months. You recall the passion of first love. You know love and lust is not bound by rules or—"

"Enough." I shrugged her off. "There are no exceptions to the rule."

"You've become a hard woman, my friend." Pricilla crossed her arms.

"You never went to prison. You never fear the day Nero will decide to kill you. Or that a senator will have his revenge on you. You don't have to deal with Nero's temper tantrums or his advisors' rants. You enjoy all the luxury of my commission and none of the responsibilities."

Pricilla wrapped her arms around herself. "You're right." She walked out of the room.

Tensions between Pricilla and I festered like a sore over the next few days. She told me the students were upset over Helene's expulsion. She told me Helene was a friend to everyone. Nothing changed my mind.

Weeks passed. Our easy banter returned. Almost. But it was like a slub in an otherwise perfect swath of linen. Noticeable. Unfixable. Our argument had woven into the fabric of our friendship. I bought her gifts. A ring, a necklace, had her bedroom ceiling painted with gods. Nothing restored our closeness.

"Helene and Daniel are married." Pricilla adjusted a thick palla about her shoulders one winter morning.

"That's nice."

"Daniel hopes you might reconsider letting her come back."

"No."

Two seasons passed before Pricilla broached the subject again.

"There's a woman waiting for you in the atrium."

It was Helene. With a baby in her arms.

"I wish to thank you for allowing me to attend your Herbal Academy. I broke your rules and have no excuse for my bad behavior."

I stared at the babe. So small and perfect and new. My heart clutched tight.

"Pricilla told me about the day we met."

Helene nuzzled her babe. "It seems like a lifetime ago."

"We're both in a better place now." I touched the babe's head. "Boy or girl?"

"A girl."

A girl. One who would grow up to be common, without an education, with few prospects for wealth or advancement.

Helene took a deep breath. "Daniel and I have a small apartment—the owner allows me to grow herbs on the rooftop—provided I supply him with a certain elixir. I was wondering if I could ask you a few questions about—"

"Do you want to be readmitted?"

Her eyes lit up. "With every breath in my body."

With Helene back in school, my relationship with Pricilla returned to normal. We did not speak of those months of stilted conversations and awkward meals.

I recalled Cicero's wise words. What sweetness is left in life, if you take away friendship? Robbing life of friendship is like robbing the world of the sun. A true friend is more to be esteemed than kinfolk.

I HELD Helene's baby while she prepared a tincture. Her tiny fist closed around my finger and her eyes gazed at me with wonder. My heart squeezed tight. A baby...I wanted a baby.

My sexual liaisons were far too infrequent to stimulate my womb. And although Lucius pressed me to be his mistress, I declined. Frequent intercourse might urge my womb to bloom, but my heart knew the truth. Pricilla's overdose of pennyroyal that horrid night long ago rendered me a barren woman.

I closed my eyes, kissed the infant's sweet-smelling head and dared to dream the impossible.

MID JULY WAS hotter than usual. My handmaid, Iris, waved a palm frond over me as I reclined on the sofa under the portico and sipped a cool mixture of honey and lemon. Lupus sprawled out in the shade.

"I canceled classes." Pricilla plopped down on the opposite sofa. "Heat melts away intelligent thoughts."

I pointed to her elegant stola. "Are you going somewhere?"

Pricilla adjusted her turquoise and gold necklace. "I'm visiting a woman I met at the baths. We're of like minds."

"Friendship or pleasure?"

"If she pleases me, a pleasurable friendship may blossom." She winked. "Rome seems quieter than usual the past few days. Is it the heat?"

"Nero left for Antium and many nobles are summering at their seaside villas," I yawned. "It's too hot for intrigue and betrayal. Anyway, I'm rather enjoying this peaceful week."

Pricilla left for the baths and the day passed with neither tearful requests for the love elixir by a jilted lover nor demands for a calming tonic by wife who caught her husband cheating.

Too hot to eat. Too hot to make love.

I sniffed, an acrid tang in my nostrils.

"Is something burning?" I asked Iris as she carried a bundle of dirty linens down the hall.

"Daniel says smoke has been rising from the Circus since morning."

"Another fire?" I crossed the atrium, walked through the ostium where a guard kept vigil at the front door.

Fires were common. The multi-storied insulae of the poor were especially prone. Accidents with oil lamps, braziers, and cooking charcoals ignited and spread quickly in the ramshackle timber dwellings.

I walked out of the villa to find Daniel in the middle of my fountain. He sat on Minerva's marble shoulders, his ebony legs wrapped around her back, his hand shielding his eyes as he stared into the valley beyond.

"I hope you have a good reason for climbing my fountain."

Daniel dropped his hand, his face carved with fear. "Domina, Rome is burning."

FIFTY-ONE

Burning?

"Which part of Rome?" I asked.

"All parts." He pointed into the distance. "What started as a small plume of smoke in the Circus took flight like a flock of birds. The breeze fans the embers and flames leap from building to building. And since there are only small shops between Palatine and Caelian Hills—no concrete temples or buildings—nothing stops the fire's progress."

Daniel tended toward the dramatic. Or rather his facial features were very expressive.

I looked where he pointed. White tendrils rose from the merchant area around the Circus. Where Pricilla was meeting her new friend. "Keep a close eye on the fire's course."

"I'll keep two."

The sharp smell grew worse, and by the time the sun reached its zenith Daniel brought unwelcome news.

"The fire spreads through the city." He wiped his eyes, red from tears and smoke.

I followed him outside to find both sun and sky obscured by a gray shroud. Black plumes ascended into the sky like charred messengers from Vulcan, the fire god. A blanket of onyx cloaked the low grounds. Pungent air stung my lungs with each breath.

Pricilla, where are you?

Daniel dropped to his knees and lowered his forehead to the ground. "Gracious domina, my family lives where the fire burns. My wife, Helene, is one of your students. You've held my daughter in your arms. Please permit me to go to them."

"Yes. Yes. Of course. Take as many water jugs as you can carry."

Daniel kissed my hand and ran into the villa. He was not the only one with family living in the insulae. The hand-maids, servants, and resident students also had family who lived there.

I called everyone into the atrium. Students, cooks, gardeners, stable boy, servants, and guards. "The fire spreads over much of the lower city. Many of you have family there. If you want to help them, you have my permission. May the gods grant you safe passage."

With cries of gratitude, they scattered like frightened birds. Two servants remained. Eitan, a strapping young man with the shoulders of a bull, claimed his relatives lived far away. The other, Iris, had no family.

Twilight came early, hastened by the devouring conflagration that draped the sky with an impermeable black veil. Only a pale orange glow revealed the sun's descent. It looked like Helios himself held a torch to the smoldering city below.

"Where are you, Pricilla?" I asked as tendrils of flames licked at the nearby hills.

Eitan and Iris loaded the carpentum with water jugs, herbs, linen wrappings, and a great quantity of gelatinous aloe vera fronds.

"More water." I turned at the sound of hooves pounding down my driveway.

"Locusta! Locusta!" Pricilla clung to a man's back as he galloped into the courtyard. "We must go! Rome is burning! The fire speeds toward Esquiline Hill."

"Is Nero's palace in danger?"

"It's safe for now, but any shift in winds and the imperial domus will be consumed."

A red-bearded man helped her down from the horse. He gave her a long lusty kiss before racing away.

"I thought it was a woman who—"

"Her brother—a follower of Bacchus." Pricilla tugged on my hand. "There's no time, Locusta. We must leave. Now! As we speak the fire creeps closer."

"Where will we go?"

"Anywhere but inside the walls of Rome."

"I won't go." Iris knelt down. "Oh, domina, please let me stay here. I'll guard your house."

"Don't fear a few flames. I'll take us to safety." Eitan climbed onto the carpentum and picked up the reins.

"I'm not afraid. This is my home, domina." Iris pressed her hand to her heart. "I will guard it with my life."

"We can't delay our departure another moment," said Pricilla.

I touched her shoulder. "Are you certain?" I didn't want to leave her.

"Yes." She lifted her chin. "If the fire is near, I will go into the bath."

"It's best if you come with us."

Iris shook head. "No, I must stay here. I must." Her tone was emphatic. Her expression resolute.

Lupus, his tail wagging, sat by her feet.

"If you insist on staying, you must not refuse shelter to

anyone." I tapped my shoulder. Lupus stood on his hind legs and put his front paws on my shoulders. His enormous head was far above mine. "Protect Iris."

Lupus licked my cheek.

I climbed into the carpentum, and the horses took off at a gallop.

Esquiline Hill was still undamaged. The embers had not blown in this direction.

"Perhaps we should have stayed in the villa," I said.

Pricilla squeezed my hand. "I was there. I heard the people. They said this fire is worse than the rest." She pointed to the treetops. "It takes only a subtle shift in the breeze for the fire to change course."

She was right.

A smoky shroud wrapped around us when we entered the city proper. Thick smoke covered like a blanket and burned our throats with every breath.

I ripped off a strip of linen, stuck my hand out the window, and passed it to Eitan. "Tie this around your nose and mouth."

Pricilla and I did the same.

The carpentum moved slowly through streets crowded with people, burros, wagons, and carts.

"We're not far now," said Eitan.

He was wrong.

When we turned the corner a wall of flame blocked the street ahead—the only street leading to the nearest gate.

FIFTY-TWO

People swarmed our carpentum. Within moments, we were mired in screaming citizens, their terrified wails mixing with the roar of the flames.

Weeping mothers, children in their arms, struggled to push past the crowds. An old man, his arm around his wife's waist, limped through the surge of panicked humanity. Two lanky youths knocked over another man who carried a chest on his shoulder. The road was choked with men, women, and children desperate to escape the encroaching flames.

I grabbed Pricilla's hand. "May the gods protect us."

Eitan cracked the whip to no avail. The horses grew skittish. A loud thud on the side of the carpentum startled me. A rock flew through the window, grazed Pricilla's cheek. Another thud. Someone pounded on the door.

"Stay back," Eitan's voice shouted over the din. "You torment a patrician! This woman is a noble healer! Get back!"

A jolt shook the carpentum, and Pricilla and I grabbed each other as it rocked from side to side.

"Get back, thieves," cried Eitan.

"Patrician swine!"

Grunts, groans, and shouts followed.

"The mob will kill us." I should have packed a weapon. A real weapon. Not the herbal kind.

With a final pitch, the carpentum toppled over. Pricilla landed on top of me. Water jugs and herb vessels tumbled on top of us. One smashed open on my head.

I wiped my eyes, water mixing with the blood from the gash. "Pricilla?"

"More blood than wound." Pricilla rolled off me. "We must get out."

We pushed aside the mess of supplies, freed ourselves from the jumble.

"This way." Pricilla pointed to the casement over our heads.

Two filthy feet pushed past the curtain, and a man dropped inside.

"Give me your coin," he growled.

"Futete." Pricilla slid a dagger from her stola and plunged it into his chest.

The thief gasped, looked down in horror as the front of his tunic bloomed crimson.

I stared at Pricilla.

"What? You think you're the only one who can kill?" Pricilla shoved his body aside. "More will come. We must go." She stepped on him, reached for the ledge. "Help me."

I made a stirrup with my hands and she hoisted herself up and through the window.

"Hurry." Pricilla stuck her arm down through the opening.

I grabbed her hand. My foot slipped and I fell onto the bloody cushion of the thief's dead body.

"Pricilla." I looked up.

Her outstretched hand was gone. Replaced by another thief sliding through the opening.

He landed with a thud. "Give me your coins and jewels."

"It's all in there." I pointed to a chest buried under the mess.

"Open it."

I crouched down and pushed off the baskets and spilled herbs on top of it. And palmed a shard of clay.

"Hurry up and open it," he growled.

I lifted the lid—there was nothing but dried plants inside —and turned around. "There!"

The thief looked, distracted for a moment. I made my move. Jammed the pointed piece of clay into the soft flesh of his throat.

"Fu—" he gurgled, blood spurting from his neck.

My knee slammed into his groin and he collapsed onto the floor. Using his body as a step, I grabbed the wooden beam above me and hoisted myself up.

"Hurry," Pricilla said as I emerged from the opening.

Three more thieves crawled like spiders over the overturned carpentum.

Pricilla, knife between her teeth and brandishing a pole, stood beside me.

Thwack! A thief fell backward from the force of her Athena-like swing.

"Jump," she shouted.

I leapt from the carpentum. Fell hard on the brick below. Pricilla jumped after me and grabbed my hand. She yanked me up, and with our fingers entwined, we disappeared into the crowd.

We did not go far and hid behind a nearby column.

"Futete!" A third thief poked his head out from the casement and hurled the aloe vera crate to the ground. "Only plants! No coins! No jewels!"

A second thief exited, climbed down, and kicked the side of the carpentum. "Stupid cunts!"

"Where's Eitan?" Pricilla asked as the thieves untied our horses.

A body lay unmoving in the middle of the street.

"There he is."

We waited until the thieves left, and then ran to him.

I crouched down, touched his bloody face. "Eitan."

He moaned, eyes fluttering. "They stole the horses."

"Can you walk? We must leave this place."

Pricilla tugged on my sleeve. "People are running. The fire must be heading this way. I smell it. We must go."

Eitan sat up, rubbed his eyes. "I'll lead you to safety, domina. I don't fear angry mobs."

"You're hurt."

Eitan rubbed his jaw. "I've endured worse beatings. My god gives me the strength to protect you."

"The Jewish god?" I knew Eitan attended secret religious meetings.

"His wrath is great, this fire he sends is proof."

"Vulcan is the fire god—Rome has no need for two. But summon your god if you like. We need every god on this terrible day."

"Help! Someone help!" A woman appeared from the smoke, a screaming child cradled in her arms. "Help my baby! Someone help!"

I started toward the mother.

"Are you mad?" Pricilla clutched my arm. "There's no time! We must go!"

I shook her off. "Bring the satchel of herbs. She needs our help."

"Don't be stupid. These are commoners, freedman, and plebeians. We'll die attending to their wounds."

"Did you forget your own humble beginnings? Has wealth blinded you to suffering? Did you forget the poor folk we tended in Gaul? You made no class distinction then—you offered remedies to wealthy and poor alike."

Pricilla's jaw shifted from side to side. "We need to go."

"We need to help people."

"The fire." Pricilla's tears streamed down her face.

"You're a coward."

"Curse you, Locusta. You damn us to Hades."

"Then the river Styx will cool our burning bodies." I squeezed her shoulder.

Pricilla snorted with resignation. "Eitan, bring our herb kits."

I hugged her, then waved to the mother. "We can help."

The mother ran toward us. "A plank fell on his arm." She stroked the child's tear-streaked cheek.

Eitan set several baskets at my feet while I examined the child's injury. The burn was bright red, a pocket of fluid forming underneath the scorched skin.

"This will calm him." I gave the boy a leaf to chew. "And this will speed the healing." I applied a poultice of aloe, chickweed, rosemary, and comfrey, then wrapped his arm with clean linen. "You must keep the wound clean. Don't let him scratch."

The mother grunted. "You must have no children, or you would know a child does nothing but scratch and itch." She offered a sad smile. "You have my gratitude."

The mother walked away, her drowsy child in her arms.

"Be sparing with the poultice." Pricilla nudged me. "All of Rome will need it."

A man, who had been lurking nearby, approached and stretched out his arm. "My hand."

I applied a compress. Others with injuries gathered

around. Gashes from falling debris, abrasions from running, and blistering skin were the most frequent.

For the worst burns, those carrying the charred body of a loved one, I offered only a peaceful death, a cessation from their agony. For others, a salve brought swift comfort.

Pricilla and I tended the wounded throughout the day. Sweat poured down our faces and our lungs burned with every breath, yet it was nothing compared to the pains of the injured.

In the midst of our efforts, a low murmur moved through the crowd.

"The fire returns." A man pointed upwards. "Look!"

A shower of bright sparklers swirled around us.

"No time to tend minor burns, wife." He grabbed her hand and pulled away.

Others departed as more sparks flew over their heads.

"Fire!" A man at the edge of the street screamed and took off running.

The remainder of our patients fled.

"The breeze changes course," said Eitan. "We're not safe, domina."

"There's nothing left here to burn." Pricilla dusted off the gray ash that fell like Vulcan's snow. "Those fools are as skittish as colts. I'm parched with thirst and ravenous with hunger."

I rubbed smoke-stinging eyes. "Eitan, there's a bakery across the street."

Eitan had to break down the door but he returned with two amphorae each of wine and water, and a loaf of bread.

"Save the water for our most thirsty patients." I hid the jugs under a pile of linen bandages while orange embers floated down around us.

Pricilla looked up from packing our supplies. "Do you hear that?"

"Here what?"

Though fire raged blocks away, the hiss and crackle of falling timber and crumbling ceilings continued. In the distance, buildings glowed red or flared gold as fire shot into the sky. Orange embers dispersed into the winds like a fiery god bestowing his wrath upon a craven city.

"I hear a baby crying. It comes from that building." Pricilla pointed across the street. "There it is again."

"No mother abandons her infant." I wrapped the aloe vera fronds in a cloth.

Pricilla cocked her head. "It sounds like a baby."

"We're weary and the ash we breathe jumbles our wits."

"Do you hear it now?"

I heard it. An indistinct and eerie cry. "It's a cat."

"That's no caterwaul. I know the difference. It's a crying baby. Someone left their child." Pricilla stepped forward.

"Don't go into the building. It's ravaged by fire."

The shops and insulae on this side of the street were fire-blackened and unstable.

"You would leave a baby to die? Maybe the mother is hurt or dead."

I grabbed her wrist. "It's too dangerous."

Pricilla yanked away. "It wasn't too dangerous for us to stop here and tend the wounded." She hurried across the vacant street.

"It's not the same. That building isn't safe. Discordia tricks you!"

"The goddess of chaos does indeed hold sway over Rome today, but I know the sound of a babe well enough."

"Don't go, Pricilla." I followed her. "Look. Sparks land on the roof."

Pricilla put her hand on the door. "It's not hot." Her head tilted back. "The cry comes from the third floor."

"Don't go."

Without a glance over her shoulder, Pricilla opened the door and disappeared into the building.

We had visited insulae like this before when we purchased seeds from a foreigner or comforted the sick. Our impoverished students often required assistance when diagnosing an illness of the merchants, freedman, or plebeians living in the squalid rooms. There was only one staircase to the upper floors. And it was always rickety and cheaply made.

I paced back and forth. Cursed the fiery shower settling on the roof. A gust of wind carried several more—as if Zephyr himself blew the red sparks. And then I saw it.

Flames shot from the roof.

"Pricilla!" I ran to the building, stood in the doorway, and strained to see into the dark interior.

I stepped over the threshold. "Pricilla!"

An acrid heat permeated the space and popping noises came from every direction.

Eitan snatched my arm. "Get out! The roof—"

"Pricilla!"

"Let me go!" I struggled to no avail, Eitan held tight.

"We must go, domina!"

A loud crack preceded the moan of wood from above.

Eitan dragged me into the street, away from the collapsing floor, away from the fire, away from Pricilla.

Tentacles of fire erupted from the rooftop. With a thundering crash, the third floor collapsed.

"PRICILLA!"

The roar of the inferno smothered my screams.

FIFTY-THREE

"Pricilla!"

I screamed her name again and again.

Black smoke belched through narrow windows. The building shuttered and whined. Fiery tongues spewed forth like the Chimera itself was trapped among the burning timbers.

The second-floor caved in. Flames shot into the air and bright sparks leapt onto neighboring rooftops.

An inhuman howl rose, mixed with orange flecks flying from the blaze.

"Pricilla!"

My scream died away, swallowed by the sizzling shriek of the conflagration. Molten sparks swirled about, their quick sting melting my courage, the heat searing my feet to the street.

Unable to move, I stared wide-eyed into the mouth of the inferno.

"Pricilla…" My voice was a whisper… a prayer… a wish.

My knees buckled, and I collapsed to the ground. Hot

tears watered the brick, my heaving sobs a hopeless plea to the gods.

Eitan tugged on my arm. "Get up."

People emerged from nearby buildings, the street once again filled with panic and wailing.

No one was safe. No building immune. Jupiter rained his wrath of fire down on the very city that worshiped him.

"I'm not leaving."

"It's not safe, domina. Please." Eitan wrapped his arms under my shoulders, pulled me to my feet. I howled in protest, refused to abandon Pricilla.

"I must save her!" I twisted and kicked but he held tight.

"There's nothing we can do, nothing left to save. The house collapsed." Eitan drew me away from the flames.

From Pricilla. From my dearest friend.

"No no no," I wailed, my chest cramping so tight I couldn't breathe.

Eitan wiped my face with a cinder-fouled tunic and enfolded me in his arms while I wept.

Pricilla…

OUR SUPPLIES RAN out the second day. The fire raged on. It laced and looped its way across the city, an igneous weaver of flame and char.

Flames devoured anything in its path. Public buildings, villas, temples—there was no obstacle the blaze did not consume. A ravenous burning beast laid waste to the glory of Rome.

Eitan and I remained within the city walls. We stayed in those areas already scorched, safe in the knowledge that fire does not return where there is nothing left to burn.

Folks wandered about in search of food, water, friends, and family. We hid in the shadows when they approached. Desperation makes violent company.

At night, molten gold snakes slithered up the hillsides. This fire-breathing serpent spewed its crimson breath into the sky, illuminating its destructive path. Several crept close to my villa. Other hills succumbed to the ravenous appetite of the fiery snake. Newly blackened summits and knolls were grim greeters of each dawning day.

I was grateful for Eitan's protection. Thieves and miscreants roamed in packs. They foraged through rubble, robbed survivors, and plundered shops.

On the third morning, Eitan and I huddled behind a low wall while vandals raided and torched a jewelry shop. Within moments, the building began to smolder, and with delighted whoops, the thieves moved on.

"You need water, domina. I'll go to the fountain." Eitan slung the jug's strap over his shoulder.

"Too dangerous," I said, weak from thirst. "Desperate men surround the fountains and demand outrageous sums or favors. They spill blood for a few trickles of water."

Eitan laughed. "I can handle a few thugs."

"I forbid you to risk your life for me."

"I'm thirsty too."

"We have no coin, no jewelry."

"I must try."

"I'll go with you." I lifted the basket. "Offer herbal remedies."

"They'll rape and kill you. No, you must hide until I return, domina. Bad men roam the streets."

We trudged through the rubble in search of a niche I could hide in.

"In here, domina." Eitan pointed to a crevice between a

fallen statue and a tumble of broken concrete. "There's a small fountain not far from here. You know the one."

"I do. Be careful."

Eitan was a burly man of intelligence, courage, and strength. I did not doubt his swift return.

I waited...

And waited...

A pale sun, barely discernible behind the soot and ash, began its afternoon descent.

Eitan did not return.

I withdrew from my cement cave, noted the silence, found safety in the quietude, and staggered down the street.

My thoughts focused on finding food and drink. A scrap of bread. Dregs from an abandoned wine goblet. Anything.

I found nothing in the fire-ravaged shops. Had no strength to break through bolted doors. Weary and weak, I trudged to the next street, hoping it held more promise.

It did not.

I walked onward and scrabbled for a hiding spot when men's shouts ricocheted off the buildings. It heralded their approach. A lone woman was easy prey. Each shrill scream renewed my fear. Thirst and hunger and fear turn even harmless scavengers into desperate beasts.

When it was safe, I continued on. I spied a potter's shop, its door torn off by looters. I trod inside with care, avoided the pottery shards littering the floor.

Had it not been for a black fly circling above, I might have missed the goblet on the worktable. Covered in ash, it was almost indiscernible among the other soot-covered items. I looked inside. A dead fly floated in the unknown beverage.

I plucked out the insect and drank. Every drop. Wine or beer or water, I did not know, because it tasted of ash. And only made me thirstier. My domus had water and food—if it still stood.

I left the shop, looked toward my villa, unable to see it through the haze.

I could, however, see the fire had ravaged much of Palatine Hill. Smoke tendrils curled skyward near Nero's palace.

A gray veil floated over the city, the sun an indistinct orb in the sky. Caustic air stung my throat, the smell of death and destruction inhaled with every breath. I moved toward home on heavy feet, slow as an old mule, my heart weighed down with misery.

And then my feet refused to move anymore. Head buried in my hands I crumpled to the ground and sobbed.

If we had not left the villa…. If we had not stopped to help strangers…

It was my fault Pricilla died. The guilt seared my heart, squeezed my chest like a vise, crushed my soul.

Smoke and sorrow concealed the passage of time. I don't know how long I sat there.

The clamor of hooves roused me enough to lift my head.

A centurion in an ash-dusty uniform reined his war horse near me. "Are you hurt? It's dangerous for a woman alone. Where's your family?"

I shook my head.

"Nero has returned to the city and set up a survivor's camp with food and shelter. May I take you there?"

His voice…

I looked up at the soot-smeared, weary-eyed, and grim-faced centurion.

"Marcus?"

FIFTY-FOUR

I was delirious.

The gods taunted me with this spectral vision.

"I am Marcus."

I scrabbled to my feet. Like the goddess Demeter after reuniting with her beloved daughter, Persephone, my heart burst with joy. "Marcus!"

Marcus narrowed his eyes, his face etched with sympathy for the filthy woman before him.

"It's me."

He smiled politely.

I wiped the hair from my face, fresh tears of hope trickling over my cheeks. "Am I that unrecognizable?"

He squinted. "Locusta?" Marcus leapt from his horse and gathered me in his arms. "Locusta. My love. My love. You're alive!" He pulled away. "Forgive my poor manners." He handed me his waterskin.

I drank and drank. Water had never tasted so good.

"Where's your husband?" he asked. "How were you separated from him? Is he hurt?"

"I'm still not wed. My heart loves and waits for only one man."

So brilliant was Marcus's smile, it was as though the sun burst through the gray blanket of smoke. He pressed me tight to his armor-covered body, then tore off his helmet. Our lips collided, our mouths greedy and joyous. His gentle fingers caressed my cheek, stroked my hair.

"I'll take you to the survivor's camp," he said. "Emperor Nero is gracious and opened the Field of Mars, his private gardens, and Agrippa's public buildings for the citizenry. And the legions he ordered bring food to the city for distribution."

"Take me home."

"The fire destroyed many of the homes on Caelian Hill."

"I don't live with Gaius Theon and Annona."

Since being in Nero's employ, I endured limited contact with the noble couple. When our paths crossed at horse races or gladiator games, we greeted each other with reserved cordiality. I was a troublesome acquaintance. Neither persona non grata nor desirable friend, my occupation deemed an unfortunate necessity. Gossip swirled about me, much of it exaggeration. Only Lucius met me with open arms and cheerful kisses.

"Please," I pointed in the direction of my villa. "I'll be safe in my home…if it still stands."

"Let's find out." Marcus lifted me onto the horse.

I told Marcus about Pricilla's death as the horse plodded past the charred debris, scorched buildings, and blackened skeletons. Sobs choked my throat. That's all that remained of Pricilla…

I blinked through the tears and stared into the soot-thick sky. How many had died? How many were grieving? How many searched for family? Or searched for their bodies? How many had lost everything. Friends. Family. Home. Business. Lovers.

I gripped Marcus's knee, dug my fingers into his skin. The love of my life found me. What were the odds? It was as if the gods decreed it.

Marcus nuzzled my neck.

"How long have you been in Rome?" My body relaxed, his arm around my waist comforting and safe.

"We just returned from Boudicca."

"Another triumph for the Roman army?"

"Yes, but our military victory came at great cost," said Marcus. "The Aenglania's battle tactics surprised us all."

"How much longer must you serve?"

"Two years."

I did not tell him about Nero. Or that my service to him had no end.

The horse turned the corner and I clapped my hands. The trees and plants were green.

"There." I pointed when the familiar archway came into view.

"You live here? In this grand villa?"

"Oh, Marcus, look! My home was untouched by the fire."

Barking and snarling, Lupus bounded into the front court-yard. He stopped short, his great tail sweeping back and forth when he saw me.

"And well protected," Marcus said.

"Go around back. I want to see if the garden is undamaged."

With Lupus at our heels, we rounded the side of the villa. Marcus stopped the horse under the portico.

"The gods favor me," I shouted. "The gardens and grounds are green! Oh, Marcus, do you know what this means?"

"Food?"

I laughed. "Water! Help me from this war horse."

"It's not safe. Looters and squatters are wreaking havoc in the city." He dismounted. "Stay behind me. There might be wicked men lurking about."

"You can see what a fierce dog protects my property. He's as vicious as Cerberus and as relentless as Laelaps."

Marcus lifted me down, and the dog rolled over on his back, legs splayed for a belly rub.

"Very vicious." Marcus chuckled and drew his sword. "Follow me."

We went from room to room. The villa was vacant. No damage done by either fire or looters. No sign of my hand-maid Iris either. The only visitor was a cat that startled us when it dashed across the gallery.

Marcus shook his head in amazement when we walked into my garden room. "Are you a… senator's mistress?"

"No. I'm Nero's herbalist."

Marcus aimed his sword at the rows of plants. "An herbalist is so well rewarded?"

"Nero is generous." I clasped his hand, drew him into the hall. "I'll stay here. There's plenty to eat and drink. My villa is out of danger. Flames don't cross spaces that have already been burned."

"Sparks are carried in the wind. I'm not leaving you alone. Not even with your one-headed Cerberus."

Lupus licked his hand.

"I'll be fine. But you must tell Nero my home is open to nobles who seek lodging. Tell Nero—"

"Tell Nero?" Marcus burst out laughing. "I can't simply walk up to the emperor to deliver your message. Protocol must be followed—a chain of command."

"Not necessary." I strode through the atrium, Lupus at my

heels, and headed for my office. "You'll deliver my message."

"My love, delivering a note is no different—passed from person to person—lost in the chaos."

"I have something better than a note—a personal item of Nero's."

Lupus rested his head on the desk as I pulled a drawer open and selected one of many thumb-sized flasks. Nero had designed them himself. I refilled them often with a special stimulating tincture made just for him. The potent mixture allowed Nero to stay awake and alert for many hours. He used it during lengthy senate meetings after a night of lustful pleasures.

I knew Nero. He would want everyone—nobles, senators, commanders, guards, common citizens—to be amazed by his unflagging stamina during this time. Nero understood the importance of rallying the citizenry, to be benevolent and courageous, to appear grander than life, to lead from a well-spring of energy.

Nero would appreciate the stimulating tincture for the long days ahead. He would recognize his flask immediately and be grateful.

I uncorked the flask and sniffed. "Give this to any member of the Praetorian Guard. Tell them it's from me. Have them relay the message that Locusta offers her villa and services."

"I'll do my best, my love, but I doubt an herbalist can sway a Praetorian Guardsman." Marcus smiled, his eyes twinkling in amusement. "Please, go to the Field of Mars, it's safe there."

"You don't understand. I can provide more assistance here. The villa is large and accommodates many people. I have medicines, healing herbs—every tincture and tonic is here. Nero knows this."

"What about looters?"

I patted the Lupus's head. "None will pass this beast."

Marcus blew out his frustration. "Nothing I say will convince you?"

"No."

"I'll send a trusted soldier to keep guard and will do my best to return before nightfall."

We shared a long kiss of promise and passion. After the galloping hoof beats faded into the distance, I wandered about, restless, Lupus at my side.

How would I manage without Pricilla? She had been my constant companion since I was a small child. She was my mother, handmaid, nanny, teacher, mentor, confidant, and friend. My only true friend.

I leaned against a column, tilted my head to the ashen sky, and cursed the gods. I railed against them. Ranted and swore until even Lupus howled with outrage.

A legionnaire arrived in the late afternoon to stand guard.

Iris returned and begged pardon for not having been here to welcome me back.

"I was tending a young boy at the neighboring villa. His body is wracked with coughing," she said.

I commended her efforts then told her to prepare for the arrival of many people.

Marcus did not come back that evening.

FIFTY-FIVE

Marcus did not return to the villa, but forty grateful nobles did. They arrived by wagon before dark.

The next morning, more people came. Most were clients who used my herbal concoctions for curative purposes. Many brought their servants.

The rooms in my villa were full that day. Every pillow, cushion, and blanket was put to use. I posted the tallest servant on the rooftop and told him to report on the fire's direction and progress.

Eitan and most of my servants returned bedraggled and hungry. I was under no illusion as to the reason for their hasty return. Food, shelter, and safety were powerful persuaders. I welcomed each one and set them to work.

Eitan fell on his knees before me. "I didn't abandon you, domina." He told me how a band of ruffians attacked him at the fountain. Eitan was an honest man, his blood-crusted wounds and black eye proof of his misfortune.

The next morning several handmaids gathered around me.

"We wish to commemorate Pricilla's death with a funeral ceremony," said Iris. "She was a friend to all of us."

I blinked back tears, felt my chest tighten. "What a wonderful idea. Pricilla's favorite stola can serve as a substitute for her...body." I buried my face in my hands and sobbed.

Later that day, we spread the garment on a table in the indoor garden, the bottom hem facing the valley. Iris wove a crown of herbs and set it above the neckline of the garment, and I set a coin below. Without a body, I could not seal Pricilla's fleeting spirit with a kiss and so I brought the edge of the cloth to my lips.

We gathered around the humble effigy and called out her name as the ritual required. We scattered seeds, buds, and roots on the stola as a testament to Pricilla's knowledge. And despite having seen enough of fire, we set the stola ablaze. We were bound by our tears, our love for Pricilla, and our grief for the thousands of dead and wounded that were scattered over Rome like dried leaves.

The lookout gave us reports throughout the day. It seemed no part of Rome was untouched. The flames even destroyed Nero's own palace, Domus Transitoria.

I tended to my guests. They kept my hands busy and my mind occupied. Nobles were a demanding group and begged to use my baths. Water was a precious commodity. No one had permission to bathe. Tired of their pleas, I had Eitan guard the entrance.

THE FIRE BURNED itself out on the sixth day.

On the seventh day, an imperial courier arrived on horseback to ask for balms to sooth burns. I had prepared for this and sent him back to Nero with bags stuffed with the poultice.

The days passed in a blur. The day began at dawn with chores. I tended wounds, provided ointments, and prepared sedatives.

It was good to be busy. Not to have time to dwell on my grief, fret about Marcus, or wonder about the future.

At night, I collapsed in bed, too weary to dream.

Marcus returned on the tenth night.

FIFTY-SIX

The villa was dark, the lamps extinguished—the best way to encourage my guests to sleep—when Marcus entered the atrium.

I ran into his arms and we held each other for a long time. Clutched one another tight. As though only together could we survive the hellish trauma of the past few days.

"The emperor needs more of your poultice," he said.

"I prepared more."

"I'm curious, my love."

"About what?"

"When I told the Praetorian guard I had a message from Locusta, he gave me the oddest look."

"You gave him Nero's flask?"

"I did. He took it and told me to wait. Moments later, Nero's servant arrived and asked about you and your villa. Tell me, how close are you to the emperor?"

"He has need of my herbal skills." For entertainment. For mental health. For murder.

"Mmph." Marcus removed his helmet, pulled off his

gloves. "So, what does a centurion have to do to get some food and drink here?"

"Kiss the villa's owner."

It was a long kiss. A kiss I never wanted to end. A kiss that took away all the horrors and made me feel as smitten as the day I met him.

I pulled back and licked my lips. "How ungracious of me." I called for Iris, told her wake the cook. "I know an enjoyable activity to pass the time while your meal is prepared."

"I'm all ears."

"That's not the part I'm interested in." I nibbled on his earlobe, then led him to the baths.

The bath offered a view of the city below, but I pulled the drapes closed. I didn't want a midnight-strolling guest to see me breaking my own rule. The bathing chamber was dark. Neither stars nor moon shone through the aperture in the ceiling. A gray blanket blocked out all heavenly light.

"Unlike when we first met in Gaul, I can only offer you the hot bath. I'm worried about the water supply."

Marcus set his helmet on a bench. "Will you bathe with me?"

"Of course. Who else will wash your back?" I unfastened the wide leather around his waist. "What's this?" I pointed to a long cane at his side.

"My vitis. It's for disciplining errant legionnaires."

"You beat your men?"

Marcus was gentle and kind with me, I could not imagine him acting otherwise.

"A centurion's responsibilities are unsuitable topics for a beautiful woman. Especially one who strips away the callousness of a soldier with each layer she removes." He kissed my fingertips.

I set the heavy belt on the bench next to the helmet, loosened the laces on his medallion-weighty lorica squamata. I unstrapped it, lifted the heavy armor from his broad shoulders. The vest underneath came off next. Then I set down his wide belt.

I knelt before him, unbuckled the greaves that protected his lower legs. He sighed, drew me close to his maleness while I untied the leather laces of his footwear.

He pulled me upright, eager hands stroking my hair, his fingers freeing my braids as I removed his tunic.

I stepped back to admire the naked man before me. Scars marked his arms and legs. Long angry wounds of battles won and lost. Marcus stood tall, my Hercules, the light of love shining in his eyes. Without a word, he removed my stola.

I led him to the table, poured cleansing oils over my hands and rubbed warm oil into his body. With leisured caresses, I savored each moan of pleasure my careful ministrations aroused.

I marveled at his musculature. Lingered over the curve and shape of his shoulders and torso. His body relaxed under my care, the frustrations of the week no longer etched on his face.

Drawing the strigil across his skin, I removed oils from his body. Each stroke heightened our need. Each scrape, a teasing prelude to our physical union.

"You torment me." Marcus pulled me close.

"Not yet, my love." I poured water on his head, applied clay to cleanse his hair.

Marcus closed his eyes as I rubbed, grunted in pleasure.

Scraped and scrubbed, we entered the bath. We made love with urgency. Fervent lovers seeking succor from each other. Two souls finding solace in the midst of a ravaged world.

Tongues and bodies expressed what words did not. There

was time enough for conversation later. Until then, our mouths were busy sucking, licking, and kissing. Fingers teased, probed, and stroked. Time stood still as we basked in the thrill of each other.

Again and again.

"One hunger is partially satisfied but another remains." Marcus scooped me up.

I wrapped my arms around his neck. "Take me to my room."

I woke a servant along the way, told her to clean Marcus's armor and tunic before morning.

The small marble table in my bedroom was set with food. Heaping plates of cold chicken seasoned with rosemary, vinegar-marinated mushrooms, radishes, and asparagus, herbed bread, and honeyed wine. We devoured the food. It was the best meal I can ever remember eating.

We made love throughout the night, his desires as ravenous as my own.

Morning came late. The gray blanket of smoke obscured the sun's early rays. Voices signaled the beginning of a new day.

I did not want to leave the bed. Or Marcus.

"The battle of Boudicca was nothing more than a senseless slaughter." Marcus lay on his back, hands behind his head. "There were so many atrocities. So much horror." His hand found mine beneath the blanket. "The images haunt me. Why should one war bring such a fever to my soul?"

"A young man's heart with something to prove no longer beats in your chest. Trials and misfortune change our perspectives as we get older."

"But as a centurion—a leader of men—I must endure the blood and violence that comes with victory. Other centurions seem to relish the gore as they slice open their enemy's throat or splay open a stomach."

I laced my fingers through his. "Years of battle took their toll on you."

"A worthy and honorable toll." Marcus kissed my lips. "Twenty-four years ago, I joined the legion a slave. In two more years I'll be eligible for equestrian status."

"I'll make offerings to the gods for your continued health and safety."

Marcus frowned. "Your villa far exceeds anything I can provide."

I remained silent, not certain of his meaning.

"Your father's vineyard must be doing exceptionally well."

"You don't believe I supply Nero with herbs?"

"Nero. You always call him Nero. As though he is a friend and not the Emperor of the World." Marcus rolled on his side, his head propped on his fist. "Roman gossip reaches into the farthest corners of the land."

"What gossip is that?"

"Britannicus was poisoned. Enemies of Nero die in their beds. Contenders to the throne drown in their own vomit. Betrayers and informers succumb to mysterious illnesses. It's all the work, they say, of Nero's poisoner." His eyes narrowed. "Every emperor employs a poisoner and a food taster—the world is rife with corruption—but when I see the lifestyle you enjoy—the servants at your disposal—your intimate acquaintance with the most powerful man in the world —I fear, sweet Locusta, that you are his notorious poisoner."

Marcus's gaze held steady. I dared not look away.

"I have no choice," I whispered.

Marcus closed his eyes. "How did this inglorious appointment come to pass?"

I revealed everything. Almost everything.

I told Marcus of Agrippina's death threat if I refused to poison Emperor Claudius. Of her treachery and my imprisonment. I explained how Lucius's recommendation granted me an audience with Nero. I disclosed Nero's need for the love elixir and other tonics.

I did not confess everything. It served no purpose to reveal sordid details. There was no need to tell Marcus exactly how I formed an alliance with Nero and Lucius.

Marcus sat up, his back to me. "You're an assassin."

I touched his shoulder. "You kill more people than I do."

"You can't compare our professions." He stood and crossed the room.

"Why not? You stab the enemy with a dagger and sword — gruesome, violent deaths—leave men to die while a river of blood flows from their body."

"I fight for the glory of Rome." He spun around, eyes hard and cold. "I serve in the legions to bring the light of Roman civilization to a heathen world. To bring culture and industry to the barbarians."

"You maim and slaughter thousands of people to fill Rome's coffers."

"How many people have you murdered, Locusta?"

"How many have you?"

Marcus lifted an amphora of wine, filled the goblet. He quaffed the drink, wiped his mouth with the back of his hand. "The Roman legion brings education, aqueducts, roads, and sanitation to primitive hordes."

"And Roman domination and slavery and taxes."

Marcus threw the goblet across the room. "You have no idea how they live! They dwell in shacks of hay and mud. Wear animal pelts. They're hungry, filthy, and piss and shit wherever they please. They're an illiterate godless people. We bring them the gift of civilization—art, literacy, medicine, philosophy."

"I, too, work for the glory of Rome. We serve the same master." I rose from the bed, my arms reaching for him. I didn't want to fight. I loved him. We both killed people. Only our weapons were different.

Marcus turned away, his gaze focused on the hazy view of Rome through the narrow window. "The sun is high. I must leave."

I went to the chair where Iris had laid his clean uniform. "So soon?"

"For many years, Locusta, I worshipped the god of warriors, Mithras." His voice was hitched, thick with emotion. "Not anymore."

"Your warrior spirit is tarnished by a lifetime of battles. I'm not surprised you worship another god." With a sad smile, I held out his tunic.

Marcus ran his hand over its thickness. "When our legion returned from Britannia, I paid a visit to Simon Peter. Do you remember helping the old man who suffered from semitertian fever?"

"The elder who speaks for the god of the poor?"

"Yes." Marcus donned the tunic. "He asked after you, said your gift of healing comes from the one true god."

I helped secure his armor. "Gift? Is that the name given to define toil and resourcefulness? The name to describe an ability that frees and imprisons? A gift!?"

"No gift is without troubles." Marcus sat on the chair, buckling and tying the straps of his greaves. "Peter spoke of forgiveness and eternity."

"The Elysian fields are a myth." I lifted his heavy belt from the table. "Have you become a follower of The Way? A believer in this god for slaves?"

"I have." It was a whisper.

"I don't understand. Why did you turn your back on Roman gods?"

"Do you remember Saul, my slave with the painful toe? The one you helped many years ago?"

"What of it?"

"On a few occasions he spoke to me of his god. I was too young and ambitious to pay heed. Now, I look about me and I see despair and greed and anger and hatred." He ran his hand through his hair. "The Way is a balm to my soul. It's as simple as that." Marcus secured his belt. "There's trouble afoot. Already the camps buzz with rumors that the emperor payed men to start the fire."

"Nero? Burn his own city?! Thieves threw torches into buildings—I witnessed this several times—but they were troublemakers bent on mayhem. Nero doesn't hire commoners."

"Another rumor claims he played the lyre and sang while watching Rome burn."

"That's a lie. Nero's own palace was destroyed, and he was in Actium at the time."

"I only repeat the gossip, Locusta."

"Rome's burning wasn't because of arson."

"Are you so sure? I heard a few patricians in the camps claim that followers of The Way started the fire."

"For what purpose?"

"To destroy this wicked city."

"Why are you telling me this?" I put my hands on my hips.

"Dark days are ahead for Rome."

"The smoke will dissipate soon enough," I said. "The sun will shine again. Rome will rise like a phoenix. Stronger and more beautiful than ever."

"And rife with corruption," Marcus clasped my hand. "Will you visit Simon Peter? Hear his words. Listen with your heart."

"I have no time for such things. I have enough gods."

"I loved you the moment I saw you. I remember how the sun shone down—you looked like a goddess—and knew you were the one the soothsayer prophesied of. The memory of your face and touch and voice sustained me during many somber days." His eyes narrowed. "Nero has changed you. Made you cruel and—"

I jerked away my hand. "Cruel? Not so cruel it prevented you from making love to me all night!"

"I love you, but I cannot—will not—wed an assassin."

"Oh?! But I can wed a centurion? You're reasoning makes no sense." I glared at him. "Is it because my job brings more wealth and prestige? Is that why? Are you jealous?"

Marcus recoiled. "Jealous of things? No. There's honor in my profession. Not yours. You kill with deception and treachery."

I stood tall. "And running someone through with a sword makes you more moral? More righteous?"

Marcus looked away. "My eyes have seen enough of death. When my commission is complete, I'll seek peace. I want to fill my days with goodness and joy."

"You can't have that with me?"

He spread out his arms. "You live in a villa of poison."

"You're jealous of my wealth and status," I said. "You're envious of my friendship with Nero."

"I don't envy your alliance or the murders you commit in his name."

My fists clenched. "How dare you come to me last night, eat my food, share my bed, only to tell me you despise my profession and that I will never make you happy! Get out!" I pointed to the door, my jaw clenched.

Marcus lowered the helmet over his head, and a battle-hardened centurion glared back. "We cannot be happy together while you're the emperor's assassin."

"You're a fool of lowborn birth whose understanding of the world has never changed," I hissed. "I see you for what you are now. A former slave boy who got lucky enough to become a centurion. You're not worthy of my love." I flung a palla over my body and stalked from the room.

VINES
&
VENOM

FIFTY-SEVEN

Marcus departed the villa. I was glad. He was a hypocrite. Stubborn. Thick-headed.

Centurions were warriors known for fearlessness and brutality. They led legionnaires into battle, fought until the end, slaughtered for the glory of Rome, in the name of Imperator Nero Claudius Caesar Augustus Pontifex Maximus.

Centurion or poisoner, the end results were the same. How could Marcus not understand that? And how could he not comprehend my predicament? He could no more desert his military post than I could defy an order from Nero. Both offenses were punishable by torture or death.

Marcus did not return. Our once bright love was forever darkened by sharp words. By my poisonous tongue.

I pushed thoughts of him aside. I had more important things to worry about. Food and water for the displaced nobles. Making more salve for burn victims.

The week's events took a heavy toll. Pricilla's death was a constant ache that squeezed my chest and filled my eyes with tears. I missed our teasing banter and our heartfelt conversations. My mind played tricks. I thought I heard her voice, felt her presence by my side, or inhaled her scent.

My villa was crowded with people, yet I never felt more alone. Pricilla and Marcus, the two people I loved and trusted most, were gone.

I had left prison a young woman, and although Nero made me wealthy, he destroyed any chances for an ordinary life. A life with a husband and children. A life with love. At twenty-nine years, I was well past the age of finding a husband. No virtuous man would wed a professional poisoner.

Power, privilege, and prosperity. I had it all. Or…it was all I had.

I looked around my villa. Graceful statues, colorful murals, polished marble, exotic urns, elegant textiles, savory meals—these were the fruits of my profession. A life built from death.

Marcus refused to see the imperial chains that bound me. Perhaps he loved the memory of a girl who no longer existed. That naïve maiden in the vineyard gave rise to a sophisticated woman who moved in elite circles. The most elite circle, Nero's laurel crown.

I could bed many men. I was beset with offers. Nobles. Senators. And, of course, Lucius. Although no man wished to wed a poisoner, they had no qualms about seducing one.

WEEKS PASSED.

Each day more guests left. The displaced nobles visited relatives or traveled to country estates while they rebuilt their fire-ravaged homes.

The fire devastated the city. Several districts razed by the flames, others scorched to ruin. Much of Nero's palace on

Palatine Hill was destroyed. Only a few districts had been untouched by the blaze.

By late September, the last guest departed. I was relieved. My body and spirit were exhausted. I had little appetite and was frequently ill. I rested much of the time and pondered my life.

Without Pricilla, I had no one to share my day, no friend to discuss new mixtures. One does not appreciate true friendship until it's gone.

I had no desire to make new friends. I declined invitations to Fire parties, which were all the rage. I was horrified when I found out servants in red tunics served flambéed meat and seafood. And orange-stained prostitutes entertained guests with morbid fire dances.

I stayed in my villa, tended herbs, created new potions, and studied Dioscorides' Medical Materials, his book of medicinal plants.

My students returned to the Herbal Academy, where we focused on healing remedies rather than love elixirs and poisonous potions.

My fatigue and bouts of nausea finally subsided in the final days of October.

I WAS BUSY. Nero's messengers made frequent visits for a supply of the energy elixir. Nero spent countless hours coordinating relief efforts. His love for the common people compelled him to authorize public housing for the homeless and lower grain prices. He used the devastation wrought by the fire to begin civic improvement. He drew plans for wider streets and established building regulations. Nero was determined Rome should rise like a phoenix from the charred ruins.

Nero's good works ought to have pleased the citizenry, but they did not.

"The people are angry." Lucius lounged on a sofa while a servant fed him olives.

I had not seen Lucius for the past two months. He was one of the lucky nobles who had been summering in Antium the week of the fire.

"The poor are ungrateful," I said. "Nero hires them for his construction projects—improves their derelict apartments. Why do they complain?"

"Because Nero appropriated one hundred and twenty-five hectares of Palatine property for his new palace."

"What?! Why so much land for a palace?"

"Not just any palace, Domus Aurea." Lucius fluttered his fingers in the air. "I hear it will be a vulgar spectacle of opulence complete with parks, zoos, lakes—"

I threw an olive pit at him. "You're joking."

"I have it on good authority." He threw it back.

I shrugged. "Well, the poor ought to be thankful, he does a lot of good for them."

"It's not just the palace inciting their wrath. Nero claims followers of The Way started the fire." Lucius grit his teeth and winced.

I knew that look.

"And?" I urged.

"You know Nero, he devised a gruesome way to punish them." He sucked air through his clenched teeth. "He calls it poetic justice."

"What does he do to them?"

"He ties them to a pole, sticks them in the ground at the palace's entrance, and lights them on fire."

ON DIES EMPERII, the celebration marking Nero's ascent to the throne, I ventured into the city proper to join the festivities. I had avoided people and the city for too long. It was time to cast off the lethargy and grief that had been clinging to me like wet clothes.

I took Eitan with me. I admired flower-festooned statues, ate delectable treats, and enjoyed gladiatorial spectacles.

Crowds of drunken revelers danced in the streets. The populace might be cursing Nero under their breath, but no one refused free food, games, and entertainment. It was difficult to believe Nero's popularity was on the decline.

My belly was full and my heart light when I decided to return home. A mob delayed us. They were freedmen and women. And they were upset. Shouting, fists raised, and wailing.

"Find out what's wrong," I told Eitan.

Eitan disappeared into the crowd.

"They're following Simon Peter, an elder for The Way. The soldiers take him to be crucified," he said when he returned.

Simon Peter? That harmless old man?

"He offers only kind words to the poor. Why is he being crucified?"

Eitan looked down, spoke quietly. "The emperor blames followers of the Christ for the fire." He shuffled close, curved his hand near his mouth. "Nero claims they used some Jewish secret code… gematria…to spread their treason."

Lucius had mentioned this gematria. It was a cipher of corresponding numbers and letters.

Eitan's eyes were watery, his face taut with restrained emotion.

"Are you a follower of The Way?" I asked.

His eyes widened. "No, domina. Not really."

"What does that mean?"

Eitan scratched his beard. "I heard Simon Peter speak once. He was wise and... gave me comfort." His eyes tracked the passing crowd.

"Shall we follow them?"

His face lit up. "If you desire, domina."

I did. I kind of liked the old man.

We trailed behind the crowd and soon there were people behind us. Before long, we were swept into the throng that headed toward the Circus of Nero.

FIFTY-EIGHT

The soldiers who led the procession halted before a great Egyptian obelisk. It was the preferred site for crucifixions. The crowd congregated around the cross, believers and gawkers vying for a better view.

Men and women wept and tore at their garments. Others lifted hands to the sky crying, "Jesus Christ" and "Lord."

Eitan and I stayed in the back.

"What's happening?" I asked.

The crowd began to moan. A man pushed passed us, his voice loud and reverential. "Simon Peter says he's not worthy to be crucified like the Christ! The soldiers nail him upside down!"

Upside down?

Eitan and I shouldered our way through the press of people. Soldiers kept everyone at bay, ordered onlookers to retreat, brandished their swords.

Followers of The Way clung to one another, their keening protests growing more desperate.

"Why does Nero order Simon Peter's crucifixion?" asked one.

"First, we are persecuted, now our elder is murdered," cried another.

"Simon Peter is innocent!"

"Don't blame us for the fire!"

Between shoulders and heads, I caught a glimpse of the execution. Simon Peter's ankles were crossed and bound tight to the plank. The soldiers had torn off his tunic and hammered spikes through his hands.

Streams of crimson flowed from his wound. Seeped into the dirt. The followers of Christ lay prostrate before him, their prayerful lamentations rising into the air like a sacred chorus.

I nudged Eitan. "It will take days for him to die like that."

Eitan's mouth hung open, his gaze fixed and oddly glazed.

A woman crawled toward Peter.

"Stay back!" The solider kicked her.

The soldiers laughed and taunted the faithful.

"This man is a traitor!"

"Where is your god now?" One soldier smashed Simon Peter's knees with a club.

"Who else wants to join Peter's Way?"

"Summon your Jesus Christ! Beg him to save Peter."

"Followers of The Way are guilty of hatred toward the human race!"

The believers cried and shouted, and yet Simon Peter's face radiated peace. I was mystified. Love, devotion, and forgiveness emanated from the elder. This god, this Jewish god, had bestowed Peter with the courage to bear his execution with serenity.

"I can't watch anymore." I turned away as the soldiers struck Simon Peter again and again.

I pushed through the crowd, sickened by the soldiers' abuse and saddened by the execution of a good man.

Followers of The Way were mere slaves, servants, and plebeians. Harmless people. An insignificant group. Why did Nero blame them for the fire?

I covered my nose with my palla and strode away, impatient to be free of the mob.

Why did these people turn their back on Roman gods?

Jupiter, god of thunder. Juno, goddess of fertility. Mars, god of war. Venus, goddess of wisdom. Neptune, ruler of the sea. Vulcan, god of volcanoes. Diana, goddess of the hunt. Vesta, goddess of the hearth.

They replaced all our gods for one god. A single deity. How absurd!

I emerged from the rabble, certain Eitan followed. He had not. I waited, impatient and miserable. And angry.

Nero had no cause to kill Simon Peter. No reason to blame these humble followers of The Way.

Eitan finally emerged from the crowd, his mouth open, a dazed look on his face.

"Are you ill?" I touched his shoulder.

"I had a vision." Eitan rubbed his eyes. "Of a grand temple rising from the blood-soaked earth where Simon Peter is crucified."

"Rome has temples upon temples. No doubt Nero plans to build more."

"No, domina, not a temple for Roman gods. This temple was the beacon of hope for all the world. A temple for Simon Peter."

"For Simon Peter?" My lips skewed. "Temples are built for gods. This man is no one, a follower of an insignificant religion."

Eitan shook his head. "I saw a great temple—shining and bright—with a great dome."

"You had a vision of Nero's Golden Palace."

Eitan's face had an odd glow. "Elder Peter will never be forgotten."

"Without their leader, these people will soon seek another god."

"As you say, domina." Eitan dipped his head.

THE FOLLOWING MORNING, I found Iris weeping in the hall, her tunic pressed to wet eyes.

"What's wrong?"

She wiped her face. "He's gone, domina."

"Who's gone?"

"Eitan. He left the villa."

"Is he on an errand?"

Iris's head swayed back and forth. "Last night Eitan told me about seeing Simon Peter's upside-down crucifixion. He told me about his vision."

"About a great temple."

"Yes, and he told me Simon Peter told him to go to Jerusalem and preach the word of Jesus Christ to everyone he meets along the way." She wrung her hands.

Eitan had left out that part.

Disobedience could not be tolerated. I gathered the servants. "I contracted a bounty hunter. When Eitan is returned, you'll witness the penalty for defiance."

It was a necessary lie. Fear made good servants. In truth, I took no action against Eitan. He had kept me safe during the first days of the fire, was beaten almost to death attempting to get me water and had returned to the villa when he could have run away. His only transgression was escaping servitude to answer the call of his new mission. One inspired by Simon Peter.

I was not a servant like Eitan, but I was a slave to Nero. Neither of our lives were our own. How could I punish Eitan for having courage enough to risk his life for freedom?

Simon Peter's crucifixion haunted me, his serenity during the soldiers' torments a testament to his faith. There must be virtue in a religion that inspires a man to bear agony with such grace.

Three days later, I heard conflicting news about Simon Peter. One source claimed the soldiers—exasperated he had not died—chopped off his head. Another source alleged he escaped with the help of disciples. I wondered, even hoped, Eitan was a party to the rescue.

RUMORS ABOUT EMPEROR NERO flowed like the Tiber. Senators spewed venom about Nero's loathsome behavior. Belched their displeasure about him during dinner parties.

I saw Nero's madness myself when I left his imperial villa one evening.

Five flaming torches lined the pathway, grisly columns of flesh that smoldered and glowed. Imperial guards dragged out a sixth person. They bound the man to a pole with cord, doused his body with oil, and set him ablaze—a human torch lighting the way to the palace.

My stomach heaved, and I retched onto the ground.

"It's a common occurrence," the carpentum driver said. "A warning to the followers of The Way."

Sickened by Nero's abhorrent behavior, I returned home, my appetite gone, the horror of charred flesh seared into memory.

The next morning my mood had not improved. My stomach twisted, the burning victims blistered into memory.

Nero's outrageous behavior continued, and it reached into all facets of his life and rule. He summoned me more frequently. Demanded a fresh supply of the love elixir.

And poison.

When he asked for poison, I asked two questions. Swift or slow? Painful or peaceful?

He wanted slow and painful for his most hated enemies. Treasonous conspirators received no mercy. Nero demanded they be in excruciating pain for days. Ignorant accomplices were granted quick deaths.

For his most hated rivals, Nero made special requests. Like death by vomiting for a licentious old senator involved in the Circensian assassination attempt.

Nero's popularity with senators was declining, but I had a far more important concern. One that grew larger every day.

FIFTY-NINE

"I'm with child." I walked between rows of plants.

Lucius snorted. "Such a shame it's not mine."

I separated belladonna with a wooden fork and studied the deadly black berries that hung from drooping green stalks. It was a profitable and versatile herb. Small doses acted as a mild sedative. Larger doses brought death.

I had stopped handling poisonous plants the moment I discovered my womb carried life. Oils, thorns, and powdery residues might permeate my skin and leak into my womb.

Helene, my best student, prepare the requested tonics under my supervision. I refused to compromise the wellbeing of my growing child. Marcus's child.

I looked from the belladonna to Lucius. "Sarra has given you many children. You don't need mine."

"You misunderstand." He leaned forward and leered.

I ruffled his hair. "I will not be your mistress."

"Yes, you will. Eventually, I'll wear you down." Lucius touched my stomach. "Why do you keep it?"

"I want the child."

"You love the man?"

I turned away. I did love Marcus. Loved his charm, compassion and dedication. Loved how he made love to me as though I was his most precious possession. But it could never be. He made that clear. And I could never leave Nero.

"I don't want to talk about it," I said.

"I'll take that as a yes." He crossed his arms. "Why did you wait so long to share the news?"

"I wasn't certain." My monthly courses were so irregular I had stopped tracking my womb's rhythm long ago. It was only after two nauseous months that I suspected. And several more watching my belly bloom that I knew. But not until I felt the quickening, did I allow my heart to bloom with real joy.

"You? How is that possible? My wife knows immediately. Her monthly blood is late."

"Long ago, Pricilla gave me a tonic to..." I fluttered my hand. "I thought I was barren."

"Well, I'm happy for you, but I have to admit, I'm envious of the man who has your heart. Now, if only my wife would stop having children. Five girls! What dowries I'll have to pay in the future." He curved his eyes to the ceiling and shook his head.

His comment stabbed my heat. Lucius's daughters had both legitimacy and a noble birthright. Their potential suitors would crave the rank and privilege Lucius's family name bestowed. My child would not have that advantage.

"Oh, Lucius, I'm an unmarried woman. What will people think?"

"They'll think the man had a lot of courage to bed Nero's assassin." Lucius kissed my cheek. "Is the father in Rome?"

"I don't know."

Lucius gave me an odd look.

"What does it matter where he is? He doesn't approve of my profession."

"He's a fool," he snorted. "As long as Nero lives you're a wealthy woman, and his child will grow up in luxury. Take heart, if you give birth to a boy, perhaps the childless Nero will adopt him."

I burst out laughing.

"I'm not joking, my pretty poisoner. Remember, Claudius adopted Nero."

"Noble tongues would certainly wag."

"Who cares what gossip a few old matrons spread? They're spiteful bitches, angry because their husbands no longer prefer lying between their legs."

"You're right, Lucius. This is a fortunate child."

MY BELLY GREW large during the autumn months. Concealed beneath a loose stolae and cloak, my condition went unnoticed until the fifth month. My breasts, however, doubled in size, or so Lucius claimed with glee each time he visited.

"If I were your babe, I'd suck on your breasts forever," he said.

I expected Lucius's advances to decrease as my stomach swelled. They didn't. Instead, his requests were bolder with each visit. I laughed at every lascivious appeal, slapped away his roving hands with playfulness. Lucius loved me. Loved me despite my continued refusal to bed him. Loved me despite my profession.

IN FEBRUARIUS, Nero requested my presence. He was singing

when I entered his chambers, his weak voice wavering as he warbled a chord. With a breathy squeak, he dismissed the slaves and told me to sit down.

"I've never heard a more beautiful voice," I lied.

"And you never will. I'm gifted with supreme vocal artistry." Nero pointed to my belly. "I thought you were getting fat. I see now you're with child. I didn't know you wed."

"I did not."

Nero's brows shot up. "I will command the man to make you a proper wife. Is he married? A senator? Is it Lucius? It's obvious he loves you."

"The father of my child is dead." It was the safest thing to say.

"Do not lie to the emperor, Locusta. I've killed others for such falseness." He smirked. "Or rather, you killed them for me."

I lowered my eyes.

"You wish to protect the father's identity, so be it. Or maybe he is dead, poisoned by your own hand." Nero hooted with delight, then changed the subject with a wave of his hand. "The Feast of the Lupercal is almost here. I decreed a host of tournaments and festivities on a scale unrivaled by any previous emperor. I ordered Poppaea to thrust her hand out to every runner. With so many athletes how can her womb not unlock its treasures?"

"A quest for fertility demands all measures be taken." I nodded despite having no faith in the superstition that the touch of a naked young noble racing through the streets healed a barren womb.

"I want to leave nothing to chance on that day. You will prepare a special tonic for Poppaea in time for the Feast of the Lupercal. I will have an heir to the throne."

I did as Nero asked.

Poppaea drank my womb-opening tonic. She touched the hand of each Lupercal runner. Nero bedded her three times a day.

Poppaea did not conceive.

SIXTY

The tightening of my womb woke me on the kalends of Maius. It was the day we sacrificed a pregnant sow to Maia, the earth goddess.

"I'll see my babe today," I told Helene while inspecting her preparation of a masticated herb.

"Such a fortunate day." Helene's hand hovered over my swollen belly. "Are you certain the babe comes today? I had many false pains."

"Today. I feel it." I took a tray from the table and eased myself into a chair. Separating the buds from the seeds should keep my mind busy.

It did not.

A second tightening came, longer than the first. I unwound the linen straps that supported my belly, set my hands on the taut skin. A half hour later another contraction came.

"Summon the midwife," I said after the fourth contraction.

I knew the midwife well. Had shared herbal knowledge with her. I trusted her. She delivered many noble babies.

During my pregnancy, she had told me to anoint my genitals with herbs, inject goose fat into my birth passage, and rub fresh olive oil into my belly to prevent unsightly stretch marks. She insisted frequent bathing provided relief from my heavy womb. She said wine baths had the most therapeutic value. But because she couldn't explain why in a way that made sense to me, I only took warm baths.

I lumbered from the garden room to the peristylium and reclined on the sofa.

The first real excruciating pain seized me a few moments later. The second stole my breath.

"Where's the midwife?" I clutched the sofa, my knuckles white, my forehead sweat-soaked.

"I'll find her, domina." Iris ran off.

Frequent contractions were good. They heralded a quick birth. I bore them with joy. For a short time. Then they lengthened, lasted so long I curled up and groaned.

Iris offered honeyed wine and meat. I declined, the pain overwhelmed all senses. After the tenth wrenching contraction I stumbled to my chambers with the help of Iris and another handmaid.

The sun was high overhead when the midwife arrived.

"I'm glad you have the sense to follow my instructions." She set a light hand on the small of my back.

I was standing beside the bed, bent over, my forehead resting on a pillow. In mid contraction, my response was a moan.

"Good, good. All is well. You have strength to stand." The midwife pulled sea sponges and lemons from her bag, then sent her apprentice for fresh olive oil and pennyroyal. "Have you taken herbs for the pain?"

"No," I said after the pain subsided.

The midwife looked amazed. "The infamous imperial poisoner does not use her own concoctions?"

"Not on the most important day of my life. I will not dull my body or mind with such potions. I want to hasten the birth not prolong it."

"Ah, here it is." The midwife watched as two servants carried in the birthing chair. "Put it here." She pointed to the middle of the room.

I made to get up.

"Not yet," said the midwife. Let's check the baby's position in the womb." With her hands covered in olive oil, the midwife slowly crisscrossed my belly. "Good, good. All is—" She drew in a hiss, eyes tapering into slits.

"Tell me!" I gripped her hand as another pain seized me.

"The baby is active—a good sign—unfortunately, the head is not in the best place."

"Breech?"

"No, thank the gods. Your son's face will be staring into the heavens when he enters the world."

"It's a boy?"

"Of course. A woman of your strength and courage only produces male children." The midwife rubbed my lower back. "Any pain here?"

"No."

"Good, good. Back labor is difficult to endure." The midwife took my hand. "Come now, the real labor of labor begins. Lying and sitting will not open your womb."

I rose from the bed on unsteady legs and stood. It was the best way to encouraging the babe to drop into the birth passage.

The day's shadows lengthened as much as my contractions.

"It's time to greet your child." The midwife pointed to the water pooling at my feet.

"I feel pressure."

"Good, good. All is well."

The midwife guided me to the cushioned birthing chair. I collapsed on its seat, whimpering from the unbearable weight that pushed down on my bottom.

The midwife's apprentice slid a stool under my feet to accommodate my short height and then a pain ripped through me with such force I screamed.

"Don't waste effort on screaming." The midwife donned an apron, covered her hands with olive oil again, and slid slick fingers inside me. "Massaging the wombs' gate will encourage it to open. Oh, good, the opening is as large as my fist—I feel his head."

Another hand covered my anus.

"My apprentice will stay your muscles to prevent tearing," said the midwife. "Bear down with the next pain."

No sooner did the midwife finish wrapping her hands in linen when a weight-filled agony erupted. My shriek rose into the air like an eagle.

"Good… good. Let the baby come. Don't hold back."

My chin dropped. My jaw clenched. I pushed! A singular fury within me thrusted downward.

"I see the head, one more pain and—"

The searing pressure was an agony unlike any other. As though my bottom would burst open. As though my body split apart. I howled, cursed, cried, and pushed.

The babe's head emerged. I felt the body wiggle past, felt the joy of life come forth from my womb.

The pressure and pain ceased.

"My baby." I stretched out my hands.

Before she placed my child in my arms, the midwife

pinched its little foot. The babe let loose a lusty cry and the babe's purple face turned bright red.

I gave birth to a son. Marcus's son. Tears wet my cheeks.

"Place him at your breast."

With his tiny head in the crook of my arm, I set my babe to my breast and coaxed him to nurse. He blinked twice, latched on, and I felt a weak tug at my nipple.

Another pull at my womb and the life cord slithered from my body. The midwife cut it and helped me to bed.

Marcus's son suckled, and my fingers caressed his round face and stroked his head. I lifted his tiny clenched hand and counted his miniature fingers. I touched each toe and tickled his feet when the sleepy babe stopped suckling.

My son. Marcus's son. My child would lack nothing. I would give him the world. All that my wealth might buy.

The midwife massaged my stomach. Pressed down the soft skin. "Rest today. Tomorrow stroll around the atrium. If your bleeding becomes heavy, summon me."

I looked at her.

"Well, if you need a second opinion." She smoothed the blanket around me. "When is the wet nurse arriving?"

"I'm nursing my own child."

"Locusta!" She laughed. "How scandalous. Why?"

My profession had exposed the truth about the human body. We absorbed harmful and beneficial substances in a myriad of ways.

"Plants thrive best in fertile soil. Everything I eat and drink is the finest quality. Who better to nurse my child?" I kissed the top of my baby's head.

"Instead of a Poison Academy you should provide well-fed wet nurses to noble women."

"The students are not taught to poison." My voice pricked like a thorn. "They're taught to heal."

"I…" She winced. "I'm sorry. Yes, of course, that's what I meant." The midwife tucked her linen wrappings into her birthing kit.

I held my son close. "A school of poison. Is that what people call it?"

"Sometimes. Healing and harming—you can't know how to do one without knowing the other. Even in my profession."

Occasionally, she was summoned to abort a child and needed my expertise when there was a complication that involved excessive bleeding.

She kissed the top of my forehead. "Juno blessed you today. Your labor was short, the delivery without incident. The gods and goddesses favor you."

When the midwife departed, I told my handmaids to leave. I wanted to be alone. To weep. With exhaustion. With joy and gratitude. With anger and resentment. With love and adoration. My emotions were a waterfall, a hundred feelings churning inside.

There was no one to share my happiness. No husband. No Pricilla. No mother. No relatives.

I wiped the tears from my eyes and gazed into my son's face. I had to be strong for his sake. I must make certain he was accepted by the right families. Without proper associations, without noble connections, he would not prosper in the Roman world.

I would do anything to secure my son's place in Roman society.

Anything.

SIXTY-ONE

"What's the name of this fatherless child?" asked Lucius.

I looked down at my chubby-cheeked son as he suckled. "Telemachus."

"You name him after Ulysses, the character in Homer's poem? The son who waits twenty years for his father's return?"

I stroked the top of Telemachus's head. "The tale ends happily."

Lucius swept his arm back and forth as though he held a sword. "Yes, father and son kill all of Penelope's suitors." Lucius swung his head from side to side. "I appear to be the only suitor present."

"You're not a suitor. You're a married man with a loving wife and children."

Telemachus pulled away from my breast and gave me a sated smile.

"I will not discuss that horrid woman." Lucius shuddered. "I came to gossip about Nero."

"Anything new?"

"Senators, nobles, commoners—everyone is angry because Nero uses prime land in the middle of Rome to build his palace."

I put Telemachus over my shoulder and patted his back. "That's old news."

Lucius sat beside me. "Not just any palace. And not a palace to live in."

"What?"

"There are neither sleeping quarters nor kitchens in the plans." He scooted closer.

"What sort of palace is it?"

"A colossal villa of revelry. Nero intends to host the most spectacular parties the world has ever seen." His hand stroked Telemachus's face. "He should have been my child. My heir."

I lifted up my son, sprinkled kisses on his chubby leg, then passed him to Iris who hovered nearby. "Set him down to sleep."

Lucius sidled closer, his hand grazing my milk-swollen breast.

I brushed his hand aside, tried to stand, but he shifted his body and pinned me down.

"What do you want?" I asked.

"I love you, Locusta. I've always loved you. From the first day I saw you at my parents' villa. You were a fleshly gift from Bacchus, vine-fresh, lips as ripe and luscious as grapes bursting to be picked." One finger traced my lips. "I'm a good friend to you." He whisked his lips across mine.

"A very dear friend."

"So dear, I pleaded with Nero to save your life." He nuzzled my neck.

"There's no need to remind me. You'll always have my undying gratitude."

"If not for me, you would be dead or very nearly so."

"You can't take all the credit. Nero needed me."

Lucius wiped away a drop of milk from my breast with one finger and stuck it in his mouth. "Mmm, sweet and creamy. Oh, now, don't frown, my love. You know me too well to be surprised by anything I do. Or want. Or desire."

His head moved to my breast.

"Lucius." I pushed him away.

"Don't reject me. Since the fire—since Pricilla's death, I've been your only confidant. Your only true friend."

"I look forward to your visits."

"Your lavish lifestyle is due to my introductions and recommendations. Without me you would have no referrals and no customers."

"You take all the credit?"

"How profitable is a skill if no one knows about it?" Lucius kissed my eyelids. "I want you."

"You know I love another." I had told Lucius about Marcus a few months ago.

"Your centurion is gone. He left on the next campaign. He left you, Locusta. He walked out of this villa and will never return."

"I sent him away. I was angry."

"You've sent me away many times. I always return."

"Marcus is proud—he did what I told him to do."

"Neither my pride nor your orders ever keep me away. Send me away a thousand times and I'll return stronger and more in awe of you than before. I'm always here for you. I will always be here for you. And for your son. Always." Lucius lowered his head, latched on to my breast, and suckled.

I did not pull away. My milk began to flow. He moaned as he sucked, and his hand moved between my thighs, seeking the desired spot.

His words stung. Marcus would never return. How foolish to wait for a lover who left without so much as a backward glance.

Lucius had been a steadfast friend for many years. He never betrayed a confidence, never judged my actions. He accepted me for all I had become. Lucius would see to it that Roman society accepted my son.

I wrapped my legs around Lucius. Yielded to the pleasures of his devotion. He took his time, teased me until I begged for him. It was only after I moaned in ecstasy that he entered and swore everlasting love.

SIXTY-TWO

I surrendered to Lucius that day. He was a dedicated friend and lover. I trusted him.

Lucius convinced me to partake in all the delights Rome offered. He promised our alliance would benefit my son. He was right. Lucius had already risen in the ranks of the Roman elite, his connections with stoic senators, nefarious procurators, and wealthy administrators extended far beyond his father, Gaius Theon. Lucius would provide the necessary introductions when Telemachus came of age.

Lucius convinced me to forge alliances with nobles, equestrians, shopkeepers, and harlots alike. He introduced me to the best and worst of Roman citizenry. Through his associations, I secured an educated nanny for Telemachus, purchased exotic herbs from foreign lands, and received invitations to coveted dinner parties.

I was determined my son become a man of wealth and power. Anything less was unthinkable.

As the Roman elite drank, gossiped, fornicated, entrapped, and conspired, I grew wealthier. Tonics for aching heads. Elixirs for seduction. Narcotics for forgetfulness. Venoms for threats. Poisons for murder.

A WILD-EYED MESSENGER raced into the indoor garden. "Domina! The emperor requires your immediate presence!"

I was in the middle of preparing a calming tonic for an unscrupulous senator. I glanced from the panicked messenger to my son, who slept peacefully in Iris's arms. "In a moment."

"Domina, I beg of you. Come now. Nero threatened to stab me if I don't bring you at once."

"Iris?" I lifted an eyebrow.

"I'll hold Tele in my arms until your return. Or until he wakes up."

My curiosity was piqued. Nero had never summoned me like this before.

I picked up my herbal kit, kissed Telemachus's forehead, and followed the messenger from the room.

The messenger sprinted down the short corridor, tore past the atrium, and jumped over Lupus sprawled in the entrance hall.

A light chariot stood outside. It had no palace insignia or distinguishing markings. A chariot for secret palace business.

"Hurry!" The messenger climbed into the chariot, extended one hand, and helped me into the three-sided enclosure.

I pulled the herbal kit's strap over my head.

"Hold on." With a crack of the whip, the two-horse team bolted away.

My hands gripped the ledge as the horses galloped down the driveway. The chariot turned so sharply into the road I almost fell off. We hurtled through the streets of Rome. Commoners scattered like crickets. A vegetable stand demolished as the chariot cut a corner.

My first chariot ride. How exhilarating! No wonder Nero traveled great distances to participate in races. The speed and thrill were more intoxicating than any tonic.

I clenched the wicker frame, knuckles white, heart pounding in my throat. We passed under the palace arch all too soon.

A handmaid waited at the entrance of the imperial palace. "Hurry," she cried.

I ran behind her, imagined all sorts of misfortunes. Wondered if this was a bit of theatrics. Nero might just have a bad headache or be out of the love elixir.

The handmaid stopped in front of Poppaea's private chambers. "In there." She made no move to push away the heavy fabric.

Another arm reached through the drapery, seized my arm, and pulled me inside.

Blood was everywhere.

SIXTY-THREE

Poppaea lay curled in a ball, bloodstained towels draped across the bed.

"Locusta," she whimpered. "Help me."

I placed my hand on her forehead. It was wet with fever.

"Are you with child?"

"Yes…but look at the blood….look."

"What stage of pregnancy are you?"

"The end of the pica stage—oh, Locusta, stop the bleeding. Save Nero's child. The soothsayer portended a male child —an heir to the throne."

"How long have you been bleeding?" I pulled the blanket away and set my hand on her swollen womb.

"Since before noon—oooh." Poppaea writhed, clutched her belly.

"Did you fall?"

"No." Her voice was too small, too hesitant.

"Fetch boiling water," I ordered a handmaid. "This is common, empress." I pulled the herbal kit over my head, opened the flap. "Did you call the midwife?"

"I'm here." The midwife, the same woman who

attended Telemachus's birth, sat in a shadowed corner of the room. "It was I who summoned you." She wrung her hands.

I untied a leather satchel. "Chew these." I poured a small quantity of small crimson berries into Poppaea's hand. "It's fruit from the chaste tree."

The demand for the berry's healing properties required cultivating great quantities of it.

I mashed a good portion of black haw bark into hot water. The bleeding must stop, or the child would be lost. A mixture of berries from cramp bark usually reduced bleeding, although I suspected there was another reason for this heavy blood flow. A reason Poppaea did not wish known.

"Drink." I tipped the cup to Poppaea's lips.

"Shall I summon the emperor?" I asked.

Poppaea's eyes widened. "No! If he sees what happened —" She choked on her heaving sobs.

"He won't be angry. This happens to many women. The bleeding will stop. All will be well." One glance at the midwife sobbing into her hands told me otherwise.

Poppaea cried out, grabbed her stomach, and began to thrash and moan. With a face as white as alabaster, she tore away the blanket. "My son!"

Between bloodied thighs lay the babe.

With great tenderness I lifted the newborn. The size of my hand from wrist to fingertip, the infant's body was unmoving, thin arms folded, legs bent and crossed. I marveled at the miniature facial features and tightly closed eyes before dabbing at the motionless fetus with a cloth.

Like the she-wolf who suckled Romulus and Remus, Poppaea's howl sent the handmaids fleeing from the room.

Poppaea stretched out her arms. "Give me my son. My son. Nero's son!"

The soothsayer's prediction proved true. His untimely progeny was a boy.

"He's perfect," I whispered as I passed the lifeless babe to the empress.

She cradled her son in both hands before setting the tiny body on her breast. Poppaea stroked his skin, kissed the top of his head, her tears bathing his skin. "My son...my son... my boy..."

I looked away, tears blurred my vision. I was an intruder in this heartbreaking scene.

Poppaea's emotional and physical health were precarious. One linked to the other. She needed comfort, so I prepared a mild sedative of black haw bark.

"My son." It was Poppaea's murmured chant. She was delirious with grief.

"You must leave," I whispered to the midwife.

The midwife wept. Hadn't stopped since I entered the room. I suspected it was not for Poppaea or the baby but for herself. Nero would order her death.

She lifted her head, stared at me with red-rimmed eyes. "Leave?"

"Flee Rome. Now." I nodded toward the empress. "If you want to live."

The midwife's eyes widened, and she gasped. She leapt from the chair, grabbed her birthing kit, and flew from the room.

The empress was still, one hand covered her dead babe at her bosom. I put my fingers to her neck. She was weak, her pulse slow, her face paler with each passing moment.

I held the tincture of cramp bark to her mouth. "You must drink, empress."

She shook her head, closed her eyes, and murmured a curse between barely parted lips.

"Please, empress. The tonic will stop the blood flow."

"I hate him." She shook her head, her words breathy and small.

I used a thin reed to administer the tonic. Forced the precious fluid into Poppaea's mouth and massaged her throat to encourage her to swallow.

Poppaea's breathing grew labored, each breath more shallow and ragged than the last. And still the bright red lifeblood flowed. The empress was dying. My ministrations were futile.

I arranged the blanket around her before leaving the room. Her handmaids, eyes red with weeping, cowered like beaten dogs against the wall.

"The empress suffers from the untimely death of her son. What happened?" I asked.

This didn't seem like a miscarriage. Something else caused it.

A dark-haired handmaid buried her head in her shawl. "He'll kill us."

I crouched down, set my hand on her shoulder. "Please tell me. I may be able to help the empress."

The handmaids looked down the hall. Each face was tight with terror. Palace spies were everywhere. An untoward remark or a thoughtless quip might result in torture or death.

Roman walls have ears.

"They argued," said another, her voice so quiet I barely heard.

The others nodded.

"She fell."

A fall during pregnancy was not uncommon. Women usually suffered no ill effects, but I suspected this was more than just a fall.

"How did she fall?"

The handmaids' eyes darted from one to the other. The dark-haired girl lifted both hands and pushed them toward me.

Nero pushed Poppaea?

"The empress was angry," said a tiny wisp of a girl. "She said he was a pusio—the woman in his other relationships."

My lips pressed together. So, the rumors were true. Poppaea did not approve of Nero's orgies with other men. She must have heard that Nero played the female—a shameful act for a Roman man. And an especially scandalous behavior for an emperor.

The girl continued, her voice hushed. "He kicked her in the belly."

"Many times," said another.

"Even after she was on the ground and begged him to stop."

The awful secret bound us together.

"Let's sit with Poppaea until he arrives." I took each of their hands. "The emperor would not wish his wife left alone."

We returned to the room and spoke comforting words to the unresponsive empress. Her lifeless hand covered a silent babe lying on her milk-less breasts.

I arranged a clean coverlet over the empress who felt only the coldness of death. A handmaid, careful not to disturb the morbid tableau, swaddled the unfortunate infant in fine linen.

An empress and an heir were murdered by the most powerful man in the world. Wife and son slain by an arrogant monster.

I sent a servant to find Nero.

Shadows lengthened as we waited. A servant entered the dark chamber to light the oil lamps. I sent a second servant to notify Nero. Then a third.

As the moon climbed high in the sky, we mourned an empress whose political ambitions were no match for a twenty-seven-year-old miscreant.

It was late when several of Poppaea's grief-stricken relatives appeared to prepare the body.

I took my leave, horrified Nero had abused his beloved wife in such a hateful manner.

SIXTY-FOUR

"You must attend Nero's nuptials to Statilia." Lucius, arms crossed, blocked my progress down the garden pathway. "He'll notice your absence and be displeased."

"What a farce." I yanked up a weed with more force than necessary. "Only a half a year has passed since Poppaea's death. Did Nero forget the spectacle at Poppaea's state funeral and internment in the mausoleum of Augustus? Did he forget his outrageous eulogy when he proclaimed her divine?"

"It was a grand performance. Maybe one of his best."

"Proof of his guilty conscience." I tossed the weed into a basket.

Lucius frowned. "Nero's grief was genuine."

"He murdered her," I hissed.

The nanny arrived with a fussy Telemachus. "Domina, your son is hungry."

Although Telemachus had reached the age for weaning, I gathered him in my arms. "You're wrong, Lucius. Nero felt no grief. He bedded another woman without delay. I heard he had Statilia's husband killed."

"No, she ordered that murder herself." Lucius gave Telemachus a peck on the cheek. "Nero needs an heir." He tickled Telemachus's toes. "You spoil him."

I passed the basket of herbs to Lucius, sat in a nearby chair, and put Telemachus to my breast. "Statilia is ugly. Her eyes bulge and her nose is pointy."

"Nero thinks she's beautiful."

I looked down at my son. His blue eyes reminded me of his father. Should Marcus ever see his child he could not deny the resemblance.

Lucius sat beside me. "I'm moving into your villa."

"Are you divorcing Sarra?"

"No, her political connections are too important." Lucius took a small carved dog from his tunic and gave it to Telemachus. "I adore you, Locusta, and I adore your bastard child."

"Is that your idea of flattery."

"Tele needs a father. A legal father. I need an heir. I want to adopt him."

Telemachus held the wooden dog in his fist as he nursed.

"Adopt Tele?"

"Why not? Claudius adopted Nero. Julius Caesar adopted Octavian. It's a great Roman tradition." Lucius set his hand on my other breast and rolled my nipple between his thumb and forefinger until I slapped his hand away.

"Is that a no? With my political connections and our combined wealth, your son will go far."

"The offer is tempting but Tele is too young and he has no political value."

"Today he does not. But five daughters taught me how fleet of foot is Time. Tomorrow, the boy will need a tutor, and the day after he will don his toga virilis marking his status as a Roman citizen. By week's end, he will have a wife—that's the speed in the Race of Life."

I looked down at Telemachus and smiled. He was so young...

"You wait for a man who will never return to you," said Lucius.

The smile slipped from my face.

"Marcus—the love of your life—your brave, strong centurion no longer loves you—abhors your profession—is jealous of your social status and despi—"

"Enough!"

Lucius touched his lips to mine. "I love you. I love Tele. Permit me to adopt him, to give him the life he deserves. Be my mistress."

"You already have several."

"Yes, I have sex with many women—a mistress is another matter—a matter of the heart."

I laughed. "You don't understand the heart of a woman at all."

Lucius's hearty laughter startled Tele. He turned his head, my nipple still in his mouth.

I had no political goals. Was all too familiar with its deadly consequences. And yet the thought of Telemachus being shunned because he was without proper connections burdened my heart. My aspirations were not selfish. They were not ambitious. I only wished to give my son the best advantages in life.

My babe sated, the nanny took him to his room to nap. Lucius and I were alone in the garden room once again.

"Yes," I said. "You may adopt Tele."

Lucius beamed at me.

"But..."

He frowned. "Tell me."

"You cannot adopt him just yet."

"When?"

"Soon," I breathed in his ear and slid my hand up his thigh.

"Anything for you," he groaned, "my pretty poisoner."

Unfortunately, as my optimism for a secure future grew, Nero's began to crumble.

SIXTY-FIVE

Domus Aurea. Nero's pleasure palace. It rose Phoenix-like from the ashes of the fire-ravaged city. Impatient for a swift completion, Nero coerced architects, Severus and Celer, into purchasing my stimulating tonic. Nero wanted them to work all day long and well into the night. Domus Aurea was the talk of Rome. The talk at every Roman dinner table and every Roman bath.

"The senators rail against Nero's wasteful extravagances. They criticize the asymmetrical architecture of Domus Aurea and complain that the Temple of Claudius was demolished." Lucius handed me a lacquered box.

"Nero never concerns himself with senators' complaints." I lifted the lid. "Ooh, emeralds."

"The commoners are turning against him as well."

"The rabble are fickle." I handed the necklace to Lucius. "You spoil me."

"I'd give you the world if it were mine, my love." He secured the emerald necklace around my neck. "Nero is losing favor with everyone. He took one hundred and twenty-five hectares of prime land in the middle of Rome from them."

"Last week you said they draped Nero's statues with flowers to honor his new building regulations."

"Yes, because the construction project adds coins to their pockets. But that also means merchants charge more for sex, food, and wine." Lucius kissed the nape of my neck. "Tell me, what have you heard from Nero's own mouth?"

"He still rages over the senators' assassination attempt."

"Old news." Lucius cupped my breasts.

"He's becoming more suspicious and mercenary." I directed his touch downward.

"And?"

"He ordered the death of forty men, the poisoning of several ruthless women, and exiled thirteen others."

Lucius unfastened the broach on my stola and peppered my naked shoulder with kisses. "You've been busy."

"I don't want to talk about Nero." I felt his eagerness through the tunic.

"Me neither. Tell me about all the ways you'll show your gratitude for the necklace."

I straddled Lucius on the sofa, politics and professions forgotten.

"You surprise me," Lucius murmured in my ear as we lay entwined under a blanket.

"Why?"

"You didn't mention Seneca's death. I thought you held the man in high esteem."

"What?" I sat up. "Seneca's dead?"

"I thought you—"

"Poisoned him? No! What happened?"

"Seneca was implicated in the Pisonian conspiracy. Nero ordered him to commit suicide. The man cut his veins and died in the customary manner. I heard his blood left his body so slowly he was given poison—"

"Not by my hands." I burst into tears. I was fond of the stoic. His quick wit and intelligent speech were precious nuggets of wisdom.

"I really thought you—"

"I like him! Admired him! I don't think I could have ever…." I buried my face in Lucius's shoulder and wept for a great man. And I cried for another reason as well. Relief that Nero had not made me poison him.

That night I startled awake, my skin cold with sweat, my heart battering against my chest. Another horrible dream. This was the worst yet. I dreamt of vines that dripped with venom. Of tendrils that climbed up the walls of my villa, green shoots creeping into every nook and recess of my home. Bright red poison leaked from their buds onto the marble floor.

NERO'S thirst for vengeance increased. As did my coffers. I was happiest when Nero traveled to other places. I didn't have to begin each day wondering what poisons he would order me to make.

But not this time.

Before Nero went to participate in the Greek games, he demanded a supply of his favorite tonics and elixirs. Nero also left Helius, his freedman, to take care of daily imperial tasks. This included poisoning his enemies complicit in an assassination plot. Business was brisk.

Rome, however, was in unrest. Senatorial conspiracies grew like weeds in an untended garden. The common folk rebelled over the food shortage. Helius, overwhelmed and ill-prepared, fled to Greece to plead for his master's return.

Nero did. And he did it in style. With a party to celebrate the newly completed Domus Aurea.

"You must come," pleaded Lucius.

"Take Sarra." I would rather stay home and play with Tele.

"She refuses to attend Nero's parties, says they're wicked and wanton."

"She's right."

"That's the best kind." Lucius sprinkled kisses on my hand. "Look, I'm begging." He got down on his knees. "Domus Aurea is unlike anything you've ever seen. Aren't you even a little bit curious?"

I agreed the next day. But not because of Lucius. Nero demanded a potent dose of the love elixir be delivered the night of his party.

SIXTY-SIX

"You're so beautiful my cock is as hard as a marble statue of Priapus," said Lucius after the servant closed the carpentum door.

I patted his leg. "Why settle for me? There will be hundreds of lovely courtesans at the party. All of which, I hear, have unparalleled talents."

Lucius shrugged. "It's the poisonous Locusta I love, that I desire, that I want so badly my balls ache."

I laughed and slapped his roving hand away.

"Have you seen Nero since his return?" Lucius asked.

"No, he sends his servants for his favorite elixirs. He only sees me when there are matters of a more delicate nature."

"Then what a treat for you to see him tonight at Domus Aurea. It's a feast for the eyes. A palace worthy of the gods." Lucius rubbed his hands together in anticipation. "Xerxes himself never lived in such a fine palace. Roman engineering defies the laws of heaven."

Like hundreds of other guests, we waited in line, ensconced in carpenta, litters, and chariots at the east Sacra

Appia entrance where the portico halo separated Domus Aurea from the city proper.

I stared at the towering colonnades. "Nero is not content with ordinary walls?"

"Nero is content with nothing. No ambitious politician ever is." Lucius kissed my cheek. "Look."

An incredible sight loomed ahead.

My jaw dropped.

"Nero must think he's the embodiment of the sun god." I gaped at the gleaming bronze statue looming like a titan over us.

"It's Colossus Neronis. The similarity to Sol is striking, isn't it?"

"Uncanny. Who sculpted it?" I asked.

"Zenodorus."

"Never heard of him."

"He's Greek, and like you, began his illustrious career in Gaul. Nero was so impressed with his statue of Mercury, he commissioned him to make this monstrosity."

A guard stopped us at the entry. "Names?"

"Lucius Gaius Theon and Locusta Parisii."

"The emperor granted you both a private tour of the estate before attending the banquet." He pointed towards a modified chariot.

Lucius waggled his shoulders. "Lucky us." His hand snaked around my waist and pulled me close. "We would make a formidable couple. And Tele would reap the benefits of our union."

My eyes narrowed. Lucius's politically connected wife was a valuable asset. Or had some aspect of her worth changed?

The ebony-skinned driver, waiting by the chariot, greeted us. "Servus sum."

"What a curious chariot." I stepped inside, wrapped my hands around the gold handrails.

"The emperor wishes his guests experience the thrill of the ride without sacrificing luxury." Lucius dug his hand into a furry pocket on the lion-skinned interior and pulled out a flask. He uncorked it and inhaled. "Nero's a genius."

With a crack of the whip, the chariot took off.

"Which of us warranted this royal tour?" Lucius asked as the horses moved along a tiled path.

"What a ridiculous question," I said. "Nero loves his poisoner more than his childhood friend."

"Nero loves only Nero."

The stallions cantered through a landscaped park. We passed sculpted shrubs, alabaster fountains, marble statues, and Zeus-sized swans floating on a large pond. The imperial trail wended past a pasture of grazing cattle, then continued its way along a high-walled wooded sanctuary.

"What's beyond the wall?" I asked.

"Beasts from distant lands," said the charioteer. "No one may enter without permission."

"I hear the emperor feeds naughty slaves to the lions," Lucius said.

"The beasts enjoy fresh meat," explained the charioteer without a trace of dismay.

Next, we dashed under a grapevine arbor in the midst of a vineyard.

"Familiar surroundings, my dear?" asked Lucius.

"My home in Gaul is a distant memory."

"How long has it been?"

"Fourteen years." A lifetime.

"Do you want to return?"

My home, my profession, and my son were in Rome.

Nothing else mattered. "There's nothing for me there." Not anymore.

Each curve of the path revealed new delights. Elegant nymphaeums, whimsical waterfalls, romantic grottos, and flower-festooned porticoes—each a feast for the eyes.

"Look." I pointed to a temple-shaped barge floating in the center of the lake. "Surely Mount Olympus pales in comparison."

"We approach the Golden House," the driver said.

"The dining room?" I assumed the tour had concluded.

"No. Another masterpiece." The driver urged the horses faster. "There."

A gleaming pantheon crested the hilltop.

When we reached the summit, the charioteer stopped. "The emperor wants you to go inside."

Lucius and I climbed the wide steps, pausing to gape at the yawning marble maw before us.

"I do believe we're about to enter Mount Olympus," Lucius said.

"Oh!" I stopped, feet rooted to the ground with amazement.

Every surface glittered with gems.

Lucius ran his fingers across a gleaming mosaic. "It's inlaid with mother of pearl."

I strolled the wall's length. "How appropriate. The story of Narcissus and Echo. Here, Narcissus is admiring his reflection in the water."

Lucius tapped his finger on another section. "And here, Hera condemns Echo to a life repeating only what others say."

No part of the vast lobby was bare, no wall without adornment.

"I heard a brave man named Fabullus painted the frescoes," said Lucius.

"Why does a painter need bravery?"

"Fabullus convinced Nero that his finest work is achieved only with perfect lighting—the daylight available during a few precious hours—and only when the sun shone. Nero was furious but conceded."

"Nero believes himself an artist, he understands an artist's temperament."

We stopped to admire the gilded furniture, chaises inlaid with precious jewels, and tables fashioned from rare stones. We gawked at the indigo ceiling, sparkling and glittering, its colors mimicking the sky's starry heavens. Lucius and I peeked inside rooms, each painted and furnished to reflect a theme.

"Greek myths," Lucius stuck his head behind a curtain.

"Roman conquests," I pointed to another.

"Oooh, the trials of Hercules. Extraordinarily lifelike. I never knew Hercules had such a big—"

"The wrath of the titans! My, my," laughed Lucius. "These murals are the most outrageous and imaginative I ever saw."

"Nero brings the glory of Rome to life."

Lucius and I followed the hallway into a courtyard with statues and fountains. Gilded chaises offered sumptuous places to admire the decadent displays.

"Divine," I said.

"A palace for a god!" The familiar voice caught me by surprise.

I spun around and dropped to my knees. From beneath a bright coral-hued tunic protruded two bare feet with gold-lacquered toenails.

Nero held out his hand. "I take delight in your excellent

opinion, Locusta. I have indeed built the most magnificent palace in the world."

I kissed Nero's hand. Lifted my gaze to him.

An array of multicolored scarves draped over Nero's unbelted tunic. His hair hung past his shoulders, golden strands entwined in womanish braids.

I stifled a cry of surprise. A young man stood beside him. He bore an uncanny resemblance to Poppaea. His features, hair, and demeanor were almost identical to Nero's deceased wife.

"Domus Aurea is a testament to your artistic vision. Its grandeur leaves me breathless," I said.

"Arise, Locusta and Lucius." Nero turned to the fresh-faced boy. "Sporus, this is Locusta, the finest and most lethal herbalist in Rome, maker of the love elixir you beg for." Nero drew the boy close and stuck his tongue in his mouth for a lusty kiss. "Sporus is my wife."

I lowered my eyes to hide the shock of Nero's pronouncement. Roman edicts did not sanction homosexual marriages. But Nero, it seemed, made his own laws.

Nero held his hand out. "The elixir."

I lifted the vial from a tiny leather pouch beneath my stola.

"The potency is increased?"

"It is."

"Did you test it?"

"Heightened euphoria and prolonged desire—exactly as you requested," I said. "My servants were happy to test it."

"Of course they were." Nero slid his hand to the boy's crotch.

Sporus cooed in reply.

I dropped my eyes again, saw that Sporus's toes matched Nero's gold-lacquered ones.

Nero tipped the vial to his lips. "Sporus and I will exalt this room with our love." His hand flapped in dismissal. "The servant will escort you to the festivities."

Lucius and I kissed Nero's hand before following the servant from the room.

Lucius bent close to my ear. "I heard he castrated the boy."

"It's as though he wants to bring his beloved Poppaea back to life," I whispered.

"He'll soon tire of the boy," he muttered from the side of his mouth, then he cleared his throat and spoke loudly. "No one hosts better revels than the emperor."

The servant led us down a hallway where fanciful statues vied with red-tinted water spouting from sculpted plinths. At the end, we entered another extensive hall where there were more feats of artistry.

Light poured through an oculi in the ceiling, which created a snaking dappled path. The mosaic floor appeared to undulate, its pattern mimicking a thousand vipers slithering beneath our feet.

Fantastical creatures enhanced the serpent-themed walls. Medusa's head, teaming with onyx snakes, extended from floor to ceiling. Perseus hid behind a column in the grisly fresco. A multi-headed Hydra leered, a hundred eyes tracking passersby. The beautiful face and taut breasts of the Python gleamed with sensuality, her dragon wings spread wide across the wall's length.

The setting sun met us on the other side. Its crimson glow was reflected in an enormous pool where a hippocamp-carved skiff floated at the water's edge. With a carved paddle in his hand, an alabaster-skinned servant waited to ferry guests across the pond.

The horse's head at the bow bobbed as if in deference to

its visitors, and the creature's fishtail pointed toward the string of flowers stretched across the watery expanse.

Lucius and I stepped into the boat and took our seats on a couch carved into the hull.

"The emperor demands each guest drink his Bacchus offering before entering the dining room." The servant handed us two wine goblets.

Lucius lifted the cup to his mouth. "Undiluted wine. Already this party exceeds my expectations."

My hand hung over the side, the water rushing past my fingertips. I took a sip, recognized the odor, the delicate sensation. "This wine has an additive."

"An herb?"

"You don't recognize the feel of it on your tongue?"

"The love elixir?"

"Not my celebrated concoction, but Nero did imbue the wine with an intoxicant."

"What a gracious host." Lucius quaffed it, then tossed the empty goblet aside. "Is this your doing?"

"Not at all." I smiled coyly, revealed nothing of my part in the enhanced wine.

With eyes closed, I surrendered my body to the invigorating sensations. Heat coursed through my limbs. My head grew light, all concerns lifting from my shoulders.

"Be careful, Lucius, or you'll have no memory of the delights you partake in." I traced the edge of a mink pillow.

"In the morning, my pretty poisoner, your head will rest on a pillow while I make you scream with pleasure." He gathered me close, his lips greedy for mine.

The little boat rocked gently at the dock until a hearty guffaw caused Lucius to break our embrace.

"Lucius! Already? Don't wear yourself out. Save your

energy for all the exotic delights inside." The plump man's belly shook with laughter.

Lucius nuzzled my ear. "Your familiar pleasures are all I want." He removed his hand from my breast.

We exited the skiff to the sounds of music and laughter and a hundred conversations.

I walk into the dining room. "The room moves."

The dining room rotated!

"Nero's gift for architecture is extraordinary. Genius does have its benefits," Lucius said.

"And faults."

Lucius gazed upwards. "It's the ceiling that moves, not the room."

The eight-sided space was breathtaking. Every wall glittered with gems and sparkling murals. Rose petals floated down from a fretted ivory ceiling, a flowery shower of corals and reds perfuming the air. Hundreds of feet tread on the blooms and released fragrance with every step.

Towering Corinthian columns, festooned in ribbons and flowers, rose skyward. Dining sofas encircled a raised platform where naked musicians played seductive songs on the sambuca, tintinna'bulum, double flute, cithara tympanum, and aulos.

Bare-chested gladiators roamed among the guests, flirting with old women and young maidens. They lifted sofas into the air while women and men lounging on them shrieked with laughter. Several gladiators engaged in mock combat or imitated sex acts. They encouraged the guests to join the fun.

Lucius and I made our way toward one extravagantly fringed tent.

"What naughty amusement does Nero hide behind these thick drapes?" Lucius poked his head inside.

"Well?" I bobbed my head toward the entrance.

"Witness the pleasures for yourself."

Tangles of flesh, rolled, heaved, and gyrated on the thick furs spread on the floor. They moaned, grunted, and squealed. I dropped the drape on the orgy.

"I recognize a senator." Lucius lifted both brows in mock surprise.

A pale hand grabbed Lucius's shoulder. "And I recognize you." Two thin arms wrapped around him and a smooth face burrowed into his neck.

Lucius kissed her cheek. "Lamia, did the emperor hire every courtesan in Rome?"

The voluptuous woman snaked around Lucius, kissed him again, a long passionate kiss he endured with grace.

Naked, but for a whisper of gold silk fluttering over her body, the famous courtesan pouted prettily. "Lucius, my love, our services—every delicious and decadent service—are at the emperor's and his guests' command." A long-pointed fingernail trailed down his chest. "You brought your wife?"

Lucius erupted with laughter. "And miss the fun? No. This is my dearest friend, Locusta."

"Locusta. Nero's Locusta? The poisoner?"

I pressed my lips into a polite smile.

Lamia sidled beside me, then glanced around before whispering her question. "Is it true you've killed ten thousand people?"

I gasped, stunned.

"Lamia, my favorite courtesan, you know Locusta can't discuss her profession. Do you reveal your clients? Or their sexual proclivities? The esteemed senator who enjoys being violated by a boy while you service his manly parts with your mouth? Or the praetor who demands you—"

Lamia clapped a hand over Lucius's mouth. "Shhh. He's here." She slid me an impish look. "If someone dies tonight, I won't tell." She tugged on Lucius's hand. "I miss you. I miss your cock, your stamina, your fingers pushing into my…" she whispered the rest.

Lucius cleared his throat. "Maybe later."

Lamia pointed to a gold and silver striped tent where a muscular servant guarded the entrance. "Take your pretty poisoner in there. I'll pleasure you both. At the same time."

Lucius clasped my hand as Lamia sauntered away and led me through the maze of tables and sofas.

"Do you visit Lamia often?" I asked.

Lucius frowned. "Basking between your legs is far more pleasurable than Lamia's costly ones."

"You didn't answer my question."

"Before we became lovers, I was a frequent visitor."

"Is what she said true? Do people think I've killed that many?"

Lucius sat down and pulled me onto the sofa with him. "I don't know, and I don't care." He sprinkled kisses on my neck.

Servants arrived and offered plates heaped with delectable delicacies. Leek-stuffed lobster. Oyster with fig. Honeyed shrimp. Fish and cherry compote. Date-filled pork. Cucumbers stuffed with marinated asparagus. Cheese soaked in truffle oil. Snails swimming in garum. Platters of pomegranates, quinces, and pears. Radishes, mushrooms, and hard cheese seasoned with vinegar.

Wine flowed and our goblets were never empty. The herb-infused wine took hold, loosened tongues and encouraged vulgarity. By dessert, guests were ripe with lust.

A troupe of fire dancers entered the room. They juggled blazing torches, did cartwheels, handstands, and curious athletic feats.

Musicians played a hypnotic tune when the belly-dancers

gyrated into the dining room. They swiveled among guests with shimmying hips and clacking castanets. They spun around, their long black hair fanning out as they twirled.

Two women balanced knives on their heads as they undulated. Three danced with serpents. Rouged nipples peeked through their sheer garments and their belts dangled with hammered gold disks that quivered as they writhed.

One belly dancer arched her back over a gray-haired consul. Her fingers dragged a scarf over his face. He howled with delight, jumped up, and began to dance. She whirled around him. The guests shouted for more more more. He tugged on her sash and it floated to the floor. Her hips moved faster. She urged guests to join them. The consul stepped on the table, waved her sash about, then doffed his own garment.

The room erupted with noise. Men jumped up, removed the other dancers' clothing.

Hands clapped.

Dishes banged.

Platters clanged.

Guests laughed.

Drums thumped.

Then Nero strode into the dining room.

Everything stopped. The music. The dancing. The conversation.

Nero lifted his hands to the heavens. "Welcome to Domus Aurea! Eat! Drink! Fornicate! My Palace of Pleasure demands fleshly offerings!"

The guests roared their approval.

"Every courtesan, every entertainer, and every servant is yours to enjoy!"

More shouts of delight.

Nero thrust his hands out to quiet the crowd. "Look at the gladiators, my friends." He pointed to several who flexed their muscles. "On this night and this night only, I grant the gladiators a unique privilege! They may copulate with any man or woman they desire. No one may refuse a gladiator's advances. To do so constitutes contempt for the most powerful emperor the world has ever known!"

A low murmur rushed through the room. Whispers of indignation and amazement.

As emperor, Nero enjoyed the privilege of indulging his whims, but this command defied the rules of decency. He ignored honor and pissed on social privilege.

I put my lips to Lucius's ear. "Several senators brought their virgin daughters to this party. Is Nero mad?"

SIXTY-SEVEN

Nero was oblivious to the shock on his guests' faces. He just condemned innocent virgins to rape. Did not care that he unraveled the moral fabric of Roman society. Nero scorned long-held rules of civility.

Some guests whooped with delight. Others stared, slack-jawed in horror. Stoic senators eyed the exit. Their wives and daughters were at the mercy of lusty gladiators. No one was safe.

Emperor Nero kicked aside plates of food and stepped up onto a table. "Sol himself is envious of Domus Aurea. At last," he shouted, "I begin to live like a human being!"

Surely, the sun deity heard the cacophony of cheers that rose into the indigo sky.

The gladiators strolled about the room. A few highborn women and their virgin daughters slid from the sofas and cowered under tables while their fathers and husbands covered them with cloaks.

"Why is Nero doing this?" I swayed, the tainted wine began to weaken my hold on reality.

"Because he thinks it's amusing," said Lucius, his eyes

following a gladiator who was meandering our way. "Locusta…"

A piercing scream cut through the din. Every head turned.

A girl of no more than thirteen years wailed as a gladiator hoisted her over his head.

"Mine!" He trampled over tabletops and stomped over couches with his virgin prize.

The maiden reached out her arms. "Help me! Someone help me!"

The gladiator walked into a tent. The mother burst into tears. Her husband smiled wanly at the guests. He dared not challenge the emperor.

My mind grew foggy. Perhaps the water was also tainted. I had employed this trick myself several times.

An intoxicating haze smothered my reason, and yet stabs of pity and sorrow pierced my soul. Had I brought my herbal kit I would have offered the virgin a tonic to help her forget. She would wake tomorrow with no memory, only the sting between her legs.

I had a tonic for almost everything. But the pain I suffered from most.

My dreams. They woke me from a deep sleep. Nestled in my mind during the day and gnawed like mice through papyrus.

My dreams…

Faces contorted in agony. Eyes wide with terror. Bodies writhing in pain.

My victims plagued my slumber. Lovers victimized by romance. Senators corrupted from scandal. Praetors seduced with power. Dishonest friends. Inconvenient employees. Treacherous slaves. Sickly wives. Abusive husbands.

The dead tortured me during unexpected times. While

sorting berries or measuring a tincture. My subconscious summoned these specters like unwanted guests.

Their faces flitted through my mind now. The terrified expression of the soon-to-be-ravaged virgin would live forever in my heart.

"My love." Someone whispered in my ear. "My love."

A warm liquid filled my mouth. I latched on, swallowing the intoxicating nectar. I wanted to forget my inglorious deeds. Wanted to forget the virgin's screams.

Lucius's smiling face loomed before me. He promised pleasure and lust and love. My arms draped over him, yielded to his desires.

As the moon climbed high over this island of wickedness, the party grew more frenzied.

Only brief recollections remain. Scandalous acts in which I engaged. With Lucius. With Lamia. With a gladiator. With servants. Shameful debaucheries I might never partake in if not under the influence of tainted wine. My will was not my own, my body succumbed to sheer sensation. Unquenchable lust.

I was a party to each erotic excess and every sensual indulgence.

SIXTY-EIGHT

"**M**y sweet Venus." Lucius's voice floated into my wakefulness.

I squinted. The sun bathed my bedchamber in bright light. A dreamy-eyed Lucius reclined beside me.

"Are we in my room? Am I still dreaming?"

Lucius ran a light finger across my shoulder. "Pretty poisoner, you should consume more of your own love elixir. Frequent doses left me quite impervious to the minuscule amount Nero added to the wine."

"I don't remember everything."

"I recall every wonderful decadent moment." Lucius kissed my cheek. "Be my wife."

"You already have a wife."

"What if I were suddenly unencumbered?" His tone grew serious.

I sat up to waves of nausea. "Sarra is healthy."

"She might fall ill…"

His horrid suggestion descended on my shoulders like a toxic yoke.

I stood, the room spinning around me. "I will never—

never harm your wife. Sarra bore you many children. She ignores our affair—your numerous paramours—your inattentiveness. A man of honor ought to pay tribute to such a long-suffering woman."

Lucius leapt from the bed, wrapped me in his arms. "Together we make a formidable team. Think about it, Locusta. My wife births only female children. Useless, costly feminine appendages."

I pushed him away.

"She refuses to fuck me anymore, claims her body is weak from bearing my children."

"That's not a reason to murder her."

Lucius grabbed my wrist. "I will adopt Telemachus. Your son will know power and prestige. Wouldn't Marcus choose the best for his son?"

I yanked my arm, but he held tight. "Your casual suggestion to murder your wife is repugnant."

Lucius cackled mirthlessly. "An odd statement from one who wraps herself in the silk of poison. Who treads on the marble of narcotics. And who bathes in the water of depravity. You delude yourself, my sweet. You're more dangerous than I. My vices come from crooked dealings with corrupt merchants and greedy politicians. Your sins far exceed my own. A special whirlpool awaits you in the river Styx. There you will meet everyone you sent to an untimely death."

"I heal people!" My cry rang false, even to my own ears. "I have no choice. To defy Nero is to die." I struggled from his grasp.

Lucius released his hold. "Why didn't you escape Rome with Marcus after the fire? It was the perfect time. Nero would have presumed you perished in the blaze. You might be free of Nero now. Free to be with your beloved centurion." His voice took on a cool measured tone. "Instead you remained here in this villa of herbs. Surrounded by luxury. Enjoying your wealth and status in society. Admit it, Locusta, we're cut from the same cloth. We belong together."

"I no longer desire your presence. Leave at once."

"Your youth has vanished, my love. Your very name sends possible suitors cowering in fear." He set a finger to his lips. "You serve a depraved master. Join me and we will revel in Nero's madness."

"I refuse to murder your wife."

"Then I will have Nero order you to do so." Lucius blew a kiss before striding naked from the room.

"No!" I raced after him, my cry startling the servant in the hall.

Lucius stopped, turned around. "I neglected to share a bit of information I learned the other day. Marcus is dead. He died during battle in the pitiful town of Jerusalem. I'm the only one who loves you now." He puckered his lips, made smooching noises, and vanished around the corner.

Air left my lungs. I staggered back, his words like a blow to my gut.

Marcus. Dead.

Dreams of his triumphant return crushed in an instant. Visions of a life together flew away like a startled bird.

I leaned against the wall and vomited. Heaved chunks of my ambitions. Gagged on vile aspirations. Retched the very herbs of my trade.

I stumbled into my chambers and rifled through my herbal kit. Herbs for nausea. Herbs for headaches. There were no herbs for heartache.

TELE GRABBED a lock of my hair. "Mama."

He squirmed until I set him down, then he raced across the room and climbed on the bed.

"I jump! I jump!"

I sat on the bed as he bounced, giggling each time he landed on his back among the tangle of sheets.

My little Telemachus. He grew so fast.

Without proper political connections, my son would join the ranks of hundreds of insignificant patricians with neither influence nor jurisdiction.

I could not send him to the family vineyard. My brother's exceptionally intelligent firstborn son had already reached the age of majority. Uncle Amando oversaw the young lad's struggle to manage the grapes, workers, and finances. There would be no room and no love for a bastard child in a house bursting with male heirs.

Neither could I send Telemachus to my sister Camilla's home in Sicily. And although it was I who paid her dowry to the wealthy noble, I dare not send my child to a distant island to live among strangers.

Telemachus flopped on his back. "I fly. I fly," he demanded, arms outstretched.

I scooped him up and, cradling him in my arms, swung him back and forth over the bed. "One…two…three…"

"Weeee!" He landed in a pile of pillows. "Do it again."

I was a woman, barred from politics or commerce. My alliance with Nero might garner the best tutor for Tele, but unless my son learned my trade, his success hinged on Nero's whims.

I tossed Telemachus on the bed again. Each happy squeal brought me closer to the awful realization about his future. It was time Lucius adopted Telemachus. It was the only way to insure my son's position in society.

But I didn't need to marry Lucius. I hoped he had come to his senses after I ordered him from my home this morning.

It could be done easily enough. After the esteemed senator Gnaeus Calpurnius Piso's attempted assassination, Nero suspected treachery in everyone.

Lucius had only to convince Nero that Sarra was involved in treason. No evidence needed. Lucius's word would be proof enough. And then a messenger would arrive at my doorstep with Nero's command. A command I must obey.

Wedding Lucius might not be so terrible. We enjoyed each other's company. We understood each other, shared secrets, accepted one another, overlooked each other's faults and misdeeds.

I trusted Lucius. I did not love him. Love was a luxury for a Roman woman, especially for a woman like me.

And yet, to refuse Lucius was dangerous. I had no desire to make him an enemy.

I knew what I had to do.

"Higher! Higher!"

"Yes, Tele, Mama has high ambitions for you." I plucked him from the bed and swung him about.

"Pardon the intrusion, domina." Iris held a headache tonic in her hand.

I swallowed the vial's contents and handed it back to her. For a brief moment, I envied Iris's simple life. It was a life free from political machinations and intrigues.

"Iris."

"What do you require, domina?"

"You served me well for many years," I said.

"It's been my pleasure, domina."

"How long have you attended me?"

"The emperor sent me the day you took up residence here."

"You report my actions to him?" I kissed my squirming boy. "Or to someone in his employ?"

"There's nothing to report, domina, and he has made no imperial inquiries for the past three years."

Iris's honesty was a comfort.

"What about the other servants? Do they report to Nero?"

"If I may speak plainly, your servants are loyal and devoted to you. You don't beat us, and you treat us well." Iris hesitated. "Pricilla…"

"What about her?"

"Pricilla told us that you granted her freedom. She spoke of your bravery and…past." Iris dropped her gaze to the floor.

"I miss Pricilla."

"We all do," she said.

"I would like to make an offering to your favorite god. Which one do you honor?"

Iris's reaction was immediate. Her face bloomed red, her mouth parted in surprise.

"You follow an exotic god from the east?"

Iris shifted from foot to foot. "Yes."

"What's the god's name?"

Iris stammered, her shoulders dropped. "I-I-I'm a follower of The Way." She wrung her hands. "Will you punish me? Or have Nero throw me to the lions?"

"I don't share Nero's contempt for The Way. You're courageous. An admirable trait." I lifted Telemachus from the bed. "I promised to make an offering to your god and I will. What do you require of me? Coin? Incense? Wine? A lamb?"

"My god requires no such offerings."

"You make a liar of me?"

Iris's hand flew to her mouth. "Oh, domina, no. Forgive me. That wasn't my intent. I'm grateful to attend you.

Grateful for your healing tonics. Without your remedy my friend would have died."

"Are you certain there's no gift I can offer your god?"

Her lips pressed together in thought. "Our god is honored when his followers bring others to listen to his words."

"Your god speaks?"

"Oh no," she giggled. "An elder speaks. One of Simon Peter's most faithful.'"

"I once provided him a tonic for the semitertian fever. His crucifixion upset me."

"Eitan mentioned that."

The name brought a sad smile. After this god gave Eitan a vision, my trusted servant disappeared. I told the servants Eitan would be captured and punished, in truth I never pursued the matter. Somehow, I found it difficult to fault Eitan for having the bravery to follow his destiny.

My own bondage prevented such bold behavior. Nero would kill me if I fled the city.

"Well, since your god does not accept goats or food, I'll go with you and listen to your elder's words." It was the least I could do.

This god of the poor. A Jewish god. A deity for slaves. Marcus claimed there was truth in this god's words. That was years ago. The night I conceived Telemachus.

Iris's face lit up. "Really? I'll let you know when we have another meeting."

I nodded, then led Telemachus to the indoor garden. It had become a daily habit. Mother and son walked up and down the rows of plants together. Our ritual was comforting. It reminded me of the times when Pricilla and I strolled through the vineyards in Gaul.

Telemachus scampered down the rows while I inspected buds and grafts. I stuck my finger into the soil to assess dampness. Telemachus tried to imitate and plunged his fist into the dirt.

Later that afternoon, Telemachus fell asleep in my arms. I caressed his cheek as he dozed, gazing with wonder at the perfection of his face. The very likeness of his father.

Marcus would have burst with joy to see his fine son, who already showed signs of intelligence and strength. Tears rolled down my face, dropped onto Tele's cheek. He would never know his father.

"Domina." Iris, mindful of the napping Telemachus, spoke softly. "The emperor sent a messenger."

I wasn't surprised. Nero often sent messengers after his parties. And last night's revel was the party of all parties.

I passed Telemachus to Iris, shouldered my herbal kit, and went into the atrium.

"The emperor orders your immediate presence. You must go to Domus Aurea."

Not the palace? How odd.

SIXTY-NINE

A servant showed me into a gold-painted room. It was devoid of furniture or statues, but the colorful frescoes and glittering gems imbedded into the wall were adornment enough.

"I don't care for your rendering of Diana." Nero lay on his back in the middle of the room, his comment directed at the ceiling.

"What features do you deem worthy of the goddess?" Another voice. This one from high above.

Suspended from the domical ceiling, a man lay on a platform.

"Portray Diana as Julia Agrippina, my mother and the noblest of woman who ever lived."

"A brilliant suggestion, emperor. How better to glorify your esteemed mother than for her likeness to be forever engrafted with Diana, goddess of the hunt. My apologies for not anticipating your genius."

"My artistry is without compare. Now, the chin and jaw are misshaped—the breasts too large. My mother had lovely pert breasts. The curve of the hip must be reduced. Mother had the hips of young woman. Ah, Locusta, don't stand there, come closer."

I hurried to his side and knelt before him.

"I have a tedious task which requires your skill."

"It's a pleasure to serve the glory of Rome."

"You heard the rumors?"

"Rumors?"

Nero's question troubled me. Rumors swirled like Kharybdis in Rome's murky waters the past few months. Every noble senator, wife, and shopkeeper whispered of the emperor's tenuous hold on his imperial position.

Commoners groused over the public land used to build Domus Aurea. Military leaders grumbled about their frustrations with his political leadership. Senators complained that Nero's extravagant lifestyle destroyed Roman morals.

Agree with him and he might get angry. Disagree and he might call me a liar or an idiot.

"The love of intrigues flows deep in the blood of Romans," I said.

"We follow in the footsteps of our gods." He looked at the ceiling. "Amulius!"

"Yes, emperor?"

"The blush on my mo—Diana's cheek must glow with youth and vigor! You paint a sickly goddess!"

"My apologies emperor."

Nero's eyes flicked my way. "A certain senator is using his daughter to promote insurrection among the patricians."

"I haven't heard that particular rumor."

"My source is a trusted friend, and he shares this information at great personal expense."

"Disloyalty cannot go unpunished."

"This small snake hides venomous fangs," said Nero.

"What's the name of this sly serpent you wish me to poison?"

"Sarra, daughter of Senator Balios, and wife to your lover, Lucius."

SEVENTY

The room blurred. I swallowed the bile that clawed up my throat. "Sarra?" I white-knuckled the strap on my herbal kit.

"Lucius suggested I throw his wife to the lions, but I prefer my beasts feed on Christians and criminals," said Nero.

Sarra was harmless. The selfless woman found politics boring, her pleasures found in managing the household and rearing five daughters. She was a plain and docile wife, one who had shown only hospitality and kindness to me.

I cleared my throat, bitter with the taste of disgust. Dare I question Nero? He was mad. Likely to do anything. "A swift or slow-acting poison?"

His eyes narrowed. "The traitor must suffer for her crimes. A painful death must serve as a warning for those bent on treason."

I did not avert my gaze, my face bearing no trace of the despair squeezing my heart.

Nero frowned. "You should be happy. Why aren't you?"

"I…"

"Her death frees you to wed Lucius."

I bowed my head.

"Why aren't you kissing my hand with gratitude?" He lifted his hand.

"Forgive me." I sprinkled it with kisses. "I'm humbled and honored by your kindness."

"Of course you are. Now, tell me, what was your favorite part of the party?"

I praised everything, the food, wine, and entertainment.

After Nero dismissed me, and as I walked away, he called out, "Locusta, wed Lucius. As soon as possible."

I closed the curtains on the litter as slaves carried me homeward. Silent tears streamed over my cheeks. Rivers of regret drowned all my misguided ambitions.

Murder Sarra!

She was a loving wife to Lucius. She took no lovers, involved herself in no intrigues, and respected the gods. A kind woman. Without ill-will. Obedient and long suffering.

Lucius's only complaint was her dull lovemaking, her inability to respond with passion and vigor to his frequent requests. Not reason enough for murder.

Except reason played no part in this treachery. Lucius found political gain in our matrimony. He loved me. I saw it in his eyes. Confessed to being smitten since our first meeting. I wondered now at the truth of this murder. Was it me he loved or was his love inspired by my alliances with the most powerful man in the world?

A marital union between a notorious poisoner and a shrewd noble. A formidable alliance. One that guaranteed high status for me, power for Lucius, and worth to Nero.

How could I reconcile murdering a woman I aided in childbirth? Provided healing herbs for? How could I kill a wife who treated me kindly even though she knew her husband loved me?

The sway of the litter stopped. Twittering birds and rustling leaves replaced the sounds of people and city.

I hid my sorrow-swollen eyes under a hood, climbed from the litter, rushed past the guard and into my villa. My domicile of poison and death and lust.

"Mama!" Telemachus ran towards me with wide arms. "Up. Up."

I gathered the innocent babe into my guilty arms. Fresh tears dropped on his head like a corrupt blessing.

There was no task I would refuse for Tele's sake.

"THE WAY MEETS THIS EVENING." Iris set a plate of fruit and bread before me.

"Not tonight. I have other tasks for you," I said.

Telemachus required looking after while I pondered the ingredients with which to poison Sarra.

Iris wrung her hands. "I beg your forgiveness, I only thought you…you said…"

A meeting of Christians. My mood was too dark for such a gathering. "I remember, but I'm busy with other matters right now. I'll attend another day."

"Domina, you look sad today. Sadder than usual. We…." She spread out her hands. "Several of us have noticed and we're worried about you."

"How dare you."

Iris dropped to her knees. "You show us so much kindness. Let us help you if we can."

I was beyond consolation. Shame poisoned me. I touched

her shoulder. "Thank you for your concern but don't worry yourselves. Bring me some wine."

Iris hurried from the room. When she returned, she brought a carafe and my favorite foods, stuffed figs and asparagus soaked in honey-vinegar.

I drank the wine. All if it. But it did not stop my dark thoughts. Nor did it stop me from seeing Sarra's face and other faces of those I poisoned. These apparitions were no longer content to destroy my slumber, now they haunted my wakeful hours.

I hurled the plate across the room.

A bit of poppy and more wine ought to cure this illness of the soul.

Poppy did indeed improve my mood. The spirits of the dead faded, and I began to ponder Nero's request. Sarra's death must be a warning to his enemies.

Did Nero truly believe Lucius's claims of his wife's treachery? Nero's suspicious nature was notorious. My wealth, the proof. But this?! Something deep inside me told me this was Nero's way to get what he wanted. And he wanted me to marry Lucius.

Roman noblewomen were known for their overzealous political ambitions. Malicious gossip, sexual favors, false flattery, and feminine deceit their weapons. Agrippina, Emperor Claudius's previous wives, Caligula's sisters. Roman history was rife with ambitious women.

Perhaps Sarra was not the innocent she pretended. Behind the sweet voice and demeanor might lurk a duplicitous heart.

I laughed. I could not lie to myself.

My resolve strengthened. Poison Sarra. Wed Lucius. No other choice remained.

I swallowed a small vial of calming tonic and summoned Iris. "I'll go to your meeting tonight. I don't neglect promises made to a valued handmaid." It was the truth. But also because I wished to be rid of the obligation. "Are you quite sure this god will not be content with coin or a slaughtered beast?"

"My god requires only your presence."

"Then he shall have it."

SEVENTY-ONE

Dim light glowed through the narrow windows of the meager abode. No carpenta waited outside. No one lurked by doors. The street was quiet and dark. No one would have suspected The Way met inside.

"Here?" I asked as we stepped from the carpentum.

"Tonight. It changes every day," said Iris.

I followed her inside. A bearded old man sat in the shadows. Iris signaled him with a peculiar hand gesture, and he nodded.

"If the Praetorian Guard come, the old man tugs on the string above his head, which rings a bell in the meeting room."

Followers of the way took a great risk. Roman soldiers died putting down rebellions in Caesura and Jerusalem between Greeks and Jews.

"Worshipping a god should not be so dangerous," I said.

Iris turned, her brow creased. "Says the most famous assassin in Rome."

"I'm well paid."

"Your reward is fleeting, mine is everlasting." Pricilla

paused at a narrow entrance. "I hope you find some small comfort tonight." She pushed the drapery aside.

A few curious worshipers glanced our way.

The woman extended her hand. "Welcome." She indicated a bench. "Tonight, the elder will share the story of a man named Saul and the reason our Lord blinded him for three days."

How horrible! What sort of god causes a man to lose his sight? This Lord was not a kind deity. I crossed my arms and prepared for a stern lecture about another malevolent god.

My face shadowed by my hood, I cast a quick glance at The Way's followers. There were freedmen and women, laborers, bondsmen, and shopkeepers. All commoners.

Several seats forward, a cloaked man shifted in his seat to let a worshiper squeeze by. The man was tall. His head and shoulders above the others.

"Do you know these people?" I whispered in Iris's ear as we took our places on the bench.

"A few."

The cloaked man turned to speak to someone sitting next to him. Although his hood obscured his features, the slope and girth of his form unsettled me.

As if the man knew my suspicious eyes were trained on him, he lifted his head to stare back.

The angular jaw. Full lips. Straight nose.

Marcus.

SEVENTY-TWO

J oy brightened my heart, poured light into my dark soul. Marcus lived!

Concealed by my head covering, I gazed at the face I loved so well. Despite his contempt for my profession. Despite his refusal to believe we fought a common enemy.

Marcus tilted his head, the hood flapping back to reveal his face. There was the briefest narrowing of his eyes, as though he recognized the hood-shaded curves of my face.

Iris pressed close to me. "Does that man know you?"

"Impossible. I don't associate with followers of The Way."

Marcus's gaze bounced from me to Iris and back again.

My heart sounded in my ears. My pulse quickened. I was happy and distressed at the same time. Joyful he lived. Miserable I was still yoked to Nero. That I had to poison Sarra. That I had to murder a woman so my son could be a senator one day. A son Marcus did not know existed.

I hung my head in shame.

A man in a dun-colored tunic cleared his throat. "Welcome, my friends. Tonight, we learn of God's great love and how this love changes hearts, minds, and destinies." The elder's voice was soothing and resonant with wisdom.

Marcus turned around, and I had to content myself with listening to the elder's homily.

The elder spoke of Simon Peter, the old man I gave a wormwood remedy to for semitertian fever. The rebel, senators considered dangerous. The insurgent, Nero had crucified upside down. And the apostle, my servant, Eitan, had risked his life to spread The Way's message for.

I learned Simon Peter was a fisherman by trade. A disciple of a Jewish prophet, one of the first. The elder spoke of his subsequent denial and his witness to the crucifixion and resurrection of Jesus. The elder recounted Simon Peter's good works in Jesus's name.

The elder next spoke of a man named Saul, another Jew and persecutor of all those who converted to this new faith. All that changed when God blinded Saul for three days with a vision.

The elder spoke of other people, men and women, transformed by this Jewish God. The tales of redemption intrigued me. Forgiveness. A new beginning…

It was an appealing idea. Except it did not apply to me. Forgiveness was for laborers, bondmen, fishermen, prostitutes, carpenters, and merchants. The gift of forgiveness did not apply to an imperial poisoner.

The elder's message of hope stirred up a cauldron of emotions. A cruel fate had guided my life, one that had corrupted my innocence and was marked by desperate decisions.

The Roman gods blessed me with herbal skill, prestigious connections, great wealth, and a healthy son. Their curses were equally potent. Although a free Roman citizen, my freedom was an illusion. Nero owned my villa, my earnings, my status, and my body.

But Nero did not own my heart.

I gazed at Marcus's broad back, and the memory of his leaving was as potent as though it happened yesterday.

My centurion was a man of ethics and honor. Two traits at odds with attaining wealth and prominence. Honor was righteous. Fame and fortune deceptive. If Nero fell, I would fall with him.

I wished Marcus could meet his son. How proud he would be! But I couldn't risk it. It would complicate my upcoming nuptials to Lucius.

"Domina," Iris laid a hand on my shoulder. "You're shivering. Are you sick?"

"I'm fine."

When the elder spoke of Jesus I listened in earnest. How could a human's death redeem my life? I closed my eyes, the words enveloping me like a warm shawl. Forgiveness of sins. No Roman or Greek god made such promises.

The elder spoke of a wondrous afterlife. One that contrasted with the horror of Hades. An afterlife filled with light and love and peace. My mother belonged in such a place.

The elder held a loaf of bread aloft. "The Lord Jesus on the night he was betrayed took bread, and he gave thanks. He broke the bread and said, this is my body which is for you. Do this in remembrance of me. In the same way, he took the cup also, after supper, saying, this is the new covenant in my blood. Do this, as often as you drink it, in remembrance of me."

The elder passed the bread and wine to the worshipers. Each partook of the humble offering.

A woman passed me the cup and bread. This was not my

faith. Not my ritual. My beliefs required giving offerings to gods, not receiving them.

I now understood why the poor flocked to this new religion.

I lifted the cup to my face yet did not drink. I did not eat the bread. Instead I crushed it in in my fist and slipped the mash into the slim satchel under my palla. My heart was too heavy with the burdens of my profession, and neither wine nor bread could lessen my guilt. To participate in this ritual felt false.

Afterwards, the believers stood and talked among themselves.

"We must leave." I tugged on Iris's hand. As much as I wanted to speak with Marcus no good could come of it.

"Locusta." A whisper. Marcus's voice reached me as I walked through the door.

I lowered my head, took another step forward.

"You refuse to speak to me?"

I shook my head, not daring to turn around.

"Have you become a follower of Jesus of Nazareth?"

I said nothing and hurried down the hall. Once outside, I gulped the cool night air. It had been too warm in the meeting room, too warm with memories.

Iris looked up and down the street. "I don't see the carpentum."

I squinted into the dark, the slim crescent moon offered little light.

"There's a tavern close by," I said. "Perhaps the driver passed the time there." I quickened my pace, cursed the foolishness of attending The Way's worship.

Most Roman streets were safe at night. Roman soldiers patrolled places frequented by patricians and equestrians. The infamous brothels, the Circus, and other Roman dens of entertainment were free from thieves—at least the plebian kind. But this was a neighborhood of the poor. And rarely patrolled.

"Lost your way?" A man emerged from an alley.

"Move aside." I strode towards him.

The man blocked our path. "Only a wealthy woman hides her face behind such a fine wrap. Meeting your lover?" The decayed mouth grunted foul air, and his hand sprung out and grabbed my cloak.

I tried to pull away, but the thief held tight. He cinched his arm around me.

"Iris," I shouted as she fled down the street.

The thief slammed me against the building, touched the tip of his dagger to my throat. "Jewels and coin."

I thrust my bag at him. "Release me or I'll have my guard kill you."

He laughed, his spittle spraying my face.

"Let me go!"

The thief yanked me into the alley by my hair. His hand clamped over my mouth. A punch to the stomach doubled me over. The next instant I was on my back in the street. He straddled me, pinned my wrists to the ground.

"Patrician whore," he hissed and hit me.

Blood exploded from my nose. My vision dimmed. My head spun. I felt him tug at my garments.

A shadow loomed over me, and with a metallic flash, my assailant toppled over onto the street.

Marcus extended his hand. "Why didn't you bring proper protection?"

"Domina!" Leather crop snapping in his hand, my driver raced into the alley and cracked it at Marcus.

"Stop," I said. "This man saved my life."

The driver advanced toward the motionless figure

sprawled on the ground. "Is this the attacker?" His whip thrashed down on the thief. Again and again.

"Enough," Marcus said.

My driver dropped to his knees, his head bowed. "Domina, I beg forgiveness. I followed your instructions. I waited around the corner."

Iris, breathless and with a hand pressed to her side, ran into the alley.

Marcus bent over me. "Let's get you home." He wiped blood from my nose with his cloak.

"You know this man?" Iris asked.

"An old friend." I turned to the driver. "Bring the carpentum at once."

The driver sprinted from the alley as though running the stadion event in the Games.

"Thank you." I lifted the palla over my head.

Marcus touched my arm. "Don't cover your face. You grow more beautiful with the passing years—lovelier than I remember."

"I'm not the same woman."

"You're not Nero's poisoner anymore?"

"My profession is the same."

Marcus helped me up. "May I see you safely to your villa?"

"I…" I touched my throbbing nose. "Okay."

The carpentum rattled into view. I stepped forward and stumbled, my legs shaking. Marcus wrapped an arm about my waist and guided me out of the alley.

"I'll sit with the driver. You're safe now, Locusta." Marcus shut the door.

Once inside, I buried my head in Iris's shoulder to muffle my sobs.

Safe? I wasn't safe. I would never be safe from Nero.

"It's my fault, domina." Tears ran down Iris's cheeks as well. "I shouldn't have insisted you come to the meeting. Please forgive me."

Forgiveness. The word was spoken many times tonight.

"There's nothing to forgive," I said. "The fault is mine."

Iris shed more tears. "You're so kind, domina."

I was not a kind woman. Kind women did not murder for wealth. Kind women did not devise ways to murder a lover's spouse for political gain. I was as evil as the attacker in the alley.

"It's not your fault. I don't blame you." I closed my eyes, leaned against the fur-draped seats, and debated the wisdom of telling Marcus about his son.

I was tired of a lifetime of calculated decisions, measured words, and practiced gestures.

We arrived home too quickly. Before I had figured out what to say—and how much—to Marcus.

Marcus held my hand as I descended. His eyes searched mine, sought for a sign that my love for him had endured.

"May I offer some refreshment for your troubles?" I asked before I could stop myself.

"Yes, thank you. I'd like that."

Once inside the villa, I sent Iris to fetch food and wine.

Marcus moved towards me. "Locusta."

I retreated. "Don't."

"Just hear me." Marcus stepped closer. "I've done many horrible things in my life. For Rome. Always for the glory of Rome. I'm not sorry for those whose lives I took—they were our enemies—but one dishonorable action presses on my heart."

I shook my head. "Don't…"

Marcus took my hand. "I made a terrible mistake several years ago. One I regret every day of my life."

"Don't say it."

"I spoke harsh words to you. Accused you of vile deeds I've done myself. You ordered me from this villa. My pride compelled me to go. My heart, however, remained."

"You're too late."

"Regret is not bound by time. God bestowed a gift that day. The fire was a chance for a new beginning together. I should have carried you to a land far away from the evils of Rome."

"Marcus…"

"I know where we could go. It's a beautiful land full of exotic spices and mountains that touch the sky." Marcus gathered me in his arms. "Let me take you away. Tonight."

"I cannot." Hot tears wet my cheeks.

"My military commission is complete, and Nero will not suspect your absence until he needs you. By then we will have crossed the sea."

"Nero ordered me to poison someone tomorrow. He'll send a messenger. If I'm not here…"

Marcus's lips touched mine, gently at first, then with increasing fervor. "Tonight. We leave tonight."

"Mama." The small voice sang from down the hall. "Mama."

Tele darted into the room, sturdy legs and bare feet padding past the stranger without a glance. Arms, warm from sleep, encircled my leg. He tilted back his blonde head and gazed up with a drowsy smile. "Mama."

Marcus stepped back in surprise, peered down at the boy.

"It's late. You should be sleeping." I lifted him up.

"No sleep. I hungry. I want figs. And honey."

"Forgive my disrespect." A shadow crossed Marcus's face. "I didn't know you were married." He looked about, as if expecting a husband to enter the room.

"I'm not." I nuzzled Tele's cheek.

"You're a widow?"

"No."

Tele twisted in my arms, wriggled around until he faced Marcus.

Marcus stared at him. He swallowed, his face growing pale. When his eyes met mine, they were moist, and his mouth moved silently with a single word. Mine.

I nodded, clutched the squirmy child tighter.

Iris entered the room with a tray laden with food and drink. "Oh domina, I didn't realize Telemachus was awake."

"He's a hungry little man this evening and requests figs and honey." I set him down on the couch.

"Play horse." Telemachus hopped up and down on the cushions.

Marcus's gaze held steady on his son.

"Horse," Telemachus shouted. "Play horse." His jumping grew vigorous.

I sat on the couch, set him on my knee, and bounced him while he giggled and laughed.

"Faster."

A myriad of emotions swept over Marcus's face. Joy. Pride. Regret. Sorrow. Pain. He longed to touch his child, the sentiment misting his eyes.

I remained silent. Did not want words to intrude on the moment.

Iris returned, set a plate of honey-drizzled figs on the table. Tele snatched a fruit, stuffed one in his mouth. After gobbling several more, he paused to look at Marcus.

"Honey fig?" His sticky fingers offered a fig to his father.

Marcus held out his hand, beaming with delight at his son's small courtesy.

"Eat," Tele urged.

Marcus plopped the fruit in his mouth. "Delicious. The best fig I've ever eaten in my entire life."

Tele clapped his hands and offered another.

Many mouthfuls later, Tele licked the sweetness from his fingers and curled in my lap. He closed his eyes, and I felt slumber overtake him when his head grew heavy in my arms.

"I have a son." Marcus's words were husky. "You kept my son from me."

"You left me."

"You should have sent word."

"Why? You disapprove of my profession."

"You're an assassin," Marcus whispered.

"Everything I do is for your son."

"Is that the lie you tell yourself?"

"I wanted your son, our son, to have the benefits of a noble upbringing," I said. "Education. Privilege. Wealth. Opportunity. You never had those advantages. Your rank, profession, and income are the result of a gracious benefactor. Your profession was the very reason you refused to make me your wife."

"I refused to see the woman I love live in the follower's camp like a whore."

"Then you understand why I continue serving Nero." I met his eyes. "I have no choice. Just as you had no choice."

Marcus rubbed his forehead. "What will we do?"

"There's nothing to be done. The gods doomed our love long ago. Perhaps, they knew we were an ill-fated pair."

His brows lifted, hurt in his eyes. "You believe this?"

"I'm not the young maiden with whom you made love to in the flowery field. You're not the same man. We both participated in Roman conquest and bloodlust. I've done... things...I could never speak to you of...shameful things." I stroked Tele's cheek. "We're not destined to be together. Nero will hunt me down. Kill me. Murder our child." Tears blurred my vision.

Marcus sat beside me. With a gentle caress, he touched his son's face. "Nero has many enemies. The senators grow angry over his missteps. The citizens are disgusted by his extravagances. They fume over his land appropriation. Only the poor love him. They enjoy the free grain, games, and festivities he provides. Nero is not long for this world."

"Are you suggesting there's an assassination plot?" I frowned, shook my head. "There's always an assassination plot. Nero uncovers them all. I know. I'm a party to his deadly vengeance."

"Those were incompetent amateurs. A greater enemy waits in the shadows."

"Who?"

"After defeating Vindex, the northern armies pledged allegiance to Verginius Rufus."

"What does this mean?"

"Nero's own army turns against him," said Marcus. "Not only that, Servius Galba waits in Rome, his adherents gnawing at the remaining senators still loyal to Nero."

"Nero is powerful. He has more friends and alliances than you can imagine. His reign will have no end."

"His reign will end and sooner than you imagine." Marcus ran his fingers through his son's hair. "Without senatorial support and backing from the army, it's only a matter of time before Nero is murdered. Should his own Praetorian Guard turn against him— "

"Impossible. They'll never do that."

Marcus stood. "I'll return tomorrow for you and my son. Together we will leave Rome."

"You don't understand. Nero ordered me to wed another man."

"Who?"

"A well-connected and influential senator who wants to adopt Telemachus."

"No man, senator or otherwise, will adopt my son while I draw breath."

"If Nero doesn't kill you, the senator will."

"Do you love him?"

"I…"

My feelings for Lucius ran deep. He rescued me from prison. Supplied countless customers. Attended to financial tasks from which I, a woman, was excluded. Our friendship had strengthened after Pricilla's death. Lucius was ambitious, extravagant, unscrupulous, and his devotion to me was unwavering. And although his lust for women and intoxicants were insatiable, he respected my decisions and profession. "He's always been there for me."

Marcus swallowed, his voice thick with resignation. "You love him."

"I owe him my life."

"Of course." Marcus touched his forehead. "Lucius."

"He loves me and will do anything for me."

Marcus knelt before me, one hand on his son's leg, the other atop mine. "I love you, Locusta. I never stopped loving you. I know Lucius freed you from prison, but I questioned his intentions then and more so now. I detest his hold on you."

"He doesn't have a hold on me. Nero does."

Marcus set a kiss on my hand. "One word, Locusta, one word, and I'll move mountains to be by your side."

We kissed and it tasted like a bittersweet acceptance of our fated love.

"I love you, Locusta," Marcus said, then kissed the top of Tele's head. "And I love my son."

He told me where he lived and left me to my thoughts. To decide my life. My future. Our son's future.

I touched my nose, bruised and tender, clotted with blood. Like my life.

I carried Tele to his room, tucked a blanket around him, and gazed with wonder at his peaceful face. How many years would pass before he would lose his innocence? Before the Roman elite demanded his obedience to politics and subterfuge?

I wept that night. Wept for a destiny that was not in my control. Wept for an ill-fated love. Wept for my estranged family. Wept for the innocent and guilty people I murdered.

My dreams were a gyre and spun my ambitions into a murky abyss.

THE MORNING SUN was a welcome sight. A new day. And not a new day. Another day of poison. Another day of obedience to Nero.

Nero's courier arrived with a parchment while I pushed around the fruit on my plate. The previous night's tears and dreams left me too full with emotion to swallow a morsel.

Nero's message was brief: Poison Sarra by day's end.

With a sigh, I pushed back the chair and headed to the workroom. A potent mixture must be prepared. I did not want Sarra to suffer. Lucius's wife deserved a swift and painless death.

SEVENTY-THREE

The guard dog growled when I entered Lucius's villa. Perhaps the beast smelled death on me. Or recognized the scent of poison in my basket.

A servant led me to into the exedrae where Sarra lounged on a sofa.

I kissed her cheek. "You look well."

"Thank you for coming, Locusta." Only a flicker in her eyes hinted at her dislike of me. "I must have mentioned my little problem to Lucius months ago so imagine my surprise when he told me you had just the cure."

I struggled to meet her gaze, to return her open smile with one of my own. "It's a common woman's ailment."

"Is it? My friends do not bleed that much." Sarra rested her hand on her belly. "It frightened Lucius when I fainted the other day. I told him a day of rest is all I need."

I patted the basket. "This should help."

"It won't close my womb, will it?"

"No, it only reduces the flow for a day or two."

She nodded. "Lucius wants a son. He deserves a son. He's

443

very good to me." She touched the turquoise necklace at her throat.

I withdrew a small flask. "I wish I could concoct a potion insuring male children. I'd be a wealthy woman."

"Surely you have enough wealth." Sarra looked down, fiddled with her gold bracelets. "And lovers to satisfy your needs."

I said nothing, pretended to look for an item in my basket.

"Sit with me a moment." Sarra patted the chair.

Courtesy left me no choice but to do as she asked. I held the basket in my lap and steadied myself for the discussion I would rather avoid.

"I love my husband." Sarra tugged at her silken mantle. "Our bond is unique. Special. Our union is more than just a political arrangement between our parents. Love—real love—strengthens the bond between us. I have always loved Lucius. Our friendship began when we were small children. Did you know that?"

"I did not."

"We played together while our parents talked politics. Lucius…my husband—my husband—is my world. I am his. We keep no secrets. I know everything."

I met her steely gaze with one of my own.

"Everything," she repeated.

I smiled, silence my shield.

Sarra held out her hand. "You have my gratitude."

"I…" Words eluded me.

"Ah, you're surprised. You, Locusta, provide my husband with a form of vulgar entertainment I refuse to grant. Then, you see, he returns to me content, and loves me more for my virtuous behavior."

I struggled with a suitable response. "Sarra— "

"Your gift of healing is beyond compare." She took the

proffered vial. "Never forget your success is due to my husband's fondness for you."

"Lucius has my unending gratitude."

"He told me how he rescued you from prison by persuading Nero to grant you an audience."

I nodded.

"My husband is a generous and loving man. My faith and trust in him are unwavering." Sarra opened the seal to sniff at the tincture. "Lucius loves me. Me."

"You're a fortunate woman to possess the heart of such a man."

Sarra lifted her chin. "I'm very fortunate."

"But I believe Lucius is even more fortunate because you're a paragon of matronly virtues."

She set her hand over her heart. "Thank you."

I stood tall, looming over her prone figure. "Drink the liquid at once. Your monthly blood will soon decrease."

"I'm glad we have this understanding. I'm glad you know your place."

"Yes, I do." I inclined my head. "I belong to Nero. I do his bidding." I kissed her cheek and walked from the room.

From the atrium, I heard high-pitched squeals echo down the hall. Five girls lifted their voices in an ebullient chorus. A happy household.

I climbed into my carpentum, determined not to look back.

"It's done, then?" Lucius poked his head through the window.

"She'll fall into a deep sleep before dying peacefully."

Lucius narrowed his eyes. "Why the scowl?"

"Your wife is a treasure. Noble in more than social standing."

Lucius snorted. "This is how it has to be. I could never

divorce Sarra. I need to create alliances, not make enemies. Together, we'll mourn her passing. Then, my pretty poisoner, you and I will become a formidable team."

"Will we? Have you heard the latest gossip about Nero? About all the senators who turn against him?"

"Today they hate him. Tomorrow they'll love him again."

I shook my head. "Maybe not."

"Have you heard something new?"

"I heard there are many senators who plot to assassinate Nero and replace him with General Galba."

"My love, there are always rumors about that." He laughed, glanced over his shoulder. "I'll see you after playing my part as the grieving husband."

"Papa." Lucius's blonde-haired daughter ran outside. "Come watch our play. I wrote it. I did." She patted her chest. "Come. Hurry."

His other four daughters burst through the door, laughing and singing. "Papa, Papa, watch us!"

I waved goodbye and watched with a heavy heart as Lucius's daughters took his hands and tugged him into the villa.

SEVENTY-FOUR

I lifted Telemachus into the air. "Play horse?"

"Yes! Yes!" His mouth, sticky with honey, kissed my cheek.

To love a child was the greatest joy and the worst misery. I wanted to give Tele the world, the best in life.

Yet I was a mere mortal and only the gods know what was best for each person. Only gods know the future path of one's life. If the gods gave us misery, then it is to make us strong. Joy, only a brief reward.

The sun began its descent. A breeze, fragrant with new blooms, cooled the Roman populace. In my garden, tree boughs danced in the gentle wind, diffused the scent of blossoms into the air. The sweet smell of life surrounded me. My child's scent, herbal bouquets, dinner aromas. A heady mixture.

Telemachus pointed to a dove that swooped over our heads. "Bird."

I followed the bird's flight over the statues of Minerva and Venus and wondered if it was an omen. The dove was sacred to Venus, goddess of love and beauty. I did not ponder its meaning. I was no soothsayer, and Roman gods were a capricious lot, their warnings and blessings meant to mislead mortals.

Telemachus in my arms, I strolled past the ornamental shrubs and topiary in my garden. It was only six days before the Ides of Iunius and already warm weather encouraged sprouting new life.

Telemachus squirmed, struggled to reach the low branches while I continued down the cobbled walkway that meandered around flowering fruit trees and fragrant woodbine.

Under one tall tree I paused to stare into its heights. Thick low boughs offered sturdy support. Slender limbs provided fruit and shade. Weak branches at the crown quivered with the slightest breeze.

"Up up!" Telemachus pointed to the lowest limb.

"It's too high. It's not safe."

Some branches grew too high. Others should never be climbed.

The stable was silent when I entered. The groomsman napped in a pile of hay. My cough sent him leaping to his feet.

"Forgive me, domina. I'll hitch the horse to the carpentum immediately."

"Not today. Saddle the horse. The old mare."

"Horse! Play horse!" Telemachus clapped.

The groomsman, confused by my request, knew better than to question me. "Well-chosen, domina. She's a placid beast." He led her from the stall, threw over a thick blanket, and strapped on a saddle.

While he readied the mare, I removed my wool palla. I wrapped it around Telemachus, strapped him to my body. He giggled but did not fuss. He knew he was going to 'play horse' on a real horse.

I donned a long thin cloak, mounted, rechecked Telemachus's makeshift harness, and with a soft kick to the mare's flanks, departed the stable.

I followed the cobbled path back to the villa and waved to the servants and handmaids who gathered to watch their domina indulge her child's whims. Then I took the path which led to the front.

The guard waved and Lupus, tail wagging, trotted behind until we reached the archway at the end of the driveway.

I urged the old mare onward and into the road.

"What's that?" Telemachus pointed to every tree, fountain, and sculpture along the way as we headed into the city.

I answered each question. A linden tree. A juniper bush. A rose garden. A statue of Jupiter. Of Ceres. After the initial excitement wore off, the steady plod of the mare lolled him to sleep.

We passed columned temples and marble nymphaeums. No one paid attention to the cloaked figure riding an old mare. I, however, paid attention to every detail. I noticed fish rotting atop a statue of Nero. Fishermen celebrating Ludi Piscatorii took their catch to the Temple of Vulcan to be sacrificed by fire. Were these decaying fish a practical joke or a message to Nero from angry fishermen?

The sky was rosy when we passed through the city gate and it was here that I cast a wary eye over the crowd.

Peddlers hawked food, trinkets, and cheap wine. Prostitutes solicited customers. Beggars lined the road, counting on the generosity of passersby to donate the coin required to enter the city.

Guards kept a vigilant eye on those who crossed beneath the gate.

My heart knocked against my chest. My fingers clenched the reins. I lifted my head, scanned the surroundings. Telemachus stirred, I felt his body shift, heard him sigh.

Beyond the crowd, a person waved in the distance. I urged the mare forward. Each step took me away from Rome. The noisy bustle faded. Each step brought me closer.

To him.

As though the old mare knew my heart, she nickered in gratitude when I stopped under a linden tree.

"Any problems?" he asked.

"None at all."

Marcus took the reins and walked off the road. "A carpentum waits just ahead. We must leave your horse."

"I understand."

"The Praetorian commander abandoned Nero."

I gasped. "He's lost all support then. It happened just as you foretold."

"Nero will probably seek refuge in the eastern provinces. Many think he'll try to escape by boat."

"I'm certain someone will help him."

Marcus shrugged.

"If Nero is assassinated then I'm truly free," I said.

"What about Lucius?"

"It'll only be a matter of time before General Galba kills all of Nero's friends and supporters," I said.

There was no need to remind Marcus that Galba would hunt down and murder Nero's imperial poisoner as well.

A battered old carpentum with an old horse and a wrinkled driver waited behind a grove of trees. Marcus helped me off the horse, tethered my old mare to a tree, and opened the door.

Once inside, he drew me close and kissed me with yearning and devotion. "I'm a happy man."

Blue eyes blinked open. "Play horse," Telemachus murmured.

I unwound my palla, transferred Telemachus to Marcus's waiting arms, then lifted a small satchel from under my cloak. I withdrew a piece of dried bread.

"What's that?" Marcus asked.

"This is the offering I was given during the ceremony of your Christ. I didn't feel worthy then. I only pretended to eat the bread and drink the wine."

"And now?"

"I realize the offering is not about worthiness. No one is without shame or regret. Your God knows this and still offers his believers forgiveness." My eyes welled with tears. "I have much to learn about your God. I...I'm ready and I want you to watch me take this first step in this ritual of redemption."

"I'm gladdened by this news, but..." A shadow crossed his face.

I touched his arm. "I didn't poison Sarra. I gave her a potent sedative. She'll sleep for a whole day and when she awakens, she'll feel quite refreshed. But..."

Marcus's brows lifted. "Go on."

"If the assassination plot fails and Nero lives, he and Lucius will hunt me down and kill me for my treachery." I put the bread in my mouth.

"They'll look for Locusta of Gaul, a woman who no longer exists."

"I don't understand."

"Your new name is Lila."

"Lila." I liked its lyrical quality. "It's beautiful. What does it mean?"

"It's Hebrew for 'you are mine.'" Marcus draped an arm around me.

SEVENTY-FIVE

R oman gossip was swifter than the fastest racers. When a courier arrived the next morning at the villa we stayed in, I hid behind a drape to listen.

"Every slave fled the palace," said the courier. "Informants said Nero was amazed his Praetorian guards had abandoned him. In the middle of the night, he ran outside and saw one of his freedmen—a man with dubious connections—and bribed him for help. Supposedly, the twice-bribed freedman—pocketing coin from Praetorian commander Nymphidius Sabinus as well—took Nero via a circuitous route to his other residence on the far side of town."

"And?" asked Marcus.

"Nero hid there until soldiers found him."

"Nero is alive?"

"Nero killed himself—stuck a knife through his throat."

"Who's the new emperor?"

"Servius Galba, although rumors suggest he's no better than Nero."

"Galba has the support of the senate and army," said Marcus.

"Indeed, and he wasted no time issuing his first imperial command. Galba decreed that Nero's consorts were now enemies of Rome and he seeks to kill every last one."

Including Nero's poisoner. Me.

After the courier departed, Marcus finalized our plans to flee the country. We had to escape before Galba found me. Punishments for crimes against Rome were horrific. Death by torture, fire, wild beast maulings, public floggings, brutal gang rape, and crucifixions.

"We must leave immediately. Galba will search for you. I've heard it rumored he holds you responsible for the deaths of thousands of good Roman citizens." Marcus spread a map of the world across the desk. "Here." He tapped his finger. "Rome has begun trading spices with the people in this land."

"Do we go by boat?"

"Yes, and we'll leave tonight when darkness cloaks our escape."

We left at sundown. Headed for the nearest port. One might suppose the dark roads would be empty but changes in Roman leadership meant couriers carried sealed scrolls and soldiers hunted for new enemies. Death squads bent on murder and revenge galloped by our rickety wagon. One fierce group thundered past in the opposite direction.

"Don't look back." Marcus said.

We arrived at the port with the rising sun. Marcus wasted no time finding the first merchant vessel bound for our destination and negotiating passage with the captain.

Fearful of being recognized, I kept my face hidden beneath my cloak.

Marcus proved a shrewd persuader. His easy manner belied the urgency of our departure. He told the captain he was a centurion turned ivory merchant whose shipment was detained at the Berenice port. The captain was likewise clever, well aware that citizens were fleeing Rome to escape persecution. Fortunately, Marcus's story convinced the captain.

I had set one foot on the gangplank when soldiers hurried toward us.

"Halt!"

Marcus set down our belongings, his arms open and palms turned outward.

"State your name and destination," said the grim-faced leader.

Marcus submitted to their questioning, their attempts to fluster him useless. Centurions were not cowed by intimidation.

"An unfortunate day for travel," Marcus said.

"Why is that?" asked the leader.

Marcus pointed to the scroll in the soldier's hand. "Who do you search for?"

"Enemies of Rome."

"I was a centurion who only just completed my commission. What's the name of your Primus Pilus?"

Marcus steered the conversation to talk of prefects and strategies and battles. No longer suspicious, the soldiers lingered, their discussion amiable.

In an effort to end the banter, I pinched Telemachus's toes. He let out a long shrill howl.

The soldier tossed an amused look at the screaming child. "A future centurion?"

"There's no greater glory for a man than in serving Rome," said Marcus.

"Ave atque vale, my friend. May your woman give you many more sons."

We gave a cheery wave to the soldiers and boarded the boat.

"We'll soon be free of Rome," Marcus said as the vessel pulled away from the dock.

I clutched his hand, smiled bravely.

Marcus's words, meant to comfort, were inaccurate. Only after Galba was no longer emperor might I be safe. I needed to be two emperors removed to be forgotten.

We left for a distant foreign land where we hoped the long arms of Roman dominance did not extend. Marcus left his home and his friends. I left my villa of poison and the wealth contained within. Coin, gold, jewels, clothes—those shackles of wealth belonged to a woman who ceased to exist. They were the property of a poisoner who suffered fools, miscreants, and deviants in the name of Emperor Nero.

SEVENTY-SIX

M arcus and I made this foreign land of blue-skinned gods, monkeys, elephants, and spices our home. And it was while fanning ourselves and drinking lassi during a sultry afternoon when a long-awaited visitor arrived.

Marcus's friend, Vitus, newly returned from Rome, brought news of Galba's horror-filled reign.

Vitus told us General Galba slaughtered Lucius, Sarra, and his five daughters as they boarded a boat attempting to escape.

Gaius Theon and his wife Annona were also slain in their villa.

Noble families who supported Nero or who shared blood ties were murdered as well.

Statilia, Nero's wife, managed to escape death, the shrewd woman already promised to another.

Marcus's patron, Gellius Septimus, was spared, since he was one of many senators bent on ending Nero's sovereignty.

"Galba wasted no time and killed everyone aligned with Nero," said Vitus. "Even his notorious poisoner."

"His poisoner?" Marcus stroked his beard, never glanced my way. "He killed her too?"

"He paraded the old hag through the streets before flogging her to death."

"She was an old woman then?" asked Marcus.

"Old and ugly." Vitus signaled the servant to refill his minted yogurt drink.

I cannot explain the sorrow I felt that day. I grieved for the woman and wondered what circumstances led her to suffer a cruel punishment meant for me.

"Why did Galba murder an innocent woman?" I asked.

"Galba must assert his dominance," Marcus explained. "Unable to find you, he probably chose some old woman already in prison. Justice must be met. The emperor's assassin must be punished for crimes against Rome. Galba's use of an imposter is an old ploy."

"Do you think he still searches for me?"

Marcus kissed my cheek. "Perhaps, but Galba's men will never find her. You left Locusta of Gaul in Rome."

Yes, I thought, the assassin and peddler of poison disappeared. In her place, a wife and mother. I set my hand over my belly and marveled at the life once again growing inside. The fruit of our love and result of many weeks crossing the Erythraean Sea.

I was not worthy of this joy.

I was not worthy of the chance to begin anew...

To be forgiven.

AUTHOR'S NOTE

Locusta of Gaul is a real person. She killed Emperor Claudius with poison mushrooms, Brittanicus, and thousands of others on Nero's orders. Some allege she had a school of poison. There are different accounts of Locusta's death. All horrible. That she was raped to death by wild beasts is one of the most gruesome. In works of art, she is portrayed as either an old hag or a young woman. She remains shrouded in mystery and, as we know, it is the winners whose accounts fill our history books.

Sadly, there was very little I had to make up or embellish about Nero. I stayed true to the people and events of Nero's time, including his lovers, the sordid gossip, crimes, and imperial dictates. History contends that he did indeed say, "At last I begin to live like a human being" upon completion of Domus Aurea.

For Latin purists, forgive me if the tenses are incorrect. I used Latin words to add historical flavor.

A Few Terms

Salve – greetings

Optimum est pati quod emendare non possis – it is best to endure what you cannot change

Ave atque vale – hail and be well

Servus sum – I am your slave, but means "at your service"

Aut viam inveniam aut facian - I will find a way or make one

Quid agis mane – How are you doing this morning?

Non omnia possumus omnes – you can be anything you set your mind to

Nos morituri te salutant – we who are about to die, salute you

Futete – fuck you

Need another decadent and delicious story by Autumn Bardot? There's more!

OTHER HISTORICAL FICTION BY AUTUMN

The Impaler's Wife

A young woman is swept into a life of intrigue, revenge, passion, and betrayal when she falls for the world's most notorious prince, Vlad Dracula.

The year is 1464. King Matthias controls Hungary, his family, and the fate of the world's most notorious political prisoner, Prince Vlad Dracula.

Ilona Szilágy, the king's cousin, is young and ambitious. Dracula is determined to marry into the family. It is love at first sight, but the king has other plans. The Impaler Prince, however, never takes no for an answer.

This begins Ilona's journey into the treacherous world of court intrigues, family betrayals, and her husband's dark desires. Eager to become Vlad's trusted confidant, Ilona soon discovers that marriage to a man tortured by his past comes with a price.

Read now.

Dragon Lady

Prostitution required the violation of my body. Piracy required my soul. The first enslaved me. The second set me free.

Against all odds, a prostitute becomes the most powerful pirate chieftain in the South China Seas. Sold into slavery by her parents, Xianggu works on a floating brothel for ten years before a midnight pirate raid changes her life. Determined to rise above her lowly status, the fearless young woman embarks on a journey requiring beauty, brains, and brawn. The Red Flag boss, Zheng Yi, is captivated by the spirited Xianggu and soon makes her his wife. This begins her adventure into the violent world of sea banditry. But Xianggu must do more than learn to wield a sword, sail a ship, and swim across a bay. She must become indispensable to Zheng Yi or risk losing everything, even her life.

In 18th century China, when men made and enforced the rules, the Dragon Lady lived by her own.

Read now.

HISTORICAL EROTICA

Legends of Lust, Erotic Myths from around the World is fourteen romantic and erotic tales of Vikings, goddesses, shape shifters, jinn, and fae that are sure to take your love of myths to a whole new level!

Read now.

Available March 10, 2020

Confessions of a Sheba Queen

A temptress. A jinni. A queen. A determined young woman pursues revenge, lust, and wealth but instead finds friendship, love, and purpose.

During a sandstorm in the ancient lands of Saba, a powerful jinni in hiding gives birth to a daughter. An intelligent, curious child, Bilqīs does not inherit the super human physical gifts of her mother, a being born of smokeless fire. Yet deep within burns the courageous spirit of her fearsome parentage. Her rite into womanhood however, reveals a sexual hunger that may be her undoing.

Tragedy forces Bilqīs to leave her home and travel to the city of Ma'rib where she seeks revenge on the king. Danger lurks around every bend and corner for a young woman with only her wit, courage, and body as her weapons. Bilqīs soon masters the art of seduction and finds it the most pleasurable method to achieve her goals.

Fate intervenes, and what began as a quest for vengeance becomes a mission to make the land of Saba the wealthiest kingdom in ancient history. Bilqīs, the enigmatic Queen of Sheba, battles prejudices, jealousy, corruption, and her own unquenchable hunger for carnal pleasures. But it is only after meeting King Solomon that Bilqīs discovers her greatest battle is not with others but within herself.

With a host of unforgettable characters and unbridled sensual escapades, *Confessions of a Sheba Queen* is an erotic and triumphant retelling of an indomitable woman succeeding in a man's world.

Never miss sneak peeks, giveaways, discounts, and opportunities to read Advanced Review Copies. Subscribe to Autumn's newsletter at: www.autumnbardot.com

Connect with Autumn and visit her at:

www.AutumnBardot.com
Facebook
Instagram
Twitter
Goodreads

Never miss sneak peeks, giveaways, discounts, and opportunities to read Advanced Review Copies. Subscribe to Autumn's newsletter at: www.autumnbardot.com

Connect with Autumn and visit her at:

www.AutumnBardot.com
Facebook
Instagram
Twitter
Goodreads

ABOUT THE AUTHOR

Autumn Bardot is an author of historical fiction and historical erotica. Her debut historical fiction is *The Impaler's Wife*. Her debut historical erotica is *Legends of Lust*. Autumn, a pen name, has worked as an educator for over fifteen years. She has a passion for history and has a special affinity for the unsung courageous females that history has neglected. Autumn lives in Southern California with her husband and every-growing family. She wishes she was one-tenth as brave as the women she writes about.